Sugarland

Graham Mcglone

This book is a novel. Unless otherwise noted, the author and the publisher make no explicit guarantees as to the accuracy of the information contained in this book, and in some cases, names of people and places have been altered to protect their privacy.

The right of Graham Mcglone to be identified as the author of this work has been asserted in accordance with the Copyright, Designs, and Patents Act 1988.

© 2020 Graham Mcglone.

All rights reserved. No part of this publication may be reproduced, stored in a retrieval system, or transmitted, in any form or by any means, electronic, mechanical, photocopying, recording or otherwise, without the prior permission of the author.

ISBN – 979-8630263230

Also by Graham Mcglone

In the line of fire (Sailing Today 2001)

The Silvertown Kid – Tales of a Randy Deckhand (2012)

Exchanging Islands (2012)

Lazy Daze – A voyage around my past (2013)

A Lazy Day – Anthology 1 (2018)

A Quiet Day – Anthology 2 (2019)

Death of a Planet (2020)

1	Chapter 1	Death at Christmas
11	Chapter 2	Inspector Stranks
19	Chapter 3	The Demise of Rita Harrison
36	Chapter 4	The Reverend Samuel Hogan.
47	Chapter 5	Hazel's Arrival.
61	Chapter 6	The Railway Tunnel
68	Chapter 7	Peeping Tom
87	Chapter 8	Carnal Desires
95	Chapter 9	A Cosy Love nest
103	Chapter 10	The Knocking Shop
119	Chapter 11	Inspector Maitland
129	Chapter 12	A Child Goes Missing
135	Chapter 13	The Night-watchman
150	Chapter 14	The Orphan's Charity Fund
167	Chapter 15	Rose Blewitt
176	Chapter 16	The Montana Brothers
210	Chapter 17	Follow the Money

Front cover image. Geison Esteves, Sao Paulo. Brazil.
My thanks to Sue Bonsor and Dave Fennessey for proof-reading.

1: Death at Christmas

Above the entrance to North Woolwich police station in London's Docklands is an elaborate cast iron lamp with tinted blue glass. It was from beneath this lamp that police constable Noah Sheppard stepped out to begin his patrol on a snowy afternoon in January of 1955. The day promised to be uneventful, with only minor crimes being reported, but circumstances would quickly change.

Before venturing out, Sergeant Ambrose had briefed Noah to keep an eye out for a quantity of lead sheathing that had been stripped from the vestry roof of St Mark's Church; and to watch for school kids stealing sweets from the corner shop near the local school.

Noah's regular beat extended a mile or so to Silvertown, including the side roads that branched off the main thoroughfare of Albert Road. The area was bordered on one side by the River Thames and on the other by London's Royal Docks. Within this area, thousands of two-up – two-down houses were packed tightly together. In effect, the whole district, from Tidal Basin to North Woolwich, was a peninsula.

The far end of each street butted onto the tall wooden fence which marked the perimeter of the docks. The Royals were the largest enclosed dock system in the world, and from where vessels would be loaded with cargoes that were manufactured in the industrial heartlands of Great Britain, and which would set sail across the oceans to deliver the goods to Britain's empire.

Beyond the dock fence and the warehouses, Noah could see the funnels and masts of the ships being loaded or discharged by the dozens of tall electric cranes that lifted the heavy freight into their deep cargo holds. And soaring high above the rest of the factories and the docks was the giant orange-painted factory of the Tate & Lyle sugar refinery.

This neighbourhood, with its morass of factories, docks, corner-shops, pubs, cafes and poor housing, felt so alive and vibrant. Noah loved it here. He loved its pulsating energy. He loved the noise and the smells of the factories, and even liked to hear the raucous cacophony of the factory hooters and the ship's sirens. But most of all he enjoyed living and working amongst the down-to-earth cockney East Enders of Silvertown and North Woolwich.

Despite their low wages and doubtful employment, they always appeared contented and cheerful. He smiled at the thought of their flamboyant cockney accents with its rhyming slang words, which to his unaccustomed ears had initially seemed like unintelligible gibberish.

Noah turned the corner into Winifred Street, taking care not to lose his footing on the icy pavement. Earlier this week his feet had slid from under him as he'd skidded on an icy patch outside the secondary school, and had landed heavily and ignominiously onto his backside. His police helmet had lay spinning in the gutter as a nearby crowd of schoolboys had jeered for all they were worth.

An elderly woman dressed in a blue pinafore with hair curlers and a head-scarf was brushing a fresh carpet of snow from the front entrance of her house into the street. All the houses were of the basic two-up-two-down variety, but generally, the housewives would keep them neat and tidy. The dwellings had an outside toilet, but possessed no bathroom. Bathing was accomplished, perhaps once per week, by using a tin bath that usually hung from a nail in the back garden. The bath was filled by a succession of kettles of hot water. The houses were known far and wide as Dockers' Mansions.

She called him over. "Mornin', Constable Sheppard. Bloody cold again, ain't it?" she said in her broad London accent. "It's cold enough to freeze the balls off a brass monkey." The colourful language made Noah grin.

"Hello, Edith. How are you?" he enquired. Edith Brooks was a salt-of-the-earth cockney who loved to chat.

"I'm a bit worried about old Ernie Samuels who lives next door," she said, indicating the house on her left. "I ain't seen nuffink of 'im since before Christmas. He moved in just last summer, so I don't know 'im all that well, but I'm worried cos I ain't seen him these past two weeks."

Noah was aware that the close-knit citizens of Silvertown usually knew every family in their own street and would take an unhealthy interest in their private business. Not much went unnoticed by the busy-bodies, and he often picked up interesting snippets of information during the course of a friendly chat. "Let's knock on his door, shall we," suggested Noah, walking the few yards to Mister Samuels house.

"I've already tried that," said Edith. Noah gave a smart rat-a-tat-tat on the door-knocker and rang the bell. No answer. He bent down and looked through the letterbox. The house was quiet. He decided to try to enter the house via the back door, because the old man may possibly have fallen ill.

"I'll make us a cuppa tea while you're 'aving a look around," suggested Edith.

He gained entry to the small rear garden and found the door on the latch. As he entered the kitchen, the smell hit him, and he instinctively knew what he would find. He climbed the stairs, and on the top landing found the body of Ernie Samuels. He was hanging from a rope that was attached to a length of timber placed across the open loft hatch. Below the body was a chair that he must have stood upon to slip the noose over his head, and had then kicked it over. The cord had bitten into his neck and his tongue protruded from his open mouth. Noah didn't bother to search for a pulse because, judging by the putrid smell, he guessed that the old man had decided to end his life sometime before Christmas. Noah's eyes were drawn to the man's fingers. Several of his fingernails were torn and streaked with blood, as if Ernie Samuels had changed his mind about committing suicide when he had felt the noose tightening, and had scrabbled wildly at the cord in an attempted to loosen the rope. But once he had kicked over that chair, his fate had been sealed and it was far too late.

He had a cursory look around the gloomy rooms, but found no sign of a suicide note. There was nothing more that he could do, and he simply wanted to escape from the sickening smell. He left the house and walked to the nearby police call box to phone the duty sergeant. The Coroner's Office would deal with it from now on.

That had been two weeks ago. Like clockwork the usual police procedures had swung into place. The police doctor had attended the scene, quickly followed by an unmarked black van from East Ham Coroner's Office who had transported the body to the mortuary where an autopsy was performed by the coroner. His post mortem examination, as expected, revealed that death had occurred some two weeks previously, a day either side of Christmas. The cause of death was suicide by reason of hanging. After formal identification, supported by means of his ex Army identification card, there remained only to discover if the deceased had any next-of-kin, so that the family may arrange for a funeral service; but that was easier said than done. A thorough search of the house eventually turned up a birth certificate for a male child named Raymond, born in 1925, and a search of the local electoral register uncovered an address in nearby Plaistow.

Unluckily for Noah, he was on scheduled duty when Sergeant Ambrose had handed him an address with orders to get over to Plaistow and inform the late Ernie Samuel's son. Noah had never shied away from any job, but informing next-of-kin that their loved ones were dead was a task he dreaded. On almost every occasion the news came as a shocking body blow for the family, and often resulted in screaming and tears. Bert Ambrose, who had performed this grim task many times over the years, had advised Noah to simply and quickly state the facts and get the hell out.

It was late in the afternoon when Noah tapped on the door of the terraced house in the backstreets of Plaistow. His knock was answered by an

unshaven man in his early thirties who was dressed in pyjamas. He had obviously been sleeping, and from his grumpy demeanour, Noah guessed that he had disturbed the sleep of a shift worker.
"Hello, sir. Are you Mister Raymond Samuels?" he asked.
"Yeah, wassup?" the man had answered belligerently. It was obvious that he wasn't an admirer of the police force.
"Are you the son of Ernest Samuels of Winifred Street in Silvertown?"
"What if I am? What's the stupid old bugger gone an' done now?"
"I'm afraid I've got some bad news for you, sir. I had better come inside and explain."

Fifteen minutes later Noah left the house feeling utterly despondent. On hearing the news of his father's death, Raymond Samuels had muttered, "Well, at last he's done summfink right. Good riddance to him." Further enquiries elicited the information that father and son hadn't spoken for the past five years after an argument regarding his father's mistreatment of his mother, who had died some years earlier. He appeared more upset because he expected to be burdened with the expense of his father's funeral and had asked Noah if he thought the old man had many assets, which as his next-of-kin, he expected to inherit. Noah remembered Bert Ambrose's advice and made a quick exit.

Inspector Peter Stranks was not a happy man. He had barely passed the police examinations for the inspector's post two years ago, and had been extremely lucky to have secured this posting to North Woolwich. He desperately needed more income, and the only way he could achieve it would be to obtain further promotion to Chief Inspector, which would attract a much higher pay scale.

But in his heart of hearts he realized that his problems didn't stem from any lack of promotion, but rather from his wife, Rosemary. He was at his wits end because she constantly berated him if they couldn't afford to buy the latest gadgets. Last week she wanted to purchase a new gramophone; the one she'd seen in the High Street store with the walnut surround and the smoked glass doors. The week before that, she had demanded they get the latest washing machine. He had remonstrated with her, "But what's wrong with the wash-board and mangle?" he asked. "Housewives have been using them for years." She had rolled her eyes at what she viewed as his obvious stupidity and reminded him that, as a police inspector's wife, she had a certain position to uphold in the community and she was damned if she would look like a throwback to the 19th century, especially if the wives of other senior police officers came around for coffee. "Their husbands buy them these things so as to make their lives easier, so why can't you?" she had argued. She then piled on more pressure. "Surely you don't want me to get wrinkly dishpan hands, do you?"

Rosemary, he recognised, was a very strong willed woman, and she will argue and complain until she gets what she wants. And that's exactly what happened last week. He bitterly recalled that she had insisted that they go straight to the electrical store and purchase the washing machine. He had tried to explain that they really couldn't afford it, but she had got upset and turned on the waterworks. "Oh darling, sometimes I don't believe you love me," she'd cried. Of course he'd had to purchase the damn thing on a hire purchase agreement. That was in addition to the bloody gramophone that he'd also bought on the never-never.

Two months previously, Rosemary had cajoled him into joining the Freemasons and then the Rotary Club, because, she said, "You've simply got to move in the same circles as the other senior police officers, darling. Getting further promotion is all about projecting a good social image. Can't you see that, Peter?"

And now she was making even further demands. Just two nights ago, after allowing him the rare privilege of making love to her, she sweetly announced that she thought they ought to purchase a larger house in the suburbs, and perhaps even a motor car. Stranks had insisted that they genuinely couldn't afford it, but after performing the exceptionally rare act of fellatio upon him, she had secured his agreement that he would strive harder to afford a larger mortgage.

Peter Stranks crossed to his office hand-basin and splashed water over his face to clear his head. He stared into the mirror and studied his features closely. He looked older than his 38 years. He noticed a few more grey hairs and his hairline was receding rapidly. He was a big man, with big bones and a heavy frame, but the obvious paunch of his belly told him that he was getting seriously overweight. He lifted his chin, so as to stretch the skin on the underside of his jaws, but the dewlaps of a double chin returned as soon as he lowered his head. He wasn't at all happy with the result, or the face that stared back at him.

To make matters worse, just days ago he'd overheard two constables chatting in the corridor where his name had been mentioned during the conversation. But what had caused him to spend the afternoon quietly fuming was the nickname they used when referring to him. His constables had called him, The Weasel.

Then, just yesterday, he had been summoned to a meeting with the chief superintendent at his headquarters office. Chief Superintendent Humber hadn't beaten about the bush, but came straight to the point. "I've noticed that the arrest record of your officers is abysmal. Your constables have arrested far fewer villains than any other station in my division. It isn't good enough, Stranks." He had attempted to offer up excuses, but Humber had waved his lame arguments aside. "If you want to be in line for any promotion, then you'd better make sure that your men's performance improves. Do I make myself clear?"

Noah decided to check out the corner sweet shop located opposite Elizabeth Street School. The elderly shopkeeper had complained that she was being distracted by the younger schoolchildren, whilst the elder ones stuffed their pockets full of anything within reach. Noah looked at his wristwatch. It was almost chucking-out time at the school, so he stationed himself outside the tuck shop and looked at what was on offer in the front window display. The goods looked old and dated, as if they had laid amongst the flies and bluebottles for an eternity.

He caught sight of himself in the reflection of the plate glass window. The face that stared back appeared younger than his 24 years and he thought his facial features had become more sharp and angular, but at least he looked slim and healthy. His light brown hair, which was usually cut short as per police regulations, had begun to creep over his shirt collar. He decided that he would pop into the barbers on his day off-duty.

Satisfied with his self-inspection, he stepped inside the shop. The fly-blown walls desperately needed decorating with a fresh coat of distemper and the ceiling had numerous cobwebs hanging from the plaster. A grizzled tabby cat lay curled up upon the wooden counter, behind which stooped an old lady who could easily have played a character role in a Charles Dickens novel. "Have you come along to catch those little bastards who've been nickin' me sweets 'ave you?" she asked in a broad cockney voice. The old girl must have been almost 90 years of age. A strong smell of mothballs emanated from her direction as the odour of naphthalene invaded his nostrils "I don't suppose they'll try to steal anything with me around, so at least you won't make a loss today," he told her. The smell was almost making his eyes water. He bought an ounce of sugared almonds and went outside to station himself where the kids would easily be able to see him.

Within minutes Elizabeth Street School, which was known far and wide as Lizzo, began disgorging hundreds of pupils onto the street. Most were well-behaved and quietly made their way home, whilst others were being rowdy and pushing and shoving and generally indulging in horseplay.

An elderly man leading a Jack Russell dog came to stand beside him, watching the antics of the schoolchildren. "Good afternoon, Mister Tilbrook. How are you?" said Noah. Reginald Tilbrook had been a Senior Air Raid Warden during the war and he yearned for the return of those far-off days when he was a respected pillar of the community and his orders in relation to black-outs and organising bomb shelters were acted upon. "Those bloody kids. They're always making trouble. It's a pity they're too young to go into the army," said Reggie Tilbrook, who had been too old to join the regular army. "If it was up to me, then I'd stick all those buggers in a khaki uniform. They wouldn't last five minutes." Noah was non-committal; not wanting to be drawn into the pros and cons of military life.

Noah wasn't a Londoner. He'd been raised near Broxbourne in Hertfordshire, a sleepy village surrounded by agricultural farmland. As a teenager, Noah had been too young to enlist in the war effort. When he had left school at 15 years of age, the war was over, so he simply went to work upon the land as a dairy farm labourer. He fondly remembered those days when he would be out of his bed at 5am to gather and milk the cows and to toil all day in the fields and barns. He'd loved it.

All that had changed when, at the age of nineteen, he'd been called up to serve two years National Service in the Army. After two months basic training and early morning route marches at Catterick in North Yorkshire, he'd been posted to Germany to support the British Army of the Rhine. Life in the military had been harsh, but he'd made lots of friends and it had toughened him up for a career in the Metropolitan Police. Noah thought that Reggie Tilbrook didn't have a clue about life in the modern army, but he kept this to himself.

He noticed a group of a dozen or so boys furtively whispering amongst themselves as they sauntered along the pavement. They disappeared around the back of one of the many bomb sites, and Noah was certain that they were up to no good. He followed at a discreet distance, but out of sight. The bomb-sites, or debris as they were known, had become the local kid's playgrounds, and the partially demolished houses would become their den. With fractured walls and chimney pots that could collapse at any moment, they were highly dangerous places in which to play, and Noah knew of several instances when buildings had collapsed and buried children under tons of rubble.

He peeked around the corner. The boys were standing around expectantly, as if waiting for something to happen. Minutes later another boy arrived, and Noah could hear raised voices as he and another lad began to square up to each other in a classic boxer's posture. There was about to be a fight. Noah remained out of sight, intent on not getting involved unless the brawl turned ugly. He had learnt a valuable lesson from a former sergeant at Bethnal Green, "Don't go looking for trouble, son. It only creates paperwork." Noah recognized the fact that schoolboys will always get into scrapes, so he let them get on with it. He peeked around the wall. The boys were throwing punches at each other, most of which harmlessly bounced off his opponent. The shorter of the two seemed to be winning as he ducked and dived and landed some useful punches. Suddenly he landed a haymaker around his classmate's ear and the larger fellow went down into the dirt, and had the sense to stay down. A loud cheer went up, and the smaller lad's arm was being held aloft in victory. The loser was helped to his feet by the victor and they shook hands. The gang of boys began to drift away and that was the end of it. Noah continued upon his beat strolling aimlessly westwards.

Days later, he was strolling along Albert Road at a leisurely pace and in no rush to get anywhere. At Silvertown Railway Station, which marked the boundary of his beat, he would retrace his steps, and after checking in with the duty sergeant from the police call box, he would stroll back to North Woolwich nick in time to clock-off at 10pm.

It had been a quiet patrol, with nothing out of the ordinary occurring. Earlier he'd had to remind a drunken sailor who'd just had a piddle in the public toilet opposite the Kent Arms, to remember to do up his fly buttons, as his wedding tackle was on display.

Darkness had fallen and apart from the regular street lamps, bright arc lights shone down from the overpowering orange painted steel monolith of the Tate and Lyle sugar refinery. Noah had reached the corner of Leonard Street when he heard glass shattering. His senses went onto full alert. The noise had come from the Constitutional Club on the opposite side of the street. He rounded the corner, and there, in full view, was a boy about to throw another stone through a window at the rear of the club. Noah was on him in seconds, and grabbed him by the scruff of the neck. The lad wriggled, but couldn't get away from Noah's strong grip. The boy looked up and realized he'd been nabbed by a copper and his shoulders sank in defeat. The kid was about ten years old and wore short trousers held up with braces. "Why did you smash that window?" demanded Noah. The boy looked terrified, but shrugged his shoulders without any viable excuse. "I'm sorry, sir. I didn't mean to" he said meekly.
Noah took out his note book and pen. "What's your name?" he said sternly. "It's Tommy Hicks," the boy said in a scared voice. He was beginning to understand that he was in a whole mountain of trouble and thoughts of being sent away to a juvenile remand centre circled around his brain. Noah pretended to write the lad's name in his book, but wrote nothing at all. "Where do you live?" he said harshly.
The boy was almost in tears. "I live in Wythes Road," he said, jerking his thumb in the direction of the side road, just two streets away. His nose had begun to sniffle.

Noah shone his flashlight onto the lad's face and faintly recognised him. "I'm sure I know your dad. Is his name Hughie?" he asked. The boy nodded. He sincerely hoped that his dad wouldn't find out about his stupidity, because he was likely to give him a sound thrashing with his leather belt. His father had once before given him a beating and he remembered the red welts that had stayed on his skin for days afterwards.

"Well now young man, what shall we do about this damage?" asked Noah, indicating the scattered shards of broken glass. The boy looked terrified and had begun to shake with fear.

"Choice number one is that I could arrest you and take you to the police station; and after I made a report on your stupid behaviour, you'd have a criminal record. You wouldn't like that, would you?" The boy had visions of standing in the dock at the Old Bailey whilst a scowling judge, wearing a black cap, passed the ultimate sentence. Tears ran down his cheeks. "No sir, I wouldn't," he pleaded.

"Choice number two is that I could tell your dad and he would probably give you a bloody good hiding for being so silly. You don't want that either, do you?" said Noah unsympathetically.

The boy was beside himself with fear, with tears dropping onto his shirt collar and snot running down his nose. "Please don't tell him, sir" pleaded the lad. In the quietness of the evening Noah heard the faint sound of music coming from inside the Constitutional Club. No one had come outside to investigate their broken pane of glass.

Noah appeared to make a momentous decision, although he had already made up his mind to settle matters in his own way from the very start. "Okay then young Master Hicks, it's got to be the third choice for you, hasn't it?" he said. The boy looked imploringly at Noah, hoping that the third choice didn't involve a spell in Borstal or a beating from his dad.

He gazed down at the boy. Judging by the look of terror on his face, it appeared he may shit himself at any moment, which brought a wry smile to his lips. He didn't seem to be a bad lad and he was sure he would have learnt his lesson and not repeat his stupidity.

He grabbed the boy by his coat lapels and gripped him tightly. He then delivered a single sharp slap to the boy's cheeks that left a red mark upon his face. Noah wasn't too worried. The red mark would disappear within twenty minutes.

"Right Tommy, that's it - all done," said Noah, handing the boy a clean handkerchief to wipe his face. "You can go home now. I won't take any further action."

Tommy Hicks looked up at Noah as if he was the Messiah who had saved him from eternal damnation. "Thank you very much, sir," he said and walked away quickly in the direction of Wythes Road.

Noah resumed his leisurely stroll along Albert Road. He was generally pleased with the way in which he'd handled the matter of the broken window. Tommy had just received instant justice. Some people, he guessed, may view his actions as questionable, but at least the lad wouldn't be engaging in any hooliganism from now on. He was sure of it.

In any event, the East End kids were quite used to far more brutal corporal punishment being handed out by their teachers every day of the week. It wasn't uncommon to find that school teachers would punish small infractions of rules with six lashes of a bamboo cane or they would rap a wooden ruler smartly across their pupil's knuckles simply for being inattentive in class. Noah put the incident out of his mind and began to whistle a happy tune.

2: Inspector Stranks

Frankie Houlder's scrap metal business was to be found behind a high galvanized fence at the bottom end of Parker Street. The half acre of land was stacked with scrap cars, surplus army trucks, piles of sheathed copper wire, and assorted metal of every type and description. Frankie's late father, Sidney Houlder, had started the business just after The Great War so as to take advantage of the tons of redundant scrap military vehicles that he could pick up cheap, and the business had gone from strength to strength. After the death of his father, Frankie had developed the business to include a haulage company and second-hand furniture business.

Frankie's formidable wife, Jackie, was the firm's book-keeper and ran the accounts. She knew everything there was to know about the scrap metal business and she could work a company ledger sheet to perfection. On paper, the company rarely made enough profit to pay any appreciable taxes. Jackie saw to that. Their three sons, Eric, Mickey, and Ronnie did all the heavy work.

An open back truck came through the gates and two young men stepped out of the cab, looking around uncertainly. Frankie, who never forgot a face, didn't know them from Adam. "Can I help you boys?" he enquired cordially, puffing on his briar pipe.

"Erm, well we've got some sheets of lead that we thought you might wanna buy," said the tallest, jerking his thumb at the lorry. "It's in the truck. Are you interested?"

"That depends on how much you've got and where you got it from. I'm not interested in buying small quantities," said Frankie, managing to appear indifferent. He invariably began every sales-pitch as if he wasn't fussed if he bought anyone's scrap or not.

"We fink there's about a ton and a half. We bought it from a demolition firm who was clearing out their yard."

Frankie instantly knew that they were lying. Any demolition outfit worth their salt would almost certainly have sold it directly to an established scrap company who paid the best prices, and not to these two oiks. He decided to squeeze them a little. "Which firm did you buy it from?"

"Erm, I'm afraid I can't remember," he muttered. "It was someone we met in a pub." His shorter ginger haired companion stared nervously at the ground and remained silent, letting his older friend do the talking.

"Well, I usually pay ten bob a hundredweight, but seeing as the price of lead has taken a nosedive, and that you two gentlemen probably ain't got a bill of sale, it'll be a lot less."

"How much are you offerin'?" asked the brains of the outfit.

"Let's have a look at it first," said Frankie, walking over to the lorry.

He pulled back a green tarpaulin that concealed the load and began sorting through the pile of dull grey lead. Judging by the width of the sheets, he guessed that the lead flashing had once lined the roof gulleys and capped the base of chimney pots and ridge tiles on a building. Some of the sheets had been removed in a hurry by cutting though the lead with metal shears. Written on one of the sheets in indelible pen were the original roofer's installation instructions, faded, but still legible, *"St. Marks – vestry roof gulley."* It was a dead giveaway as to the lead's provenance.

Frankie didn't comment, but knew without a shadow of doubt that the lead had been nicked, and that these two characters had probably done the roof stripping. He puffed on his pipe contentedly and managed a secret smile. He had heard on the grapevine that Saint Mark's Church, which lay across the far side of the railway line, had had its roof stripped two nights ago. It didn't worry him one iota. Anyway, he thought, the Church of England's got plenty of money, why should he care? However, it made a huge difference to the price he would be offering. These lads were in no position to haggle. "I'll give you six shillings a hundredweight, take it or leave it," said Frankie. The lads went into a huddle to discuss the bad news.

"Okay, it's a deal," said the tall one.

"Right then, load it onto the weighing scales, lads," he said. "And if you get any more scrap, then perhaps we can do business again."

A half hour later, the two young men drove out of Frankie's yard wondering uncertainly if it had all been worth their while.

Inspector Stranks sat at his desk reviewing his officers arrest records. The information was entered upon a sizeable document that listed his officer's names, rank, arrests (with date), court appearance date, and sentence. His finger traced down the list, highlighting those constables whose performance was reasonable.

His index finger rested on the name of Constable Sheppard as he read the notation beside the officer's name. His mouth turned down in displeasure. Constable Sheppard had made only one arrest within the past three months, and that had been a simple drunk and disorderly for which the inebriate had been fined a paltry 40 shillings. Sheppard had, by far, the lowest arrest rate of any of his officers. Something would have to be done about him.

Peter Stranks intended getting Sheppard in for a dressing down. He wasn't going to allow his officers to shirk their duties and permit the local crime rate to increase, and ruin his chances of promotion into the bargain. He could imagine Superintendent Humber summoning him to headquarters for a further reprimand. He buzzed the duty sergeant at the front desk. "Sergeant Ambrose, would you ask Constable Sheppard to see me at his earliest convenience, please."

Noah Sheppard knocked on the office door with some trepidation. It wasn't everyday that one got a summons to see the station inspector and he wracked his brain for any clue as to the reason. However, The Weasel, as Stranks was often referred to, frequently got bees in his bonnet about minor issues, and it wasn't unusual for officers to be on the carpet for some trivial misdemeanour. He could think of no valid reason for being sent for. As far as he was aware, there had been no complaints with regard to his work, and things had thankfully been quiet on his patch just lately. He heard the word, "Come!" and entered the office.

Stranks didn't invite him to sit, but came straight to the point. He stabbed an accusing finger in Noah's direction. "Over the past three months, Sheppard, you've made very few arrests, which tells me that you're not doing your job properly." Noah was about to explain that things were quiet on the streets, but Stranks was having none of it. "Your colleagues manage to arrest villains in other parts of the division, so why aren't you doing the same? Your performance frankly leaves a lot to be desired and it's just not good enough." Noah attempted to explain the circumstances, but Stranks held up his hand against interruption. "I don't want you going around with the idea that you can spend your days mooching about Silvertown, chatting to old men and having cups of tea with gossiping old ladies. You've got to be more hands-on. Get out there and mix it up a bit, or the local villains will think we've gone soft on them. You're a police officer, Sheppard, not bloody Father Christmas. Do I make myself clear?"
Noah was devastated. He'd always thought that he was an effective police officer and did a good job, and it hurt his pride that his senior officer wasn't at all pleased with his performance. Without a further word, he silently nodded in acquiescence.
Stranks pointed at the door. "Now get out there and arrest some criminals. I shall be looking for some big improvements, understood?" Noah answered with a submissive, "Yes sir."
Stranks picked up his pen. "That's all," he said, without looking up.

When Sheppard had left his office, Stranks drummed his fingers on the edge of his desk in a thoughtful mood and contemplated how he would handle the problem of the downward turn in arrests. He wouldn't tolerate any of his constables making him look like an ineffective idiot and fouling up his chances of promotion and he certainly didn't relish another bollocking from Chief Superintendent Humber.

He needed promotion, together with the increased salary that it would generate, so as to keep Rosemary contented. Coppers like Sheppard would simply have to get in line if they wanted to keep their posts. If they didn't make arrests for any valid reason, then he'd make it a disciplinary matter. He suspected that Sheppard was probably among those constables who called him The Weasel behind his back. His finger traced down the document to search for the next on his list.

Noah was devastated when he left Stranks' office. He felt stung by the notion that his senior officer thought so little of his performance, that it required such a harsh bollocking. He had always seen himself as just an ordinary conscientious copper who carried out his tasks to the best of his ability, and it came as something of a nasty surprise to learn that his work was viewed as less than satisfactory. He had never had any complaints before, and wondered why they should surface just at this particular time.

He disagreed with Stranks' opinion, but was helpless to do anything about it, other than to acquiesce to his orders. But more than that, he disagreed with the policy of comparing the number of arrests with the local crime rate. He took the view that crime prevention, whereby potential villains or tearaways were warned off, rather than waiting for the crime rate to soar, was better than going for wholesale arrests. It may look better on paper, he thought, but not in reality. He may be 24 year old rookie, but he couldn't see the wisdom of this new policy.

He remembered when he had applied to join the Metropolitan Police Force. It had been a little over two years ago. He had been buoyed up with the excitement at joining what he naively viewed, as a team dedicated to fighting for the forces of law and order, where you could make a difference to the community and keep the streets of London free of crime. Very soon after leaving Hendon Police Training College and assigned to his first police station at Bethnal Green, he'd been brought down to earth when the station sergeant informed him that, nowadays policing was about putting in the hours, keeping your nose clean, and retiring on a nice fat pension.

Thankfully he had disregarded the sergeant's advice and embarked upon a mission to be a dedicated and committed copper. He was certain that his presence on the tough streets did make a difference. Noah was glad that he had taken that decision, because he enjoyed his work enormously and every day was different. But then his secondment to Bethnal Green had ended and he'd moved to North Woolwich.

He was of the opinion that if police officers could see problems arising beforehand, by means of cultivating good relations in the community, then information would slowly and surely flow their way and potential crimes could be nipped in the bud. He saw a policeman's role as an integral part of the community. Not someone to be feared, but someone to be respected, and to guide them onto the straight and narrow path of being decent citizens.

Noah was especially interested in the local children. If their energies could be channelled into more innocent pursuits and endeavours, then it may prevent that child taking up a lifetime of crime. If kids got into bad company, then it was a fine dividing line that could tip the scales and lead them to spend spells in juvenile detention centres. Those establishments were akin to criminal colleges, where they would rapidly learn to commit even more serious crimes.

He was especially keen to help the local kids with taking up after-school clubs, joining the Scout and Girl Guide movement and a multitude of sports activities. Kids, he thought, would often commit petty crime due to boredom. He thought himself fortunate to have been raised in a rural area of the countryside where crime was sparse. What chance did these kids have living in this industrial and poverty stricken surroundings, where the opportunities to steal and rob were much greater and more prevalent?

All these things went through his thoughts, but he recognised that he was powerless to prevent Stranks doing things his way. Noah shrugged his shoulders in futility.

At the rear of The Railway Tavern, opposite Silvertown Railway Station, stood Ryland's pie & mash shop. Noah had heard rumours that the meat in their pies was horse meat, but he'd never seen any evidence to support this idle tittle-tattle; and in any event, he found their food delicious. Noah loved eating this most traditional of cockney dishes and would sometimes pop-in for a food break during the afternoon when it was at its quietest.

Ted Ryland was removing a new batch of pies from the oven. He looked up and grinned. "Hello Mister Sheppard, how are you? Have you come in for your usual?" Noah, he knew, would always have double pie, mash and green liquor with a mug of sweet tea.

The cafe was empty. "Thanks Ted. I'm starving." He removed his helmet and sat at a bare wooden table with a bench seat. During the busy lunchtime the place would be heaving with dockers and Tate & Lyle workers as they grabbed a quick and cheap midday meal.

Ryland placed Noah's steaming plate on the table and sat on the opposite bench seat. Noah tucked into his meal and waited for Ted to make conversation; as he knew he would. Ted Ryland loved to chat about any subject under the sun and Noah often picked up small tit-bits of low level information. He wasn't exactly a copper's nark – one who traded information or who ratted on his friends - but he could at times be a rich source of information. Ryland always addressed him as Mister Sheppard, and Noah wasn't about to disavow him regarding the appropriate way in which to address a police officer. He liked to keep things on a formal footing.

Noah took a mouthful of pastry and minced beef filling and waited. Ted was rolling up a cigarette. Ryland said, "I hear that Harry Plunkett who lives in Wythes Road has caught tuberculosis and he's gone into a sanatorium." Noah nodded. He'd already heard about Harry from Mrs Plunkett.

"Did you hear about Valerie Hillman's boy?" asked Ted. Val's son was 25 years old and worked in Tate & Lyle. Without waiting for an answer, Ted said, "Him and his missus are emigrating to Australia next month. He reckons there's no future for 'em in England." Noah thought that this was hardly riveting or important information.

"What else is occurring in the parish, Ted?"

Ted Ryland was eager to be seen as a good citizen. He blew a thick cloud of cigarette smoke into the air. "I heard on the grapevine that a boatload of cheap fags are gonna be delivered next week."

"Where did you hear that?" asked Noah. This was becoming interesting.

"A bloke came in 'ere yesterday. He was tellin' his mate about it. He was sitting right there," said Ted, pointing to the adjoining table. "I overheard 'em talking."

"What did they say, Ted?"

"A boatload's coming in to North Woolwich on Tuesday night from France. I heard 'em mention the pier where the Sun tugs lay-up overnight. He said it's a nice quiet spot. That's all I heard."

Noah nodded. This was good information. If cigarettes were being smuggled, then he'd pass on the word to Andy Summers of CID, who would, no doubt, let the HM Customs black gang know about it. He pumped Ryland for any other details, but he could only give a very hazy description of the two men who had stupidly talked too loudly.

Noah continued walking his beat. The news of Johnny Hillman emigrating to Australia came as no surprise at all. Thousands of British people were packing up and leaving war-torn Britain to live on the other side of the world in what they viewed as The Land of Milk and Honey. In Australia they were becoming known as the Ten-Pound Poms because that was the subsidised price they paid for their voyage to down under. Noah couldn't blame them for leaving. Ten years after the ending of WW2, the country was tottering on the brink of bankruptcy and couldn't afford any major house rebuilding programme. In London and other major cities that had suffered air-raids by the Luftwaffe, there remained great swathes of derelict bombsites.

However, the information from Ted Ryland, concerning a boatload of smuggled cigarettes, interested him very much indeed. He phoned the station from the blue police call box and asked for DC Andy Summers to meet up with him. According to Ryland, the smuggler's boat wasn't due until Tuesday. That would give the CID another four days in which to put together a plan to nick them as they brought the cigarettes ashore.

He recalled his recent bollocking from Inspector Stranks regarding his lack of arrests. If this information should result in an important seizure, then Stranks could hardly complain about his shortcomings, could he? Furthermore, it wouldn't do the ambitious inspector's career prospects any harm either.

Noah wasn't a happy man. After notifying Summers of the intended smuggling operation, a plan of action had been agreed between the Metropolitan Force's river police division, HM Customs, and the local nick at North Woolwich. The upshot was that the Customs boys would keep watch from an upstairs room of the nearby Royal Pavilion pub which overlooked the pier, and from where they would no doubt, thought Noah cynically, be provided with snacks and liquid refreshment, whilst the river police would observe from the comfort of their warm and cosy launch on the opposite bank of the Thames. Noah and PC George Cheeseman were ordered to keep watch from aboard one of the gaggle of Sun Towage Company's tugs that was berthed on North Woolwich Pier.

From the moment they stepped onboard the tug, Noah knew that they had been given the worst possible task. The tugs were laid-up powerless and crewless for days at a time until their services were required. They climbed up to the wheelhouse from where they could observe any small craft approaching the pier. Inside, the tug was bitterly cold and rivulets of condensation ran down the steel bulkheads to form pools of water upon the decks.

"I reckon you've been given some duff information," said George, miserably after two hours had elapsed. "I wouldn't think that anyone would be so stupid as to offload thousands of smuggled cigarettes from a boat, when our police station is just two hundred yards down the road, would you?"

"I'm beginning to think you're right," said Noah. "And we're situated on a main road. It doesn't make sense that they'd bring the stuff ashore here."

Throughout the night the officers took turns at keeping watch. Nothing at all happened. At 6am the police launch came alongside. "We've been knocked-off," said the coxswain. "We're going home." He put the throttles down and the launch roared off towards London.

Noah and George found a cafe nearby and had a well-deserved fried breakfast. Tomorrow he would have a stern word with Ted Ryland. From now on, thought Noah, he could keep his damn information to himself.

Inspector Stranks was in a foul mood. The smuggling operation, which had promised to deliver some major arrests, had petered out to become a non-event. There hadn't been any sightings of small craft in the Woolwich area during the night, and it had become a complete waste of time. To make matters worse, he had personally taken charge of the operation, and requested the attendance of HM Customs and the Met's police launch. An hour ago he'd spoken to the inspector of the river police division at Scotland Yard and had felt obliged to apologise for the time-wasting fiasco.

And now, to add insult to injury, he had just got off the phone with an infuriated Chief Superintendent Humber, who had given him a right royal bollocking for wasting his division's precious time and energy. "The next time you get a tip-off, Stranks," ranted Humber, "you should check that your intelligence is accurate and that we're not all being led up the garden path. Do I make myself clear?"

The object of Peter Stranks wrath was directed at Constable Noah Sheppard. It was Sheppard who had initially reported the tip-off, resulting in the non-eventful smuggling operation. If it hadn't been for him reporting this worthless information, then he wouldn't be in this position. He could picture his chances of promotion rapidly dissipating.

To cap it all, he had foolishly bragged to Rosemary over the weekend that the imminent prospect of arrests would enhance his standing at the forthcoming meeting at the Rotary Club where senior police officers from neighbouring divisions would meet. With every minute, his anger at Sheppard's stupidity went up a notch. His thoughts at that moment centred on one particular objective. "I shall crucify the bastard."

3: The Demise of Rita Harrison

Noah was having a cup of tea with Elsie Turpin at her house in Auberon Street. He often found time to chat to Elsie, because apart from providing some fancy chocolate cakes with the aforesaid tea, she was a rich source of information and rumour about almost any subject – especially anything scandalous! She didn't just make it her business to collect gossip within her immediate locality - she knew what was happening far and wide; and most often Elsie knew the true facts rather than the idle tittle-tattle. Where gossip was concerned, Elsie Turpin was in a league of her own. She was a Nosy-Parker *par excellence*. It was well-known that she was familiar with everyone and their private business. There was a saying amongst Silvertown residents; "If you're even thinking of having a love affair with your neighbour – watch out - because Elsie Turpin will know about it, before you've had time to hold hands."

Elsie Turpin was a stout wispy-haired woman in her mid-fifties whose husband Ronnie worked in the docks. When Noah had first been posted to Silvertown, she had made it her business to cultivate his friendly manner, and he suspected that she imagined him as her own rich supply of information. However, as a serving police officer, Noah was only too well-aware that, although she provided a steady source of intelligence, one had to ensure that he didn't tell her too much, and that the exchange was mostly one-way traffic.

"I was chatting to Mrs Parry yesterday," began Elsie, as she poured more tea from the china teapot. "She lives down near the Wicket dock gate in Leonard Street. Anyway, she was telling me that her next-door neighbour - a youngish woman called Rita Harrison - seems to have gone missing."
"How long ago did she last see this Mrs Harrison?" asked Noah, becoming interested.
"She ain't been seen for over a month. Susie Parry and Rita were really good neighbours who got on very well indeed," she went on in her strong East End accent. "Rita always used to pop-in for a cuppa tea every day. Susie says that summat's not right and she's worried about Rita. She finks that if Rita was finking of moving away from the area, or visitin' relatives for a month or so, then she would have said so."
"Is Rita Harrison married? Does she have a husband?" asked Noah.
"She was married," explained Elsie. "Her 'usband worked in the docks, but he was killed about two years ago when he fell into a ship's cargo hold."

Noah winced at the thought of such a violent death. He said, "Well, that may account for why no one's reported her missing." He noted Susie Parry's address and promised to look into the matter.

The next afternoon Noah knocked at the address in Leonard Street which Elsie had given him. Susie Parry was a short bottle-blonde haired woman, who he guessed was in her middle-thirties. He related the tale as told by Elsie and asked if she could add any further information. She invited him into the front parlour and poured tea from her best china tea-set. After eighteen months among the East Enders, Noah had come-to-terms with the fact that he would be offered copious amounts of tea whilst on duty.
"I ain't heard anyfink from Rita in over five weeks," she said. "I'm really worried about her. It's unlike her to just go off and say nuffink about it."
"I understand that Mrs Harrison's husband was killed in an accident in the docks?"
That's right," she said. "It was some time back. About two years ago."
"Does Rita have a boyfriend? Is she in a relationship with anyone?" he asked. Her brow creased in thought. "She doesn't have what you would call a proper boyfriend. There's this bloke who calls twice a week. He comes on Tuesday and Friday evenings. He stays for an hour or so, and then buggers off again. I asked her about him one time, and she got quite upset and told me to mind me own bleedin' business. That's not like her to say anyfink like that. She's normally such a lovely neighbour."
"Have you seen this man's face? Would you know him if you saw him again?" asked Noah.
"I definitely would. He always wears a hat with the brim turned down, as if to hide his face. But yeah, I'd know him anywhere. He's a good deal older. About middle forties, I'd say – with thinning hair."
"Have you seen this man call here since she's gone missing?" enquired Noah. "No," she said, shaking her head. "He ain't been 'ere."
"What does Mrs Harrison do for a living?" asked Noah. "Does she have a job?"
"Yeah, she's the secretary to the works manager, Mister Mortinson, at Tate & Lyles," she said, jerking her thumb in the direction of the enormous sugar refinery.
"To your knowledge, have any work colleagues seen her within the past five weeks?"
"No they haven't," she said categorically. "A friend of hers from work knocked at my door two weeks ago and asked if I'd seen her. She said she ain't turned up for work for ages."

"Do you know of any family whom she may have gone to visit?" asked Noah, with an increasingly bad feeling about the sudden disappearance of this young woman.

"Nah, I don't fink she's got any close relations. Anyway, she would have told me if she was finking of going away for a while. Apart from that, she's left me to feed her cat."

"You're feeding her cat?" queried Noah. "Does the cat come into your house for its food?"

"No, ages ago she gave me a spare key. I go in every day and feed it."

His eyebrows lifted in surprise. "You have a key? In that case let's go and have a look around."

Noah slipped the spare key into the Yale lock and opened the door of Rita Harrison's house. Susie Parry was right behind him. It was a typical two-up two-down terraced house with a small patch of garden and a rear alleyway that butted onto the ten-foot high dock fence. The fence ran for several miles around the perimeter of the Royal Group of Docks. He sniffed the air. The place smelt stale and mouldy; as if some undiscovered foodstuff was decomposing at the back of a cupboard. "I've had to throw some food away, because it was going off," explained Mrs Parry.

They moved through the rooms, looking for any recent signs of habitation, and not expecting to find any. The rooms were cold and the fire grates contained only the grey ash of long dead coal fires. He climbed the stairs and made a brief inspection of the two bedrooms. They were neat and tidy and the beds were made-up.

Back in the lounge, a tortoiseshell cat came to brush against Noah's ankle, meowing for food. Mrs Parry opened a fresh tin of cat food and dispensed it into the food bowl on the kitchen floor. Noah spotted a cat-flap in the kitchen door which explained its comings and goings.

He opened the back door that exited onto a small garden. Like many dwellings in this area, a narrow passageway ran between the dock fence and the rear wall of the adjacent gardens. At the rear of Rita's garden, Noah spotted a wooden gate that led into the alleyway. There was a patch of coarse grass and several spindly shrubs dotted about the small plot, and Noah got the impression that Mrs Harrison wasn't a keen gardener. Halfway along the garden and butted against next-door's brick wall, lay a heavy concrete coal bunker, and stacked behind it were a half dozen burlap sacks that appeared to contain just earth and assorted debris. Against a garden wall he found some rusty garden tools, a fork and a spade, and a Dutch hoe with a broken wooden handle. The usual tin bath hung from a hook on a wall. Like a majority of the dwellings in Silvertown, this house didn't possess a bathroom, and bathing was only possible by bringing the metal bath inside the house and filling it from a succession of boiling kettles. An outside toilet was next to the kitchen, and Noah had a cursory look inside, but it revealed only a clean and tidy lavatory with a cast-iron cistern with a pull-chain flush system.

On the dining room table was a pile of mail, which Mrs Parry explained she had picked up from the hallway. There were several letters, mostly commercial flyers and suchlike. Noah decided to open them so as to shed light on her correspondence. One letter was an invoice for the overdue payment for half a ton of coal, which he presumably thought he would find, stowed in the garden coal bunker. Another invoice was an overdue account from the milkman. Mrs Parry explained that she had cancelled the milk delivery after it had begun to pile-up on the doorstep.

The furniture in the house was of the post-war utility type, and even that looked as if it were threadbare and second-hand. Nothing looked new. In the corner of the lounge was an upright roll-top desk which had pigeon-hole compartments stuffed with paperwork and stationary items. In one compartment he found a cheque book. He flicked through the cheque stubs and found nothing untoward; simply cheques made out to tradesmen. This begged the question; if she wasn't earning cash and her cheque book was in his possession, then what was she using for money? On another shelf Noah spotted a navy blue United Kingdom passport in the name of Rita Sylvia Harrison. It contained a stamp for Boulogne in France dated 1947. Could this trip abroad have been perhaps her honeymoon with her late husband? He leafed through its pages, and for the first time was able to look at a photograph of the missing woman. The photo was taken that same year, and showed a dark haired woman who would have been in her early twenties. Noah looked carefully at the picture and thought that she had an attractive fresh face. The crow's feet that radiated out from her eyes enhanced the features and made her look quite striking. He also noticed that she had a small beauty spot upon her upper left cheek. He put the passport in his pocket and the pair continued moving from room to room, searching for anything that could throw any light upon her whereabouts. One thing was for certain. Rita Sylvia Harrison was definitely not travelling abroad. Noah had her passport in his pocket to prove it. Eventually they relocked the house and Noah promised Mrs Parry that he would make some further investigations.

The next morning Noah made some enquiries and discovered the name and address of the owner of Mrs Harrison's rented property. He had found it strange that there were letters on the doormat from the milkman and the coalman demanding payment; but after five weeks there appeared to be no letter from Rita Harrison's landlord asking why he hadn't received any rent. It was most odd. Noah had gone to visit the landlord – and had discovered some very interesting information indeed.

Around lunchtime he presented himself at the main entrance of the Tate & Lyle factory and asked a uniformed commissionaire to see the works manager. He was escorted through the office building and asked to wait in the manager's outer office.

Noah was a worried man. He questioned whether he should in fact, be investigating the disappearance of Rita Harrison at all. After all, it was one thing to make some tentative enquiries and have a cup of tea with Mrs Parry, and perhaps even a cursory search of Rita Harrison's house. However, it was not his job to go barging into the Tate & Lyle manager's office to investigate reports of a missing person. This was clearly the responsibility of the Criminal Investigation Department. He should have mentioned the facts of the case to Sergeant Ambrose and submitted a written report. The incident would then have been handed over to the CID.

Noah was hesitant about his actions, even though he simply wanted to ensure that Rita Harrison was in fact missing. There could very easily be another explanation. The more he thought about it, the more worried he became about stepping on the toes of the CID detectives. What the hell was he thinking? He could get into a lot of trouble. He was a simple uniformed beat copper, and it was definitely not his task to carry out an investigation. He could visualize the plain-clothes CID boys getting very upset if they should find out. He looked at his wristwatch. He had been kept waiting 30 minutes - which he thought was rather rude - but it wasn't too late to abandon his visit. Mister Mortinson's secretary sat typing a letter at a desk in the corner of the office. He could easily tell her that he'd changed his mind and simply walk out and forget about the whole affair.

Suddenly, the works manager's office door opened and a stern faced man stepped out. He said, "I'm Raymond Mortinson. I'm rather busy. What do you want?" Noah extended his hand and introduced himself. The man was clearly irritated but waved Noah into his office and signalled for him to take a seat. Mortinson took his own seat behind his desk. "So, make it quick. What do you need to see me about?"
"I'm making enquiries regarding the whereabouts of Mrs Rita Harrison. I understand that she's your secretary."
Raymond Mortinson looked shaken at the mention of his secretary's name, but quickly regained his composure. "I don't know where she is. She didn't come into work anymore. I don't know where she's gone."
"I'm not saying that you do know where she is, sir. I'm simply asking if you can shed any light on her disappearance."
Mortinson shook his head. "I haven't seen her in over six weeks."

"How long has she been your secretary, sir?"

"She was my secretary for the past two years. Before that she worked in the general typing pool."

"Haven't you found it rather strange that she's gone absent without saying anything about her intended movements?"

Mortinson stared at the floor. "Not really. She was free to do whatever she pleased."

"Is she a good secretary, Mister Mortinson? Does she perform her duties satisfactorily?"

"She was okay, I suppose. She did her job," muttered Mortinson.

"Are you aware if she has a boyfriend?"

Mortinson looked surprised at the question. "I've no idea," he said testily. "She wasn't the sort of person to discuss her private life."

"There's just one last question, sir. Have you ever had any social contact with Mrs Harrison outside of the factory?"

"What the hell kind of question is that?" exploded Mortinson, his face and neck turning red. "Of course I haven't. I've never met Mrs Harrison socially."

"I'm simply trying to get a clearer picture, sir," said Noah, standing up to leave. "Thank you for your time."

Long after the policeman had left his office, Raymond Mortinson sat at his desk deep in thought; wondering how on Earth the police could possibly have linked him to Rita's disappearance? Surely they didn't have any evidence? The constable had simply said that Rita was missing. He hadn't mentioned anything about her body being found, had he? Perhaps it was normal routine procedure to interview a missing person's work colleagues? Even if they have found her body, would they be able to make a connection? He doubted it. He wished he'd never heard of Rita, damn her. His thoughts recalled the series of events that had led to his relationship with his secretary.

She had previously been just one of the dozens of admin staff working in the typing pool at Tate & Lyle's refinery. Raymond had been her boss. He had often noticed her attractive figure and pretty face as she worked at her typewriter, or during a lunch break in the works canteen. He would secretly fantasize with thoughts of a sexual nature; imagining her in bed beside him, but he was well aware that, not only was she a happily married woman, but that he was at least ten years older.

Then, just over two years ago, her husband was tragically killed in an accident aboard a ship in the Royal Docks, where he was a stevedore.

Rita becoming a widow coincided with his regular office secretary handing in her notice; and so on an impulse, he promoted Rita and made her his secretary and personal assistant. She was also given a small increase in salary. With experience, she became a good and reliable member of his staff, easily able to cope with the responsibilities of running his busy office. He remembered that this gave him ample opportunities to admire her shapely body, and he would often find himself covertly staring at her well-formed breasts and long slim legs. She was a well-spoken woman with a warm and friendly voice, quite unlike some of the brash girls working down in the sugar packing room.

Conversely, his wife Hilda, to whom he had been married for almost 20 years, held no attraction for him whatsoever. Before their marriage, Hilda would never allow his sexual advances to amount to anything, stating that she was saving her chastity for their wedding night. Whenever he attempted to caress her shapely curves, it was rebuffed with, "Oh darling, don't spoil things. Let's wait until we're married." This only made him ever more determined to ravish her virgin body, even if it meant tying the knot. Hilda's widowed father had been a rich city banker, whose only child would eventually inherit his fortune, and the promise of a sizeable inheritance for his bride-to-be, he told himself, was an additional compelling reason to marry into substantial wealth.

As a young man in the 1930's, his opptortunities to engage in any incidents of a sexual nature were few and far between, as most decent young ladies were brought up in the Victorian manner, to practice chastity before marriage. Consequently, his sexual experience had consisted of a single occasion when he had met an older woman in a bar.

He recalled their wedding day almost twenty years ago. The events, even now, were fresh in his memory. He recalled the ceremony in the church, the wedding reception afterwards at the country club. He remembered speeches being made, cutting the wedding cake, and dancing with his new bride. But most of all, he recalled looking forward to taking his virgin wife to their hotel honeymoon suite and making love to her.

He remembered that night with perfect clarity. Their honeymoon was at a seaside hotel, and they had travelled down on the steam train. Hilda had been laughing and bubbly throughout their journey and during dinner in the hotel dining room; but all that had changed when they retired to the bridal suite. She had insisted that they turn out the lights before getting undressed, and had laid motionless on the far side of the bed. He had tried to be understanding and at least coaxed her into letting him take her into his arms, but she lay there rigidly and immobile, and apart from allowing him to kiss her, she wouldn't respond to his overtures of love.

Their week long honeymoon had been a disaster. For three days and nights he had tried to make love to her, explaining that it was perfectly normal behaviour for married couples to indulge in sexual intercourse, but she would have none of it, arguing that it felt dirty and contrary to her Christian upbringing. "I do love you, Raymond. But why do you have to spoil things? Isn't it enough that we're together?" she had asked.

On the fourth night, after much persuasion and cajoling, she reluctantly allowed him the conjugal rights that he craved. It was a disastrous failure. He had tried, within his limited experience, to be a gentle and considerate lover, but after the actual act of intercourse, she had turned over and cried herself to sleep.

After their return from honeymoon the situation never improved. For a time they lived at her father's extensive house in London's outer suburbs, and Hilda moved into a separate bedroom, citing the excuse that he snored. Even when they moved into a home of their own, this state of affairs never changed. Outwardly, during the daytime, Hilda would be the loving housewife, keeping a tidy home and preparing wholesome meals; but come the night she retired to her own bedroom and they very rarely had relations of a sexual nature.

Instead Raymond threw himself into his career, working hard and quickly gaining promotion at the giant Tate & Lyle sugar refinery. Eventually, after a steady climb up the managerial ladder, he was elevated to the position of work's manager. Almost immediately he began to change his management style to one that was more confrontational and aggressive. Gone was the cosy arrangement, whereby his juniors could breeze into his office for a pleasant chat. He was quite aware that his subordinates now viewed a summons to his office with a certain amount of fear and anxiety, because he would often employ bullying tactics and the threat of dismissal as a means to secure their obedience. He saw no problem with that. He was, after all, the work's manager, and he required his orders to be obeyed.

It was a pity, he thought cynically, that he couldn't get his own wife to obey his orders with regard to making herself available in the bedroom department, but any hope of improvement in that area had long ago been snuffed out, when she had informed him that, "I don't ever intend to let you take advantage of me to satisfy your deviant desires."

Occasionally he would take a bus ride into the city centre; and in Soho, would employ the services of a prostitute, with whom he could do anything he wished. However, it gnawed at his pride that his prudish wife was utterly spoilt and that she gave him nothing in return.

Mortinson rose from his desk and looked down at the activity on the factory floor far below. From his high vantage point he could see one of the company's own fleet of ships as it discharged raw sugar at the riverside berth. The ship's cargo had been loaded at one of Tate & Lyle's own sugar plantations in the West Indies. On arrival in London the cargo was loaded onto conveyor belts and taken into the heart of the plant to be refined and automatically packaged into 2lb bags. He could see the employees industriously hard at work with fork-lifts, loading up trucks that would distribute the sugar to all four corners of Great Britain and beyond. He returned to his desk, pensively reflecting on the events that had led to his association with Rita Harrison.

Some months after she had became his secretary, she had warily approached him to ask if it might be possible to have a pay increase, citing the fact that she had now been his secretary for six months and had passed the required probationary period. He told her that he'd think about it. She had seemed worried and anxious, and had said that, after the death of her husband, she was finding it difficult to afford the rent on their house in Leonard Street. She added that, with only her wages coming in, she was worried about being evicted.

He had given it some consideration and had seized upon an idea taking shape in his thoughts. He told her that he valued the work that she did, and wouldn't like to see her evicted out onto the street. Therefore, the company would be willing to pay the rent in lieu of a pay rise. If he gave her a pay increase, he stated, the other office staff would undoubtedly want one too. It had seemed rather strange to Rita Harrison, that her boss, who was known to keep a tight grip on the company's finances, should be willing to become her saviour. Their arrangement, and the rent payments, he said, must remain confidential between themselves. It would, he said, be their little secret and his cash-strapped secretary had taken the offer with both hands, as a drowning man would grasp at a lifebelt.

However, he had failed to tell Rita that the rent payments would be coming from his own pocket, as she may otherwise have smelt a rat. He duly arranged with the landlord to take over the weekly payments and assured Rita that she need never worry about her rent again; it was all taken care of. Little did she know that Raymond Mortinson had a plan to be reimbursed in a more subtle fashion.

A few evenings later he turned up unannounced on her doorstep and she naturally invited him inside. He brought a bottle of wine and a bouquet of roses, and slowly and surely began to court her. Twice every week he would visit, gradually gaining her confidence. He would bring chocolates, sheer nylon stockings, and other luxury gifts. At first she was flattered that a man in such a high-ranking position in the factory should want to woo his lowly secretary; but she didn't have the confidence to rebuff his advances. He was, after all, the man who arranged for her rent to be paid and had the power over her future employment. He wasn't an unattractive man, she told herself. A woman could do a lot worse. She was quite aware that he was married, and in fact, he had openly told her about the situation with his wife. Rita was unsure if she should allow this to go further; but deep down, after so tragically losing her husband, she was desperately lonely and in need of some male companionship. In her heart-of-hearts, she knew that they would begin an affair, even though she was under no illusions that she would simply be his girlfriend; his occasional bit on the side. And then one evening, he had simply taken her into his arms and kissed her, and that small act had initiated a full-blown love-affair. She had allowed him to lead her upstairs to the bedroom where they quietly undressed and self-consciously crept into bed.

His lovemaking, he admitted to himself, had been awkward and amateurish; the result of very little sexual experience. But gradually, he thought smugly, his proficiency in the bedroom had improved considerably. He limited his visits to two times per week, on Tuesday and Friday evenings, when Hilda attended her Women's Institute meetings, and wouldn't notice his absence. He could always claim that he was working late at the office, but he was secretly terrified in case she should discover the truth. Her wealthy father had died some years ago, and Hilda had consequently inherited the whole of his estate; which was considerable. With her new wealth, he and Hilda had moved into a large sprawling house in the outer suburbs, which allowed her to indulge her passion for entertaining her circle of friends. Conversely, with all their wealth in his wife's name, he was still relatively penniless, with only his wages to his name. Therefore, whenever he arrived at the house in Leonard Street, he ensured that his hat brim was firmly pulled down over his face to hide his features. Raymond Mortinson had no intention of allowing his visits to his part-time fancy woman to become common knowledge and to wreck his marriage, albeit a loveless union.

And then, almost six weeks ago, Rita had dropped a bombshell. It was a Tuesday evening, and he had arrived at her house eager to take her upstairs to the bedroom. She seemed in a sombre mood. "I've been to see my doctor, and he's confirmed that I'm pregnant," she had told him.
"Bloody hell, Rita," he'd exploded. "Why didn't you take some precautions?"
"Me? Why didn't you? You could have worn a French letter, but you always refused."
He thought furiously, considering all the options. "Well, you'll just have to get rid of it," he told her firmly. "I'll find someone who can do the job. I'll pay for it, of course."
The horror on her face said it all. "I'm not having some amateur back-street abortionist kill my baby," she spat out. "You can forget that idea. I'm going

to have the baby and I'm intending to keep it," she had said forcefully, like a lioness protecting her cubs.

"But Rita," he pleaded, "you can't bring up a baby all by yourself."

"Says who?" she retorted. "Anyway, I was hoping you would be helping me financially."

He ignored her hint for more monetary help. If this should ever become widely known, he thought anxiously, then he would be ruined. He could imagine word spreading through the factory like wildfire. He had countless enemies at Tate & Lyle who would gladly tell his wife the awful truth. He visualized Hilda throwing him out onto the street. Their marriage would certainly culminate in divorce, and he would be penniless. His foolhardiness would be viewed by the Tate & Lyle directors as suspect, and his senior position would be at risk. His mind could see danger signals exploding like distress rockets – sending out their message - "She mustn't have this baby."

"Let's get this straight. You cannot have this child," he said firmly. "If anyone should find out that I was the father, then I'd be ruined. It cannot happen. Do you understand me?"

"Don't worry, Raymond," she jeered, "you've made it crystal clear that you have no intention of helping me. You're the last person I'd want identified as the father of my child."

He could feel the pressure inside his head rising; as if he was about to implode. "You'll have to have an abortion," he screamed. "Is that understood?"

"Are you worried in case your wife should find out?" she sneered. "Is that what you're afraid of?"

He ignored the implied threat. "If you insist on keeping the baby, then you'll be on your own," he shouted, his face and neck turning red. He decided to apply some pressure. "I could arrange matters so that this cosy arrangement is finished, and your rent doesn't get paid. What would you do then, Rita?"

"Don't threaten me, Raymond, or I may have to go have a quiet word with your missus," she said threateningly. "Don't think I wouldn't. I don't imagine she'd think very highly of you, would she?"

"You wouldn't dare," he said menacingly. "Otherwise you'll find yourself unemployed sooner than you think."

"You're a bastard, Raymond," she screamed. "You're a twenty-four carat bastard." Her outburst was a side of her personality that he'd never encountered. Usually she was an outgoing woman with a happy bubbly character; but now she was wild eyed as she shouted and screamed at him. "You come here twice a week simply to shag me – which, by the way - you're not very good at. Then you think you can make me pregnant and fob me off with threats of having me thrown out onto the street. You've got another think coming."

He saw red. "Shut up. Shut your mouth," he screamed. His hand lashed out and slapped her face, leaving a red mark on her cheek.

Raymond Mortinson arose from his office desk and opened the window, taking deep lungfuls of fresh air in an attempt to calm himself down. Events were a bit hazy after that. He remembered hitting her hard. She had tears in her eyes as she screamed profanities at him, calling him every vulgar name she could think of. He just wanted her to shut up. He recalled knocking her to the floor and violently wrestling with her until he gripped her neck with his fingers – and pressed harder. Just wanting her to shut up!

Noah Sheppard returned to Susie Parry's house in the afternoon and was invited inside. Over a cup of tea and biscuits, he said, "You told me yesterday that Rita had a visitor call twice a week."
She nodded. "That's right, he came as regular as clockwork. But he ain't showed up since she went missing."
"You also said that you would recognize him again. Are you quite certain?"
"Absolutely," she said emphatically. "I'd know him anywhere."
"In that case, I need your assistance," requested Noah. "It's almost time for the day-work office staff at Tate & Lyle's to finish work. I want you to come to the factory gate and we'll see if you can spot Rita's mystery caller."

They walked the few hundred yards to the factory's main entrance and Noah had a few words with the uniformed commissionaire manning the gate. Without any explanation, he and Susie Parry were allowed to sit inside the gatehouse, where it was warm, and from where they had a clear view of the departing sugar workers. They were not likely to be spotted, as the windows of the gatehouse were tinted. The factory hooter sounded stridently to indicate that it was 5pm, and presently the office staff began to leave. Susie Parry studied each face intently as they exited from the double doors leading from the office complex. "There's no one I recognise so far," she said.

Minutes later, a man came out of the office, striding briskly towards the gate, eager to catch the bus home. "That's him," she said positively, pointing at a suited man with a briefcase and umbrella. "I'd stake my life on it. It's definitely the same bloke."
Noah nodded in satisfaction. "Thanks Susie. That's all we need for now. I'll walk you back home."

He returned to the police station and went to see Sergeant Ambrose. The sergeant was frankly flabbergasted by the details that Noah reported. He sat him down in the duty room and insisted he write a full written statement there and then.

"Well young Noah," said Ambrose, using the constable's Christian name as he reread the report, "you appear to have solved this nasty little crime all by yourself, haven't you?"
"Thanks Sarge," replied Noah, "but there are still quite a few gaps to fill-in."

The next morning, Noah found himself in an unusual situation for a rookie police constable. With a possible murder on their hands, Scotland Yard's Criminal Investigation Department - the CID - had been called in to take over the case; and because it had occurred on his patch, and had first-hand knowledge of the incident, Noah was ordered to assist them. Bert Ambrose had taken him to one side. "You've done a good job, lad. By all means, help out the CID boys, but just make sure you let the detectives pick up all the credit. That's how this game is played; but you could come out of this smelling of roses, okay?" Noah was grinning with pride. Sergeant Ambrose didn't often give out congratulations.

The CID arrived from Scotland Yard mid-morning. They were shown into Inspector Stranks' office where they were joined by Bert Ambrose and Noah. Introductions were made, and tea and biscuits were served by the duty station constable.
"I'm Detective Inspector Marston," said the tall senior man, shaking hands. Marston appeared to be in his middle fifties and probably old enough to retire from the force on a comfortable pension, but with his worldly-wise face, and eyes that appeared to miss nothing, Noah correctly guessed that he stayed on in the job simply because he loved the cut-and-thrust of putting criminals behind bars. Marston indicated his colleague. "This is Detective Constable Raines, who will be assisting me in this investigation." Raines was a rather chubby red-faced man in his early thirties.

Marston hung his hat and gabardine overcoat upon the coat-hook and made himself comfortable. The room was quiet as he studied a document, which Noah recognised as the statement which he had written yesterday. Marston removed his spectacles, polishing them with a handkerchief. "If indeed any crime has been committed, then you seem to have solved it all on your lonesome, constable. Well done."
Noah blushed. "Thank you, sir," he murmured.
"Are you quite certain that our suspect is the work's manager, Constable Sheppard?"
"I'm fairly certain, sir, although the evidence seems circumstantial."
"What makes you so sure he's our man?" asked Marston.

"When I questioned him in his office yesterday, every answer he gave in relation to Rita Harrison was made in the past tense. It was as if he already knew that she was dead. Also, he denied any social contact with her outside of the factory – which we know to be untrue."

"Hmm, yes, I see," said the detective inspector, studying the statement closely. "I'll tell you what we'll do. We shall go visit this Mrs Parry and the landlord of Rita Harrison's house, and we'll get written statements from them. Then I think we'll have a more thorough search of her house." He pointed at Noah. "Seeing as how you've got first-hand knowledge of this case, then I'd like you to come with us, okay?"

Noah glanced at Inspector Stranks for confirmation. Stranks nodded. "That's fine. You're assigned to DI Marston until further notice."

The three police officers that same afternoon interviewed Susie Parry at her house in Leonard Street. She had felt as proud as a peacock that a senior detective - from Scotland Yard no less - was sitting in her front parlour drinking from her best china tea-set and taking notes of the crucial information which she had provided. For this special occasion, she had even worn her best frock and taken the curlers from her hair. She anticipated that her wide circle of friends would be eager to hear a full account of the affair when she met them down the pub later. She would be the centre of attention. Satisfied that she had thoroughly described the events relating to the disappearance of her neighbour, Marston had her sign a sworn statement and took possession of the spare key for the house next-door.

When they opened the door to Rita Harrison's house, a crowd had begun to assemble in the street and householders were openly gawping from behind their net curtains. After all, it wasn't an everyday occurrence to find a police car parked in the street. Already, word had spread that the police were looking for a body and rumours were rife, even though the police investigation was in its early stages.

Inside the house, it was exactly as Noah had left it, except that Mrs Parry had put fresh cat food in the bowl and some post had been laid on the lounge table. "Have a look in all the rooms and up in the loft-space," ordered Marston. "Meanwhile I want to look at the mail." Detective Constable Raines and Noah explored every room, looking under beds and in wardrobes, and searching for anything unusual.

They rejoined Marston, who sat deep in thought as he leafed through Rita Harrison's passport. Her photograph stared back at him. "She was quite a pretty lady, wasn't she, Constable Sheppard?"

He noted that Marston referred to her in the past tense. "Yes sir, she certainly was," he agreed.

The detective leaned back in the chair, his hands intertwined behind his head and his eyes half closed in deliberation. "I'll tell you what's bothering me, shall I?" Without waiting for a response, he said, "Rita hasn't been seen for the past six weeks, has she?"
"No sir," said Raines and Noah in unison.
"But according to this unpaid invoice from the coalman, a half ton of coal was delivered to this house three weeks ago," said Marston pensively. "Which begs the question; if Mrs Harrison wasn't here to order the coal, then who did?"
Noah decided to be bold. He said, "More to the point, sir, If Mrs Harrison was already missing, then why order it at all?"
"That's a very good point, Constable. Let's go have a look at the garden."

Nothing had changed in the garden since Noah had last been here. However, Raines made a point of searching the toilet and rear alleyway, simply to show his boss that he was being a busy-bee. Marston meanwhile, had taken the wooden lid from the coal bunker and was peering inside. A great heap of black coal filled the entire bunker.
"Do you reckon that you could hide a woman's body inside that bunker?" asked Marston, addressing both officers.
"It's possible, sir," agreed Raines.
"In that case, you and Constable Sheppard can grab that spade and start digging out the coal."

It took the best part of an hour to extract the coal and to lay it in a heap beside the bunker. Meanwhile, the residents of the adjoining houses had come out to stand in the rear alleyway to gawp and to whisper at the policemen's activities. Rumours would henceforth be rife with supposition; and every facet of police activity would be embroidered and embellished when it was told and retold in the pubs and factories of Silvertown.

When at last they had emptied the coal bunker, they found a sheet of thick plywood lining the base. The wood looked fairly new, and Noah instinctively knew what they would find beneath it. Under the wood, the earth looked to have been freshly dug-over. Noah carefully raked away the top layer of soil and almost immediately unearthed a human hand. Even though he had been expecting to find her, he was nevertheless shaken by the discovery of the corpse.
"Well done, lads," said Marston. "You can stop digging for now. We'll leave the body where it is until the forensics team has had a look at it." He said to Noah, "Nip along to the police box and phone the station. Tell them what we've found and ask them to contact the coroner's office and to send a forensics team down here, okay?"

The coroner submitted his findings of the post-mortem the next morning, and they again assembled in the station inspector's office to study the report. The room was quiet as Marston skimmed through the document. He removed his spectacles and vigorously polished the lens, and Noah guessed that his spectacles got this treatment whenever he needed to concentrate. "The identity of the deceased is confirmed as that of Rita Sylvia Harrison, and the cause of death was strangulation," he told them. "The exact time of death cannot be determined, but is thought to be between four to six weeks." He looked up from the report. "Another interesting fact is that she was two months pregnant."
"What happens now, sir," asked Noah.
"I think it's time we paid a visit to Mister Raymond Mortinson and we'll see what he's got to say for himself."

After they had left his office Peter Stranks quietly fumed. He had been on the verge of disciplining Sheppard for wilfully refusing to improve his performance, but now the wind had been taken out of his sails. He could hardly haul him over the coals for lack of arrests, especially when he'd been instrumental in solving the Harrison murder, could he? He was most displeased.

Later that morning, the two detectives and Noah Sheppard entered the office of Raymond Mortinson. He was shaken to see them, but quickly pulled himself together. "What can I do for you? If this is in relation to Rita Harrison, then I've already given Constable Sheppard here, all the information I'm aware of."
Marston flashed his identification card. "That's not quite true, is it Mister Mortinson?"
Mortinson looked uncertain. "I don't know what you mean. I've told you everything." Noah noticed his hand begin to shake involuntarily.
Uninvited, Marston stretched out in a leather chair. "Rita Harrison's body has been found at her house. She had some rather nasty bruising around her neck which was caused by strangulation," he said, matter-of-factly.
"I'm sorry to hear that," whispered Mortinson, his eyes fixed on the carpet. He felt numb with fear.
"I'll bet you are. Also, she happened to be rather pregnant, but I assume you already knew about that, didn't you?" The detective inspector's voice sounded relaxed and confident.
Mortinson looked scared. His eyes were searching this way and that, as if he could magically escape this nightmare, but Raines stood implacably by the door. "I don't know what you're suggesting. I know nothing about it."

"Of course you do, Raymond," Marston said in a friendly voice. "We know that it's you who pays the rent on Mrs Harrison's house in Leonard Street. We've spoken to the landlord." Mortinson stared fixedly out of the office window as his world came crashing down around him. He was silently shaking his head, hoping against hope that it was all a dream.

"We've had a chat with Rita's neighbour, and she's positively identified you as the man who turns up every Tuesday and Friday evening at Rita's house. Was that so you could get your nooky, Raymond?" Tears welled-up in Mortinson's eyes and he dabbed his face with a handkerchief. "No doubt we'll be finding your fingerprints all over her house, and I'll even bet next year's salary that we'll discover some forensic evidence that links you to her death." Mortinson was unresponsive, and with lifeless eyes, continued to stare into the distance.

"Why did you kill her, Raymond? Was it because she was pregnant? Did she want to keep the baby? Were you afraid that your wife would find out? Is that the way it was?"

Raymond Mortinson's eyes were brimming with tears and he shook his head uncontrollably from side to side, unable to speak coherently. His shoulders sagged in defeat, knowing that he was beaten, knowing that his lies had unravelled and that his world had come apart.

Detective Inspector Marston stood up. It was time to go. He looked down at Mortinson, who remained staring into space. "You didn't plan this very well, did you Raymond? You didn't prepare for the unexpected. You never know what's going to come out of the blue, do you?" He read him his legal rights whilst Noah cuffed his wrists and they marched him downstairs to the waiting police car.

In the factory area, word had somehow spread and a crowd had gathered to watch in stunned silence as Mortinson was led across the factory floor. He had once been the high-flying boss, and now he was accused of murder. None were sorry to see him get his comeuppance.

.

4: The Reverend Samuel Hogan

It was three weeks later and the only clue that spring had arrived were the trees in Victoria Park were in bud and the grass was becoming greener. Elsewhere in this industrial conglomeration, any flower or plant that attempted to bloom into life was quickly snuffed out under the heavy cloud of thick smoke that constantly belched from the factory chimneys. The only vegetation that seemed to thrive was the thick masses of weeds growing upon the bombsites.

Noah returned to the station after yet another long day pounding the beat. At the reception desk the duty constable handed him a letter. The envelope was postmarked Broxbourne in Hertfordshire, and the handwriting was in Wendy's neat and precise script. He had first met Wendy Everett at a dance held in the village hall some eighteen months ago. She lived in a neighbouring village and worked at the pharmacy in the nearby town of Hoddesdon.

During the following month, he had tentatively held her hand and stolen several kisses, and she had become his girlfriend. She would normally write a letter every week, to pass on village gossip and tell him what she had been doing; and although her news was mainly unexciting and humdrum, he nevertheless looked forward to receiving her scented letters. He took it upstairs to his room in the police section house and lay on the single bed to read it.

Usually she would fill three or perhaps four pages with her news of life in Broxbourne and the surrounding villages, but surprisingly, this was just a single page. Instead of beginning her letter with her usual, "My darling Noah," it simply said Dear Noah. She had tried to let him down gently, but the end-result was the same. She said that, after being his girlfriend for all this time, she had always hoped they would settle down and get married. Wendy explained that she couldn't hang on forever in the expectation that he would one day pop-the-question, so therefore, she was ending their relationship. She went on to say that there was a local chap with a good job, who wanted to take her out, and so it was best to break-up now.

He re-read the letter, not quite certain if he should be sad or relieved their relationship was over. On the one hand, it was depressing that she had found someone else, but on the other side of the coin; after tasting the exciting fleshpots of Germany and London, he really couldn't see himself settling down with a wife and kids in a sleepy Hertfordshire town. Life was too short not to enjoy it, he decided. He wrote a letter in reply; wishing her every success for the future.

North Woolwich police station employed just one civilian employee. She was Mrs Lillian Branson; a formidable lady in her late-40's who guarded her territory like a lioness guards her cubs. Lily's job description stated that she was responsible for cleaning the station and cooking a midday meal for duty police officers; and Lily took her responsibilities very seriously indeed. Anyone who hindered or thwarted her considerable efforts would be well advised to step smartly backwards, because once her fuse was lit, she would give the unfortunate officer, whatever his rank, a tongue lashing that would make a Regimental Sergeant Major's worst tirade seem tame by comparison. She had once given Inspector Stranks a right royal bollocking for walking across a freshly mopped tiled floor; after which Stranks had mumbled his apologies and retreated to the safety of his office.

Lily was a born and bred cockney who lived locally with her docker husband Fred and five children. She was a short dumpy woman, who always wore a wrap-around pinafore and a turban hat. Over the years her shrewd and animated eyes had seen dozens of police officers come and go. Lily's only vice, apart from her short fuse, was the cigarettes which she endlessly chain smoked. She would invariably have a Woodbine dangling from her lips which - even when she spoke - would waggle up and down almost with a life of its own. She was known throughout the station as Fag-Ash Lil.

Noah had incurred her wrath soon after being posted to North Woolwich as a rookie constable, when he had inadvertently slopped tea onto her nice clean floor. But despite her short temper, Lily was a real character who was known and loved throughout the station. With her quick wit and a knack for telling dirty jokes, she was looked upon as one of the boys.

Noah was ambling around Silvertown on his usual haphazard patrol, which meant that he went wherever he pleased. Today he'd called in on some local shops to pass a few moments in idle chit-chat and to gently pump them for information. It was amazing how much intelligence he picked up on his travels simply by starting a conversation with a smile and a bright "Good morning." Today had been the turn of Curly and George Merritt at their greengrocery shop in Albert Road. Back in the day, George had been a useful light-heavyweight boxer, and had a cauliflower ear and a flat nose to prove it. The brothers always kept their customer's gossip to themselves, so there was no information at all to impart, but Noah liked to spend a few minutes listening to stories about George's pugilistic career, when he had been an up-and-coming fighter. He had a chat with Mrs Dellamura at her grocery and ice-cream shop in Andrew Street, but today things had been slow and information had been thin on the ground.

Noah decided to go have a look at the damage to St. Mark's Church roof that had occurred a few weeks ago. Sergeant Ambrose had briefed him that a quantity of lead had been removed, but there had been no further information. Of course, Noah suspected that Frankie Houlder, the scrap metal merchant, had bought the lead from whoever had stripped the roof, but he had no way of proving it.

He bought a slab of fried cod and chips for his lunch from Staggies chip shop in Constance Street. He planned to eat it in the graveyard behind the church, where it was quiet and no one would be able to see him. He ensured that the woman serving behind the counter double-wrapped his fish in newspaper so it didn't get cold. Sergeant Ambrose took a dim view of any of his officers eating food, especially fish and chips, within plain view of the general public. Ambrose didn't think it conveyed the right message to the local residents if his officers walked around reeking of vinegar and with tomato ketchup oozing down their chins.

He walked across the footbridge that led from Silvertown Railway Station and into the morass of industrial factories that lined the banks of the River Thames. The manufacturing works belched smoke and noise all day long and their brickwork and chimneys were encrusted in a thick coating of grime. A steam tank engine pulling dozens of goods wagons screeched by under the bridge on its way to Stratford. As it passed beneath the footbridge with a chuff-chuff-chuff, a cloud of grey smoke rings were expelled from its blackened chimney and Noah was warmly swathed in acrid smoke and that wonderful smell of steam from its pistons.

St. Mark's Church was surrounded by railway sidings and factories on three sides and by vegetable allotments on its eastern perimeter. The church, built in the 1860s, was a solid looking building with a proliferation of stained-glass windows and an ornate steeple with turrets at its eastern end. Noah found a quiet spot in the graveyard where he could sit with his back against an old gravestone and stretch his legs out. It was an unseasonably warm day and it felt good to feel the rays of the sun on his shoulders. He unwrapped his fried fish lunch and almost salivated as the undeniable smell of salt n'vinegar reached his nostrils. He took a deep breath and savoured the aroma for a few seconds before biting down into the fish.

"You look as if you're enjoying that, Noah." The booming voice had come from over his shoulder. He swung around to find the Reverend Samuel Hogan grinning at him from behind the gravestone.

"Oh my God, you nearly gave me a heart attack," said Noah, almost choking on the fish.

"It wouldn't be the Good Lord's fault if you had a seizure," said Hogan. "You must have been a terrible sinner in the past. But you can repent your sins by sharing that nice piece of fish you're holding in your hand."
Noah tore off a chunk of cod and handed it over, then divided up the chips. Hogan stretched his long legs and made himself comfortable on the grass beside him. "I'm so glad I found you here, Noah. These are delicious," he said, indicating the chips.

They ate their meal in the silence of friends who have no real need to speak just for the sake of conversation. Noah had first met Sam Hogan after being posted to North Woolwich as a rookie constable. He had been attending the magistrate's court for a case involving a young girl accused of shoplifting and had got chatting to the reverend as they waited for the case to be called. Sam Hogan, it transpired, was there to speak up for the girl; which he did with much success, because she was let off with a small fine.

Approaching fifty years old, Hogan was almost twice Noah's age, but he acted much younger than his years and Noah found him like a breath of fresh air. He respected the fact that Hogan never tried to ram religion down anyone's throat. This was especially relevant because Noah was not remotely religious and had only ever attended Sunday school as a lad because his parents had insisted upon it.
"I'm actually here to look at your vestry roof. I hear it's been stripped."
"There's not much left to see," said Sam. "The bastards took all the lead flashing from the valleys, and ridges and hips, and now the place leaks like a bloody sieve." It wasn't unusual for Hogan to swear like a docker when amongst his men friends, but he acted like an angelic cherub amongst his parishioners.
"Do you think there's any likelihood that the police will ever find whoever stripped my roof?" asked Hogan hopefully. "It's going to cost a fortune to get it replaced."
"I don't think there's a cat-in-hell's-chance of that. In any case, even if we found who stripped it – they're not capable of reinstalling it, are they?"
"I suppose not," he said miserably.
"Sorry Sam, but I suspect that the lead's already been sold to some unscrupulous scrap metal merchant." He had Frankie Houlder in mind, but kept that snippet of information to himself.
Samuel Hogan was still a handsome man and his brown eyes crinkled with humour when he smiled. "In that case, Noah, I shall pray that the bastards fall off the roof and break a bone or two the next time they're nicking some poor bugger's lead."

Upon the following Saturday, the Reverend Hogan was standing on the chancel steps, awaiting the arrival of the bride and to begin the wedding ceremony. From his elevated position he could see down the length of the church. Below him the groom and best man were fidgeting at the front of the congregation. He thought the groom looked like a condemned man awaiting his fate. Behind him, approximately 100 guests were here to witness the nuptials take place. He didn't recognise any of them as his regular parishioners. His organist, Mrs Fry, was playing such sombre music that the congregation was in danger of nodding off to sleep. He wished she would play something more happy-go-lucky. It didn't seem like a joyful occasion, as there was not a single smile amongst the entire congregation. He thought that one could be forgiven for thinking they were attending a funeral.

The bride arrived and the congregation rose to their feet as Mrs Fry struck up The Wedding March. The bride and her father walked slowly up the aisle towards her groom. It crossed Hogan's mind that the wedding must be costing the bride's father a small fortune. She looked nervous. Her father seemed tense. The bride was now beside her soon-to-be husband. He didn't recognise either of them. Neither the bride nor the groom had ever set foot inside his church before, and he had a sneaking suspicion that she just wanted a grand white wedding. She glanced at him nervously. The groom took her hand and gave it a reassuring squeeze. The music stopped and the church was silent. The assembled participants and guests waited for the vicar to begin the service.

Suddenly, a cry went up from Dolly Edwards standing in the fifth row of pews. "You wait until he finds out she can't cook!" she said in a riotous voice. A roar of laughter went up from the assembled crowd and the bride was bent over in hysterics. The entire church was filled with hilarious laughter and Sam was laughing along with them. That wonderfully off-the-cuff remark had broken the ice and the rest of the wedding service was a happy occasion.

The wedding reception was held in the hall of the Tate Institute. Sam was invited to come along in the evening. He decided to abandon the dog-collar and arrived in a suit and tie. Soupy the caretaker had surpassed himself and decorated the tables with crispy white tablecloths, candles, and flowers. A band was playing dance music and the bar was doing a roaring trade. The guests are dancing and small children are skating across the polished wooden dance floor – getting underfoot of the grown-ups, but no one seemed to mind. A noisy crowd of revellers were laughing and drinking at the far corner of the hall, where they had pushed two tables together to accommodate their large family. Amongst them is Dolly Edwards. She throws her head back as she laughs at a dirty joke that someone has just told her. Sam had a drink thrust into his hand and is introduced to many of the happy couple's relations – and instantly forgot their names.

Suddenly a woman was standing in front of him. She was in her mid-thirties, with dark hair and animated eyes. "Did they teach you to dance at theological college?" she asked him in a cheeky tone of voice. He was lost for words and begins to mumble an unintelligible answer.
She took the drink from his hand and parked it on the nearest table. "Come on vicar, let's see if you can waltz," she said, and guided him onto the crowded dance floor.

As they began to glide over the floor she slipped her arm around his waist so that there was not an inch of space between them. She was above average height with an intelligent face. She looked up and smiled at him with full moist lips. Her fragrant perfume reminded him of apple blossom. She was wearing an off-the-shoulder gown. He surreptitiously glanced down and glimpsed her substantial cleavage. When he looked up again, it was obvious that she had spotted his gaze. She grinned mischievously. "Watch out, or your eyes will pop out of their sockets." He began to apologise, but she silenced him with her finger over his lips.
"Do you have a name or do I have to call you vicar all night long?" she asked.
"It's Sam. What's yours?"
"My name's Monika," she said. He detected a fruity Birmingham accent.
"Where are you from, Monika?" he asked.
"I'm from Wolverhampton. I'm a friend of the bride's sister," she said, as if that explained why she had travelled such a long distance to attend the wedding.
The band finished the tune, but she wasn't in any hurry to extricate herself from his arms, and stood there looking steadily into his eyes. There was that same mischievous smile again. "So tell me, Sam, do vicars have to swear undying allegiance to the church and live a life of celibacy?"
He grinned at her forthrightness. "No, that's for Catholic priests. I'm Church of England."
"Aah, that's good to know," she said. The band struck up with another slow smoochy number and they continued dancing.
"Are you staying here with the bride's sister?" he asked her.
"No, I've booked bed and breakfast at a guest house." She momentarily hesitated. "But the battleaxe landlady said that she locks the front door after eleven o'clock, so if I'm not in my room by then, I'll be locked out."
He decided to be bold. He hoped that he had read her signals correctly and that she wouldn't take offence at his next question. "Well, if you don't want to stay at the B&B, then you're more than welcome to stay at the vicarage." He waited while she considered the invitation.

"Would anyone here know that I'd stayed with you?" she asked, looking around the dance hall.
"Absolutely not," he assured her.
"In that case I'll accept your very kind offer." She grinned like a naughty child. "Will I need to wear my pyjamas?"
He wrapped his arms around her waist and gave her a squeeze. "I don't think that will be necessary, do you?"

St. Mark's church was quiet during the afternoons. He had carried out the morning matins prayers service and wouldn't be required until evensong, so this was his time to catch up with more mundane matters of his ministry. Sam Hogan was sat in a comfortable chair in the vestry, writing a sermon for the forthcoming Sunday service. It was one of the chores of his calling that he detested, for he found sermon writing akin to penning poetry, neither of which he was proficient at. He decided that his subject this week would be forgiveness.

He heard echoing footsteps approaching over the flagstone floor. There was a hesitant tap on the oak door and a female voice said, "Hello is anyone at 'ome?"
A teenage girl came into the room. It was Florence Brock, one of his regular parishioners. Her face was flushed and she looked embarrassed. "Can I 'ave a word wiv you, vicar?" she said.
"Certainly you can. It'll give me an excuse not to be writing this drivel," he said, indicating his unfinished sermon. "Take a seat. What's the problem?"
She sat opposite him. "I don't really know where to start," she stuttered.
"Why don't you just start at the beginning?" he suggested gently.
"I fink I'm pregnant, vicar," she blurted out. "I ain't had a show an' I'm late for me period an' I dunno what I'm gonna do."
"Oh dear," he said. He disliked having these female problems thrust upon him; mainly because he was at a loss as to how to deal with them. "Have you been to see your doctor?" he asked.
She shook her head. "I don't wanna see Doctor Imber. He'll only give me a hard time."
He nodded sympathetically. It was true enough. Doctor Julius Imber wasn't renowned in the district for being a compassionate listener, and could be quite brusque and unapproachable with his patients. He certainly wasn't known for having a good bedside manner. It was rumoured that he originally came from Germany, and his unintelligible accent was so thick you could almost scrape wallpaper off with it.
"What about your family? Have you told them you're pregnant?"

Florence was wringing her hands anxiously. "I can't tell me dad. He'll go spare."

"What about the child's father? Does he know?"

She looked distinctly embarrassed. "I dunno where he is. We was only together for one night. He was a merchant seaman," she explained. He remembered that Florence worked in the sugar packing department at Tate & Lyles. At some stage, she would need to give up work when her baby was due.

"One thing's for sure," he said matter-of-factly, "You'll have to see your doctor so as to have it confirmed that you're definitely pregnant."

She nodded, knowing that the vicar was talking sense. "Would you come wiv me?" she asked.

He momentarily wished that he'd had the good sense to have chosen another career. Oh dear God. Why do people always come to me with their stupid problems? he asked himself. Then he remembered why he had joined the church all those years ago. It was to help people like Florence who found it difficult to help themselves.

"Of course I'll come with you, Florence," he said.

It was a week later. Florence's pregnancy had been definitely confirmed by a gruff Doctor Imber. She was two months gone. She returned to see the vicar. "Will you come to my house to tell my mum and dad," she asked. "I can't do it by myself. I just can't face it. My dad will knock me into next week." Against his better judgement, Hogan agreed, and his visit was arranged for Tuesday evening.

The Reverend Samuel Hogan knocked at the door of the house in Saville Road. It was answered by a nervous looking Florence Brock. "My mum and dad are in the living room," she whispered as she led him to the back room. Ted and Iris Brock were taken aback when the vicar entered the room with a breezy, "Good evening to you." It wasn't every day that the vicar came calling and they were confused as to the reason for his unannounced visit. Ted Brock stared truculently at Hogan, somehow suspecting that he hadn't come here to convey any good news. He was still dressed in his typical docker's attire of bib and braces with a thick leather belt and a silk neck-scarf under a blue shirt. His flat cap lay upon the table.

Iris Brock looked perplexed, but remembered her manners. She said, "Good evening vicar. Would you like a hot drink?" He declined her offer, but made himself comfortable in a chair in front of a roaring coal fire. Florence made herself scarce in the furthest corner of the room, away from her father.

Sam decided to push on with it. "The reason for my visit will come as something of a shock to you, I'm afraid, so I won't beat around the bush," he explained. "Florence has asked me to tell you that she's pregnant."

Ted Brock's face took on the perfect example of a wounded lion. He scowled at his daughter. "You bring disgrace to our house and then you wanna invite the bloody vicar over here so that he knows about it as well?" His face had turned an ugly red colour. Florence cowered in the corner, with her hands covering her face.
"And whose the bleedin' father of the baby?" he demanded. "Come on. Tell me the bastard's name."
Iris Brock was visibly upset. "Now calm down, Dad, you're upsetting our little girl."
He screamed, "I'll bleedin' well give her what for if she don't tell me."
Mrs Brock looked distressed. She turned to the Reverend Hogan, "I apologise for all the bad language, Vicar, but it's come as a bit of a shock." Her husband had meanwhile arisen from his chair and made as if to take off his leather belt. Florence looked momentarily terrified; but then, for the first time in her young life, she somehow found the strength to stand up to her father. "You've got no room to lecture me," she said, pointing her finger at him. "I've worked out the dates between your wedding day and my birthday, and you seem to 'ave forgotten that Mum was pregnant when you got married, haven't you?"

Ted Brock was pole-axed. His daughter had never had the nerve to back-chat him before. But sadly, what she had said was the truth. Iris had certainly been pregnant when they'd walked up the aisle together. He looked embarrassed. He stared at the linoleum floor, unable to meet his daughter's gaze. He vividly remembered all those years ago, when Iris's father had insisted that they get married with all haste, and she had been two months pregnant on the day of their wedding.

Sam Hogan didn't feel the need to add anything to an already uncomfortable situation, so he remained silent. Iris Brock took Florence into her arms and they were locked in a close embrace. Florence was weeping. "Oh Mum, I'm so sorry."
Mrs Brock hugged her daughter tightly. "Sshhh," she reassured her. "It'll all turn out right. You'll see." Ted Brock looked uncomfortable. He'd obviously realised the hypocrisy of his outburst and wanted to make amends. He crossed the room and wrapped his arms around his family and kissed his daughter's head. "Never mind Princess, it'll all turn out okay," he whispered.
Sam suggested they sit down and discuss matters. "Florence has told me that she doesn't feel able to raise her baby herself," he told them. "Therefore I have suggested that, nearer the time of her confinement, she goes to stay at a home for unmarried mothers. Afterwards she plans to have the baby

adopted." They all nodded silently at the wisdom of her intentions. Florence, they agreed, was barely seventeen years old and much too young to bring up a child.

"In the meantime, I suggest that you give Florence all the support that you can. She's possibly going to find it difficult to cope." The Brocks nodded in agreement.

A half hour later, Sam was on his way home. He was generally pleased with the way in which the problem of the pregnancy had been resolved. He was under no illusions that, if he had not been present, then the atmosphere would have degenerated to one where Ted Brock would have used his leather belt on Florence.

He was crossing the footbridge that spanned the railway lines. Another ten minutes and he would be back in the warm and cosy vicarage. But he was in a melancholy mood. Every so often, The Reverend Samuel Hogan questioned why the hell he'd ever decided to become a vicar.

When he'd first applied to join the ministry of the Church of England, his innate conviction had been that God was an all-seeing fatherly figure; one who shaped the lives of all mankind. He truly believed that it was his mission in life to help his fellow man and to make the teachings of Jesus Christ available to everyone. It had felt as if he was about to embark upon a crusade. In those halcyon days those deep seated beliefs helped him to weather the rigours of the three year course at the theological college before eventually being ordained into the bishopric of East London.

But now, after twenty years in the clergy, he had come to accept that being a vicar was just another job like any other, except that one had to work on the Sabbath. The early years, when he had first taken over this church from the late Reverend Denison, had been most pleasurable, because he was young and keen and determined to make his mark on life in this strange community.

The size of his congregation during those idyllic days had been considerable, and he could usually count on the church being full to overflowing for the Sunday service. But after the turbulence of the war years, the citizens of Great Britain, who had lost loved ones and learnt of the atrocities of The Holocaust, lost faith in The Almighty's power to prevent such carnage; and his flock had gradually reduced in size to such an extent that he sometimes began to wonder if it was worth holding any services at all. As one year stretched into another, his regular parishioners dwindled to a level where they had all but vanished.

He was intelligent enough to recognise that the 1950s were rapidly modernising times; and after six years of war, the population of Great Britain were fed up with living in austerity, and demanded some fun and entertainment in their lives. The church had not changed its sombre and solemn services in decades and still clung to the belief that church services should be serious affairs; and so the level of active churchgoers had faded away.

Hogan also believed that the new craze of rock n' roll from America was having an undisciplined effect on the young and making them act disobediently to the authorities, and especially to the church. Youngsters, especially on his patch, were staying away from the church in droves.

On a brighter note, he'd received a letter from Monika. Without going into graphic details, she said that she'd enjoyed herself very much indeed during their weekend together and wondered if he would care to travel to Wolverhampton for a repeat performance. Even though he was broad-minded, he was somewhat shocked, because the performance she was referring to was two days of sex, interspersed with him having to hold Sunday services, whilst she, who readily admitted to being an out-and-out atheist, languished in his bed until his work was done.

Monika was a schoolteacher. Half-term was approaching and she asked if he would care to accompany her on a long-weekend caravan break in the countryside. She didn't mention any sleeping arrangements, but a few nights curled up in Monika's arms seemed rather inviting.

He could get a colleague in the West Ham diocese to cover his church services for a few days and may even be able to borrow a car. Sam was a normal red-blooded male, but he had to be very careful that he didn't get entangled in any local relationship that could turn sour. After all, he had the good name of the church to uphold, and the bishop wouldn't take kindly to him dragging the church's name through the mud. Monika was attractive and an adventurous woman in the bedroom department, so this long distance relationship seemed perfect. He immediately wrote back saying when he would arrive.

He had always found it strange that, although many Church of England vicars were married, the general public thought it distasteful for single clergy to have a girlfriend or a relationship with a female. As far as the straight-laced public were concerned, unattached clerics should not be linked romantically with a girl, and sex was definitely off the menu for a man of the cloth.

5: Hazel's Arrival

The eight constables gathered in the station's duty room, getting themselves ready to proceed out onto their respective beats. They read the briefing notes on the blackboard which detailed any crimes outstanding, and who or what to keep a sharp look-out for. The room was noisy and clamorous as the Bobbies shouted good-natured profanities at each other

The officers fell silent as Sergeant Ambrose entered the room accompanied by a fresh-faced female police officer. "Okay lads, get fell-in," he boomed. The constables quickly formed-up in a straight line and came to attention, ready for inspection. All eyes were on the girl as Ambrose inspected his constables for anything other than perfection.

She appeared to be in her early twenties and Noah thought she was quite pretty and rather tall for a girl. "This," said Sergeant Ambrose, indicating the WPC, "is Constable Hazel Leggett. She's fresh out of Hendon Training College and it's her first day in the job, so I'm sure you gentlemen will show her every consideration and kindness, won't you?" He noticed a few raised eyebrows and heard some groans from the older constables which indicated that they weren't at all pleased at the prospect of working with a female. "Constable Leggett," Ambrose informed them, "will be stationed here at North Woolwich for the foreseeable future."

Noah could see the caution in her eyes. Female officers were a rare breed in the police force and many of her new-found male colleagues wouldn't take kindly to going out on patrol with a WPC. She warily glanced along the line, searching each face for a welcome response, or at least some sign of approval. Her eyes settled on Noah. He gave her a friendly wink and she returned it with a weak uncertain smile and concentrated on what Bert Ambrose was saying.

"Now then lads, as you know I usually pair-off any new recruits with an officer who'll show them the ropes for their first three months until they've got settled in. So, which one of you lucky lads is it going to be?" he asked, largely posing the question to himself. He walked along the line of constables; mentally deleting those officers who would rather have their eyes gouged out than serve with a female officer. Eventually his eyes came to rest on Noah. "Constable Sheppard, you've served here long enough to be able to show her the routine, haven't you laddie?" Noah nodded automatically. "Right then, the job's yours. Both of you report to my office."

Twenty minutes later, after the shortest of briefings from Ambrose, which chiefly concerned Noah showing her around the station, they were sent out on patrol.

He decided to walk his usual beat and explain the territory as they strolled through the area. He pointed out the Royal Docks, the pubs, the small corner shops, the major factories, and the river. Contained within Noah's patch lay vast areas of bombsites that, before the war, had once been streets of neat terraced housing and factories, but which, at the height of the Blitz, the Luftwaffe had reduced to piles of rubble. Broken bricks and scorched timbers lay in forlorn heaps from which tall weeds grew and small boys scavenged the wasteland for firewood to sell in bundles. To the south, beyond the railway line, lay dozens of factories that belched smoke from their chimneys in the manufacture of innumerable commodities. The factories backed onto the River Thames, which on any given day, saw hundreds of cargo vessels, tugs, barges, sailing ships, pleasure steamers, colliers and tramp ships moving their cargos into and out of London on the tide.

"There seems to be ever so much to learn, doesn't there?" she said. "Have you been here long?"

"About eighteen months. Don't worry; you'll soon pick it up. Where are you from?" he asked.

"I'm from a small town called Witney in Oxfordshire. I was working in a children's nursery before I joined the police force." Her voice had an attractive throatiness but was well modulated, and inasmuch as she pronounced her words clearly, she appeared to have a neutral accent.

"What shall I call you?" she asked nervously. "Constable Sheppard seems much too formal."

"My name's Noah," he told her. He noticed her raised eyebrows. "Yes, I know it sounds very religious, but my mother liked biblical names," he explained. He grinned. "It could have been worse. She could have called me Zebadiah."

She laughed. "I know what you mean. My father insisted on giving me a middle name that makes me want to cringe." She stopped to face him. "And before you ask; I wouldn't tell you, even if you threatened to pull my fingernails out."

Noah liked the way that her eyes crinkled at the corners whenever she smiled. It showed him that she had a good sense of humour; something she would certainly require in her new chosen career. A few wisps of unruly blonde hair escaped from the brim of her uniform cap, which together with a rather luscious mouth, had the effect of making her very attractive indeed.

They walked onwards towards Silvertown, occasionally stopping to chat to local residents or shopkeepers, and all the while he pointed out anything of interest and what to keep one's eyes on. Every so often he would steer her down one of the many side roads, so that, not only would she become familiar with the layout of Silvertown, but especially if there had been trouble at a particular address.
"Do you get much crime around here?" she asked.
"Nothing too serious," he told her. "We mostly get domestic violence, when a bloke comes home blind drunk and decides to knock his missus about a bit." He saw her nose crinkle up in distaste. "Sometimes we get some petty theft. The strange thing about this place is that not many people bother to lock their doors at night. You can usually knock and walk right in. The reason being; is that everyone knows they don't have anything worth nicking."
She laughed. "Thank God for that. I don't think I'm ready to try to nick some drunken wife-beater just yet."
"Well, when that time comes – just remember that the only weapons you have to defend yourself, are a truncheon and a police whistle."
"I'll keep that in mind," she said.
"Actually, we did have a murder case here a while ago, but the suspect was quickly arrested and went to trial. They hung him a month later." Noah deliberately withheld the information that it was he who had discovered the crime. He didn't want to appear to be fishing for kudos.

They were now strolling along Newland Street, where the ten-foot high wooden dock fence ran into the far distance and he explained how the fence ran around the whole of the vast Royal Docks, from Galleons Reach in the east, to the Tidal Basin in the west, for a distance of several miles. "So, how do the dockers get in and out?" she asked. He explained the system of roads and manned check points that allowed access into the docks. She nodded in understanding, appearing to comprehend the plethora of information that, it seemed, she was required to come to grips with.
"You might think this is incredible, but I've never actually seen a proper ship before." she admitted. "We don't get many ships sailing around the villages of Oxfordshire. Mind you, we do see quite a few narrowboats on the canals. Do they count?"
"No. But never mind, you'll be seeing dozens of ships in just a few moments." Minutes later, they came to Leonard Street, just yards away from where the murder had occurred. Again, he didn't mention his part in bringing the offender to justice.

He pointed out a narrow opening in the dock fence, where groups of dockers and ship's crews were going in and out. They went to stand beside the entrance. "This is called The Wicket Gate and it's used by the dockers to quickly get to the local cafes and pubs," he explained. A comical notion came into his head. He laughed. "It's best not to stand in front of the gate at lunchtime because you'll be trampled to death by hundreds of dockers as they rush to guzzle a midday pint of ale." The gate was manned by a uniformed constable who was busy checking the documentation of a ship's crewman. The dock policeman looked up and spotted them, and to Hazel, his demeanour appeared frosty and decidedly unfriendly. Noah saw it too. The policemen simply gave a curt nod and went inside the gatehouse.

"What was that about?" she asked. "He didn't seem very friendly. Have you upset him?"

"Don't worry about him," he said. "They're not real policemen. They work for the PLA - the Port of London Authority - and their territory is only inside the docks. They're like a private police force," he informed her. "They don't like us, and we don't like them."

She was keen to understand. "Why's that?" she asked.

"Because they're a bunch of thieves," he said with a sneer. "If any sailor going on shore leave has a few extra packets of cigarettes than he's allowed, then he usually has to slip the dock police a ten bob note so that they let him out. They're all on the take. We hate them."

As a new recruit, Hazel didn't understand the complexities of inter-force rivalry, but simply nodded and let the matter drop.

Noah pointed past the police gatehouse. "Anyway, whilst we're here, you may as well take a look at your first ocean-going ship." In the distance several bulky cargo vessels were berthed alongside the wharfs, and cargo was being loaded or discharged via tall electric cranes from the dockside. Along the quayside the scene was a hive of activity as fleets of vehicles offloaded their export cargo into warehouses and fork-lift trucks whizzed to and fro. Meanwhile, men were trundling sack-trucks loaded with packing cases from the warehouses and gangs of dockers stowed the freight into the ship's cargo holds.

Suddenly, a giant cargo ship gave several blasts on its steam horn and began to move slowly astern from its berth. Two tug-boats busily pushed and pulled the ship out of its berth and along the dock towards the River Thames. To Hazel, who had never set eyes on a ship before, the whole magical scene was one of hectic chaos and the dockside was a cacophony of industrious noise.

In the distance, beyond the railway line, reared the enormous orange painted monolith that was the Tate & Lyle sugar refinery. The factory's height and sheer size dwarfed the nearby industrial plants and towered over most of Silvertown. Twenty four hours per day its conveyor belts carried the thousands of tons of raw sugar from the ships at the riverside wharf, and whisked it noiselessly into the depths of the factory, where it would be processed and purified and emerge as bags of sugar.

"That," said Noah, pointing at the sugar refinery "is the largest employer around these parts, except, of course, for the stevedores in the Royal Docks."

"How many work in there?" she asked.

"About three thousand people," he guessed. "They refine the raw sugar that's imported from the West Indies, and make granulated white sugar and brown Demerara sugar. They also manufacture icing sugar and molasses."

A passing red double-decker trolley bus hummed by on its way to Canning Town, its spring-loaded trolley poles giving off occasional sparks of arcing current as it motored almost noiselessly towards Silvertown Railway Station. On the open platform at the rear, the uniformed bus conductor stood smoking a cigarette.

Noah pointed westwards. "About two miles away, in West Silvertown, is another huge Tate & Lyle plant that employs another two and a half thousand people. They make the syrup."

"Blimey," she said "this place seems to exist on sugar. I'll remember that whenever I put a spoonful in my teacup."

Suddenly the works hooter sounded out its strident message to signal the end of another shift pattern, and a great mass of workers - hundreds of them - streamed out of the factory gate, on foot and on bicycles, and headed for home.

He grinned. "Welcome to Sugarland, Hazel."

Hazel's first day on the beat was thankfully a quiet one and they returned to the police station at the end of their shift happily footsore. She was relieved that Sergeant Ambrose had chosen Noah to be her guide and mentor, because she found him easy to get along with, and he took the trouble to explain the finer points of life in this part of London's Docklands. From her brief introduction at this morning's parade, she couldn't imagine any of the older constables being at all happy with having to wet-nurse a rookie copper, especially a female one, but Noah didn't seem to mind, and she suspected that he had even enjoyed teaching her the most relevant points of policing. In addition, and on a purely personal note, she thought that he had a kind face with the most beautiful eyes and a devastating smile.

Halfway through their shift they had called in at George's Diner for a refreshment break, and whilst they had sat in a secluded booth drinking tea, she had hesitantly asked him about his family. This had elicited the information that his parents lived in rural Hertfordshire, and that he lived in a single officer's room of the section house that is attached to North Woolwich police station. More importantly, he let slip that he had recently split up with his girlfriend.

The following days were much like her first day on the beat, except that Noah guided her down different streets and introduced her to many of Silvertown's residents. At each address, they were frequently invited inside for a cup of tea by a friendly housewife, and Hazel was amazed at the prodigious amount of beverages that he was able to consume during a shift. However, what she was supremely impressed with was the way in which, during the course of a pleasant chat, he would flawlessly extract a piece of useful information without the person even being aware of it. "That info may come in handy one day, so it all gets filed away in the back of my brain," he had joked, tapping his head.

They turned the corner into Parker Street. "We're going to have a chat with one of Silvertown's more interesting characters," he informed her. "You'd best not say anything because Frankie can be a slippery customer."

They entered Houlder's scrap yard through metal double gates and Noah instantly spotted Frankie in a far corner of the yard examining a pallet of copper tubing. He had his back towards them as they approached noiselessly from behind. "Hello Frankie, how's it going?" boomed Noah, and for a brief moment he thought the scrap dealer would jump out of his skin in surprise. Frankie had a look of panic on his face with an unannounced visit from The Old Bill.
"Bleedin' hell Mister Sheppard," he said with an exaggerated indignation, "you nearly gave me an 'art attack, ya did. Ya don't wanna be creepin' up on people like that."
"Sorry about that," grinned Noah, not feeling at all repentant. "I wondered if you've had anyone offering to sell you some lead roofing. Saint Mark's Church roof got stripped a while ago."
"Nah, I ain't had nuffink like that. You're welcome to come in the office and have a butcher's at me accounts, though," said Frankie, secure in the knowledge that any illegal transactions were always paid in cash and never went onto the firm's books. He held his arm outstretched, as if to usher them across the yard to his office. But Noah was having none of it. "I think we might have a little look around first, Frankie," he said, and he began strolling aimlessly around the yard looking at anything of interest and especially at any piles of metals that were covered with tarpaulins. Noah knew full well that if Frankie Houlder had purchased the stolen lead, then he would have quickly sold it on and cleared it out of his yard at the first opportunity. There was not a cat-in-hell's chance it would still be here. However, Noah thought it wouldn't do any harm to apply some pressure and appear to question the origins of several quantities of copper and brass. Frankie stuck with him like

glue, appearing eager to answer any queries regarding the provenance of metals that he could account for, and rather hazy about those for which he couldn't.

Even though Frankie was getting on in years, he still liked to think he was something of a ladies' man and attractive to the opposite sex. "So, who's this pretty lady?" said Frankie, pointing at Hazel with a cheeky but likeable grin. "Are the gendarmes employing double-breasted policewomen now?"

"This is Police Constable Leggett," said Noah somewhat formally. He thought he'd apply a little more pressure. "Her dad owns a scrap yard, so she knows the difference between a copper pipe and a brass tap washer. Therefore, you may find her having a look around your premises on a regular basis," he lied. Frankie's grin disappeared and he wished he'd kept his mouth shut.

Noah had seen enough. They wouldn't be finding the illicit lead from St. Mark's Church and were patently wasting their time, so they said their goodbyes and continued on their beat.

It was mid-morning and Noah had taken Hazel down to Auberon Street to meet one of North Woolwich's most colourful residents, the redoubtable Elsie Turpin. He thought it would add some interest to an otherwise humdrum day and at the same time would enrich Hazel's local knowledge of the area's more interesting characters.

Elsie had recently taken to using Noah's Christian name, rather than the proper and formal, Constable Sheppard. She presumed that by being on first name terms with him, it would curry favour and she would be privy to a greater amount of valuable information. Noah had decided not to disavow her of her grand scheme, but to keep the flow of information strictly on the basis of one-way traffic. His way!

They had been having tea and biscuits in Elsie's front parlour, for which Noah felt incredibly privileged, for he knew that most cockneys reserved their front parlour strictly for special occasions. Introductions had been made and, without the slightest attempt to be discreet, Elsie had commented, "Blimey Noah, you can't narf pick 'em, can't you? She's very pretty. Is she gonna be your girlfriend?" Noah had become embarrassed and his cheeks had turned a deep shade of crimson. He spluttered something unintelligible and the moment had gratefully passed. Hazel meanwhile had quickly offered to help Elsie to butter some sandwiches in the kitchen. "I ain't got any butter, dear – only marge. What do ya fancy in yer sandwich?" She suddenly remembered something. "I've got a lovely tin of salmon that I was saving for special occasions. That'll do nicely."

Ten minutes later, Elsie was pouring yet another cup of tea from her best china teapot and handing out dainty sandwiches from a cut-glass dish covered with a doily. Noah was trying, without any success, to extract a titbit of information as to the origins of thousands of packets of illicit cigarettes that were currently being sold up and down the parish. He suspected that these may be the very same consignment that the police and HM Customs had failed to intercept a few weeks ago after he'd received the worthless tip-off from Ted Ryland. Elsie lit another of her 'coffin nails' and mumbled that, "I don't know nuffin about anyone offering cheap fags, or I may 'ave bought some meself."

A radio, encased in its walnut surround, was playing melodiously upon the sideboard, and Noah faintly heard the dulcet tones of Ruby Murray singing on the BBC's home service station. Minutes later, the chimes of Big Ben came from its speaker to announce the midday news. Elsie leaned over and tweaked up the volume. "I always likes to listen to the news, dear," she informed them. "It keeps me up to date, dinnit?"

The BBC news reader came on the air and read out reports from far-flung outposts of Britain's empire. There was a report from Malaya, where communist insurgents had been overrun by Commonwealth troops near Kuala Lumpur and news of the savage war of attrition between British backed Kikuyu troops and Mau-Mau guerrillas in colonial East Africa.

"It's a bleedin' shame we ever got involved in Africa, dear," stated Elsie loudly. "Those blackies ought to know better." Noah didn't want to enter into a discussion about the pros and cons of inter-tribal warfare, and remained quiet.

The news reader was silent for a moment, and then, with great solemnity, he announced the next news item. "It has just been announced that Sir Winston Churchill has resigned as prime minister of Britain due to his failing health. A statement from 10 Downing Street confirmed that Sir Anthony Eden would become Britain's next Prime Minister with immediate effect."

There was a moment's silence in the room as the news regarding Britain's wartime leader was digested. Then Elsie said, "Awww, it's a pity poor old Winnie's on his last legs, ain't it dear? I reckon the war did 'im in." The two police officers nodded silently.

"But I'll tell ya summfink," said Elsie, stabbing her finger at the radio to emphasize her point, "having that Eden bloke as Prime Minister ain't gonna make a dollop of difference coz we're all Labour Party voters around these parts." Noah grinned at her colourful language. But of course, he thought, she was perfectly correct. The constituency of West Ham had, apart from a brief period, been a stronghold for Labour Party support stretching back to

1892, when the staunchly working class hero, Keir Hardie, had been elected to parliament. It had remained a Labour seat ever since.

He was brought out of his parliamentary reverie by Elsie lighting up a fresh 'coffin nail' off the end of her cigarette butt. She chain-smoked to such an extent that the room was pervaded by a thick smog of smoke. It was time to go. They quickly said their goodbyes and made their escape; but not before Elsie had the last word. With a cigarette dangling from her lips, she said, "Awww, yew two make such a lovely couple. I fink you ought to ask her out, Noah." And with that, she closed the door.

Later that afternoon, they found themselves standing outside Drew Road Primary School, where the children were dashing frantically around the playground. It was playtime. Groups of girls were playing at hopscotch or skipping and turning cartwheels on the hard tarmac surface and gangs of scruffy boys were charging around the perimeter playing war games with invisible machine guns that brought shouts of, "Rat-a-tat-tat. I killed ya. You're dead!" She smiled indulgently at Noah. "I'll bet this brings back some memories, doesn't it? Or were you too busy kissing the girls behind the toilets and trying to look up their knickers?" He grinned sheepishly, but didn't enlighten her. He was secretly pleased that Leggett had been paired-up with him on patrol, because he found her openness and her knack of plain speaking very refreshing. He liked the way in which she smiled with her eyes.

Hazel on the other hand was a little mystified. She had now been Noah's rookie trainee for several weeks, and during that time they had got along very well together. She had got to know his ways and his little idiosyncrasies (he didn't like Marmite, but adored chocolate) and she felt relaxed and confident in his company. Several times she had caught him gazing at her figure surreptitiously and on one occasion had enjoyed the fact that he had blatantly stared at her legs when her uniform skirt had got hiked up. She was quite sure that he was attracted to her, but as yet he had made no move to ask her out. Last week she had even taken off her uniform cap and allowed her long blonde hair to spill down past her shoulders. She had been rather pleased when he had appeared somewhat mesmerized and couldn't take his eyes off her. Perhaps, she mused, he wanted to keep their relationship on a purely professional footing and not have any romantic involvement, but she felt sure that, with a gentle shove in the right direction, he would show some interest. She considered simply asking him out on a date, but on reflection, she didn't want to scare him off. Consequently she decided to wait and see if anything should develop.

That very next evening brought one of the smogs for which London had become infamous. The fog was so saturated with the outpourings from coal-fired power stations and hundreds of factory chimneys, that the smog became as thick as pea soup. The air was so dank and wet, and the atmosphere so dense, that one couldn't see more than twenty feet ahead.

Noah and Hazel were on a late shift and due to finish at 10pm. Rather than try to find their way around side streets in the dense gloom, they elected to walk along Albert Road where the street lighting was marginally better, but even so, they had to use their police issue flashlights to see where they were going. Suddenly, out of the smog a trolley bus glided slowly past, barely at walking pace. The bus driver was straining to see ahead through the windscreen as the dense fog closed in around them. The bus conductor was beside him acting as his lookout.

Eventually from out of the impenetrable smog they saw the dim lights of a shop, and came upon Fry's newsagents on the corner of Parker Street. Noah was weary from peering through the swirling mist. "Come on, Hazel," he said. "Let's see if we can scrounge a cup of tea from Mrs Fry." They went inside where it was warm and cosy.

Mrs Fry was a jovial stout woman with permanently wavy hair and thick spectacles. Her secondary job was as the organist at St. Mark's Church across the far side of the railway line. From behind the counter she welcomed them with a beaming smile. "Hello Constable. How are you? And who's this young lady?" Noah introduced Hazel and asked if they might get a hot drink. Mrs Fry went out back and put the kettle on. She returned with two steaming mugs of cocoa and then reached under the counter and produced two bars of Cadbury's chocolate. His eyes lit up. He loved chocolate. He delved into his trouser pockets and came up empty-handed. "Sorry Mrs Fry," he said apologetically, "I'm afraid I don't have enough cash on me to pay for the chocolate."

She put a finger to her lips. "Shush. Don't mention it. They're rep's giveaway freebies. Just enjoy 'em."

She looked at Hazel. "And how long have you been working around these parts, then dear?"

"Not very long," she informed her. "I've only recently completed my basic training, so Constable Sheppard has been showing me the ropes."

Mrs Fry was an incurable romantic. "Awww, he's such a nice boy, isn't he dear? You two make such a lovely couple." There was a pregnant silence and Hazel could see he was embarrassed by Mrs Fry's attempt at match-making. His face was flushed. At last he said, "I think we'd better go call the nick and let them know where we are."

It was true enough. Duty patrolmen were obliged to call their station at least twice during their shift, simply to let the station sergeant know where they were or if there was anything out of the ordinary to report. They said their goodbyes to Mrs Fry who couldn't resist reminding him, "She's ever so pretty, ain't she, love? You look after her, won't yew?"

Back outside in the thick opaque smog they momentarily became separated, and within seconds she had been swallowed up in the enveloping pea soup. Visibility was down to just a few yards and Hazel panicked because she was disorientated and had no idea which way to turn. She called out to Noah and he retraced his steps and found her. Without thinking she linked her arm through his and hung on tight. "Hang onto me, Noah, or I'll disappear into the fog and you'll have to send out a search party. Think of the paperwork." He didn't resist.

They found the square blue-painted police call box three streets further on, located outside the Constitutional Club. The call boxes contained a telephone which was assessable from the outside via a hinged door, so that members of the public could call the police station in an emergency. He had often been asked what was kept inside the box, but he always kept tight-lipped on that subject. In fact, apart from the telephone, which had a direct line to the local police station, they contained just an incident book, a fire extinguisher, and a first-aid kit – nothing more. They could also be used to securely hold a prisoner until transport arrived.

Noah opened the door with his pass key and called the police station at North Woolwich. The duty sergeant tonight was Charlie Ethridge. His voice came booming down the line. "Blimey Noah, I thought you were lost. I'd almost given up hope of ever seeing you again. What's the visibility like?" he asked.

"It's about ten feet, Sarge. I can't see anything in this fog."

"Well, you'd best come back to the station, then. Is Miss Lovely-Legs Leggett with you?"

"Yes, she is," he answered without humour. He didn't much care for the latest nickname that several officers had taken to calling Hazel. He re-cradled the phone and told her that they were returning to base.

He reached out and grasped her hand, as if to lead her out into the dense smog, but suddenly and to her utter surprise he wrapped his arms around her waist and found her generous mouth and kissed her urgently. She didn't resist, but willingly came into his arms. They spent long drawn-out minutes kissing passionately, as he occasionally nibbled her ear lobes and neck. Encapsulated within his physically strong arms, she didn't want this stolen moment to end and wished it could continue forever. Inside the narrow confines of the police box, their bodies were pressed together tightly and without the prospect of anyone appearing out of the dense fog to discover their illicit embrace.

He took a deep breath and smelt the sensual aroma of her womanliness and the fresh smell of apple blossom in her hair. Time didn't seem to matter as they indulged their passion and he kissed her again and again. Within this dark and impenetrable fog they were quite alone; where no one could discover them and they could pleasure themselves without untimely haste. At last they broke apart and simply clung on to each other, breathing heavily.

She whispered flirtatiously into his ear. "Jeezus, Constable Sheppard, you took your own sweet time. I've been waiting for you to kiss me for ages."

He laughed and nuzzled her neck. "Good things are worth waiting for. You're far too impatient, Constable Leggett."

It took them another hour to navigate their way through the deserted streets. The thick impassable smog resembled a solid grey wall that grudgingly dissipated to allow them to progress forwards. But at last, through a break in the mist, they saw the bright lights of the police station shining ahead of them. Instinctively she let go his hand and checked that her tunic wasn't askew.

"Hazel, we've got to be careful from now on," he said. "I'm not sure what the rules are about police officers fraternizing, but I'm pretty damn sure that Inspector Stranks will take a dim view if he found out that you're my girlfriend."

She couldn't resist teasing him. "Oh really?" she laughed sensually. "And when did you decide that I'm your girlfriend, Constable Sheppard? Was that right after you took advantage of me and kissed me when I wasn't looking?"

He dug her playfully in the ribs. "You know exactly what I mean, you little minx."

"I understand only too well, Noah" she said seriously. "It's going to be even more difficult than you think, because most of our colleagues hate working with WPC's and would love to see me fail. They would be deliriously happy to see me fall flat on my arse."

"Yes I know," he agreed sombrely. "Most of the older constables are living in the past and think that a woman's place is in the kitchen or knitting clothes for her babies."

"Some of them deliberately use foul language when I'm around," she said. "Noah, please don't get involved or react if that happens. It will only make things worse for us. Anyway, I'm a big girl and I can look after myself."

He nodded. "Don't worry, Hazel. I'm sure it'll work out okay." The fog had thickened again and the police station had disappeared. She reached up on tiptoe and kissed him on the cheek. "Oh my darling Noah," she whispered. "You're my hero."

Their relationship was discovered much sooner than they could have imagined. The next weekend they were off-duty and Noah had made plans to take Hazel to the cinema for an afternoon matinee. There was a choice of two cinemas on the opposite bank of the river and they would need to board the ferry. Hazel took the bus to the terminus at the Woolwich Ferry, where she had arranged to meet him at the loading ramp.

She spotted Noah gazing out over the busy river, absorbed in watching two coasters making their way upstream towards the Millwall Docks. He was smartly dressed in a suit and tie. She came silently up from behind him. She giggled. "You're not thinking of running away to sea, are you?" He twirled around in surprise and slipped an arm around her waist and kissed her full on the lips.
"Steady on, Constable," she joked, "or I may have to handcuff you."
He was grinning with amazement. This was the first time he had seen Hazel not wearing her police uniform and he thought that she looked gorgeous. She wore a simple grey skirt with a white blouse and a red woollen top under a short jacket. Her blonde hair, which had for the most part been hidden under her uniform cap, now hung down over her shoulders. Some light red lipstick perfectly accentuated her clear blue eyes and he thought the whole effect was effortlessly stunning. He said, "You look beautiful."
"Thank you kind sir," she answered. "You don't look too shabby yourself."

He took her arm and they boarded the ancient ferry for the short journey to South Woolwich. "I'm sorry I'm late, but my bus got held up at the locks by a bridger," she said by way of explanation. The bridge in question spanned across the lock gates that allowed the giant cargo vessels entry into the Royal Docks. Several times per day, traffic would be held up as the lifting bascule bridge opened to admit the arriving and departing freighters access from the River Thames. Noah nodded. 'Bridgers' were an occupational hazard.

As countless trucks and cars were being loaded onboard the ferry, they made their way to the lower deck where they could look at the ferry's engine room. Four ancient ferries were used to provide a free service between North Woolwich and South Woolwich on the opposite bank of the River Thames. Noah was explaining how the massive condensing steam engines powered the side paddles, when suddenly there was a clang of the ship's telegraph bells and the ferry was on its way. They returned to the upper deck to watch the busy river traffic making their way to and from the upriver London Docks. A gentle breeze blew Hazel's hair across her face and Noah was mesmerized by her prettiness and couldn't take his eyes off her.

They choose to watch a light-hearted film at the Odeon Cinema, and as soon as the auditorium had darkened, Noah took her into his arms and kissed her. Time and time again they kissed and clung tightly to each other, not caring if they attracted frosty glances from nearby cinema-goers.

It was as they were leaving the cinema's foyer that the couple came face-to-face with Ronnie Baldwin, a rough mannered fellow police constable. He was a red-faced overweight copper who came from the East End of London. When Noah had first been posted to North Woolwich, Baldwin had not endeared himself to him, due to continually referring to him as a "Posh Git," because of his neutral Hertfordshire accent, as opposed to his own broad cockney dialect. On another occasion Noah had felt obliged to intervene when he had discovered Baldwin down in the cells giving a young tearaway a beating for what was a minor offence. "What's the problem?" Baldwin had objected loudly. "The little bastard deserved a bloody good pasting."
And now here he was, stood in front of the couple with a leer upon his face. "Allo, Allo, what 'ave we got 'ere. Are you two having a bit of hanky-panky, are you?"
Noah remembered Hazel's advice not to react. He stitched a grin on his face. "It's nothing like that, Ronnie. We just bumped into each other when we were buying an ice cream from the usherette."
"A likely story," said Baldwin sceptically, and after a curt goodbye, went off in the direction of the ferry.
After a moment's silence Hazel said, "Do you think he'll talk?"
"He probably can't wait to spread it all over the station. He doesn't like me." He explained about his past problems with Baldwin.

On the following Monday morning, Noah's prediction was swiftly proven correct. He went into the station's mess-room, where several officers were having a lunch break. Ronnie Baldwin was sat sprawled in a chair smoking a cigarette. He gave Noah the benefit of a wicked grin. "Well, well, look who we have here. It's lover-boy himself. Where's your girlfriend Miss Droopy Drawers?" Noah simply shrugged his shoulders, but Baldwin persisted in telling those present the full story of the encounter at the cinema and that he and Hazel had looked red faced and embarrassed when they had been found together. In a loud voice he bawled, "Have you shown her your truncheon yet, lover-boy?" Noah quickly poured himself a mug of tea and left the room, accompanied by Baldwin's raucous laughter.

6: The Railway Tunnel

Noah and Hazel were on a late shift and due to finish work at 10pm. As long as there were no reports or paperwork to write-up, they planned on quickly changing into civilian clothes and nipping along to a quiet pub where they weren't likely to run into any work colleagues. Since that chance encounter at the cinema, Ronnie Baldwin had continued to taunt Noah with sexual innuendo at every opportunity. If they passed by in the corridor, then Baldwin would invariably sneer, "Are you gettin' plenty of nooky, lover boy?" Noah simply ignored him, but was secretly terrified that his relationship with Hazel would become common knowledge and reach the ears of Inspector Stranks. There didn't appear to be any hard and fast rules regarding fraternisation between police officers of the opposite sex, but Stranks was a churchgoing Baptist and a stickler for high moral standards among his officers. If he should discover anything he viewed as illicit, then he could easily put a stop to the couple being paired-up on duty patrols, or worse still, transfer either of them to another police division.

Their duty shift had been a quiet one, inasmuch as the citizens of Silvertown had been behaving themselves and the town was silent. They had strolled the mile or so down to Silvertown Railway Station where the western edge of their patrol beat terminated, and now they would retrace their steps back to the police station in time to clock-off. It was a dark warm evening and the streets were quiet, with only the faint sound of a piano playing in the nearby Railway Tavern.

But Noah was in no hurry. "Let's go over the railway line and have a look around," he suggested.

Hazel was mystified. "What for?" she said. "It's as quiet as the grave over there."

He grinned mischievously. "It's just the right place to have a smooch with my girl. Let's go."

She linked her arm into his. "I hear and obey, O'Master."

They walked across the foot bridge that spanned the railway line and found a dark deserted spot among the bombsites. The last trains of the evening had long gone and the nearby factories had closed for the night. Everything was quiet. She snuggled into his arms and raised her lips to meet his in a long and delicious kiss. The kiss continued into eternity as they clasped their bodies tightly together. He heard her moan softly as their tongues met and writhed like snakes making carnal love. He slid his hand under her tunic and found her ample breast, and for the briefest of moments she allowed him to roll the proud nipple between his fingers before firmly extricating his hand from beneath her blouse.

In an ideal world she would have wanted him to make love to her. More than anything she yearned for a time when she could give her body to him, completely and utterly, and without the emotional self-reproach that comes with a quick stolen moment of illicit lovemaking. She was certain that she loved Noah. She adored being with him and he was constantly in her thoughts. But her hitherto single sexual experience, and the feeling of guilt that it had created, had reinforced her resolve to save herself for just the right moment, when there would be no rush whatsoever and she wouldn't have to hide her feelings of embarrassment. She had no idea when that moment would come, because their personal circumstances made it difficult to be alone. Whereas she lived in digs, where an eagle-eyed landlady forbade any male visitors; he lived in the single officer's accommodation of the police section house.

"I'm sorry, Noah," she whispered with regret. "Let's wait for the right time."

Minutes later she felt his body tense as he listened intently. "What is it?" she asked. "What's wrong, darling?"

"Shsssh. I can hear someone making a noise," he whispered. "It sounds like hammering." Seconds later she heard it also. It sounded like someone was striking a metal object with a large hammer. The noise reverberated from the direction of the railway line where the track meandered off in the direction of Canning Town. Five times the clamorous noise rang out, followed by deathly silence. Then they heard whispered voices.

"Someone's up to no good down on the line," said Noah. "Let's go take a look." They crept silently across to the parapet where a vertical steel ladder allowed access to the British Railways maintenance crews who regularly worked on track repairs. Noiselessly they descended the ladder onto the track, taking care to walk upon the wooden sleepers so as to make the minimum of noise.

They were getting nearer. They could clearly hear the men's voices now and more blows rang out from the hammer. Only the faint moonlight shining on the high concrete walls of the railway embankment prevented the track from being cloaked in utter blackness. Carefully they stepped along one sleeper after another, gradually getting closer. The men had no idea they had been discovered and carried on hammering. They heard one man whisper, "Go on, Lennie, hit the bloody thing harder." Noah and Hazel were now within twenty feet. He took out his flashlight and indicated to Hazel that she ought to get hers ready also.

Suddenly he flicked on the powerful torch and flooded the scene with bright light. Hazel also shone hers and revealed two young men crouched at the side of the track where they had been attempting to remove lengths of copper cable, from what was presumably a part of the railway signalling equipment. Noah shouted. "Stay where you are. You're under arrest. Don't move." For the briefest moment the men remained motionless; staring at the flashlight like rabbits frozen by the headlights of a motor car. One was older and wore a woollen cap; the other was chubbier and had ginger hair. The eldest screamed, "It's the Old Bill. Run for it, Lennie!" and in a flash they were running along the tracks to evade capture.

Within seconds the men had sprinted between the tracks and were running like the wind towards the quarter mile long railway tunnel further down the line. Noah and Hazel set off in pursuit, but in their heavier uniform overcoats, couldn't hope to match the younger men who ran like their lives depended upon it. For several minutes the pair could only watch as the men receded further into the distance, and it seemed that they would make good their escape. However, the police officers had a distinct advantage with their flashlights, whereas the two men were running blind. The offenders were almost at the mouth of the tunnel when Noah's toe caught the edge of a railway sleeper and he went flying and landed heavily onto the steel railway line. The wind was knocked out of him and he lay there, unable to continue the chase. He was in a great deal of pain and he thought that he may have fractured a rib. Hazel bent down to help. "Darling, are you alright?"
"I'll be fine," he said through gritted teeth, "but I reckon those bastards will get away."
She stood up. "Not if I can help it," she shouted, and raced off in pursuit.
Noah yelled after her, "Hazel, come back here. Don't try to get them by yourself. You might get hurt." But she kept running and never turned back.

Hazel ran into the tunnel and could hear the two men ahead of her attempting to make some headway in the stygian blackness. She was gasping for breath and slowed her pace to a fast walk, for she knew that up ahead of her, the men would be staggering around in the darkness, unable to see even a few feet in front of them. They would be tripping over railway lines and sleepers and would make almost no progress, whereas with her powerful flashlight, she could turn night into day.

She found the men two hundred yards further inside. She shone the light on them. They were sat upon the gravel with their backs against the tunnel wall and looked exhausted. The ginger haired kid had a bloody nose and was holding his chest in pain. The elder man's foot was at a strange angle. "I think I've broken my ankle," he said morosely.
"Tough luck," said Hazel. "You shouldn't be out nicking stuff." She got them both to their feet and placed them under arrest. After reading them

their legal rights she led the way out of the dark tunnel and back towards Silvertown. The man with the broken foot had to hold onto his friend as they hobbled along the track. Almost as an afterthought she realised that she had only one pair of handcuffs. Noah had the second set. She slipped the cuffs onto the ginger kid's wrists. The one with the broken ankle wouldn't be running anywhere.

The two men were sat in separate interview rooms waiting to be questioned by CID detectives, and the uncertainty of the outcome was getting under the skin of at least one of them. The elder of the two, George Taylor, had been taken to Queen Mary's Hospital, where his fractured ankle had been encased in a plaster cast, and promptly returned to a cell at North Woolwich nick.

Taylor wasn't particularly worried. After all, he argued, what could they charge him with? He and Lennie hadn't managed to actually steal any copper cable before being discovered on the railway line, so no offence had been committed, other than trespassing. Anyway, he'd already served a nine month stretch at the Borstal in Kent for theft on a much grander scale, so he doubted that he'd be put away for trespass. He sat back and relaxed.

Meanwhile, in another room along the corridor, his younger friend, the ginger-haired Lennie Phillips, was shaking with fear. Although he had sprained a rib and broken his nose in the tunnel, these things were insignificant when compared with spending time in jail. The thought of being sent to a young offender's institution for many months filled him with dread. He doubted that he would be able to cope with being locked up with the tough hard-cases that he may share a cell with. He'd heard stories that it wasn't uncommon in such places for stabbings and beatings to occur on a regular basis. But chief among his concerns was what his father would do to him. His dad was a strict disciplinarian, and it wasn't unusual for the old man to administer a beating with his leather belt for the smallest of misdemeanours.

In the CID office, Detective Constable Andy Summers offered Noah Sheppard a mug of tea and indicated he take a seat. "How are your ribs, Noah? Are they still sore?"

Noah rubbed his ribcage and winced. "They're not too bad, Andy, but still a bit painful. They've strapped me up with bandages and the rib should begin to knit together again soon."

Summers grimaced at the vision. "I would have thought that you'd be on sick leave."

Noah nodded. "I'm going on sick leave just as soon as we question these two idiots," he said indicating their prisoners. "I wanted to wrap this little caper up first."

Summers was in his middle thirties with a shock of fair hair. His midriff was beginning to become flabby due to a fondness for fish n' chip lunches, but on the plus side he had a bizarre sense of humour that endeared him to his colleagues.

He picked the crime report off his desk and briefly studied the wording. "Well, I'm sorry to have to tell you, but these two young tearaways are going to be let off with just a warning. I'm afraid there's nothing we can charge them with – other than trespassing on British Railway's property. Anyway, they've both sustained injuries, so perhaps they've learnt their lesson." Noah nodded. He had come to the same conclusion.

Summers stood up. "But let's go have a chat with young Mister Phillips. Perhaps we might learn some useful information." He smiled broadly. "Let's play good cop – bad cop. I'll be the baddie."

They entered the interview room and took seats on the opposite side of the table to Lennie Phillips. The youngster looked scared and his leg began to shake involuntarily.

"Right then you piece of shit," shouted Summers, "you can begin by telling us whose idea it was to pinch the copper cable. And don't even think about telling us any lies because we've already spoken to your mate, Taylor."

The boy began to shake. "It wasn't me – honestly."

Summers changed tack to confuse the lad. "What were you going to do with it? You could hardly have carried away two tons of copper cable over your shoulder, could you?"

"We was gonna come back for it later – after we'd disconnected it. George has got an open-backed truck."

"Then what? Did you have a buyer for it?" asked Summers.

Lennie Phillips squirmed in his seat and remained silent. He wondered if George, who was presumably in another room, had already spilled the beans. Perhaps they already knew the facts. He remembered the advice that his mother had often repeated. "Never tell any lies, Lennie. You'll never go wrong if you tell the truth, son." His mind was in turmoil.

Noah leaned over the table. "Come on, Lennie," he said in a soothing voice. "If you tell us the truth, then perhaps we can help you out - so that you don't have to go to jail."

Wet tears ran down Lennie Phillips face. "Frankie Houlder was gonna buy it off us," he whispered. The two police officers exchanged looks of comprehension. Bingo! A good result.

Summers said, "Let's talk outside," and they left the room.

Out in the corridor Summers lit a cigarette. "Even though he's just admitted to it, we won't be able to arrest Frankie, because no crime has been committed, and he'd simply deny it. It would be their word against

Frankie's." Noah nodded in understanding. "Don't you worry about Frankie Houlder. I may not be able to arrest him, but I'll put the fear of Christ up him."

Noah wrote a full report of the incident, which landed onto Inspector Stranks desk the next morning. In it he recounted his own mishap of suffering a fractured rib during the chase, and Hazel's part in capturing the two men single-handed. He deliberately omitted the reason why the two officers had been together on the dark bombsite.

Inspector Stranks forwarded a copy of Noah's report up to the head office of London's Metropolitan Police Force at Scotland Yard. He had also attached his own report, which positively highlighted the part that Constable Leggett had played in apprehending the criminals without any thought to her own safety. Stranks was aware that Leggett had simply chased these tearaways into the tunnel, and due to their self-inflicted injuries, they had given up without a fight. He was of course conscious of the fact that, if the arresting officer had been a man, then the incident would have been viewed as nothing out of the ordinary. But in these rapidly modernising times, when women police officers were a rarity, the powers-that-be would be keen to recognise the part played by its women officers. He felt that some sort of official recognition would reflect positively on his police station and improve his men's standing in the community. On a more personal note, he argued, it wouldn't do any harm to enhance his own career prospects by association. Within a week, word had been sent back from Scotland Yard that Hazel had been nominated to receive the Chief Constable's Commendation for Bravery.

Two weeks later, on a Thursday afternoon, every police officer at North Woolwich station was dressed in their finest uniform as a cavalcade of police limousines swept into the courtyard, accompanied by police motorcycle outriders. The elderly Chief Constable - appearing patrician and statesmanlike - was shown into the building, along with his entourage of senior police officers who sported uniforms decorated with medals on their chests and laurel leaves upon the peaks of their caps. As Bert Ambrose succinctly put it afterwards, "There was enough brass and fruit salad on their outfits to sink a battleship."

All police constables were on parade as Hazel's name was called out, and she stepped smartly forward to receive her Commendation for Bravery. The Chief Constable shook her hand, and after bending down to whisper some kind words of congratulations, presented her with a boxed medal and the commendation written in calligraphic script on vellum parchment.

Later that evening, after the top brass had returned to central London, dozens of police officers went for celebratory drinks at the nearby Royal Pavilion pub, where Hazel was the star attraction. Noah found her at the bar surrounded by fellow officers, all eager to offer congratulations and admire the medal. During a quiet moment, he asked, "What did the Chief Constable say to you?"

Hazel grinned and wrinkled her nose. "I can't actually remember. I told him that I was only doing my job, but the old goat was too busy staring at my tits!"

The following day Bert Ambrose took Noah aside. "I've had a word with Inspector Stranks and recommended that you and Constable Leggett remain paired up as a team after her probationary period has ended, okay?" Noah was over the moon with the news. After showing Hazel the routines and procedures of his own patch for the past three months, he fully expected her to be transferred onto another beat. "Thanks very much, Sarge," he said. "Constable Leggett's a very good officer to have around."

Bert Ambrose fixed Noah with a piercing look, and then smiled. "Just as long as you two don't get caught kissing or holding hands, okay?"

7: Peeping Tom

Hazel and Noah's shift would end at 10pm. Prior to setting out on patrol Charlie Ethridge took Noah aside. He explained, "A woman from Silvertown came into the station this morning complaining about someone peeping into her bedroom windows at night." He grinned and gave him a slip of paper with the address. The house was in Holt Road. "Pop by and see if she's imagining it, would you?"

Noah was aware that it would be difficult to apprehend anyone for this type of offence because, not only are Peeping Toms normally active when its dark, but they largely remain motionless – which makes it difficult to spot them.

They turned into Holt Road and walked towards the dock fence. Beyond the fence, in the King George V Dock, tall electric cranes were loading tons of freight into a cargo ship's holds. The work would continue until the evening, when the docks would again fall silent.

An elderly rag n' bone man was driving his horse and cart down the middle of the road. He wore a scruffy overcoat, with its waist tied up with string, and on his hands he wore fingerless gloves. Over his unshaven face he wore a balaclava to keep out the chill. He rang a hand-bell and shouted his mantra loudly, "Any old iron – cash for old iron." His cart was piled high with scrap metal and his old mare looked clapped out from constantly pulling heavy loads. The horse lifted its tail and deposited a great pyramid of steaming horse-dung onto the road. The streets around Silvertown got their fair share of dung deposited by the horses of the coalman, the milkman and of various merchants that traded on the streets of the town. An elderly man came out from his house and swept the dung carefully into a bucket. The back gardens of Silvertown were tiny, but the residents would often spread horse manure onto a few treasured rose bushes to enrich the soil around them.

They knocked at Number 22. A woman dressed in a pinafore and turban hat answered the door. "Oh I've been expecting you," she said, ushering them indoors.

"I understand that someone's been peeping into your windows at night?" said Noah.

She nodded. "Yeah, for the past three nights I've noticed a bloke staring into me bedroom window and its bleedin' making me nervous. Can you do summfink about it?" They were shown into the front parlour and the police officers introduced themselves. She went to the kitchen and returned shortly with the ubiquitous pot of tea and biscuits.

He took out his notebook and wrote down some details. "What's your name?"

"It's Mrs Fletcher. June to me friends," she said smiling. June Fletcher was a mousy-haired woman in her mid-thirties who Noah thought was reasonably attractive without being eye-catching. She was of average height with a plumpish figure.

"Have you seen this person's face? Is it anyone you know?" he asked.

She shook her head. "No, it was pitch dark and I only saw the silhouette, but I fink it's a bloke coz of his size. He was a bit on the chunky side," she explained. "He stands in the rear alleyway and just stares."

"What time of night was it when you've noticed him?" enquired Noah.

"It's been 9 o' clock for the past three nights. I turn out my bedroom light, but he's still there – staring at me."

"Couldn't you simply close your curtains?" asked Hazel. Noah thought it was a valid point.

"I always close my curtain, dear, but when I 'ave a peep, he's still crouching behind my back fence. I can see his head moving."

Hazel noticed a wedding ring on her finger. "Have you told your husband about this?"

"My old man works away. He's in the Merchant Navy. His ship's somewhere in the Mediterranean at the moment and he ain't due back 'ome for six weeks," she explained.

Hazel nodded in understanding. She thought it must be terrifying for the poor woman to be all alone in the house and having some pervert out there staring into her bedroom. Noah stood up. "I think we'd best have a look from your bedroom window."

The bedroom was neat and tidy with a double bed, wardrobe, and chest of drawers. A thick flowery rug for the most part concealed the linoleum covered floor and he noticed that the curtains were of thick material, but would nevertheless allow anyone peering in to see the outline of the occupant. They looked out of the window. The garden was small and neat and was enclosed by close-boarded fencing. Borders planted with flowers stretched down both sides of the garden with hydrangea and rose bushes at the far end. The woman was obviously a green-fingered gardener. A narrow alleyway divided the gardens of the adjoining properties between Holt Road and Lord Street, and Noah guessed that the mystery visitor would gain access via a side passageway. June Fletcher pointed to the spot where the man had stood watching her every move. Noah had seen enough. He looked at his wristwatch. "We're on duty until 10pm," he told Mrs Fletcher. "We'll return at 8:30pm when it gets dark and we'll see if we can spot him."

They said their goodbyes and continued upon their patrol. As they walked side-by-side along Albert road, Noah said, "Damn it. That's put a dampener on my plans for this evening."
"What do you mean? What plans?" said Hazel, curiously.
He grinned wickedly. "Well, I was planning to take my darling girl to a dark spot tonight and give her a snog and a squeeze."
She gave him the benefit of a sexy laugh. "Well, we could always work some overtime, couldn't we?"

On the corner of Wythes Road stands the Tate Institute. Noah and Hazel were outside the main entrance as he educated her in the colourful history of Silvertown and its institute. In 1887, he told her, Sir Henry Tate, the noted philanthropist and the benefactor of London's Tate Gallery, had the institute built for the social needs of his sugar workers. Henry Tate's empire merged with that of Abram Lyle in 1921 and they had more sugar refineries built at West Silvertown, Liverpool and Greenock.

He pointed to the dance hall that was attached to the library. "Inside the institute, they have a public library, snooker and billiard room and a dance hall with two bars." Noah had been inside many times, but mainly to borrow books or to play snooker.
Her eyes lit up. "Oh Noah, can we come to a dance here sometime?" she asked excitedly. "I love to dance."
Noah looked embarrassed. "We could do, but I can't dance. I think I've got two left feet."
She laughed. "Don't worry. I'll teach you. It's quite easy."

It was late afternoon as they watched the comings and goings of the refinery's employees as they finished their shifts. Factory workers poured out of the plant in their hundreds and headed across the railway lines to board the trolley buses and trains that would take them home.

The institute's caretaker, Soupy Edwards, came out to say hello. Noah had met him soon after arriving on the scene as a rookie copper almost two years previously. "Hello matey, how you doing?" said Soupy with a huge toothy grin. He could never remember anyone's name, so everyone was called, "Matey."
"I'm fine, Soupy," said Noah. "And how's the dance hall business going?"
"We're doing a roaring trade," he told them. "We're packed to the rafters every Saturday night."
Hazel was introduced and she shook his hand. She was at least four inches taller than the short and rotund caretaker. She was curious. "Why are you called Soupy?" she asked him.

He scratched his greying head. "I think it's because - many years ago - there was a brand of soup made by a company called Edwards. I've been called by that name for so long that I've forgotten why."
He wiped the sweat from his animated chubby face with a handkerchief. "Would you like to come inside for a butchers?" Soupy asked her, jerking his thumb towards the dance hall. Her puzzled look told him that she didn't understand one word he'd said.
"Butchers – its short for butcher's hook – which is short for look," he explained.
It sounded like complete gibberish to Hazel - but then the penny dropped. She consulted Noah. "Can we?" she asked expectantly. He nodded agreement and they went inside.

She was beginning to understand why Noah enjoyed working in this part of London's Docklands, amongst the East Enders. She liked the friendly characters such as Soupy and Mrs Fry. She liked the closeness of their community spirit and the camaraderie amongst its residents, even though she was often confused by their fractured cockney language.

She was shown the dance hall. A generous sized stage took up the space at one end, with tables and chairs arranged around the remaining three sides. High above the dance floor, a net holding hundreds of multi-coloured balloons was suspended in readiness to be spilled out onto the dancers below. "That's the hardest part of this job," said Soupy, indicating the balloons. "Every Saturday I've somehow gotta blow that lot up, and I always seem to run out of puff."

Soupy loved to chat and this elicited the information that, far from simply being the Tate Institute's caretaker, he organised every aspect of the entertainment, from booking dance bands, to ensuring that the bars never ran short of liquid refreshment. He was a founding member of the T & L amateur dramatics society and on Saturday nights he could either be found serving behind the bar or up on the stage dressed as a pantomime dame.
"I've also gotta stoke up the boiler so the place don't get freezing cold," he grumbled good naturedly, "but my boy gives me a hand with that."
"Can we buy a ticket to next Saturday's dance?" asked Hazel impulsively. Noah started to object, but thought better of it.
Soupy reached into his jacket pocket and extracted two entry tickets. He grinned. "There you are - compliments of the house." Hazel was ecstatic and couldn't thank him enough, whilst Noah was hoping that he wouldn't trip over his own feet on Saturday night.

Soupy walked them back out to Wythes Road. He shook hands. "It's been nice chatting to you," said Hazel. As they walked away, she turned to wave goodbye. Soupy returned her wave and called out, "Cheerio Matey." He'd forgotten her name already.

They returned to Mrs Fletcher's house after dark and the pair went inside to check that all was ready. June Fletcher agreed to keep the bedroom light on and to parade back and forth facing the window with the curtains tightly closed. It was now simply a case of waiting to see if the Peeping Tom showed himself.

Before entering the house, Noah and Hazel had reconnoitred the area around the alleyway and worked out any escape routes, just in case the suspect should do a runner. There appeared to be only one way in and out of the alley, which was via a side passageway.

Mrs Fletcher made tea and sandwiches and they settled down to await the voyeur's arrival. Hazel took up position at the adjoining top landing window where the lights were switched off and she could keep watch through a slit in the curtain. There was nothing more to be done. Noah made himself comfortable in the parlour reading a newspaper. He had no intentions of hiding out in the dark and muddy alleyway.

He looked at his wristwatch. It said 9pm. Ten minutes went by and Noah wondered if this was a waste of their time. Maybe the man wouldn't show tonight.

Suddenly he heard Hazel whisper urgently from her vantage point on the top landing. "Noah, I think he's here. I'm sure I can see someone moving down in the rear alley." Noah went up the stairs, two at a time. He carefully parted the curtains and had to wait a moment until his eyesight adjusted with the ambient light. Then he saw an imperceptible movement. A man raised his head above the line of the back fence and he saw his eyes staring upwards at June's bedroom window. "Okay, let's go get him," he said, heading for the front door. Hazel was close behind.

They crept into the alleyway between two houses that led into the rear alleyway. The man would be twenty yards away on their right. It was deathly quiet in the close confines of the dark pathway as they advanced slowly forwards. They placed their feet carefully so as not to make any noise and alert the intruder. They crept ten yards and Noah could see an indistinct shape ahead of him, next to June's fence.

Suddenly he stepped onto a dry twig, which in the stillness of the night, snapped with the sound of a rifle bullet. The dark shape suddenly exploded from his hiding place, running blindly away from them through the overgrowing bushes and wild foliage towards the far end of the alley. Noah knew that it came to a dead end and that the man would be trapped. All pretence of keeping quiet was now abandoned as Noah and Hazel shouted at the man. "Stop where you are. You're under arrest." They flicked on their flashlights and could see him ahead, bursting through undergrowth.

Noah thought the man must surely have injuries from cuts and scratches caused by wild rose and blackthorn barbs. Hazel was close behind him and lighting the way with her torch. The man came up against the solid fence barring his way at the end of the alleyway. It was now just a matter of grabbing and cuffing him.

But without warning, the man crashed through a picket fence on his left and burst into a neighbouring garden. The pair could hear him climbing over walls and clambering over one fence after another as he garden-hopped to escape. Noah shouted to Hazel, "Run around to the next street and head him off," and he heard her racing back the way she had come so as to intercept him on the opposite side of the block. He didn't attempt to follow the man across the resident's gardens, as he doubted if he would be coming back this way. He retraced his steps back to Holt Road. He looked right and left along the street, but Hazel was nowhere to be seen. He quickly walked around the block into Lord Street, hoping to catch sight of the intruder.

Under the glare of a streetlamp he found Hazel sat upon a front garden wall calmly picking thorns from her tunic. Her feet were firmly planted upon the torso of a young man who was lying on the ground, securely handcuffed. The man was moaning in agony from lacerations across his whole body and blood oozed out of the cuts. She harrumphed in mock indignation, "Oh how nice of you to turn up, Noah. Did you stop-off at the pub for a pint?"

Noah was impressed. "Well done, love. Did he give you any problems?" he said, indicating her prisoner.

Hazel jabbed her toe into the detainee's buttocks. "Are you okay down there, sunshine?"

The man was in a great deal of pain. "I'm bleedin' from everywhere," he moaned.

"You're a bleeding pain in the arse. It serves you right," she said, without the slightest trace of sympathy. "Oh, and by the way, did I mention that you're under arrest for behaviour likely to cause a public nuisance?"

She leaned across and whispered softly into Noah's ear. "And don't forget, Constable Sheppard. You owe me a snog and a squeeze."

It was a warm but overcast day as the couple strolled westwards along Newland Street, with the dock fence on their right stretching into the far distance. On their left, street after street of terraced houses competed for space among the bombsites and the newly-built prefabricated housing. The prefabs were being quickly erected all across cash-strapped Great Britain in place of the generally more expensive houses that were built of bricks and mortar. Ten years after the end of World War Two, the economy of the United Kingdom had remained teetering on bankruptcy as she valiantly fought her way back into financial solvency, but there was little government money available to finance a major house rebuilding programme. Prefabricated houses, which were cheap to build and quick to erect, appeared to be the short-term answer.

Hazel pointed as they passed a row of prefabs. "When you were on sick leave I got chatting to a lady that lives in one of those," she said. Noah didn't respond, but simply nodded. "She said that they were ever so warm and cosy and lovely to live in," continued Hazel. Still she got no response, except for another nod of the head. She ploughed on. "Yes, this lady, whose name is Mrs Reese, said that she wouldn't go back to living in a proper house – not after living in a lovely prefab. She said that they're the best thing since sliced bread." Still Noah said not a word. She looked at him sharply. He appeared to be in a world of his own.

"Noah, have you been listening to one word that I've said?" she asked sternly.

"Of course I have. You've been telling me about prefabs."

"Well, for your information," she said in exasperation, "I've been trying to drop some very heavy hints that you perhaps might like to live in one someday."

"Me? Live in a prefab? Whatever for?" he said, not remotely recognising any of the heavy hints.

Hazel shook her head at men's stupidity. She was getting annoyed. "I didn't mean just you live in it, you dumb ox. I meant us living in a prefab together. I presume that you want to marry me at some stage, don't you?"

Notwithstanding her inescapable proposition, things began to click into place. "Oh of course I do, my sweet. I may even pop the question some day," he grinned.

"Hmmm," she hummed doubtfully. "I may have died from old age by then."

Walking beside her, Noah was contentedly grinning. And then he began whistling a snappy tune.

They came to Kennard Street, where he had decided to buy a slab of Cadbury's chocolate at the Cooperative Society department store. But just as they were within twenty yards of the entrance, the door burst open and a young lad darted out into the street and almost collided with them. The store's manager, Alfie Symonds, came rushing out, looking flustered and out of breath. He caught sight of the youngster and shouted, "Stop him. He's a thief." The boy was wild eyed with fright, but quickly sidestepped around them and made off towards the dock fence. "Stop him," repeated the manager, but he was too breathless to give chase. As quick as lightning, Hazel swiftly took in the scene and ran after the boy. With her long athletic legs, she rapidly caught him up and grabbed him by the scruff of the neck. They walked slowly back towards the store, where Alfie Symonds stood with a look of smug satisfaction upon his face.

They took the boy upstairs to the office. Symonds rifled through the lad's pockets and came up with two Mars Bars. "Aha, just as I thought," he said, so as to justify his accusations of theft. They sat the boy in a chair. The kid was so small his feet didn't even touch the floor.

Hazel knelt beside the lad. "What's your name, young man?" she asked sternly.

The boy had angelic blue eyes. "It's Billy. Billy Baldwin."

"And how old are you, Billy?" she enquired in a calm voice.

"I'm eight and three quarters. I'll be nine soon," he said with a melodic voice that was full of innocence. He swivelled around in the chair to address Alfie Symonds. Regretful eyes looked up for forgiveness. "I'm sorry that I pinched your Mars Bars, mister, but I was hungry."

"Which school do you go to?" asked Hazel.

"Drew Road Primary School," said Billy.

"Why aren't you at school today?"

"I didn't want to go," he whispered.

"Why's that? What's wrong with school?"

"I don't like some of the boys," he said in a faint tone. "They pull my hair and bully me." A tear ran down his cheek and Hazel handed him a handkerchief. She looked up at Noah with eyes that pleaded with him to take mercy upon the lad and not take this incident any further.

She returned to questioning the youngster. "Well, perhaps your mummy could go see your teacher and tell him about that, eh Billy?"

"My mum died when I was seven years old," said the lad with a faltering voice full of sadness, and Hazel almost found herself crying in sympathy. She tousled his light brown hair and smoothed it all in one movement.

"Is your dad at home?" asked Noah. He had already decided that he wouldn't pursue this petty theft any further, but the boy's father would have to be informed.

"I think he is," said Billy uncertainly.

Noah took Alfie Symonds aside. "I don't think we ought to make any official reports on this matter, Alfie. He's just a kid. Best if I simply have a word with his dad, okay?" Symonds agreed. He was glad to let the affair drop and avoid any paperwork on his part. Hazel picked up the chocolate bars and, reaching into her pocket, handed Symonds a shilling coin. "That should cover the cost of the Mars Bars," she said. "The boy's hungry."

"Right then, young man, let's take you home, shall we?" said Noah. "Where do you live?"

"In Muir Street," said Billy. It was just around the next block. They set off to walk the few hundred yards to Billy's house, and without a word the boy took hold of Hazel's hand as they walked side by side. He munched on a Mars Bar with his free hand.

Muir Street was a backwater of just a dozen houses that had remained standing after being bombed by the Luftwaffe and where acres of derelict bombsites littered the landscape. They arrived at his house and Noah rapped on the doorknocker. The house was a typical Dockers' Mansion of a two up-two down terraced residence. Tufts of weeds grew vigorously from between the cracks of the concrete at the front entrance and the place exuded an uncared for appearance. Some grubby net curtains hung in the windows, which were covered in a patina of dust and cobwebs. The boy was still holding Hazel's hand when the door opened - and framed in the doorway, dressed in grubby grey trousers and a loose fitting shirt - was Police Constable Ronnie Baldwin.

Hazel's mouth opened in surprise. She'd never given any thought to where Baldwin lived, but was surprised to find him residing in this near derelict house amongst the bombsites. Baldwin's brow furrowed in a question mark and his eyes narrowed in suspicion. "Whatcha doin' 'ere?" he said in a low growl. "What's going on?" The unmistakable cockney accent was patently evident.

Noah stepped forward to diffuse the heavy atmosphere. "It's nothing to worry about, Ronnie. We've just found young Billy around at the Co-op and wondered why he's not at school."

He decided not to mention the matter of the wayward Mars Bars.

Hazel said, "He's told us that he's being bullied at school by some bigger boys. That's why he played truant today."

Baldwin relaxed and took a less confrontational stance. "Oh righto. Fanks for telling me. I'll give Billy a spanking and send him to bed for his cheek."

Hazel spoke up for the boy. "Actually Ronnie, what he needs right now is some food. He's very hungry. As far as the bullying is concerned – would you like me to go see the head-teacher about it? I don't mind doing it."

After the previous snide remarks and innuendos on his part, Baldwin had never expected any friendliness at all from Noah or Hazel, and in fact he had assumed quite the opposite, but it was clear to him that the pair didn't appear to hold a grudge. He was won over. "Erm thanks very much," he said. "That would be very much appreciated." He was more than happy that they seemed content to let sleeping dogs lie. He reached out his hand and Billy detached himself from Hazel and ran over to his father and wrapped his little arms around his dad's protective legs.

By way of explanation, Baldwin said, "It's been a bit hard bringing him up alone ever since I lost my wife. I haven't got the hang of this cooking and cleaning lark yet." He looked down at his boy and tousled his hair. "But we'll be alright, won't we son?"

Hazel's eyes were on the verge of becoming moist, as she could see that Ronnie Baldwin clearly loved his son and would take better care of him in the future.

"He's a lovely boy, Ronnie," she said through wet eyelashes. "He's a credit to you."

Ronnie invited them inside for tea, but the couple needed to get back onto their beat and said their goodbyes. Little Billy Baldwin stood waving until they had turned the corner out of sight.

As the pair ambled along, heading in the direction of Drew Road School, Hazel decided to wind him up. She said, "I've come to the conclusion that you're not the big roughy-toughy copper that you pretend to be, but just a big softy."

"Really?" he said arching his eyebrows in feigned surprise. "Whatever's given you that impression?" He was somewhat used to her goading him by now, and in fact, he quite enjoyed the light banter.

"You," she said, pointing an accusing finger, "could have carted that little boy off to the nick and had him charged with stealing, and earned some brownie points from Stranksy in the process. But you didn't because you're such a soft touch for a sob story." Happy with her mock accusation, she waited in smug expectation for Noah to defend himself.

Instead of answering, Noah began to whistle a catchy tune, which annoyed her even more.

"And," she said - again pointing her finger to press home her point - "you could have got your revenge on Ronnie Baldwin for his snide remarks by arresting his light-fingered kid." Noah continued to stroll along with a contented look upon his face.

"What's up, Noah? Cat got your tongue?"

He smiled indulgently at her. "You're only miffed because I didn't get excited at the prospect of living with you in a prefab."

She opened her mouth to deliver a well-aimed wisecrack, but couldn't think of a suitable barbed reply. She reached into her pocket. "Whatever. At the end of the day, my gallant Noah, it's me that's about to scoff this spare Mars Bar."

The pair entered the playground at Drew Road Primary School. The kids had just eaten their midday meal and now it was playtime. Whilst small gangs of boys ran around playing war games like demented maniacs, a gaggle of girls appeared to be playing shopkeepers. He heard one girl ask her friend for, "Two panda spuds, ta very much." Some of the lads were playing with marbles and swopping cigarette cards, whilst girls played fivestones or hopscotch. The school was a tall imposing Victorian building with high vaulted ceilings that was spread over four floors. They climbed the front steps and made for the head-mistresses' study.

Miss Green was a skinny grey haired spinster who was nearing retirement age. Noah had met with Miss Green many times since taking over the Silvertown beat, and he found it helpful to exchange information so that the kids didn't mix with the wrong crowd and take up a life of crime. As he introduced Hazel, they discussed young Billy Baldwin being bullied. The head-mistress promised to have a word with his class teacher and nip any rough-stuff in the bud.

Meanwhile, she was brewing up the ubiquitous pot of tea. Hazel hadn't yet become accustomed to the huge amount of tea that would be consumed each day whilst on patrol. Whenever they called at an address to speak with a householder or a shopkeeper, then the teapot would be immediately brought out. Miss Green looked into the tea caddy. "Oh dear," she said, disappointedly, "We seem to be running out of tea leaves." But then her face brightened up as she remembered something. "Never mind, our ship's due in shortly from China. They're certain to have a cargo of tea onboard and I'm sure they can spare a small amount for the school."

Noah exchanged bemused glances with Hazel. What was the woman blathering on about? What's all this about her ship coming from China with a cargo of tea? Had she lost her marbles?

Miss Green saw their confusion and explained. "Oh yes, it's quite true," she said in her frail voice. "The school has adopted a cargo ship through the Ship Adoption Society, and our ship, named Glenorchy, will be berthing at Number 1 berth right next to the school this very afternoon. She belongs to the Glen & Shire Line," she told them. "In fact we'll be taking the children up onto the flat roof to welcome her home at any moment. Would you like to join us?"

Hazel was excited. She caught Noah's eye. "Please, can we watch?"

"Yes okay, but first nip down to the police box and tell Sergeant Ethridge where we'll be."

Over two hundred pupils and teaching staff were gathered noisily upon the flat roof of the school. It stood 120 feet above ground and had a commanding view of the whole of Silvertown and as far as Galleons Reach on the River Thames. The kids were quite safe up here because it was securely enclosed by solid six foot high steel fencing.

The view encompassed the entire length of the King George V Dock and beyond, so that one could clearly see the whole vista of how the docks operated. More than a dozen ocean-going cargo and passenger vessels lay alongside the berths, and their cargoes were being loaded or discharged by tall electric cranes. On the quayside, fork-lift trucks whizzed to and fro between the quay and the warehouses, and stevedores, looking like armies of ants, wheeled sack-trucks loaded with packing cases or steel ingots or machine parts that had been manufactured in the industrial heartlands of Great Britain.

A black hulled vessel had just entered the docks from the River Thames and was making its way slowly and majestically up the dock, assisted by two tugboats. She was a handsome looking vessel with a tall black and dark red coloured funnel. Gradually it got closer until they could plainly make out its name painted on the bows. It said Glenorchy.

The deputy head-mistress came over and introduced herself. Much like the head-mistress, Miss Lawley was also an ageing spinster. She was a well spoken woman with brown wavy hair and dressed immaculately in a tan coloured suit. She had a ready smile and seemed to be well liked by the children. She pointed to the approaching ship. "She'll be tying-up just there at Number 1," she said, pointing to a vacant berth. "She'll be here in London for about three weeks whilst she unloads her cargo, then re-loads for her next voyage."
"Where's the ship come from?" asked Hazel.
"It's been on a five month voyage to the Far East, calling at Suez, Bombay, Colombo, Hong Kong, Shanghai and Japan. I should imagine the crew will be keen to be going home on leave."
Miss Lawley explained why the school joined the ship adoption scheme. "Mainly it means that the children write letters to the crew, and they send us information regarding their voyage, such as what ports they're calling at and what cargo they're carrying. We mark her position on the map in the assembly hall so that the kids know where the ship is. The children like reading the letters from the crew, but they especially love going onboard whilst she's in port."
"The kids get to go onboard?" exclaimed Hazel, excitedly "I've never been aboard a ship."
Miss Lawley smiled. "Would you like to go onboard the Glenorchy? We've got a visit arranged for 30-odd children for next week. You could accompany them if you like."
"We'd love to," answered Hazel before Noah could respond. "Wouldn't we Noah?"

The ship was now close to the school and the tugs began to push her gently into her berth. It was time for the kids to make some noise. "Three cheers for the Glenorchy," someone shouted, and a huge cheer went up. Other children waved the Union Jack and the Glen Line house flag and it seemed to Hazel like organized but happy pandemonium.

At the bottom end of Parker Street, abutted onto the dock fence, was a convent. The main single storey building and several out-buildings were set in over an acre of agricultural land on which the nuns grew vegetables and soft fruits. The entire acreage was surrounded by a four foot high wall. The local community had very little contact with the nuns because they kept themselves to themselves and appeared to be mostly self-sufficient. During the period that Noah had patrolled the Silvertown beat, he had never had any dealings with its residents.

It therefore came as a surprise when he and Hazel were waylaid by one of the nuns who spotted them as they visited Kath Lomas' off-licence, located opposite the convent. "Good mornin' to yae, constable," said the nun, in a broad Irish brogue. "Oim Sister Bernadette. The Reverend Mother would loik to be havin' a word with ya, if yae please." She led the way into the convent.

The Reverent Mother was an ancient woman whose entire body, except for her hands and the small area of her face, was hidden beneath voluminous layers of her black and white habit. A silver cross and chain hung around her neck and she held a set of rosary beads in her left hand.

She held out a spindly hand. Noah wasn't sure if he should shake it, or go onto his knees and kiss it in benediction. He shook her hand and introduced himself and Hazel.

"I'm Sister Evangeline, the Reverend Mother" she said in a frail voice. "We've had some of the sister's clothing stolen from our washing line, and I would like you to investigate the matter."

Noah glanced cagily at Hazel. This was a type of crime that was both unusual and difficult to apprehend any perpetrator, as most clothes stolen from washing lines were taken in the dead of night. It was something that he didn't really want to get involved in, but he would reluctantly have to show some willing.

"Erm yes, we'll certainly try to help," he said with not much certainty of success. "Perhaps you'd like to tell us what items have been stolen?"

The Reverend Mother looked embarrassed. "They're items of a personal nature," she stuttered.

Noah was uncertain what she meant. "Erm, could you be more specific?" he said.

Hazel leaned over and whispered into his ear. "I think she means knickers, you dumb ox."

Sister Evangeline rose from her chair and led them out into the garden. The washing line in question was strung between two gnarled apple trees. A half dozen bath towels were flapping in the light breeze. Sister Bernadette began removing the towels and folded them into a wicker basket. Noah had a quick look around. Nearby was a rickety wooden shed which sat clear of the ground upon some old breeze blocks.

"How many times have these items been stolen?" asked Noah.

"On four occasions," said the Reverend Mother. "Our sisters can ill afford to lose their clothing."

"And have they gone missing at the same time on each occasion?" he asked.

"It's always during the night-time," she said with certainty. "When the sisters come to collect it in the morning – several items have gone missing."

"I see," said Noah, thinking furiously. He didn't have the faintest idea what he could do about it. He was buggered if he was going to spend the whole night on a stake-out in this pitch dark garden. "Couldn't you simply remove your washing from the line at night?" he suggested.

She fixed him with a frosty glare. "Young man, I have fifteen nuns residing here. Their laundry needs to be washed and dried on a regular basis. Cleanliness is next to Godliness."

Noah was flummoxed. He mumbled, "We'll come back later when it's dark."

They continued their patrol by meandering aimlessly around the quiet streets. The light had faded, but it would still be another two hours before full nightfall. Work in the docks had ceased for the day, and apart from a lively tune being played on the piano in Cundy's pub, only the regular hum of the machinery from within the giant Tate & Lyle sugar refinery could be heard. They were on duty until 10 o' clock and Hazel suspected that Noah would want to take her somewhere secret and isolated where he could wrap her in his arms and hold her tightly. She wouldn't be complaining if he did. They needed to make the most of every opportunity.

"Have you ever thought about becoming a nun?" he asked her out-of-the-blue. She was shocked at the mere thought of it. "Me? You've got to be joking?"

"It's just that I think you'd look quite tasty in a habit and wimple," he said, plainly mocking her.

She roughly elbowed him in the arm. "Listen buster, I could ensure that you take up a life of celibacy if that's what you want."

"Don't get mad. I'm only asking."
Another minute passed. It had gotten darker. They were now strolling towards the dark innards of the Silvertown By-Pass. "Do you fancy checking out the area under the arches?" he asked her innocently. It would be pitch black under there and she knew he would be kissing her.
"Aha, now you're firing on all cylinders," she said. "Lead-on lover boy."

They returned to the convent. The building was in darkness. He guessed that the nuns went to bed early so as to rise for early morning prayers. It didn't matter. In fact he preferred that the place was as quiet as the grave. They made their way silently around the walled garden to the approximate location of the washing line. They leant on the wall and looked over. In the dim light they could barely make out the string of white underwear flapping on the clothes line. He presumed that the nuns deliberately dried their underwear at night so that it wouldn't be on display to all and sundry during the daytime. Judging by the voluminous width of the knickers and with legs down to the knees, they looked like the type of bloomers that were often parodied in music hall sketches and lampooned on saucy seaside postcards.
He whispered in her ear. "I think you'd look great in a pair of those."
She said, "Sshhh," and gave him yet another dig in the arm.
Minutes went by. There was not a sound. Then without warning, one of the items of underwear dropped from the clothes line and fluttered to the ground. They could see movement on the ground, and in almost total blackness the light coloured material slowly began to move inch by inch along the ground towards the shed. Noah flicked on his flashlight and illuminated the area. He switched it off and they continued to watch as the dim white shape was inexorably dragged in the direction of the shed.
"Crime solved, Constable Leggett. We'll come back tomorrow and inform the Reverend Mother. What do you reckon?"
"I'm tired. I reckon I need to go to bed and have erotic dreams about a police constable that I'm acquainted with. That's what I reckon."
"You're right," he said, grinning. "You would never have made a virtuous nun."

They returned to the convent the next afternoon. "We've solved the mystery of your items going astray," Noah said to Sister Evangeline. "And we think we know where they've gone." The old woman gave him a crooked grin. "Oh bless you my son. Who's taken them?"
"Follow me," he said. The Reverend Mother, Sister Bernadette and four other nuns followed the pair out to the washing line.

He got down on hands and knees and looked under the garden shed. The floor had rotted away and there was a foot wide hole. He opened the wooden shed door. The rusty hinges creaked in protest as the light streamed in. From inside an old wooden crate, six pairs of angelic eyes looked inoffensively back at them. The packing case had been lined with numerous pairs of knickers for the imminent arrival of the kittens, who now looked out on the world with the innocence of new-born babies. He stood to one side to allow the nuns to inspect the guilty parties.
"Oh, how wonderful," beamed the Reverend Mother. The other postulants gathered around billing and cooing.
"We shall feed and look after these little darlings from now on," she said. "Thank you, my son, for bringing some joy back into our lives."

The pupils from Miss Austin's class were gathered in the school assembly hall when Noah and Hazel arrived. Today the kids would be going onboard their adopted ship, the Glenorchy, and Noah and Hazel would accompany them. The pair had cleared their outing beforehand with Sergeant Ethridge.

The children were led in a long line out of the school and into the docks via the Wicket Gate entrance, with the police officers bringing up the rear. They snaked their way across the lock gates of the King George V drydock where a Shaw Savill Line cargo ship was undergoing its annual maintenance and hull survey. The water had been pumped out of the dock and the ship now stood high and dry on wooden blocks and with what looked like dozens of telephone poles that were jammed between the sides of the dock and the ship's hull to prevent the vessel from tipping over onto its side. Down in the bottom of the dock, scaffolding had been erected around the stern, and men were working upon the twin phosphor-bronze propellers and the massive steel rudder plate.

The kids were escorted to Number 1 berth where the Glenorchy was moored. They gathered excitedly at the bottom of the gangway. Close up, the ship was much bigger than anyone could have imagined. The slab-sided steel hull rose high out of the water and the tall funnel towered above them. They gingerly climbed the gangway to the upper deck where they were met by a ship's officer and taken inside the opulent accommodation.

The group were taken on a guided tour of the vessel, where they were shown the wheelhouse with its steering wheel and navigational equipment. A deck officer explained how the ship was safely navigated across the oceans and where the ship had been on its voyage to the Far East. Onwards they were taken to see the immense cargo holds, where thousands of tons of freight from the Orient were being discharged. And lastly they climbed down into the bowels of the ship to visit the engine room, where the enormous twin Sultzer engines now lay silent, but which could easily drive the ship across the oceans at 17 knots. Noah and Hazel found the visit fascinating.

With the guided tour over, the schoolchildren were taken into the officers' dining saloon where they were seated at tables set with sparkling white tablecloths and silver cutlery. The forward facing saloon windows afforded a superb view, and the walls – or bulkheads – were lined with dozens of exotic types of polished veneered wood. Affixed to each panel was a discreet label that described each type of timber. The room had the pleasant aroma of beeswax polish. Noah read off the different names. There was Teak, Mahogany, Sapele, Burmese rosewood African olivewood, Mopane and Sandalwood.

Attentive uniformed Chinese waiters served tea with salmon and cucumber sandwiches and fancy cakes; and to the cockney children, many of whom came from impoverished homes, it must have seemed like having high tea at the Ritz Hotel.

The ship's captain came to introduce himself. He was a tall patrician figure who looked magnificent in his navy blue uniform with its four gold bands on the arm; but thoughtfully, he took the time to tell the children about the ship's latest voyage to the orient. The kids sat there spellbound as he described the voyage as they sailed through the Suez Canal or ploughed through a typhoon in the South China Sea. At last the ship's tour was over and they reluctantly made their way back to the school.

It was a Saturday night and the couple had tickets to the dance at the Tate Institute. They found a secluded table for two at the back of the dance-floor and hoped that they didn't bump into anyone connected with the job. Noah was nervous; not only because of the possibility of a chance encounter with a fellow constable, but he was panicking because he couldn't dance to save his life. It was Hazel's idea to come dancing, whereas the very thought of having to perform on the dance-floor filled him with dread.

He fetched drinks from the bar and settled at their table. The music hadn't yet started so he had some breathing space before he was required to make an ass of himself. High above the dance hall, the balloons had been inflated and lay in their netting, ready to be spilled out onto the dancers below. A rotating glitter ball sent out kaleidoscopic rays of multicoloured light beams into every corner of the room. The stage was equipped with a set of drums, piano, electric guitars, and microphones, but the band had yet to appear.

He spotted a gang of four Teddy Boys gathered in the far corner of the hall. They were dressed in what was, to Noah; quite bizarre clothing that was styled on the Edwardian era. They wore long drape coats with velvet trim on the collar and pocket flaps and with narrow drainpipe trousers that stopped halfway down their ankles to reveal white socks. Their similarity to an Edwardian dandy was completed by a fancy brocade waistcoat and a pair of suede brothel-creeper shoes. Noah found their hairstyles the weirdest feature of all. Most of the Teds sported a greased quiff that was carefully combed around the sides of the ears to form a duck's arse at the nape of the neck.

As they congregated around the bar, the four Teds looked quite menacing, and Noah hoped that they weren't going to start any fights. He was off-duty and didn't fancy taking on a gang of men in weird clothes. The recent rise in their popularity was a strange phenomenon and he was aware that some Teddy Boy gang's idea of a good weekend, was to cause fights and mayhem at the seaside resorts. He'd heard of riots taking place in Bognor and Brighton.

Then from the direction of the women's toilets they were joined by four Teddy Girls who were dressed in drape coats and pencil skirts and beehive hairdos. Noah breathed a sigh of relief. The Teds weren't likely to start any fisticuffs if their wives or girlfriends were with them.

Soupy Edwards stopped by after taking a break from serving behind the bar. "Hello Matey," said Soupy. He'd long ago forgotten their names. "I'm glad you could make it tonight. Hope you have a great time."
Noah indicated the Teddy Boys. "I hope we're not going to get any problems with that bunch tonight, are we Soupy?"
"Them?" Good God no! They're a great bunch of fellas," said Soupy. "They're tonight's band."

As the band started up with a Bill Haley number, Hazel was halfway to the dance-floor and dragging Noah with her. "It's dead easy. Just watch what the others are doing," she suggested. She guided him in a few dance steps and within a few minutes, he found he was jiving quite reasonably. The song finished and she threw her arms around his neck. "Darling, you were really good. You still need some practice, but that weren't bad for a first attempt." Noah stood there grinning. Hazel was a good teacher.

The band went into another Bill Haley song and the pair were jiving again as he became more confident. The Teds girlfriends came on stage and did backing vocals on a couple of Johnny Ray numbers and then slowed the pace with some Ruby Murray hits. Noah was tired out. "Let's sit this out," he said, and flopped into his seat.

She smiled across the table at him. "I knew you could do it. I'm proud of you, darling."

8: Carnal Desires

Frankie Houlder and his sons were out on a job when Noah and Hazel arrived at their scrap metal yard. They went inside the yard office, where Jackie Houlder was sat at her desk totting up columns of figures in a ledger.

Jackie was a 50 year old ex-dancer who had met Frankie thirty years ago at a club, and after a whirlwind romance they had married and produced three strapping sons. Jackie was a moderately attractive curvaceous peroxide blonde who fashioned her looks on film starlets like Monroe, Jayne Mansfield or Diana Dors; and to further her film star image, she invariably wore a mink coat whatever the season or the time of day. However, although some unkind remarks referred to her as "Brassy" or "Mutton dressed as Lamb," she was a financial wizard when armed with the company's account books or a ledger sheet. What she lacked in good taste, she made up for with good business sense. Jackie could cook the books to perfection, so that the company's profits were minimal and the taxman got next to nothing. In short, she was the brains of the outfit.

She gave him the benefit of a radiant smile. "Hello Constable, how are you?" she said, closing the ledger quickly.
"I'm fine, Mrs Houlder." He introduced Hazel, and after being seated, he continued. "I'm glad I bumped into you, because there's something important which you might want to pass on to your husband." Without further ado Noah related the saga of the two lads arrested on the railway line and their admission that Frankie had arranged to buy the copper cable from them. At this point Jackie was about to interject with a denial, but Noah held up his hands against interruption. "What those lads were about to do with the railway signalling cables could have caused a train smash or derailment, and that's what concerns me. Just talk some sense into your husband and let him know that I'll be keeping my eyes wide open from now on. If I even suspect that there's any dodgy dealing going on, then I can easily turn up here with a search warrant and crawl all over this yard with a fine tooth comb. Is that understood?"
Jackie Houlder understood perfectly. She said in a meek voice, "Of course it is, Constable. I'll pass that on."

Back out in the street, Hazel gazed at Noah with something approaching hero-worship at the way in which he'd effortlessly handled the problem. However her admiration was summed up in very few words. She said, "My God Noah, you've got some balls."

Hazel Leggett lay in bed at her digs. The room was furnished with cheap utility furniture that had seen better days and the worn out bed springs creaked and protested every time she turned over. The bright street-lamp outside the house cast beams of light into the room, which was only partially diffused by the thin curtains. She turned onto her side to escape its glare. Hazel was tired after a long shift and craved some well-earned sleep, but her thoughts were keeping her awake.

Her feelings, as always, concerned Noah. She was sure that she was in love with him, and quite certain that she adored every fibre of his body. But her feelings, she told herself, were much deeper than that, and heading off into directions that she had never before experienced. Just recently she had began to have erotic visions of Noah that caused her to question if this was normal behaviour in women generally. There was no one whom she could talk to or confide in who could say whether these emotions were normal behaviour in a woman. All her close female friends were back in Oxfordshire, and she very much doubted if they would be of much help.

Hazel felt hot and flushed as these uninhibited desires and emotions fluttered in and out of her thoughts. She lifted the eiderdown to one side so as to allow him admittance into her bed. Deep down she knew that these carnal desires were wrong, but she couldn't help herself. She wanted to feel the warmth of his body next to hers and feel his limbs wrapped around her, so as to envelop her body in its warm cocoon. She imagined him kissing her and sensing his warm breath as it expelled onto her cheeks. She visualised him forcefully turning her onto her back and feeling his dead weight on top of her, with the sensation of being heavy and substantial and immoveable, and smothering her body with his masculinity.

She felt a hot flush in her cheeks and took a sip of water from the bedside tumbler. She laid her head back onto the pillow and closed her eyes, gradually wavering on the edge of sleep, but unable to evict him from her thoughts. He returned to her bed and again slid his muscled body on top of hers in one easy movement. She felt him forcefully gripping her wrists, pressing them down into the mattress, so that she was held hostage and there was no escape. He bore his weight down onto her; holding her captive with his manliness. She was utterly helpless to deny him whatever he desired. He manoeuvred himself between her legs and she opened them wide to allow him unfettered access. Her head began to swirl with an erotic kaleidoscope that she had never experienced in her 22 years. She wanted him desperately; wanted to give herself to him completely and without limits. She could feel his urgency and spurred him on, raising her hips to meet the onslaught that was to come, and finally to experience that exquisite sensation as he thrust the thick core of his body deep inside her own.

She awoke from her dreams in perspiration, breathing heavily. She lay with her eyes wide open, squirming in her bed and unable to settle comfortably with these unspeakable thoughts that were wildly darting in and out of her emotions. She questioned her own morality. Should she be having these wild carnal desires swirling through her consciousness? She felt sure she shouldn't. Nothing made sense.

They were about to begin another shift as they exited the police station. "Let's take a short detour through the park today, love," he said when they'd got clear of the nick. They turned left into the Royal Victoria Park, which was next to the police station. The park was in the opposite direction to their regular Silvertown beat, but Noah fancied a change to their usual schedule. "I want to see some greenery and foliage and flowers instead of factory chimneys belching out smoke; even if it is just for half an hour. What do you think?"
"Whatever you say is okay by me o' magnificent one," she said, trying to goad him.
"Stop taking the Mickey, wench. I just thought you might like a change of scenery, that's all."
"Gosh Constable, you sure know how to show a girl a good time, don't you?"

It was a sunny afternoon and mothers were out in force, pushing their toddlers in prams or letting them play on the swings and see-saw in the play area. Some older children were paddling in the shallow end of the bathing pool. A park keeper, dressed in the brown uniform of West Ham Council Park Service was planting out dozens of freesias into a flower border. It was hard to believe that everything could be so green and peaceful in this oasis of tranquillity set amongst the noisy and smoky industrial conglomeration of the docklands. The park's southern perimeter butted onto the banks of the River Thames and the pair strolled along the pathway that ran beside it. For a while they watched the changing river activity as tugs with strings of barges were making their way up on the flood tide, whilst fully-laden coasters and colliers were heading for their upriver berths. Noah and Hazel ambled along a shady avenue of plane trees and exited the park via Bargehouse Road where they rejoined the main road. The noise of the heavy traffic reminded them that they were back into the world of reality. They swung around, heading back towards the west – towards the factories of Silvertown.

The hours flew by as they ambled around the streets of their patrol area, often stopping to chat to shopkeepers or householders or simply to take up the offer of a hot drink and to put their tired feet up for a few minutes. Noah was amazed at how some of the local people were so impoverished that they would pawn their best Sunday suit or a wedding ring on a regular basis; and yet they were generous enough to invite you into their homes for tea and biscuits. He knew of one particular elderly couple who were as poor as the proverbial church mice, and were so destitute that they would walk down the centre of the local streets singing songs in the hope of some kind soul putting some coins into their collection hat. "Gaw'd bless ya, governor," they would say to any kindly benefactor. It wasn't uncommon in Silvertown for residents to take in washing or scrub the floors of better-off neighbours so as to make ends meet, and he knew of one local woman who would make girl's pretty taffeta party dresses for the paltry sum of ten shillings so as to feed her children.

The pair resumed their sedate but stately progress until, by evening, they were walking leisurely around the streets of Silvertown. In the receding twilight the enormous steel leviathan of the Tate & Lyle sugar refinery could be heard constantly humming as it refined countless tons of sugar for the consumption of Britain's working masses.

It was a warm but dark night as they strolled westwards along Drew Road. At its junction with Saville Road, where the ever present dock fence marks the perimeter of the Royal Docks, a giant passenger liner sat in the dry dock where it was scheduled for annual maintenance and hull painting. The ship-repair yard had closed for the evening and the deck cluster lights onboard the ship cast an eerie glow over the street. They briefly popped in to Cath Lomas' off-licence. Cath offered a glass of lemonade and they passed a few minutes chatting about that most English of subjects – the weather. Two boys entered the off-licence laden with empty lemonade bottles and Cath handed over the small refund that they could rightfully claim for returned glass bottles. Onwards the couple strolled past Eid's bakery, where in a few hours time; Mister Eid would arise from his bed at the crack of dawn to begin baking the fresh loaves and rolls for his customers. It was a pleasant evening and the town was quiet.

Their patrol usually took a haphazard route, which was dependant on the random direction that Noah had chosen, but tonight Hazel knew exactly where they were heading. Ahead of them, the dark shape of the Silvertown By-Pass loomed out of the night; its thirty foot high elevated roadway supported by massive concrete pillars. During the daytime, the roadway was teeming with heavy traffic taking manufactured goods into and out of the Royal Docks; but come the night, when work in the docks had ceased, the by-pass was deserted. The area beneath the road was a dark and dingy forgotten backwater, where kids played during the hours of daylight and winos would sometimes doss down for the night.

They walked beneath the road and Noah flicked on his flashlight, ensuring that no one was around. They found a quiet corner, deep within the confines of the roadway's foundations, where they discovered an old wooden packing crate that would function as a seat. She quickly came into his arms, eager to be kissed. These stolen moments, were few and far between, and apart from these clandestine kisses, it was impossible for them to be together. Hazel could never enter the single man's section house at the police station without every constable instantly being aware of it, and the news would spread like wildfire. Conversely, male visitors were prohibited by the hawk-eyed landlady at her digs in East Ham. She had made that rule abundantly clear from the outset.

What if, she wondered, Noah moved out of the section house and rented a house? At least they could be together in an idyllic love nest. But even that idea was strewn with difficulties. If it should become known that they were shacking-up together or "living in sin," then the cosy arrangement of Bert Ambrose turning a blind eye to their romance would vanish in an instant, especially if the righteously upstanding and supercilious Inspector Stranks should get wind of it. The upright pillars of society within the police force wouldn't stand for the force's name being brought into disrepute, and both their careers would be at stake. She felt uncomfortable with any scheme that may put Noah's career at risk, and so they decided to delay any decisions regarding their future.

Noah had loosened her tunic and his hand was inside her blouse. She allowed him to unsnap her brassiere so that her breasts were easily accessible and he could stroke and gently squeeze them. She had completely changed her attitude with regard to heavy petting on duty. She knew how much Noah wanted her, and it didn't seem fair to withhold herself when she knew that it would bring him so much pleasure. If she was honest with herself, she loved him caressing her and it made her feel desirable and needed.

She felt comfortable and safe in his protective arms and casually she let her head rest onto his shoulder as he stroked her hair. Her finger traced over the faint scar tissue on the underside of his chin, caused as the result of a bicycle accident as a boy. It was barely noticeable, but he was self-conscious about it and despite these small imperfections, she knew that she loved him dearly.

They had been sweethearts for some months now, ever since he had kissed her on that foggy evening; and yet their lovemaking had consisted of only an occasional stolen moment, when full intercourse was impossible and definitely off the menu for Hazel. She was adamant that they would save their desires until an opportunity presented itself when they could snuggle up together in complete privacy, and afterwards, not feel cheap and devious.

Their romantic interlude continued as he wrapped his arms around her waist and pulled her tightly into a close embrace. Noah's hands reached behind her and squeezed the soft cheeks of her bottom as he kissed her. She could feel the hardness of his erection through the material of her uniform skirt, and wished they were in a secret and private place, where she could allow him to make love to her.

The headlights of an approaching vehicle made them suspend their canoodling until it had passed by; but instead, a goods vehicle pulled into the side of the road and switched its engine off. The couple were out of sight under the stygian blackness of the roadway, but Noah let out an oath at being disturbed. Two men alighted from the truck and stood whispering on the pavement, as if waiting for something or someone to arrive. The men lit cigarettes and talked in low voices. Meanwhile, Hazel readjusted her clothing and buttoned up her tunic.

She whispered, "This doesn't look right, Noah. They're up to no good."

He nodded. "I think you're right. Let's wait and see what happens. They can't see us here."

Ten minutes went by. The two men were nervous and Noah heard them discussing whether to simply drive away. The driver's mate wanted to disappear, but the truck driver insisted they hang on a while.

Moments later they were joined by a third man who had silently walked from the direction of Connaught Road. The men whispered amongst themselves, but neither Noah nor Hazel could hear what was being discussed. The third man was tall and slim, and from his dialogue and demeanour, he seemed to be in command of the discussions.

From his jacket pocket the truck driver brought out a thick envelope and handed it to the new arrival, who tucked it safely into his windcheater. "That's it," whispered Noah. "I'm damn sure that some money's just changed hands. That tall bloke's just been paid off. Let's go." Silently they crept from the shadows and made their way around the far side of the truck. The three men were unaware of their presence and continued talking. Hidden from view, Noah leaned into the open window of the vehicle and removed the ignition keys and pocketed them. "They won't be driving anywhere," he whispered to Hazel.

He unclipped his torch and Hazel did likewise. In unison they flicked on their flashlights and flooded the area with light. The three men were taken completely by surprise and stood stock still. Hazel casually positioned herself behind them, in case they decided to make a run for it.

"What's going on?" asked Noah. "What are you doing here at this time of the night?"

"We ain't doing nuffink," said the driver.
"Nah, we was just having a chat. That's all," said his sidekick.
The third man remained silent, but looked around warily, as if looking for a way out; but Hazel stood ready to grab him.
"What's in the truck?" asked Noah, jerking his thumb towards the vehicle. They all played dumb.
"Okay then, here's what's going to happen," said Noah. "We're going to search your vehicle, but while we do so, you're all going to be handcuffed. We wouldn't like you going for a long distance run, would we constable?"
"We certainly would not," grinned Hazel. She unclipped her cuffs and slipped one onto each wrist of the driver and his mate. Noah handcuffed their tall companion.

Hazel climbed onto the rear of the truck and searched around with her torch. She opened some packages, checking on the contents and any delivery notes. She climbed down. "It's electrical goods - refrigerators, washing machines, radios, gramophones, and a few television sets. It's loaded to the roof. There's thousands of pounds worth. It's all marked for export."
Noah spoke to the driver. "Where did this come from? Have you got any documents?" The driver shrugged his shoulders and looked away.
"Okay, I reckon this lot's stolen," said Noah. "You're all under arrest." He instructed Hazel to read them their legal rights. It would be her arrest, and go onto her personal arrest tally. Noah stayed with the three men whilst she went to a nearby police call box and requested Sergeant Ethridge to send a Black Maria to transport their prisoners to the nick.

It was a long night for the pair as they booked their prisoners into custody and made full reports regarding the incident. From here on in, other police officers, notably the CID, would take over the case and prepare the documents to enable the men to be charged. In the meantime, they were held on a simple theft arrest warrant and held in the cells overnight. Arrangements were made to recover the truckload of stolen items, which would be categorized and stored as evidence.

One surprising fact that came to light occurred when the men were searched in the custody room. The driver and his sidekick's pockets revealed only the everyday items that people routinely carry with them; but the third man, whose name was revealed as Arthur Kensett, whom Noah had witnessed receiving a package, was found to have an envelope containing £150 in used banknotes. In answer to why he was in possession of such a huge sum of cash, he simply shrugged his shoulders and said he wanted to see a lawyer. He would say no more. It was clear to Noah that the electrical goods had been stolen from the nearby docks. Why else would they be marked up as "For export?"

Having witnessed the handover of the cash, Noah suspected that this was a payoff for Kensett's part in the theft, but was no wiser about his actual role. It seemed to him that the two drivers were simply low-level thieves. One thing was for sure, Kensett's part in the theft must have been crucial; bearing in mind that his own salary as a police constable was only a small fraction of what Kensett had been paid.

With their prisoners safely tucked up in the cells for the night, Noah and Hazel went off to their respective beds for a well-earned sleep. In the morning the CID detectives would take on the task of digging out more facts and interviewing the three men.

The next day, as the pair reported for duty, Hazel had some startling news. "I knew I'd seen Kensett's face somewhere before, but I couldn't recollect where," she told him. "But now I've remembered. Do you recall that sulky looking PLA copper who was on duty at the Wicket Gate some months back, when I'd first joined the job?" Noah's brow knitted in concentration as he tried to recall the incident.

"That's him," said Hazel with absolute certainty. Her finger pointed in the direction of the cells, where Kensett was locked up. "That fellow we've got in the slammer is a policeman."

It was all beginning to make sense to Noah. He'd tried – and failed to offer up any sensible reason why Kensett had been paid such a huge amount of cash. Now it became clear that it was payment for turning a blind eye to the theft of goods from the Royal Docks warehouses.

The pair went off to see Detective Constable Andy Summers.

9: A Cosy Love-nest.

Hazel wondered if it might be possible to take a holiday together. They had been sweethearts for many months, and yet it was impossible for them to have any time alone, apart from the stolen moments when they were on night duty. Even those pleasant interludes, when she allowed his hands to run unhindered across her body, were becoming frustrating. She was a normal red-blooded female, she told herself, and she wanted him to make love to her without the need to hide and to duck and dive. In short, she concluded, she didn't want to feel cheap and deceitful.

If they should be found out, then she was under no illusions that the supercilious Inspector Stranks would transfer them to opposite ends of the division and make it impossible for them to get together – if at all. Even the recent award of the Chief Constable's Commendation for Bravery would count for nothing with Stranks. Anyway, Hazel felt certain that the award was just a public relations exercise to bolster his reputation and flagging career. It was window dressing – pure and simple.

She and Noah had both accrued some annual leave and it was a case of "use it – or lose it." She had always wanted to visit Devon on England's south west coast, and to discover its sandy beaches and tiny harbours tucked away in idyllic coves. The thought of walking barefoot through the surf whilst hand-in-hand with Noah, filled her with a delicious anticipation and an eagerness to go pack a suitcase.

She thought they may be able to book a room at a seaside hotel, but even that straightforward matter was sprinkled with difficulties. Many hotels would not accept unmarried couples sharing a room, and it wasn't uncommon for courting couples to wear fake brass wedding rings as evidence that they were wed. Hazel had heard stories that in some guest houses, strict battleaxe landladies with Victorian attitudes would even demand to see a marriage certificate. She shook her head in frustration. What should have been a simple matter of enjoying a romantic holiday together was being frustrated with complications.

One week later, after submitting annual leave forms, they were granted their time off. However, Bert Ambrose had spotted that the requested dates coincided, and had given her an old-fashioned look which seemed to convey the fatherly message, "Watch yourself, young lady." But then his face had split into a wide grin and he said, "I hope you have a lovely time."

Noah had insisted on making all the arrangements so that their holiday itinerary would be a complete surprise. She didn't have a clue where they were heading for. He had taken care of everything. She was instructed to simply pack a suitcase. The days before departure were excruciatingly exciting as she attempted to wheedle any hint of their destination out of him, but he was adamant that, "You'll find out when we get there." The weather forecast promised warm and sunny days, all thanks to a high pressure weather system which sat squarely over the British Isles. They agreed that he would collect her from her digs early on the Saturday morning.

She was ready and waiting when he knocked at the door. She gave him a quick kiss and said, "Come on, lover-boy, let's get going on this wonderful mystery tour." She was dressed in a maroon two-piece outfit that accentuated the curves of her figure and her blonde hair hung down below her shoulders. A little light make-up emphasised her perfectly shaped blue eyes and her lips were a deep red. Noah thought she looked gorgeous.

Out in the street, she was surprised to find that he had arrived with a Morris Minor motor car. "Where did you get this from?" she asked, as he stowed her suitcase in the luggage space.

"A chap I know who owns a garage let me borrow it," he explained. "He owed me a favour." The prospect of motoring along country lanes to their holiday destination, wherever that may be, filled her with excitement. She made herself comfortable beside him in the little car. "I didn't even know you could drive."

"I learnt when I was in the army doing my National Service," he explained.

He put the car into gear and set off. Once clear of the city they made good time along the trunk roads, where the traffic was sparse and their little motor car chugged steadily westwards.

At Stonehenge they pulled over to spend a half hour idly roaming around the huge monolithic granite stones that had stood sentry for thousands of years. Soon afterwards, near the village of Cricklade, they stopped at a roadside diner for a late morning English breakfast. As they sat eating, she said, "Are you going to tell me exactly where we're going, Noah?"

He grinned. "Not yet. You'll need to have some patience."

She was serious for a moment. "Noah darling, there's something I need to ask you."

He picked up on the solemnity of the occasion. "Okay sweetheart. Fire away."

She looked steadily into his eyes. "Do you love me?"

"But of course I do," he said. "I've loved you from that very first day when we went out on patrol together."

She squeezed his hand and smiled with relief. "Thank you. I've been worried because you've never actually told me and I had to make sure."
"I haven't?" he said. "In that case, from now on, I'll tell you every day."

Two and a half hours later, she was ecstatic as they came upon a road sign that announced, 'Welcome to Devon.'
"Oh Noah, this is wonderful," she said, grinning from ear-to-ear, "How did you guess that I wanted to come to Devon?"
"I must be able to read your mind," was all he would say.

It was evening when they pulled into the town of Dawlish on Devon's south coast. They found the caravan site, tucked away in a leafy orchard on the edge of town. He parked the car next to a blue and white painted caravan and unlocked the door. They went inside. "Oh Noah, this is perfect....It's just perfect. What a lovely surprise." Whilst he connected the gas bottle and filled the water tank, she explored the little caravan which would be their home for the next ten days. She looked into drawers and cupboards and unearthed bedding and made their love nest neat and cosy. He produced a box of groceries that had been hidden in the car's boot space. She said, "I think I'm going to enjoy looking after you in our little home-from-home. I'm going to cook you lots of tasty dishes." She had never mentioned the subject of her culinary expertise, but he was more than happy to let her spoil him with home-cooked meals. "That's great," he said, "but I spotted an old country pub just down the road. I could do with a pint. Let's go."

Later that night, after an evening dinner and beer at the pub, they lit the gas lamps that cast a warm glow throughout the caravan. He was lying in the bed, expectantly waiting for her to finish her preparations in the small bathroom at the far end of the caravan. A soft night-light cast a faint glow over the tiny room. He moved to the far side of the bed, making room for her to get in beside him. He could hear her brushing her teeth and combing her hair. He heard the bathroom light-switch flick off as she opened the door and stepped out.

She remained motionless in the semi darkness, and he could see that she was naked. She stood in the caravan's dim shadows, and the wraithlike vision was enhanced by the weak light of the gas lamp. She waited silently and perfectly still, with her arms at her sides, and her chest pushed outwards, as if she was standing to attention prior to inspection. It seemed to Noah as if she wanted him to feast his eyes upon her and to allow his gaze to roam unhindered across the hitherto unseen valleys and canyons of her body. He stared unashamedly at her beauty, taking in the curves of her figure and flat tummy. Her delicate ribs were faintly outlined below breasts that stood out proudly with pronounced nipples that were encircled by light brown areola.

His eyes took in the long slim legs and travelled upwards to the forbidden triangle with its thick bunch of light brown hair. But his eyes were predominantly drawn to her lovely face with their delicate features and lips that were full and shouting to be kissed.

He whispered, "Hazel, you're the most beautiful creature I've ever seen."

The following day was warm and sunny with a barely perceptible light wind. They idly window shopped in the narrow streets or browsed through antique bookshops and had a cream tea in a cafe. The town was busy with holiday-makers who strolled around streets that were lined with grand Georgian manor houses alongside rustic cottages with quaint gabled roofs.

Hazel had read an information brochure on the town's history and discovered that the author Jane Austen had spent a considerable time in Dawlish. She could imagine her, as she idly shopped perhaps for muffins or a quill pen and dressed in crinolines and a wide-brimmed Regency bonnet.

Hazel felt a liberating relief that they could walk anonymously arm-in-arm around the streets of the town without fear of discovery by a fellow police officer; and with this new-found freedom, it seemed that they were a million miles away from London.

They made their way to the seashore where the railway line ran close-in alongside the promenade as it snaked its way from London to Exeter. Within minutes they heard the strident whistle of an express train as it approached the station on its non-stop service from London. Suddenly, it appeared from around a bend, travelling at full speed with black smoke and soot belching from its smokestack and hot steam hissing from its madly pulsating pistons. The Great Western train, with its dark green coachwork, was pulling a dozen Pullman carriages, and each was decorated with lacy curtains at the windows and a brass lamp with a gingerbread design on the fabric shade. The train made a thunderous noise as it roared along the track, so close to the seashore, that its passengers could almost reach out and touch the sand. They noticed a group of boys standing on a bridge; and as the train sped towards them, they leaned over the parapet so that they momentarily disappeared in a cloud of smoke and ash as the train flashed beneath them. Within seconds it was out of sight and they could hear only its low rumble as it disappeared into the distance.

Arm in arm they strolled along the foreshore to Coryton Cove where they planned to swim and sunbathe. He bought sixpenny ice cream cornets from a kiosk before choosing a deserted space among the sand dunes. At the top of the beach, above the high-water mark, were rows of beach huts, where holiday-makers were relaxing in deck chairs or brewing up yet another pot of tea on their portable gas stoves. Down on the beach they spotted children collecting seashells and exploring the rock-pools for limpets and small crabs and investigating fronds of kelp. And wheeling above them, were eagle-eyed seagulls that stood ready to swoop down and scavenge a leftover sandwich that a picnicker had carelessly left unattended.

They stretched out onto bath towels that Noah had unpacked from his knapsack and self-consciously slipped off their clothes and arranged them in neat piles. Hazel was relieved that he had suggested they wear their swimming costumes under their day-clothes. Hazel was wearing a one-piece blue costume that perfectly accentuated her curves, and he unashamedly ran an admiring eye over her figure without feeling at all bashful.

She spotted him staring. "Do you like what you see, or do you want to trade me in for another model," she teased him.

He laughed. "You look perfect. Come on, I'll race you into the water," and with that, he ran headlong down the beach and dived into the surf.

In the late afternoon, after swimming among the breakers and diving down to the sandy seabed, they relaxed on their bath towels and watched the offshore fishing boats with their ochre coloured sails and flocks of attendant seagulls, ever watchful for a discarded fishtail.

She sat with her back towards him and with his arms safely wrapped around her in a warm cocoon. Her arm rested on his leg and she could feel his soft breath in her hair as he nuzzled her neck. Hazel felt a warm glow of contentment being in the strong arms of the man that she adored. "Mmmm, that's nice darling," she whispered, as he blew gently into her ear. "Do that some more."

She was still glowing from their lovemaking last night. She really hadn't known what to expect; but without a doubt, she knew that it had been perfect. As she had stood naked beside the bed, she had adored the way in which he had taken his time, unhurriedly exploring her body with his eyes and making her feel beautiful and desired. He had peeled back the bedcovers, making room for her to slip in beside him and she had luxuriated in the glowing warmth of his body next to hers. He never rushed her with any urgency for their passion to be consummated, which she knew had been simmering just below the surface for many months. Noah had been attentive and understanding and sensitive to her needs, and although they hadn't previously discussed the subject, he had somehow guessed that her prior experience was minimal.

Her one and only previous sexual encounter had occurred when she was 19 years old, with a boy who had been an ex school-friend. The act of intercourse itself had been over in minutes, and afterwards she had felt cheap and used and the boy had subsequently ignored her just days later.

Conversely Noah had taken his time and took great pains to make her feel relaxed in his arms and never rushed matters, but simply kissed her and held her tightly. She had felt safe. A little later she had felt his hands wandering across every part of her body, exploring the deep uncharted areas untouched by any man. She had enjoyed the exquisite feelings as he kissed her breasts and down her tummy and buried his face in her hitherto unexplored and uncharted erogenous zones as he had taken possession of her body.

When at last he had manoeuvred himself above her, she had willingly opened herself up to accept him, although she was nervous with anticipation for what was about to occur.

She whispered, "Please be gentle, Noah."

He kissed her forehead as he spread his weight onto his forearms. "Of course I will, darling. We've got all the time in the world." And then, with infinite gentleness, he slid deep into the nucleus of her body.

Their lovemaking had been slow and almost languid at first as he had kissed her passionately on the lips and across her cheeks, but as the urgency overtook them, her mind felt free and uninhibited, and she found herself soaring from one high plateau to another on a journey of powerful emotions. She sensed his approaching climax and began grinding her hips to meet his thrusts and to spur him on to even greater efforts. And then, finally, there had been that wonderfully intense moment when he had exploded deep within; and as she arched her spinal column in a rigid intensity, an unknown force caused her to involuntarily cry out in a guttural animal sound. They lay motionless for some minutes, breathing heavily as she wrapped her arms around him, secure in the knowledge that her fulfilment had been total and complete. Afterwards, they had remained locked in their passionate union as the afterglow of their lovemaking had slowly dissipated.

The following days of their holiday had been wonderful as they explored the small harbours and coves across the length and breadth of Devon. Under warm sunny skies they would bathe on the sandy beaches or eat a picnic lunch in the shade of a tree or visit the ancient castles that littered the landscape, and on one shameless occasion they had made love beside a slow running river with only some swans and cygnets to watch them. Their little motor car had dependably taken them wherever they required, and never once complained or faltered, and the small caravan, that had provided them with complete privacy and a snug home in which to lie in each other's arms, had likewise served them faithfully. And as they walked hand-in-hand along the grassy cliff-tops on yet another excursion, it all seemed so far away from their life back in London.

But eventually the time came for them to return to Silvertown. The journey home had set a sombre mood, and Noah could feel Hazel becoming more despondent with each mile they drove nearer towards the capital. At last, after negotiating the bleak streets of London's East End, they sighted up ahead, the solid brick facade that was North Woolwich police station, where on the following Monday morning, they were due back on duty. Noah intended to drive by the station without slowing down. He didn't want any familiar eyes spotting them. Hazel leaned over and put her hand upon his arm. "Thank you so much, darling, for making the past ten days the happiest of my life."
He nodded. "I've loved every minute of it, sweetie." His eyes indicated the approaching police station. "But now, I'm afraid it's a case of welcome back to reality."

Noah was nervous when he reported for duty on Monday morning. He didn't want to answer too many searching questions concerning their holiday, just in case someone put two and two together and came up with the fact that he and Hazel had been in each other's company. He didn't want to set tongues wagging or it could cause untold problems. He needn't have worried. Bert Ambrose simply said, "Welcome back to chaos. I hope you had a good leave," and ambled off to check on the drunk locked up in Cell 4.

After morning parade he and Hazel set off on a leisurely stroll around their patch with no clear destination in mind, but to simply patrol where the mood took them. For no particular reason Noah decided to branch off the main Albert Road and wander into Fernhill Street where the public baths were located.

With most local residents having to make use of a portable tin bath, many took the opportunity to luxuriate once a week in Fernhill's full-sized deep baths, where the water was hot and unlimited. The public baths contained a separate men's and women's section and had white coated bathing attendants on hand to provide fresh bath towels and sell small tablets of soap at 1d each. They also made a little money on the side by offering to shave the men with a cut-throat razor. Noah had no need to use its facilities as he had a splendid bathroom at the police section house.

They were halfway along the street when the door at Number 26 opened and a stout woman came rushing out to meet them. "Oh God," whispered Noah urgently with a voice close to panic. "Let's get out of here. It's Kathleen. She's a bloody pest." But they were too late and the woman buttonholed them with a tirade that never stopped.
"You're just the man I wanna see, so it is," she said, pointing a finger at Noah. Kathleen was a flame haired Irishwoman with a broad Irish brogue

that originated in County Tipperary and became even more Gaelic as it sailed across the Irish Sea. The dialect was so thick that she often couldn't understand it herself. Kathleen McGinchy complained bitterly about everything and everyone and, he guessed, could even find fault with the Virgin Mary. Once she got her voice into gear, there was no stopping her, and she would be off and running like a non-stop express train. She hardly paused for breath, and certainly not to let anyone get a word in edgeways. When Kathleen got a bee in her bonnet, it was best to let her mouth run its course until she was too physically drained to speak any more. Noah had first come upon her shortly after arriving in North Woolwich as a new recruit, and had almost been traumatised by it. His colleagues back at the nick had laughed uproariously and offered their sympathy, but said that he'd been lucky to survive the encounter.

Kathleen was in full flow by now. "So the little shite thinks he can pull the wool over my eyes, does he? I'll bloody well show him what's what, so I will...." The tirade continued without Noah ever becoming aware of who she was referring to. He glanced across at Hazel. She had her mouth agape with astonishment. She'd never heard anything like it. Meanwhile Kathleen was off on another hunting expedition where she intended stringing up whoever had upset her by the testicles and ripping his entrails from his body with her bare hands. Noah caught Hazel's eye and winked at the ridiculousness of the situation. Kathleen's voice was getting louder by the minute and the decibel levels were approaching the sound barrier. "The lazy gob-shite thought he could get one over on me...So I told him....I said, 'Hell will freeze over before I'll let ya get da better of me, ya feckin thick Paddy...." Noah grinned and whispered Hazel's ear, "Have I told you that I love you just lately?"
She laughed, enjoying the implied suggestion of completely ignoring the redoubtable Kathleen McGinchy. "I love you too," she mouthed back.
"You're all a feckin' bunch of thievin' gob-shites - and I'll see ya in hell, so I will..." screamed Kathleen, unaware or unconcerned that they weren't listening to one word she said. By now she had blasted herself into outer space and was heading for the moon.

Eventually Noah solved the problem of the non-stop Kathleen by taking Hazel by the arm and simply walking away. They were twenty yards along the street when they looked back to find that she was still in full flow.
"Darling, can I ask you a question concerning your ancestors?" asked Noah seriously.
Her eyes cagily narrowed in suspicion. "Okay. But keep it clean."
"Excuse me for asking," he said, "but do you have any Irish blood running through your veins?"

10: The Knocking Shop

Whilst Noah and Hazel were being harangued by the redoubtable Kathleen; five miles further to the west, in Canning Town, a car pulled up outside Lloyds Bank on Barking Road. Three men got out and went inside the bank whilst the fourth man stayed with the car; which had been stolen yesterday in nearby Stratford.

As the men entered the bank's double doors they pulled balaclavas down over their heads and one of the gang pulled a sawn-off shotgun from his overcoat. A second man, the shortest of the three, withdrew an ex-army Webley revolver from his jacket and fired a round into the ceiling. The noise was deafening as chunks of ceiling plaster rained down and the atmosphere smelt of gunshot propellant.

Several women cashiers screamed. "Shut up," shouted the man who'd fired the weapon. "You," he yelled, pointing at the youngest female cashier, "put all the cash into this holdall." He turned to the three customers who were in the process of being served. "Get down on the floor," he shouted, as he waved the revolver in their direction.

The third man, who wore a check jacket, opened the mouth of the holdall and stuffed wads of banknotes into the bag as they were handed over by the girl. They moved from one cash-drawer to the next, emptying the tills as they went. At one stage she became flustered and handed over a bag of half-crowns. "No coins – I don't want any coins," he screamed. "Banknotes only."

The tall man with the shotgun had remained silent throughout. He looked at his wristwatch. "It's time to go," he said to his fellow bank robbers in a calm voice. The three men exited the bank and leapt into the car. Seconds later they drove away with their wheels spinning blue smoke.

The time elapsed during the robbery was three minutes and thirty five seconds.

It was their first night shift since returning from their holiday. Nothing out of the ordinary was occurring, and even the pubs, which were regularly packed with dockers and merchant seamen, were unusually quiet. Only a group of kids playing a noisy ball game of rounders on a street intersection spoiled the tranquillity.

They had obviously discussed the Canning Town bank robbery earlier that day, but it had occurred outside their own K division's patch, so the police officers at North Woolwich weren't directly involved and had taken no active part in its investigation. Detectives from the CID's Flying Squad Serious Crimes Unit were in charge of the ongoing enquiries, and they wouldn't appreciate any uniformed flat-footed coppers trampling all over their case. Apparently the robbers had escaped with over three thousand pounds. Obviously if any information should come the way of K division, then they would act upon it, but none of their fellow officers were busting a gut to solve the case.

Hazel was in a sombre frame of mind. She had felt downhearted and in a pessimistic mood since their return from Devon. For ten days they had tasted the freedom of being able to hold hands in the street or steal a kiss, but now they had returned to work, their relationship was back at square one.

"Darling, how do you feel about getting a flat together?" she asked.

Noah had been expecting this, and had frankly been thinking along the same lines. He'd also been finding it hard having to hide his feelings. "I think it's a superb idea, love. We'll still have to act prim and proper when we're on duty, otherwise Stranks would split us onto different beats, but at least we'll be sleeping in the same bed every night."

She reached out and squeezed his hand, smiling with relief. "I was hoping you'd say that. I don't think I could go on like this. It seems so unfair that people in other jobs are free to have a relationship, and yet the police frown upon it as if we were a couple of perverts."

He nodded. "We'll still have to hide the fact that we'll be living at the same address, but otherwise it should work out okay."

"Oh darling, I can't wait," she said. "When shall we start looking for a place together?"

"We've got two days off next week. Let's look in the classified ads, shall we?"

Their decision instantly bolstered their mood. Suddenly they had a great deal to arrange. What area to search for accommodation. What furniture they would need and the buying of crockery, bedding, kitchen utensils and tableware. The list was endless.

A blazing orange sunset was fading into the western sky as they reached the limit of their patrol area at Silvertown and for a while they gazed at the lights onboard the dozens of ships berthed in the Royal Docks.

Hazel said, "I know we'll be living-in-sin, but I don't care. I just want to snuggle up with you every night."

"That sounds wonderful, but we'll still have to watch our step when we're on duty. We can't go around holding hands, so we'll still need to find a quiet spot for a cuddle, won't we?"

They had reached the footbridge that led over the railway lines to the deserted factories and bombsites. The light had faded and it was pitch dark. He grinned salaciously. "Do you fancy going for a stroll across the line?"
She dug him playfully in the ribs. "I thought you'd never ask."

It was a week later when they were haphazardly strolling in the general direction of Silvertown. Every so often Noah would guide her down a side-street, simply to break up the monotony of pounding their regular beat. This time they deviated into Auberon Street.
As they drew abreast of Elsie Turpin's house, she came out into the road and stood grinning at them. "'Allo you pair of lovebirds," she said. "I ain't seen you around the area for a couple of weeks. 'Ave you been away on holiday?" Noah momentarily panicked and wondered if Elsie had inside information about their trip to Devon, but he quickly realised that, although she'd guessed correctly, it was an accidental shot in the dark. However, it had been a tense moment. If a chatterbox like Elsie Turpin should get wind of their private lives, it would be all over the parish within days.
"No such luck, Elsie," he said nonchalantly. "We've been busy elsewhere." Elsie changed the subject. "We've got new neighbours moved in across the road," she said. "They can't be short of a few bob coz they drive a big shiny limousine."
Normally Noah wasn't remotely interested in Elsie's idle tittle-tattle, but this sparked his curiosity. Very few citizens of Silvertown could afford a motor car, so anyone driving around in a limo was definitely worth further enquiries.
"Have you found out anything about them yet, Elsie?"
She gave him an indignant look. "Blimey Noah, gimme a chance, will ya? They've only just moved in last week. Come inside and I'll see if I can remember anyfink more." They went into Elsie's house and she seated them in her front parlour, where she served the ubiquitous cups of tea and side plates of biscuits.
"So, what else do you know about them, Elsie?"
"Well, it seems to be two blokes who own the place. They arrive in the limo and they've got a chauffeur. But they also have four or five women who show up there every day. They get lots of blokes visiting as well. Some of 'em turn up at all times of the day."
"Are they young women?" he asked.
"Yeah," said Elsie, "they're only in their early twenties."
"It sounds like they've opened up a knocking shop," he said.
Hazel had never heard that word. "What's a knocking shop?"

"It's another name for a brothel."

"Oh my Gaw'd," said Elsie with a look of horror. "I hadn't fought of that. D'yew mean to tell me that they're over there right now doing disgusting things?" Elsie could be quite a straight-laced and an upstanding citizen when the mood took her.

"Seems like that may be the case," said Noah.

Elsie happened to glance through her net curtains. "There's a bloke just turned up." They watched as a middle aged man wearing a gabardine raincoat nervously checked both ways, and then knocked at the door. A woman opened the door and he was quickly allowed inside.

"What you gonna do about that then?" said Elsie, jerking her thumb at the house. "We can't be 'aving no brothel around here. This is a respectable area."

"I'll make some enquiries," he assured her. Meanwhile Hazel had been writing some details in her note book. He said, "Remind me to talk to CID regarding finding out who owns the house. We'll do a search via the Land Registry and West Ham Council's rates department."

Days later there was news from Andy Summers. Noah had asked him to investigate the suspected brothel and now they were sat in his office drinking a brew.

"Have you ever heard of the Montana brothers?" asked Andy. Noah shook his head,

"The owners of the house are Anthony and Josef Montana. They arrived in England just after the war from Malta, where the local police had shown plenty of interest in their activities, which mostly centred around prostitution. Anyway, they set up shop in the Whitechapel area. It was mostly small-time black marketeering and fencing to start with, but then the local villain went into prison and there was a turf war. Unsurprisingly, the Montana brothers came out on top and they took over the prostitution and protection rackets. Then they moved into armed robberies. They were very smart. They never got personally involved, but set up the planning and supplied weapons and took a percentage of the take."

Noah was astounded at such bare-faced criminality. "Didn't the local police get involved?"

"They tried," said Summers, "but the Montanas always left it up to lesser mortals to do the dirty work. If the police wanted to talk to them, they always insisted on having their solicitor present."

"So why have they set up here in Silvertown?"

"Because eventually the Whitechapel police enlisted the help of the Flying Squad and they made life too hot for them. The Sweeney constantly harassed them and shut down several brothels, so presumably they've moved here for a quieter life."

Noah was aghast. "We cannot let them settle in here. We've got to get rid of them somehow."

Andy Summers grinned. "Don't worry, Noah. I've got a plan."

Along the Albert Road was a seaman's pub called the Kent Arms. On most nights of the week it was jam-packed with sailors and dockers getting more legless as the night wore on. Sprinkled in amongst the revellers were some of the more flamboyant members of the ships' crews who were clearly homosexual.

As they approached the pub, Noah decided to give Hazel a ringside seat and educate her in the strange characters that came ashore each night from the ships. They stood in the shadows across the street from the bar. "What are we waiting here for, Noah?" she asked. "I thought we were going back to the station."

"Have some patience, Constable Leggett. I'm going to show you some weird and wonderful sights. We're just waiting for some people to leave the bar."

Moments later a group of loud and rowdy women came out from the public bar of the Kent Arms and made their way towards them. On closer inspection Noah could see that they weren't women at all, but a bunch of queers dressed up in female attire. He guessed that they were probably stewards aboard the cargo and passenger ships berthed in the King George V dock; and they were out for a good time. They gathered around the police officers in a noisy babble. One of them, dressed in a long sequined gown and pearl necklace with a blonde wig, staggered over, clearly the worse for wear. She buttonholed Noah. "Oh hello gorgeous, how are you?" she said in a deep and resonant voice which was clearly male. Her face was plastered with foundation cream and her cheeks were reddened with rouge. On her lips was a bright red lipstick and her eyes were heavily layered with mascara. Noah thought she looked like a caricature of a pantomime dame, but he simply smiled benevolently and said, "Good evening ladies. How are you?" Her companions were likewise covered in gaudy cosmetics and dressed in the most bizarre clothing and wore an assortment of wigs and hairpieces.

Noah glanced at Hazel. Her face was a picture as she stared open mouthed at the first homosexuals she'd ever encountered. He guessed that, around the narrow lanes of Oxfordshire, she had never before stumbled upon queers dressed in drag. Although homosexuality, even between consenting adults, was illegal in Britain, these individuals were simply dressing up and committing no crime, so Noah had no intention of arresting anyone.

"Where are you ladies off to?" he asked.

"We're going down to the Round House for a little drinky-poo's," lisped one of the group, pursing her lips for effect. The Round House was another sailor's pub that was frequented by homosexuals from the ships. It was a lively bar which was to be found opposite Bargehouse Road and was always thumping with loud music.

"Well I hope you girls have a good time. Goodnight," he said, and the queers went off noisily in the direction of the Round House.

Still in shock, Hazel said, "I would never have believed it unless I'd seen it with my own eyes."

Noah smiled and did a decent impression of Humphrey Bogart. "Stick with me kid – I'll show ya a good time."

They found a perfect property via the classified ads in the local newspaper. The two-bedroom house was located in a quiet backstreet of nearby Beckton; close enough to get a bus to work, but away from the prying eyes of any police colleagues. They met the landlord to view the unfurnished property, and agreed an affordable weekly rent.

They scoured the nearby second-hand shops and bought a double bed and other essential furniture which would be delivered early the following week. He allowed Hazel to choose the furniture. She would instinctively know what they required; whereas he didn't have a clue. Further shopping expeditions for kitchen equipment, bedding and the mountain of other articles they would need, reminded Noah that he had never had to fend for himself in the past. His accommodation with his parents in Hertfordshire, in the army in Germany and living in the police section house, had all come fully furnished. They would move in next week.

Monday morning's parade brought a switch from their usual patrol area. One of their older police constables, Percy Longstaff, had called in sick and his beat needed to be covered. Percy's beat was in West Silvertown, further towards Canning Town. Charlie Ethridge was the duty sergeant. "Sheppard and Leggett, you'll take on Percy's patch for the time being. You can grab a couple of bicycles from the bike-shed. Understood?"

Ten minutes later they were cycling side-by-side along the Albert Road. Stray wisps of Hazel's blonde hair were streaming behind her as they pedalled furiously over the tarmac surface. With her strong calf muscles she had no problem keeping up with Noah and within minutes they had cycled past the Tate & Lyle refinery and Silvertown Railway Station and past the limit of their usual beat. This was now strange territory to Hazel, although Noah had worked the West Silvertown beat during his first rookie days after arrival. They pedalled over the Silvertown Viaduct with its twin reinforced concrete spans resembling ungainly rainbows. Onwards they cycled past acres of desolate bombsites that had once been row upon row of snug terraced streets before being flattened by the Luftwaffe some fifteen years previously.

Across the railway lines to their left stood grim and dirty factories churning black smoke from their numerous chimneys, and in the far distance on their right, the giant Ranks Millennium Flour Mills soared high into the sky. The River Thames, which lay out of sight beyond the chemical plants and factories, meandered around the Isle of Dogs and up into the City of London, whilst over to their right, in the Royal Victoria Dock, stevedores were frenziedly loading and discharging the cargoes of dozens of freighters.

As they neared West Silvertown an awful smell permeated into their nostrils. Hazel had never smelt anything so rancid in her life. "What the hell's that rotten stink?" she shouted to Noah breathlessly. The stench was getting stronger and she attempted to hold a handkerchief over her nose as she pedalled. "That's coming from Knight's soap factory," he told her. "They make Knights Castile scented soap and they use animal bones as part of the production process. Keep pedalling until we pass it. It smells worst when there's a westerly wind."

They cycled past the soap factory and the smell dissipated somewhat. A sign above the arched entrance said, John Knight Ltd – The Royal Primrose Soap Works.

She said, "Blimey, you'd think that with a name like Primrose, the place would smell sweeter." Next door to the Knight's factory stood the imposing Tate & Lyle's Plaistow Wharf sugar refinery. Noah explained that it's where they manufactured the syrup.

They cycled into Lyle Park, the only oasis of greenery within this stark industrial morass of noisy factories. They pedalled to its far end, where the park meets the river and the noise and bustle of the manufacturing works dissolved into semi-tranquillity. After briskly cycling the two miles from the police station they needed to take the weight off their feet. Besides, Noah knew from earlier visits that, although many thousands of people worked in the nearby factories, West Silvertown was a quiet backwater as far as crime was concerned and not a lot happened here to cause him any worries.

Hazel found a bench and they sat watching the busy traffic on the river. Two ocean-going freighters were negotiating the sharp bend around the Isle of Dogs as they made for the lock entrance at the West India Docks, whilst closer inshore a Thames sailing barge was heading for Bow Creek to discharge its cargo of cement. Further near the riverbank a string of barges were being towed upstream by a steam tug, while downstream they could see the tall smoke-stacks of the Woolwich ferries criss-crossing the river.

The tide was flooding upstream into London, taking dozens of vessels with it on its silent journey as it filled the River Thames. In a few hours time the tide would change direction yet again and dozens more ships and barges would depart from the docks and quays and take advantage of the receding ebb tide to assist them down towards the open sea.

They had brought a satchel of food and a flask of tea. Noah took a bite of a cheese and tomato sandwich and carefully poured sweet tea into beakers. He passed one to Hazel.

She squeezed his hand. "I'm so excited about moving into our house tomorrow. We'll have a lot of work to do, but I'm looking forward to making it nice and cosy."

He wiped crumbs from around his mouth. "Me too, sweetie. Can't wait."

They spoke about the million and one domestic items they needed to buy – from tea cups to a toaster and bath towels to T-towels.

"What do you think about getting a television?" she asked. Television sets were becoming more and more popular; ever since a large chunk of Britain's population had watched the Queen's 1953 Coronation on TV. They were now all the rage and dozens of people he knew were getting one. Even Elsie Turpin had a TV, although Noah suspected that hers had fallen off the back of a lorry.

He mulled it over. "The trouble is, that TV sets cost a fortune – and it's not as if they're broadcasting for very long. They go off-the-air completely during the evening so as to get the kids off to bed. Have you ever heard anything so ridiculous?"

"I know they're expensive," she agreed, "but perhaps we could rent a TV from Radio Rentals. What do you think?"

"How about we hang on a while?" he suggested. "At the moment we've only got one BBC channel to watch; but there's the new ITV station opening up later this year. Anyway, we've still got the radio, haven't we?"

"You're joking, surely? You only ever listen to that stupid Goon Show on the radio."

He felt mortally wounded. "What's wrong with The Goons?"

"They're just four silly men talking with ridiculous voices," she said dismissively.

They returned to their Silvertown beat the next day. Miraculously Percy Longstaff had made a complete recovery and was back at work, although Noah suspected that his illness yesterday had been a thumping hangover. It was well known that, every once in a while, Percy would go on a bender.

As they neared the police box outside the Constitutional Club, its blue light began flashing. Noah went inside and picked up the handset. Charlie Ethridge's voice came on the line.
"Get yourselves around to the nunnery in Parker Street. Someone's been exposing himself to one of the young trainee nuns."
"How long ago did it happen, Sarge?"
Noah could hear Charlie turning the pages of the station's incident log. "It was called in just a half hour ago. Go see what you can do, will you? Mind you, the flasher will probably be long gone by now."

Noah opened the heavy wooden door that led from Parker Street into the gardens of the nunnery. Hazel was right behind him. To their right he noticed the wooden shed where, last year, they had solved the case of the nun's missing underwear. "I wonder if the cats still live inside," said Hazel.
"I doubt it," he said. "They'll be all grown up by now."
He spotted a group of nuns on the far side of the smallholding, busily digging over the soil. Among them was the mother superior, Sister Evangeline. They walked over. Noah thought he ought to moderate his wording when speaking to the nuns. He recalled when Sister Evangeline had been reticent to report that the nun's knickers had been stolen from the washing line; and had simply referred to the missing bloomers as 'items of a personal nature.' They led a solemn and reclusive life within the walls of the nunnery and he had no wish to embarrass them when it came to taking details of a man exposing himself. He needed to phrase his language accordingly.
"Good afternoon, Reverend Mother. We understand that you've had an unwelcome visitor?"
She recognised him from the earlier incident. "Good afternoon Constable Sheppard. If you've come to find that dirty bugger, you're too late. He's gone."
Noah was taken aback by her descriptive language, but he ploughed on. "What time did this occur?"
"It was about two hours ago. It happened right over there," she said, pointing towards the potting shed. "He jumped out from behind the shed and dropped his trousers."
"Do you have a description of the man? What was he wearing?"
"I didn't see the incident. I was in my office. Sister Dymphna here witnessed everything." She ushered over a young nun who, judging by her tear-stained face and puffy eyes, had been traumatised by the whole affair.
Sister Dymphna was young and slim and Noah thought was far too pretty to be a nun. "What happened?" he asked.

She began describing the circumstances in a soft Irish accent. "I was taking the washing off the line...when a man...he jumped out...I asked him what did he want...and he..." She couldn't continue and broke down in tears. Noah suspected that young Dymphna was one of life's innocents who originated in rural Ireland and perhaps had led a naive and secluded life. He doubted whether her parents had ever coached her in the ways of the world or the birds and the bees.

Sister Evangeline on the other hand was a hard-hearted woman. She chastised the young postulant. "Oh for God's sake. Pull yourself together. These officers need to gather the facts of the case so stop being a silly girl and tell them what's happened." Sister Dymphna's face crumpled with further tears.

Sister Evangeline scowled. "I happen to know that you have three brothers back in Ireland, and I'm sure you all had a bath together at some time when you were youngsters, so it's not as if you've never seen a boy's privates before, is it?" The Irish postulant stayed silent.

Hazel stepped forward. She said, "Perhaps it might be better if Sister Dymphna gives me the details." She spotted a garden bench behind the shed. She took out her notebook and pen. "Let's go sit over there, shall we?"

They escaped from the nunnery a half hour later. As they strolled along Albert Road, Hazel brought him up to date via her notebook. "According to Sister Dymphna the flasher was about 18 years old. He was around 5ft 7in tall and had curly black hair. He was a little overweight and she remembered that his hair was slicked back into a duck's arse." She laughed. "That's not the way the nun described it though."

"What was he wearing?" asked Noah.

"He wore jeans and a T-shirt with a black leather jacket. She also said he wore a thick leather belt with cow horns on the buckle."

"Did he say anything to her while he was exposing himself?"

"No, he just leapt out from behind the potting shed and stared at her whilst he dropped his trousers. Then, she said, he waggled his willy from side to side. After that she ran back into the convent."

Noah wasn't confident regarding solving the case. They had no evidence and only a vague description to go on. "Perhaps we may get lucky and pick him up."

Hazel laughed and gave him a sharp dig on his arm. "Maybe I ought to slap some handcuffs on you tonight. You waggle your thing at me every time we climb into bed."

It was later that evening back at the police station that Hazel realised she may have cracked the case. "Noah, you remember that peeping tom we dealt with a while back?"

He nodded. "Yes I remember him. Why?"
"I've just realised that he matches the description of the flasher. Not only was he the same height and build, but he also had a duck's arse haircut and wore a leather jacket with a fancy belt buckle."
He grinned. "You clever girl. I think we ought to go have a chat with him."
She went off to find the peeping tom's file so as to get a name and address.

      The next afternoon they rang the doorbell of a terraced house in Oriental Road. A man in his early fifties opened the door. He was tall and heavily built and wore the typical docker's attire of bib and braces with a thick leather belt and neckerchief.
"Mister Duncan?" The man nodded.
"We want to talk to your son, Jeremy. Is he at home?"
"No, he's not here. What's this about?"
"When will he be at home?" said Noah, ignoring Duncan's question.
"You haven't told me what it's regarding."
Noah thought he was being uncooperative. He said, "We simply want to ask him some questions. We need to know where he is, Mister Duncan."
Harry Duncan appeared to cooperate with the cops whilst at the same time being unhelpful. "I don't know where he is. He's in the Merchant Navy aboard a ship somewhere."
Noah glanced at Hazel. It seemed to be at a dead end. Hazel shrugged her shoulders, as if to say there's no more we can do.
Noah tried one last attempt. "What's the name of the ship he's onboard?"
The man shook his head. "I've no idea. He don't tell me nuffink."
Noah tried one last question. "Will Jeremy be coming home on leave?"
The man seemed to answer him honestly. "I sincerely hope not," he said.
Noah fixed him with an intent look. "I hope not also, Mister Duncan. If he does, we'll be waiting for him."

      After the police had gone, Harry Duncan sat in his living room and recalled the conversation. The officers hadn't given him details of why they wanted to question Jeremy. That didn't matter because he already knew exactly why they wanted him.
      His son had come home yesterday and confessed that he'd done something stupid and that the police may come knocking on their door. When, at last, Jeremy had owned up to getting his cock out and waving it at a young nun, he had gone crazy and taken off his leather belt. The boy needed to be taught a lesson.
      This wasn't the first time his son had been in trouble with the law. Last year he had been caught gazing into a housewife's window at night and been hauled up before the magistrate. He'd been damn lucky he got away

with a stiff fine. If he should be charged a second time with exposing himself, then he may end up being sent to Borstal. He knew that his son wouldn't have been able to cope with being locked up with the vicious thugs imprisoned in those awful places.

Life had not been easy. After he had come home from the war in 1945 he'd went to work as a stevedore in the Royal Docks. Jeremy was just eight years old when he'd come home from work one day and found a letter on the mantelpiece from his missus. She said she'd met an American sailor during the war and he wanted her to join him in the USA. She simply packed a suitcase and jumped aboard a ship bound for a new life in America.

Jeremy had always been a problem child. From an early age he struggled at school, and because he was mentally backward, he was bullied in class. He had trouble finding a job, or couldn't seem to hold down a job for very long. Then yesterday he had dropped the bombshell regarding exposing himself at the nunnery and Harry Duncan had come to the end of his tether.

A friend from his army days who now worked for the Merchant Navy Shipping Federation owed him a favour. He made a phone call and within an hour his friend had arranged for Jeremy to be issued with seaman's documents and join a ship sailing shortly for Australia.

This morning he escorted his son into the docks and they said their goodbyes at the gangway. He remembered Jeremy's words as he was about to board the ship. "I'll be back home in six months time, Dad."
Harry Duncan had stuffed a bundle of banknotes into the boy's pocket and taken his son's hand in his own. He said, "Sorry Jeremy, you won't ever be able to come home again. Have a good life son."

The pair was scheduled to have the following two days off as rest days and the next morning Noah left the section house for the last time. He boarded a bus for the new house at Beckton. Hazel was already at the house with the landlord as he handed over the keys. Now they had the place to themselves as they walked about the empty rooms discussing what would go where. Noah had decided to leave all those decisions to Hazel as her grasp of homemaking was far better than his. By mid-morning the furniture truck had arrived and she took charge of where everything was to go. Into the late evening they worked tirelessly on making their house into a cosy home, but at last, satisfyingly exhausted, they crept into bed and almost immediately fell into a deep sleep.

It was a few days later and Noah had arranged for them to visit his parents in Hertfordshire. He again borrowed the Morris Minor and they set off for the house in Broxbourne. It had been months since he'd last seen his parents and he felt guilty about it. Hazel was excited - but nervous - to be meeting them for the first time. It took them only an hour and a half to arrive at the house on the outskirts of the town.

Arthur Sheppard and his wife Valerie made Hazel welcome and told her to make herself at home as they settled into comfortable seats in the lounge. Valerie Sheppard went off to the kitchen to brew a pot of tea, accompanied by Hazel who had offered to help.

"It's ever so nice of you to invite me to stay, Mrs Sheppard," said Hazel as she helped to lay out the cups and saucers.

"No need to be formal, love. Just call me Val," said the wife as she put slices of fruit cake on a plate. "My husband's name's Arthur."

Meanwhile in the lounge, Sheppard Snr winked at his son. "Blimey Noah, you've gone and got yourself a real pretty one there, haven't you?"

"I certainly have, Dad," he agreed.

"Any plans to get married yet?"

Noah was saved from giving an answer as the women returned with a tray of tea and cake. They sat around making small talk; asking Hazel about her upbringing in Oxfordshire and bringing out an album containing photographs of Noah as a child. He was red with embarrassment as Hazel commented on a photo of him aged three, with wavy hair and wearing a plum-coloured velvet suit. "What a cute little chap he was," she laughed. "He hasn't changed much, has he?"

Arthur was a big boned man with a toothy grin that split his face into a caricature of The Laughing Policeman; although he was in fact a bus driver and his wife was a school secretary. The conversation mainly centred on their work together as police officers and describing the people of London's Docklands. Val Sheppard was a slim dark haired woman who appeared to be bubbly and outgoing, but whom Hazel suspected could be easily shocked.

"What's your house like, Noah? Is the rent expensive in London?" his mother asked innocently.

Noah was instantly wary. The stigma of an unmarried couple living together was frowned upon far more in the religious and pious countryside than in the streets of London. Noah had forewarned Hazel that his mother was a regular churchgoer. "It's fine, Mum, it's got two bedrooms and a sitting room."

She turned to Hazel. "Do you live very far away from Noah, dear?"

Hazel felt her cheeks redden. "No – not too far away," she said. The room fell silent.

Arthur Sheppard broke the ice. "I daresay you two lovebirds will be going down the pub tonight, won't you?" It opened up a whole new topic of conversation as Noah told his parents what their plans were for the weekend.

That evening they went to The Crown pub. Before they'd left the house Val Sheppard had shown Hazel where she would be sleeping. It certainly wouldn't be anywhere near her only son.

Noah brought their drinks from the bar. "I'm sorry about all the secrecy," he apologised, "but my mum would go spare if she even suspected that we're shacking up together. It's her religious upbringing."

"It's not your fault, darling," she said. "But I do wish we didn't have to duck and dive like this. It's bad enough having to hide our relationship from our colleagues, never mind our parents."

"It won't always be like this," he said, attempting to cheer her up. "One day we'll be married and then we can do what the bloody hell we want, can't we?"

She let out a loud belly-laugh. "Oh my God. Was that a proposal?"

He grinned. "You know very well that I want us to get married. But when the time's right I'll ask you properly. Okay?"

She laid her head on his shoulder. "I shall look forward to that, but right now, we're not in any great hurry, are we?"

Whilst Noah and Hazel were sleeping in separate beds in Broxbourne; thirty miles to the south, in Canning Town, Peter Stranks was in an unusually happy and ebullient mood. He and Rosemary were driving home in his gleaming new motor car. He rubbed his hand over the soft padded steering wheel. It had that smell of new fresh leather and fluffy carpets that one gets with a newly purchased vehicle.

Of course it had been quite a different story a week ago. Rosemary had forcefully pointed out that, although he had frequently driven police vehicles in the past, he had never owned a car of his own. Why couldn't they buy one - even if it was bought on the never-never? They would be the first family on their street to have one and their neighbours would be green with envy, especially that toffee-nosed Mrs Willard at Number 27.

He had given the perfectly valid excuse that they really couldn't afford it, but she had been quite adamant that his status as the officer-in-charge at the police station deserved its just merits and that his men should see him arrive in a shiny new car, and not on an old bicycle wearing bike clips around his ankles.

Later that night, she had for the second time in many years, performed fellatio upon him and afterwards encouraged him to make vigorous love to her. The next morning, after yet another lovemaking session, she had insisted they go see the bank manager for a loan, followed by a visit to the car showroom.

And now here they were driving home from a meeting of the Rotary Club at Canning Town, where his fellow members had stared enviously at his new Wolseley car. It was the model with the polished walnut dashboard and the fully synchromesh gearbox. The club president had enviously commented, "You must be doing very well, Peter, to afford a brand new car." Stranks couldn't wait to drive into the courtyard of the police station on Monday morning and see their jealous faces. He would be the only officer in K Division to own a motor car.

It had been a good night out. He had consumed a half dozen pints of bitter and one or two whiskies for the road. Rosemary had had a few gin and tonics and was very tipsy, but she had whispered into his ear that sex was definitely on the menu when they got home. He pushed the car a little faster along the Silvertown Way, eager to get her into the bedroom before she could change her mind or pass out.

It was almost midnight as he roared through Silvertown towards North Woolwich. He felt somewhat befuddled as he drove down the middle of the road, but dismissed it. He'd be okay, he told himself. There were just a couple of miles to go to their house in nearby Barking. He steered the car with the aid of the single broken white line running down the centre of the road's surface as a guide, but the vision he saw in his bleary eyes showed as triple lines, but he never noticed them.

He reached the intersection at Pier Road, just yards away from the police station on the opposite side of the road. It was his responsibility to give way to traffic coming from his right, but he barely reduced his speed. He didn't see the approaching vehicle, but felt Rosemary grip his arm moments before she screamed. Without warning his car smashed into the side of the other vehicle and there was the noise of an almighty bang and a screech of brakes and twisted metal.

Inside the police station's canteen, several constables were on a tea break. Sergeant Bert Ambrose was making himself a sandwich and Percy Longstaff was brewing up a pot of tea for George Cheeseman and Dave Roberts. They all heard the crash and ran outside where they were presented with a scene of pandemonium.

The two cars were mangled heaps. Steam was wafting from the front end of a Wolseley which was twisted beyond recognition and a Ford Consul had its nearside bodywork crumpled and had come to rest against the Royal Standard pub on the adjacent corner of the road. The driver of the Ford was uninjured and was helping his female passengers to get out. They were screaming. The female passenger of the Wolseley was out of the car and shouting profanities at its driver, who remained remote and motionless in his seat.

Whilst Percy assisted the passengers in the Ford, George was the first to reach the Wolseley. He ignored the woman on the basis that if she was on her feet and shouting, then she had probably not suffered any serious injury. He opened the driver's door and recognised Inspector Stranks immediately. He was conscious, but staring into space. He also stunk of booze. He called Sergeant Ambrose over and they helped Stranks out of the car. He could barely stand upright and slurred unintelligibly, "Shorry Rosemary, I sheem to 'ave 'ad an accshident." He then sat down in the road before he fell down.

The Ford's driver came over ranting and raving. He pointed accusingly at Stranks. "He caused all this," he said, indicating the carnage of twisted metal. "He smells as if he's pissed."

Things moved swiftly after that. The Ford driver and occupants were ushered into the station where they were given tea in the canteen. They would be transported home later. Mrs Stranks was made comfortable in the inspector's office until she also could be taken home. Ambrose then arranged for a local recovery truck to attend and tow away the wrecks.

As for Inspector Stranks, he could barely walk, and had to be assisted into the station's custody room. As far as Ambrose was concerned it was a straightforward case of drunken driving. He had no interest in covering up the incident for the benefit of Stranks. In any case, there were far too many witnesses. He called in the police doctor who would arrive shortly and take a blood sample to determine if Stranks was inebriated. In the meantime he put the inspector into a cell and slammed the door.

11: Inspector Maitland

Three days later a tall man dressed in civilian clothes came into the station sergeant's office. Charlie Ethridge was on duty. The man held out his hand. "Good morning, old chap. How do you do? My name's Charles Maitland. I'm your new station inspector." Charlie's mouth dropped open in astonishment. Maitland was about 50 years old with silver hair and a handlebar moustache. He was dressed in a smartly tailored suit with highly polished shoes and a Brigade of Guards tie. His accent was pure upper crust, or as Charlie put it later, "A very posh gentleman indeed."
"I apologize that I'm not here in uniform," he said, "but my suitcase hasn't arrived yet, so this will have to do."
"That's not a problem, sir," said Charlie, smiling. He liked Maitland instantly.
"Perhaps you'd like to show me around the station?" suggested Maitland.
Charlie nodded. "That would be my pleasure, sir."
"Then lead on, old bean."

The next morning the eight duty constables were brought to attention as the tall figure of Maitland entered the parade room. His suitcases had arrived and he was dressed immaculately in his Inspector's uniform that appeared to have been custom-made in London's Savile Row. Sergeant Ethridge was the duty sergeant, but Ambrose had come in, eager to see the new boss who everyone was describing as resembling royalty. Word had travelled fast. Even Fag-Ash Lil's curiosity had got the better of her and she sat at the back of the room listening intently.
Maitland's eyes ran over his assembled officers and seemingly satisfied, ordered them to stand easy. They relaxed. "You will all have heard of the circumstances regarding the departure of Inspector Stranks," he said, shaking his head. "It's a terrible shame when a senior officer's career ends so ignominiously, but we have to move on and repair the damage."
He asked Ethridge to introduce him to the men and the sergeant presented each man as they worked their way along the line. As he came to each constable, Maitland shook him briskly by the hand and asked a pertinent question as to his length of service or if he was married. As Ronnie Baldwin said later; he felt as if he were being presented to a prince at a royal gathering. Noah found Maitland to be genuinely interested in his men's problems. He asked Noah what he thought would prevent crime in his area.

Without hesitation, he answered, "The young kids tend to commit petty crime when they're bored, sir. I would like to see an after-school club and sports activities to keep them out of trouble." Maitland had nodded thoughtfully. "That's a very good point, Constable Sheppard. Well done." When Hazel's turn came, Maitland's eyes seemed to sparkle and he spent an inordinate amount of time talking to her.

It had been raining non-stop for the past five days and the pair were thoroughly fed up. A brisk northerly wind whisked the raindrops underneath their waterproof capes and found its way down the neck of their tunics. He could feel a rivulet of cold rain travel down his back and he involuntarily shuddered. He momentarily felt envious of the few constables that went out in patrol cars and who could stay dry and warm within their heated cocoon.

They were strolling westwards along Albert Road towards Silvertown. Occasionally they would have to step around deep puddles on the pavement or take avoiding action from the spray as a vehicle sped by. He peered around at Hazel walking beside him. She looked thoroughly miserable as she lowered her head against the all-pervading downpour, which served only to dampen their spirits. A single bead of drizzle ran down to the tip of her nose and hung there, until she wiped it away with the cuff of her tunic.

She was feeling sorry for herself. "Whose bloody silly idea was it to become a policewoman?" she moaned to herself. "If I'd had half a brain I would have become a typist and would be happily sitting in a warm office."
Noah chuckled. "But then you would have never met me, would you, sweetie pie?"
She laughed at him in mock derision. "Huh, right now, Constable Sheppard, I would gladly forego that pleasure if only I could get warm."
"We'll get down to Leonard Street in about ten minutes," he promised. "We can go inside the police box and I'll give you a cuddle. That'll make you warm n' cosy."
"Mmmm, that sounds wonderful." She peered from under the hood of the cape and laughed. "I always knew you'd come in useful someday."

But it was not to be. Far out in the North Sea, a low pressure weather system had generated a northerly wind-storm that had caused a tidal surge all the way down to the Dover Strait. Together with the frequent heavy rain, this triggered the incoming spring tide to become far higher than its predicted height. The tide had overwhelmed the sea defences and drained into the sewers, only to flood back out of them again and into the streets.

The flooding became most severe as they approached Leonard Street, and Noah could see that the police call box was filled with flood-water. That, he thought grumpily, put paid to their plans for a secret smooch inside. Further along, Saville Road, Wythes Road and Parker Street were inundated with two feet of sewer water and people had come out into the street with devastated looks upon their faces. They wouldn't be able to start clearing up their houses until the high tide had receded. On the corner of Saville Road, Harry Gee's grocery shop was awash, with packets of foodstuffs floating on the brackish water. Noah hoped that Harry had taken out a flood insurance policy. Some small boys, who seemed to think it was great fun, were wading thigh deep in the flood-water.

Noah and Hazel couldn't help much, except to signal the occasional vehicle that it was causing a tidal wave, and to slow down. For a few private cars it was already too late, as the depth of water had covered their engines and they'd been left abandoned; but very few residents of the neighbourhood could afford to buy a car, so those cases were few and far between. He was aware that the citizens of Silvertown were quite used to the floods that regularly gushed out of their drains, and somehow they would shrug it off with that same spirit that had enabled them to survive the Blitz. Rather than stand out in the rain, they went for a cup of tea in George's Diner, which had narrowly escaped the worst of the floods.

Over the following weeks Inspector Maitland interviewed each of his police officers in his office. Noah had heard from other constables who had already been summoned, that Maitland was a real gent and listened to their views and their problems.

As a civilian employee, Lily Branson hadn't expected to be called upon, but she'd been surprised when Maitland had asked her, "to pop in for a chat." She had decided beforehand that she would stand her ground and give him the sharp end of her tongue if he tried to change the manner in which she worked around the station. She wouldn't be standing for any of that old palaver, she stated belligerently. Lily had worked herself up into a lather and was ready for action.

She stepped into his office and was instantly captivated when he had offered a filter tip from a solid silver box and had struck a match to light her cigarette. He poured tea into bone china cups whilst she sat mesmerized by his attentiveness. Far from discussing any changes to Lily's working arrangements, Maitland asked about her family and her origins in the East End district of Poplar. When Lily mentioned the street where she had been born, Maitland inexplicably knew all the local shops and pubs thereabouts. She was instantly won over.

Afterwards, when she returned to the canteen to serve the midday meal, her previous opinion that Maitland was, "That posh git who's turned up 'ere to change fings," had been transformed. Now she was singing his praises. Fag-Ash Lil lit another cigarette and announced to the assembled constables that Inspector Maitland was, "a bleedin' gentleman, and much nicer than you load of tossers!"

It was Noah's turn for an interview with the inspector. Maitland shook his hand, and after being seated, he offered a cigarette from a box. Apart from Hazel and Bert Ambrose, Noah was one of the few non-smokers in the station, so he held up his hand in polite refusal. Charles Maitland lit up a briarwood pipe and spent some minutes tamping down the tobacco in the bowl before lighting it. Upon the desk Noah noticed a framed photograph of a much younger Maitland in military battledress and wearing the stripes of a major. Maitland followed Noah's gaze. "That was taken in Germany in 1945," he explained.

He asked about his upbringing in Hertfordshire and then moved on to his crucial role in the Mortinson case. He remembered Noah's thoughts on getting the local kids involved with sports and clubs. "Yes, we must do something about that soon, shouldn't we?" he said.
The inspector consulted a document on his desk. "According to this, you're on a foot patrol with WPC Leggett."
"Yes sir, that's correct," he answered.
"And how do you get along together?" asked Maitland innocently.
Noah's senses went onto full alert. "We get along fine, sir. She's a very competent police officer."
"She's also a very pretty girl, Sheppard," he said in a faraway voice, as if recalling a distant memory. "One could be forgiven for falling in love with her, couldn't they?"
Noah wasn't sure if to respond. He could be on dangerous ground here. He simply said "Yes sir. She's very pretty." He was sure that Maitland must know something.
The inspector's eyes bored into his. He got to the point. "Do you two have any plans to marry?"
Noah was dumbstruck. He didn't know what to say. If Stranks had been asking the question, he would have instantly denied it, but Maitland seemed to be asking out of genuine interest. He cautiously said, "Perhaps we shall at a later date, sir."

Maitland puffed on his pipe and smiled. "Oh good show," he said. "There's nothing quite like a decent wedding to buck up the spirits of a bunch of coppers, is there?"

Noah smiled nervously. "No sir. I'm sure there isn't," he said.

Inspector Maitland pointed the stem of his pipe at Noah. "In the meantime, I'm sure I can count on you to be discreet. Understood?"

Maitland stood up. The interview was concluded. He shook Noah's hand. "The very best of luck," he said.

PC George Cheesman had called in sick with a stomach bug. In actual fact he had a hangover, but no one from the police station would be checking up on him. Bert Ambrose switched the pair to cover George's regular beat around Savage Gardens.

In the afternoon they climbed aboard some spare bikes and set off on a shift that would finish at 10pm. They walked their bicycles through the Royal Victoria Park, the only public gardens amidst the dirty factories of North Woolwich. The frontage of the park bordered onto the River Thames and for a time they watched the busy river traffic steam past on their way upstream to London or downstream to the river estuary.

They cycled beyond the vast engineering works of Harland & Woolf, whose fitters repaired the cargo ships that berthed in the Royal Docks. Up ahead, the bascule bridge that spanned the locks had been raised to allow a ship to enter the docks. "Damn, we've caught a bridger," said Noah. They would now have to wait until the ship had transited through the lock and into the swinging basin of the King George V Dock before the bridge could again be lowered. At the barrier they waited in line with a queue of cars, trucks and cyclists. "I don't mind," said Hazel excitedly. "I like looking at the ships. It makes me wonder what exotic part of the world they've come from."

The lock gates opened and a steam tug took the strain and began slowly towing the laden cargo vessel through the narrow opening. It passed a mere 40 feet in front of them and Hazel stared in awe as the huge cargo liner sailed majestically past. She could hear the throb of its engines and smoke wafted upwards from its smokestack as it glided sedately by. Up in the ship's wheelhouse she could see the captain and dock pilot relaying orders to the tugs and the deck crew so that the ship slid through the narrow gap without a scratch to its paintwork. Ten minutes later the ship was clear. The bridge quickly lowered its roadway and the traffic surged forward as the barriers were opened.

Onwards they pedalled, cycling across the Royal Albert Dock Basin and around numerous streets, simply to become familiar with them. They weren't especially looking out for any particular crime, but if it should happen to find them, then that was another matter. Noah pointed out the extensive Tate & Lyle sports ground that was regularly used by the employees. He showed her the Galleons Hotel, built in the 1880's of the Victorian era for passengers joining the P&O liners bound for the Far East, but now largely under-utilised. The author, Rudyard Kipling, he told her, had stayed at the hotel prior to sailing off to India.

The pair had been cycling around the district all afternoon and they'd found nothing out of the ordinary occurring. All was quiet. Noah called the station from a police call box to report where they were and that all was peaceful. Charlie Ethridge was the duty sergeant. Noah liked Charlie and had a healthy respect for the way in which he treated his junior constables.
The tall, but pear-shaped sergeant, had over 30 years service under his belt and could have taken retirement long ago, but he stayed on because he loved the job. Charlie noted their report and went back to eating his fish and chip supper.

It was evening now and darkness was approaching as a brilliant orange sun set over the London skyline. They went down to the water's edge to watch the traffic on the Thames, and saw several sailing barges laden with cargo, making their way upstream towards the city. Noah found a sheltered spot off the beaten track, where they couldn't be seen from the road. It was as quiet as a graveyard. Hazel suspected why he had brought her down here, but she wasn't about to complain. She looked forward to their illicit romantic interludes whilst on duty. It somehow added an extra dimension of excitement to their canoodling and she didn't see any problem with it, even though they would probably make love when they went to bed later tonight in their own home.

She'd known from that very first day as a rookie WPC that she was attracted to Noah. Later, when he had smiled and his eyes had crinkled at the corners was the moment she knew they would fall in love. Although he hadn't yet popped the question, they often talked of marriage and she was quite satisfied with the present status quo of living together in their love nest.

Noah removed her uniform cap so that her long blonde hair hung down over her shoulders. It was pitch dark now as she came into his arms, eager to be kissed. He wrapped his arms around her and pulled her in close as their lips met in a passionate embrace. She felt his tongue search out her own as his hands wandered unchallenged across her body. Her breathing rate increased as he reached behind and took the soft orbs of her bottom into the palms of his hands and squeezed them tightly together. She was in heaven. He reached under her tunic and unclipped her brassiere; then he turned her around, so that she had her back towards him. He wrapped his arms around her and caressed her breasts, gently squeezing the erect nipples between his thumb and forefinger. Her breathing became more rapid as he nuzzled her neck and nibbled the lobes of her ears and breathed heavily through the tresses of her hair. She could feel his erectness through the thin material of her uniform and felt full of pride that she could be the source of his uncontrollable urges. She knew that they really should have waited until they were safely at home in the privacy of their own bedroom, but she didn't want to wait. She wanted to feel him holding her – loving her - caressing her – kissing her passionately – and for a small moment in time, she wanted to feel like a wanton woman who would give herself unquestionably and without restrictions.

Towards the end of their patrol the couple were cycling side-by-side returning to the station. They had their lights on and thankfully the traffic was sparse. Soon their shift would end and they could go home for some well-earned rest. Apart from their amorous interlude it had been a non-eventful day; when they had found no crimes being committed, and it had simply been a matter of pounding their beat and making their presence felt.

They had reached the Albert Dock Basin when a Number 101 bus overtook them and quickly came to a halt. The bus conductor leapt off the rear platform and waved them down.

"There's a girl onboard who's in a bad way," he said. "Can you take a look at her?"

They stepped onto the bus and found a girl in her late teens laying prone on the side bench seat. She was curled into the foetal position and her face was creased up in pain. She let out a loud animal moan as she clutched her lower abdomen in agony. Noah noticed the other passengers staring. Hazel knelt beside her and whispered, "What's the matter, love? Where does it hurt?" Hazel listened intently as the girl spoke in a low voice. Noah couldn't hear what either was saying. She lifted the girl's skirt and inspected her undergarments.

Hazel got to her feet. "She needs to get to hospital. She's bleeding heavily from between her legs. How long will it take to get back to the nick?"

Noah guessed about ten minutes. He went into a huddle with the bus driver and conductor. The bus was heading for the terminus at the Woolwich Ferry, but they would, they said, stop outside the police station. Noah threw the two bicycles onboard and they set off. The driver kept his foot on the pedal as he made his best speed. Hazel knelt beside the girl and spoke with soothing words and gently stroked her hair. Meanwhile the other passengers continued staring at the scene at the rear of the bus. Hazel beckoned to Noah. "I think she may have had a miscarriage," she whispered. "She's losing a fair amount of blood."

On arrival at the police station Charlie Ethridge and two constables came out and helped to get the girl inside whilst Hazel called for an ambulance. It arrived inside ten minutes. The couple volunteered to accompany the girl in the ambulance, which would take her to Queen Mary's Hospital.

The ambulance set off with bells ringing and lights flashing. Hazel sat beside the girl and wrote down some details in her notebook. The medical orderly inserted an IV drip of saline solution into her vein and noted her vital signs. Throughout the journey Hazel stayed with her, whispering words of encouragement and persuading her to say what had happened. Noah didn't attempt to get involved. Hazel was quite capable. He sat in the far corner of the ambulance and held on tight as it bounced along the roads.

On arrival at the hospital, the girl was loaded onto a stretcher and wheeled inside. "This is more serious than we thought," said Hazel. "That poor girl's almost bleeding to death because she's had an abortion." That was a big surprise for Noah. Of course he was well aware that for any female with an unwanted pregnancy, the chances of undergoing a legal termination under medical supervision were few and far between. The laws regarding legal abortions were very restrictive and rolled up in red-tape. Therefore, the only avenue open to many women was to find a back-street abortionist to carry out the procedure, which of course, was illegal. In many cases the abortion was carried out in the back room of a private house by an abortionist who was untrained in medical procedures and whose hygienic measures left a lot to be desired. Very often the poor woman would either suffer massive loss of blood or be extremely ill with septicaemia.

They followed the stretcher into the emergency room and took a seat in the waiting area. Hazel took out her notebook. "The girl's name's Alice Clarke. She's 19 years old and lives in Canning Town," she told Noah.

"Where does the abortionist live? Did she give you an address?"

"No she didn't," said Hazel. "A friend accompanied her to the address, but then left her there. All she knows is that she was taken to a house in Barking." The town of Barking was a little further to the north of their own house at Beckton.

"Some friend," commented Noah sourly. "So, she has no idea where she was?"

Hazel shook her head. "No she doesn't. But I do have the name of her friend. It's Vera Doherty, and she works with Alice in the sugar packing department at Tate & Lyle in Silvertown."

"In that case, I think we'll pay Miss Doherty a visit, don't you?" he said.

"We most certainly will," agreed Hazel.

An hour later, they were able to talk to Doctor MacInnes, who had examined Alice Clarke. "She's lost a lot of blood," he told them, "but she'll be okay. I've put her on a course of antibiotics which should fight any infection. Now she'll need lots of bed rest." MacInnes pointed his finger in the direction of the ward where Alice was resting. "Whoever did this abortion needs to be caught. They almost killed her. If you hadn't helped her – she'd be dead."

"Don't worry, Doctor," promised Noah, "we'll catch her."

"Another thing to keep in mind," said the doctor. "The abortionist made such a bodge-up, that she won't ever be able to conceive again." The doctor shook their hands and returned to his busy tasks in the emergency room.

It had been a long day and Hazel was exhausted. She took hold of his arm. "Come on Noah, we'll just about catch the last bus home."

The following afternoon they were back on duty. George Cheesman had got over his hangover and returned to his regular beat, which meant that Noah and Hazel could resume their Silvertown patrol area. But today's work would be different. They teamed up with DC Andy Summers and drove in his unmarked car to the Tate & Lyle refinery. They introduced themselves to the manager of the packing department and he made an office available for their use.

Vera Doherty had been pulled off the assembly line and looked extremely nervous as she entered the office. She guessed that it was in connection with Alice. She had called at Alice's flat in Canning Town yesterday evening, and had expected her to be back at home after the abortion, but of course, she had no way of knowing that her friend was in hospital. And now the police were at her place of work and would no doubt be asking some awkward questions. She was very nervous indeed.

Andy got her seated and read her the legal rights. Without any preamble he told her of last night's events on the bus and that Alice was damned lucky to be alive.

Doherty looked genuinely shocked. "I was sure she'd be alright. That's why I left her there."

"What's the name and address of the abortionist?" demanded Hazel. Doherty gave her the details without a second's thought.

"You can go back to work now," said Summers, "but we may come back next week and charge you with assisting an illegal abortion. We'll see."

Tears welled up into Doherty's eyes as she finally realised the seriousness of her situation; and with a nervous look of apprehension, she returned to her sugar packing duties.

Hazel accompanied Andy Summers to Barking in his car. As he would most likely be arresting the woman in relation to an illegal abortion, he required a female police officer in attendance.

With paint peeling from the window sills, the house in the back streets of Barking looked dilapidated and uncared for. In answer to

Summers' persistent knock, the door was opened by a careworn woman in her middle fifties who knew exactly why they were there. She silently held the door open for them to enter. It was as if she was resigned to her fate.

    Fifteen minutes later, after witnessing the woman's crocodile tears and hearing her lame excuses as to why she had allowed Alice to almost bleed to death, Hazel slipped handcuffs onto her wrists and they led her out to the police car. Back at the police station she would be charged with behaviour likely to endanger life.

12: A Child Goes Missing

The choir were putting their coats on and leaving the church almost before the last notes of the hymn had died away. It was always the same every Wednesday after church choir practice. They were always in a hurry to leave the dark and chilly church and get back to their warm and cosy homes.

St. Mark's Church choir consisted on two adults – Bob and Audrey Davis - and three youngsters, Alec Howell and his sister Sandra, and eight year old Jackie Pope. The organist was Mrs Fry, who also ran the newsagents in Albert Road. She would normally remain behind and tidy up the hymn sheets and wash the tea cups.

The Reverend Samuel Hogan meanwhile sat with his feet up in the second row of pews and tried to make sense of the sermon he was attempting to write for the forthcoming church service on Sunday. He hated sermon writing with a vengeance and thought that it was an utter waste of time because hardly anyone ever took notice of the message he was trying to convey, and mostly his small congregation had a glazed look in their eyes as he read from the scriptures. His sermon this week was to be based on virtuous purity and chastity outside of marriage.

He stopped writing and laid down the pad. He could hardly lecture his flock on the righteousness of celibacy, he argued, when he, the vicar of St. Mark's, was making definite plans to spend the forthcoming weekend with the lovely Monika, where sex would definitely be on the menu. He thought that would be unacceptably hypocritical. He ripped the rough draft from the writing pad and scrunched it into a ball.

As she came out of the church Jackie Pope turned up the hood on her Duffel coat against the chilly evening. It was dark, and not a glimmer of moonlight showed from behind the thick grey clouds scudding across the night sky. Even though she'd previously walked home by herself after choir practice, she still felt a little scared. She took comfort from the fact that her mum, who worked at the Tate & Lyle sugar refinery, would be home by now and preparing a hot meal and lighting up the blazing coal fire in the living room. She had only to walk past the allotments, and then cross over the railway bridge to her house in nearby Andrew Street. Anyway, she wasn't totally alone. She could just make out the dim figures of Bob and Audrey 100 yards ahead of her as they made their way home. Right now her mum would be cooking her tea. Good – it was always sausage n' mash with baked beans on Wednesdays with jam roly-poly for afters. She was starving hungry.

Jackie heard footsteps behind her. They were rapidly getting nearer. She heard the metallic sound of hob-nailed boots on the pavement. They were a man's heavy footsteps. Within the stygian blackness of the night she began to feel frightened. Suddenly, from behind her, a man's soft voice said, "Hello Jackie."

Doris Pope was anxious. She had finished her shift at Tate & Lyle and had arrived home shortly afterwards. Jackie should have been home a half hour ago. Choir practice always ended at the same time every Wednesday evening; as regular as clockwork. She knew that she wouldn't have gone elsewhere. Her daughter was a shy girl and she didn't have any friends outside school; and other than attending choir practice and Sunday church service, she stayed indoors; mostly reading or listening to the radio. She put on her hat and overcoat and set off on the ten minute walk to St. Mark's Church. If Jackie was returning home late, then she would bump into her. There was no other route home she could take.

The church was in darkness except for lights coming from the vicar's residence. In answer to her knock, he opened the door wearing jeans and a sweater. "Have you seen my Jackie?" she asked him. "She should have been back home ages ago."
"I'm sorry, Mrs Pope. She left at the same time as the rest of the choir." He invited her indoors. The Reverend Hogan asked sensible and pertinent questions with regard to Jackie's possible movements. Would she be at a friend's house or have wandered off anywhere else? Was she having any problems at home? Mrs Pope explained that Jackie was a shy and reserved girl who didn't easily mix with her classmates. She could think of no other place where she would be. Sam Hogan picked up the phone and called the home of Alec and Sandra Howell. It was unusual for any residents of Silvertown to possess a telephone, and if they did, then it would usually be a shared party line. The kid's father, Tom Howell, picked up the phone. He was a sales rep for the Pearl Assurance Company. In answer to Sam Hogan's inquiry he said that his two kids had come home by themselves. He thanked him and rang off. Next he rang Bob and Audrey Davis and got the same answer.

Doris Pope was distraught. Her thoughts tried to blot out the possibility of her estranged husband finding out her whereabouts and taking Jackie away from her. Surely he couldn't have found her, could he? One thing was for sure. Reggie Pope wouldn't have bothered to trace her whereabouts in order to win her back. He had made it abundantly clear on that painful night two months ago. He'd stated that, as far as he was concerned, their marriage was over.

She recalled that night with perfect clarity. Somehow he had discovered her illicit affair with Lennie Clarke, with whom she'd had a fling. When Doris had come home from her work at the Tate & Lyle packing room, Reggie had intercepted her as she alighted from the bus. "Let's take a walk," he said, taking her roughly by the arm. "I know all about you and your fancy man. Don't you worry; I've already taken care of him. I don't want you back at our house. You can go live with your lover boy." She learned later that her husband had been around to Lennie's house and used him like a punch-bag. He'd broken his jaw, two ribs, and knocked out three teeth. She hadn't seen her husband since that dreadful day.

And now she was sure that something awful had happened to her daughter. She was crying and inconsolable and begged the Reverend Hogan to call the police station. He lifted the handset.

The duty sergeant was loath to instigate a search for the child; after all, he said, she had been missing for a mere hour and a half; but the Reverend Hogan had used his powers of persuasion and vouched that Jackie was a shy and reserved child and wouldn't have gone off anywhere by herself. The sergeant had promised to send an officer to investigate and suggested that Mrs Pope return home just in case Jackie should turn up and so that the police had a point of contact for their enquiries.

For Noah and Hazel it had thus far been an uneventful foot patrol as they leisurely strolled through the side streets of their patch. All that changed as they passed the Royal Albert pub on the corner of Tate Road. In the near distance, the police call box located outside the Constitutional Club began to flash its blue light. It was a signal for any officer to contact the police station. It was a rare event for the station to activate the light, so Noah set a rapid pace.

He lifted the telephone from its cradle. Charlie Ethridge came on the line. He didn't beat around the bush. "You and Leggett get yourselves around to Andrew Street and speak to Mrs Pope. Her eight year old daughter's gone missing," he told them. "She was at choir practice at St Mark's Church this evening and didn't return home."
This sounded serious. "What time was this reported, Sarge?" he asked.
Ethridge consulted his shift log. "It was called in just 15 minutes ago. The girl was due home about an hour ago and her mum got worried when she didn't arrive home by half past seven."
Noah looked at his wristwatch. It said 8:30.
"Okay Sarge, we'll get round there straight away." It was going to be a long night.

"Mrs Pope stated that her daughter's quite a shy girl and she doesn't have many school-friends who she may be out with – but check it out anyway. And Noah – keep in touch."
"Okay Sarge, will do."

    Noah and Hazel were shown into the front parlour of the house in Andrew Street and immediately began gathering facts. Hazel was taking notes. They started with the basic questions – full name – age – eyes – hair – build general description – clothing. Doris Pope looked tired as she answered their enquiries nervously, but managed to keep her composure. Noah shifted the focus of his investigation onto more generalised questions. What school did Jackie attend? Has she ever gone missing before? Who were her friends?

    Doris Pope seemed distracted as she recounted the timeline and sequence of events of her daughter going missing. Hazel looked down as Doris Pope began to fiddle nervously with her hands. She noticed that she wasn't wearing a wedding ring. "Where's the child's father, Mrs Pope," she asked. "Are you married? Does a Mister Pope live here?"
Doris Pope's eyes wouldn't meet hers. For a full ten seconds she didn't answer. Then she said reticently, "He's not around anymore." She didn't elaborate and Hazel let the subject drop.

    Mrs Pope went out to the kitchen to make a pot of tea. Hazel whispered, "Something's not right, Noah. I can't put my finger on it, but I don't think she's telling us everything."
He nodded. "Yes, that's the impression I was getting. She seems to be holding something back." He considered the situation for a while. "There's not much we can do at this time of night, other than to have a quick look around the local streets; but tomorrow I'll ask Andy Summers to look into the case."

    Early the following morning Silvertown was flooded with police officers who'd been drafted in from all parts of the division. Some of the officers searched the area around St Mark's Church, and especially the church graveyard and the adjoining allotments. Others went door-to-door making enquiries and asking residents to search any sheds or outhouses.

    Noah and Hazel went to see Miss Green, the headmistress of Drew Road School. As expected, Jackie Pope hadn't turned up for school, and of course, Miss Green knew nothing of Jackie's disappearance. Noah brought her up to date. Miss Green accompanied them along to Jackie's classroom where they had a word with her teacher, who confirmed that the girl was somewhat shy and hadn't easily made friends. Miss Green said that she would make an announcement at the morning school assembly and would ask if any pupils had information regarding Jackie's disappearance.

It was as they were preparing to leave that Miss Green said something which made a huge difference to their investigation. She said, "I don't suppose Jackie's been here long enough to make many friends, has she?"

"Really? How long has she been a pupil at Drew Road?" asked Hazel.

"Oh, only about two months," said Miss Green.

"What school did she attend before coming here?" asked Hazel.

Miss Green consulted her files. "She went to Pretoria Road School in Canning Town."

They returned to the house in Andrew Street. Andy Summers met them there. Noah brought him up to date regarding the Pope's recent arrival from Canning Town. They went inside to speak with Doris Pope.

"Why didn't you tell us that you've only recently moved here?" asked Hazel.

Mrs Pope went on the defensive. "You didn't ask me."

"Where's the girl's father?"

"He's still living in our house in Canning Town, I suppose."

"What's his name?"

"It's Reggie....Reggie Pope."

"When we last spoke, you stated that Jackie's father, 'Wasn't around anymore,' whereas you certainly do know where he is and I wouldn't be at all surprised to find Jackie with her father. When did he last see his daughter?"

Doris Pope couldn't look them in the eye. "About two months ago," she replied in a whisper.

"I think you've been wasting our time, Mrs Pope." Hazel was livid. "What's his address?" she demanded.

Ten minutes later the three police officers were driving to Canning Town. They knocked at the house which Doris Pope had once shared with her husband and daughter. A tall stocky man in his mid-thirties answered the door.

"Reggie Pope?" asked Andy.

"Yeah, that's me. If you're looking for Jackie, she's upstairs in her bedroom listening to the radio." He held the door wider for them to step inside.

Hazel went upstairs to check on Jackie, whilst Andy and Noah had a chat with her father. They had discussed matters on the drive over to Canning Town and had agreed that, if Jackie was indeed with her dad, then no crime would have been committed because the law doesn't differentiate between each parent having lawful access to their children.

Reggie Pope was very cooperative and even served up mugs of tea to the police officers. However, they did advise him to allow Jackie to return to Silvertown with them so that she didn't miss any more school lessons. Reggie Pope agreed with them, but stated that he would seek a court order to enable regular and unrestricted access to his daughter.

13: The Night-watchman

In late October Noah got the surprise of his life as he walked into the mess-room prior to going out on patrol. In place of the recently retired Jim Andrews, a new constable had arrived at the station and was now busy making himself a mug of tea. Noah recognised him instantly. He couldn't believe his eyes. The new man was called Patrick McEachen and they had served together in an army regiment in Germany during Noah's National Service.
Their eyes locked in recognition. "Well, well, look what the cat's dragged in," said McEachen in a strong Irish accent. "It's the pride of the British Army, so it is."
The other two constables in the room, Ronnie Baldwin and Les Jones, raised their eyebrows in surprise that Noah and McEachen were acquainted, but could instantly detect a frosty atmosphere. The room fell silent. Noah simply said, "Hello, long time – no see," and walked out.

Minutes later the duty constables were called into the parade room for inspection, and Sergeant Ethridge introduced McEachen to the other policemen. As a new arrival, McEachen would be paired up with an experienced officer and the task was thankfully given to Les Jones to show him the ropes.

As Noah and Hazel strode along Albert Road he related the story of Patrick McEachen. He had first met McEachen, he told her, when he had been posted to the Royal Army Service Corps – the RASC – at Bielefeld in Germany. Noah had been a raw recruit of 20 years of age and fresh from his basic training at Catterick Camp in Yorkshire. He had been billeted with fifteen other men in a cold and cheerless Nissen hut and tasked with driving 3-ton army trucks which delivered various loads of stores and equipment to a wide range of military outposts across the length and breadth of Germany.

McEachen had been a senior storeman at the vast army distribution centre from where the trucks loaded their cargoes. Soon after he arrived, Noah was approached by McEachen, and without going into details, he asked if Noah would like to earn some serious cash. Noah gave it two seconds thought and said that he wasn't interested. McEachen simply shrugged his shoulders and said, "You'd best forget that I ever asked you, understood?" and walked away. Noah didn't have a clue what McEachen was up to, but he was pretty damn sure that he was up to no good and he didn't want any part of it.

A few days later, he spotted the storeman and one of the drivers check that the coast was clear, then suspiciously slip behind the truck maintenance sheds. They had failed to notice that Noah was observing them from a distance. Some money changed hands and the storeman and driver went their separate ways. Over the coming weeks, after hearing some of his hut-mates whispering amongst themselves, it became apparent that McEachen had several of them in his pocket. Noah suspected that he doctored the delivery notes, and with the connivance of his pet drivers, a truck-load of goods would be mysteriously sent elsewhere.

"So what you're saying – is that McEachen's a crook?" stated Hazel.

"That just about sums it up," said Noah. "The problem is that I never reported it because I couldn't prove anything. And anyway, I didn't want to get involved. I was just a raw recruit of 20 years old."

"So he got away with it?" she asked.

"Not exactly," said Noah. "Some weeks later, McEachen was caught red-handed when the regimental quartermaster decided to carry out a surprise stock check, and tons of army stores were found to be missing. Mind you, they eventually let the matter drop, because any official action would have shown that the army's stock control system was open to abuse, and that would have caused some bureaucratic embarrassment, if you see what I mean?"

"So he escaped by the skin of his teeth, then?"

"Yes, however, our light-fingered Corporal McEachen was forced to resign from the army." As they ambled along Albert Road, Noah's mind recalled the chain of events from several years ago. "He must have received an honourable army discharge though; otherwise he would never have been allowed to join the Met Police, would he?"

"No, I don't suppose he would," she agreed.

"I reckon that McEachen blamed me for getting caught," said Noah, pensively. "He must have thought that I'd reported his activities to the quartermaster."

"Why do you think that?" asked Hazel.

"Because the night before he was due to leave the army, and return to being a civilian, he came to my billet and said to me, "You can take that smug look off your face, Sheppard. Don't think you've got away with dropping me in the shit. If I ever see your face again, then you'll live to regret it."

"But there's nothing that he can do to you, is there Noah?"

"Let's hope not," he said, optimistically.

On a cold morning in October, a middle aged woman came into the station to make a complaint that she'd been assaulted by her husband. Noah and Hazel were about to go on duty when Bert Ambrose called them into his

office. The woman was sat in front of Bert's desk. Her face looked in a terrible state. Both of her eyes were purple and she had a nasty cut above her right eyebrow that was turning yellow. Her lip had been split and dark bruising showed around her neck. Her nose looked to be broken. Ambrose indicated Noah and Hazel to take a seat.
"This is Mrs Fowler," said Bert. "Her old man's beat her up last night. She's moving out and I need you and Constable Leggett to escort her back home so that she can get her things."

Noah hated dealing with these domestic violence situations. In most cases they never came to anything. Either the woman simply packed her bags and left the bloke to go off elsewhere, or she refused to sign an official complaint and went back to him once the dust had settled. In a few weeks time he would again come home from the pub blind drunk and use her as a punch-bag - and the whole sorry story would start over once more.
"Where do you live?" asked Noah.
"Our house is in Muir Street," the woman whispered.
"Is your husband likely to be at home?"
She shook her head. "No, he works in the docks. He doesn't usually get home until after six o' clock. He mostly has a few beers in Cundy's pub before he gets home."
Noah was glad to hear it. He didn't relish getting into an argument with her old man or having to listen to a slanging match right there on the doorstep.
"Why did he hit you?" asked Hazel sympathetically.
Mrs Fowler was shaking her head. "I'm not sure why he did it," she said. "George is usually very good to me. I was bathing our youngest kid when he got home. She's only four years old and she'd had an accident and shit her knickers. Anyway, I hadn't had time to get his tea ready on time, so he gave me a doughboy and split me lip."
"How many children have you got?" asked Hazel.
"We've got three; a boy and two girls. They're at school right now. I took them around to my friend Judy's place last night and we slept on the floor. Now I dunno where we'll sleep, coz she ain't really got the room to put us up."
"Let's see, shall we?" said Hazel. "I'm sure she'll put you up for another couple of nights if needs be." The woman nodded nervously, but she was secretly afraid of what George would do if she walked out on him. She couldn't just leave the area. Her job was at the sugar packing room at Tate & Lyles and their kids went to local schools, so she couldn't just pack her bags and vanish. George would be sure to find where she was staying.

It was almost lunchtime when Noah and Hazel escorted Mrs Fowler into her home in Muir Street. She invited them in whilst she packed some clothes and essential items into bags. Hazel went upstairs with her to the bedroom whilst she packed away her stuff. Noah didn't feel the need get involved and remained downstairs.

Minutes later Hazel called down, "Noah, could you come up here, please." He climbed the stairs, complaining under his breath. She was waiting for him on the top landing. Mrs Fowler was in the children's bedroom packing away their clothes. "Come and see what I've just found," she whispered.

They went into the main bedroom and she pointed to a bundle wrapped up in towelling which lay on the bed. "I found it on top of the wardrobe," she explained. Noah carefully uncovered the bundle. It was a heavy calibre revolver. Noah inspected the weapon, careful not to wipe any fingerprints off the lightly oiled gunmetal. "This is a Webley Mk V1," he said. "I've seen plenty of these when I was in the army. They were mostly used as officers' side arms."

Hazel jerked her thumb towards the woman in the next bedroom. "But her old man works in the docks. What would he be doing with a gun?"

Noah whispered in her ear. "We'll let the CID boys sort it out. Nip down to the police box and call Bert Ambrose and let him know what's happened."

Forty minutes later the Flying Squad – The Sweeney – had arrived from Scotland Yard. Mrs Fowler wasn't a suspect in the matter of the gun and had been allowed to go stay with her friend Judy for the time being. The gun was taken away to undergo a ballistics test where it would later emerge to be an exact match of the slug that had been extracted from the ceiling at Lloyds Bank.

Meanwhile, at the same time as the house in Muir Street was undergoing a thorough search, George Fowler was arrested aboard a cargo ship in the docks where he was working as a stevedore. He was taken to North Woolwich nick to be interviewed by the CID. After being advised that his fingerprints had been lifted from the gun (which was a lie – the gun was clean.) and that he was in line for a 10-15 year stretch of porridge at one of Her Majesty's prisons, George Fowler decided that he wasn't one of life's gallant heroes, and promptly spilled the beans and told them everything in exchange for a softer sentence. It subsequently transpired that Fowler hadn't taken an active part in the bank raid, but had been given the gun for safekeeping by a member of the gang. The rest of the bunch were picked up that same evening.

Some months later, after the trial at the crown court had resulted in long prison sentences, a small ceremony was held at North Woolwich nick when Hazel and Noah were the recipients of The Chief Superintendent's Commendation Award in recognition of discovering the vital evidence that wrapped up the Lloyds Bank robbery case. Chief Superintendant Humber personally presented the awards and was full of praise for the pair. Later that evening the sergeants and beat coppers assembled en-masse at the Royal Pavilion pub for a celebratory booze up.

It was a sunny autumn day when Noah, Hazel, and several officers arrived at Drew Road Primary School to give the kids a demonstration on police work. Noah had set up the demo after having a word with Inspector Maitland, who had given his blessing to make use of the station's officers, even though it entailed using up some overtime.

Les Jones had set up a loudspeaker sound system in the school playground and now all the children and teachers were gathered around the perimeter seated on bench seats. Also present were some parents and local dignitaries, including the Reverend Samuel Hogan. Les would be doing the commentary. The kids were waiting with eager anticipation for the fun to begin.

Suddenly they heard the rapid ringing of a siren and bells as a police car approached from the direction of Saville Road and raced through the school gates. It did a fast and dramatic lap of the playground before screeching to a halt in front of the children. Several police officers leapt out as if searching for someone.

"These policemen are looking for a burglar," said Les gaily through the microphone. "Has anyone seen him?" The officers, who included Percy Longstaff and Dave Roberts, did a creditable imitation of thoroughly searching for the criminal from amongst the ranks of assembled children and grown-ups. "Has anyone spotted him yet?" asked Les. The children all craned their necks to look, but shook their heads.

"Shall we call in the police dog? He'll be sure to sniff out the burglar," shouted Les enthusiastically through the Tannoy.

"Yes," shouted two hundred young kids. They were getting excited.

"Here comes the police dog," announced Les, as the station's dog unit van screeched into the playground. One of K division's five dog handlers, Hamish McMurdo, brought the German Shepherd bitch out from her cage and snapped on a long rope lead.

"This is police dog Honey and she's three years old," broadcast Les over the speakers. "Do you think she'll be able to find the burglar?"

"Yes," screamed the kids. Some of the younger infants were squirming in their seats with excitement. Meanwhile Hamish allowed Honey to go sniffing around the playground, seemingly looking for a scent.

"Can you help Honey to find the burglar, kids?" asked Les. "If you see him, then I want you to shout out as loudly as you can, okay?" The whole school, including the teachers cheered a resounding "Yes."

Without warning, a dirty and shifty looking man dressed in a black and white striped jumper, a flat cap, a black face mask, and carrying a bag over his shoulder marked SWAG, appeared from around the back of the playground. Underneath the archetypical burglar's outfit was Ronnie Baldwin, who had been waiting in the head-mistresses' study for his cue to make his appearance. The police officers ensured that they were facing away from him, but it didn't stop the kids going wild. They all shouted and screamed in unison, "There he is." Ronnie ducked back behind the wall.

"Where is he," shouted Les exuberantly, the decibels were getting higher, but Les was loving it.

"He's behind you," screamed the children. Some of them were standing up and pointing and going berserk. It seemed to Noah as if the kids were exposing the pantomime villain. Then Ronnie broke cover and tried to escape by running across the playground.

Suddenly, Hamish McMurdo let Honey off her leash and shouted a command, "Honey – Attack!" In seconds the dog raced like an arrow across the playground and clamped her jaws around the arm of Ronnie who was doing his best to escape. He didn't stand a chance as Honey's sharp teeth sank into his especially thickly padded jacket and pulled him to the ground. Hamish shouted, "Honey – sit," and the dog sat a few feet away, but without taking her eyes off Ronnie. Percy and Dave Roberts ran over and snapped handcuffs on him and a huge cheer went up from the kids. But out of the blue, from amongst the children seated on the benches, one solitary child stood up and shouted, "Hey leave him alone. That's my dad!" It was little Billy Baldwin.

The remainder of the afternoon consisted of a display from West Ham Fire Brigade, who arrived noisily with their big red pump tender and turntable ladder sounding their two-tone horns. Whilst the pump sprayed water dramatically across the playground, the other carried out the rescue of a damsel in distress who was trapped on the fourth floor of the school. She was dressed in a blonde wig, bright red lipstick, and a flowery frock, but looked suspiciously like one of the beefy firemen. Meanwhile the kids were allowed to sit inside the police cars and fire engines and watched a demo of fingerprinting and other police work.

Later that evening the coppers and sergeants again gathered at the bar of the Royal Pavilion for a few beers and to relax. Noah thought that these drinking sessions were getting to be a regular occurrence, but he wasn't complaining. It had been a successful day. Bert Ambrose shook Noah's

hand and thanked him for arranging all the separate departments to take part.
"Well done, Noah," he said. "What's next on your list?"
"I'm going to organise a football team for the local lads," said Noah. "It might help them to stay out of trouble."

Moments later, he was leaving the toilets at the back of the pub, when he came face to face with Patrick McEachen. He hadn't seen the Irishman for some weeks, which suited him just fine. McEachen scowled. "Well, look who we have here. It's the blue-eyed boy of North Woolwich nick." McEachen fixed him with an intense look. "You may have thought I'd forgotten about you, Sheppard, but I'll be lining up a suitable settlement for you, so I will."
Noah began to explain that the cause of him being forced to leave the army was none of his doing, but McEachen sidestepped around him and headed back to the bar.

Hazel was in a foul mood. Her mother had written to say that they hadn't seen her in months, and so she and dad would be arriving to visit next weekend. This put Hazel into a tight spot because she couldn't take them to the house she shared with Noah and would have to find alternative accommodation for the days when they would be here. If they even suspected she was living-in-sin with him, then she would never hear the end of it. Her parents, Bob and Audrey Leggett were God-fearing churchgoers who presumably thought that their only child was a virgin, even at 22 years of age. Hazel didn't know what to do.
"It's all your fault, Sheppard," she complained as they strode along Albert Road. "If you hadn't made me fall in love with you, then I would never have been in this predicament." Noah thought it was a novel line of reasoning and began whistling a catchy tune, which exasperated her even more. "And you took advantage of me when I wasn't thinking straight," she said, to add weight to her argument. He carried on whistling.
"Come on then, Sherlock Sheppard. Help me out. How do I hide the fact that their virginal daughter is cohabitating with a big strapping copper?"
"Oh that's an easy one to solve," he said, and gradually began taking longer strides so that she was unaware of the fact until she was almost running alongside him to keep up. It had recently become his favourite pastime as he knew that it infuriated her.
She stopped in her tracks and faced him. "So? Are you going to tell me or do I have to wring your neck?"

He grinned back at her, as happy as a mackerel that he'd been successful in baiting her. "I'll make a deal with you. You tell me what your middle name is, and I'll give you the answer."

On the first day they'd met and had gone out on patrol together, she had revealed that her middle name was a source of embarrassment, but she had never divulged what it was. He was aching to find out.

"If I told you what it was, then I guarantee that you wouldn't love me anymore."

He laughed. "I'll take the chance. Come on – tell me."

"Do I have to?" she pleaded.

"That's the deal," he said smugly. She wasn't in a position to argue.

"Alright then." She took a deep breath. "It's Britannia," she said, her face and neck turning red. "I was named after my grandmother," she explained.

"It sounds very patriotic. I'll bet your grandfather had a good laugh, though," he said, his face creasing up with laughter.

"So, do you still love me – you bastard?" she snarled.

"Hmmm, I'll have to think about it," he said, winding her up. "It could go either way."

"So how am I going to solve the problem of hiding our living in mortal sin," she asked.

"That's easy. I'll move out my few clothes and go live in the section house for the weekend. Then you'll be able to put-up your mum and dad in our spare room, and everyone'll be happy."

They were crossing Saville Road, located opposite the towering steel monolith that was the Tate & Lyle sugar refinery. Smoke was belching from the chimneys of the nearby factories as they worked at full blast. Silvertown, in the middle of the day, was a cacophony of noise and strange odours. A steam train pulling three carriages chuffed by on its way to the terminus at North Woolwich. Black and grey flecked smoke belched out of its smokestack and steam escaped from its pistons as it gathered speed. Noah looked at his wristwatch. It was almost time for the T&L early morning shift to knock-off. At any moment the factory hooter would sound, and hundreds of sugar workers would stream out of the gate on foot and riding bicycles, to go across the railway crossing, and then either make their way home or dive into the pub for a pint of ale.

Two small boys were sat on the pavement outside Harry Gee's grocery shop. They had their backs against the shop-front wall, and squashed between them was an effigy of Guy Fawkes. The boys called out to a passing factory worker, "Penny for the guy, mister." The man reached into his pocket and threw a few pennies into their collection plate.

Hazel and Noah stopped to inspect their handiwork. The effigy was made up of old clothes that had been stuffed with rags. The kids had put in some extra effort so as to make the effigy as realistic as possible and they'd attached an old pair of boots and a floppy hat. They'd presumably used their mum's cosmetics to paint on the face and sewn on the glass eyes from one of their sister's dolls. It looked quite lifelike.

Parked beside the boys was a home-made barrow. It reminded Noah of when he was a youngster and had built a similar barrow. He told Hazel how they were built. Traditionally the wooden barrows, he told her, were constructed by the boys from scratch, using a length of builder's plank, to which an old set of pram wheels were fixed. The wheels at the front could be steered with the feet or by attaching a length of rope and pulling in whichever direction one wished to steer. Some lads would attach a padded seat on which to sit, and a wooden box in which to stow odds and ends. Many local boys used their barrows to take bundles of kindling around the streets and sell it door-to-door. The one thing that was essential with one's barrow was to have a good friend who would usually push it along the pavement, and then leap onto the tailboard. This barrow was no different.

Noah recalled his own childhood back in Broxbourne when he and his friends would make up their own guy and collect pennies with which to buy fireworks. If one's guy was realistic, then you usually collected more money, but no one wanted to contribute for an effigy that resembled a pile of dirty rags.

Noah looked down at the urchins. "How're you lads doing? Having any luck?" He could see that their collection plate held just a few pennies, but their fortunes may change in a few moments.
"We've only just got 'ere, but we'll get plenty of pennies when that lot knock off," said the eldest, jerking his thumb at the sugar plant.
"What are you going to buy with your takings?" asked Hazel.
The boys looked at her as if she were stupid. "We're gonna buy fireworks, of course," said the elder one. "We gonna get bangers an' rockets an' squibs an' roman candles an' caffrin' wheels."

They continued on their beat. In both Silvertown and North Woolwich, the landscape was littered with several bonfires that were under construction by local lads. The stark terrain of the bombsite between Saville Road and Leonard Street was courtesy of the German Luftwaffe, who had levelled dozens of houses there in 1941 with a single high explosive bomb. The bonfire being built upon the site was currently ten feet high and getting higher every day as the local urchins scavenged whatever scrap timber they could lay their hands upon.
These bonfires and firework displays were largely unsupervised affairs and Noah was aware of several instances when children had been injured.

As promised, Hazel's parents arrived for the weekend and were pleasantly surprised that she could accommodate them in the spare room of her house. Noah had packed his meagre set of clothing into his suitcase and moved back into the single officers' accommodation in the section house, citing the excuse that his landlord was carrying out essential repairs.

Beforehand they had discussed him being introduced to them. "After all, darling, I am your boyfriend and you're a twenty two year old red-blooded female, so it wouldn't make sense to hide the fact, would it?"

"Of course not," she had said uncertainly, "but they're a bit fuddy-duddy and I don't want them to be faced with the shock that we're living together."

She needn't have worried. Noah was duly 'invited' for Sunday tea just hours before they were due to catch the train back to Oxfordshire. He was introduced to Jim and Rose Leggett and must have made a good impression, because they got on like a house on fire. Her dad was a tall rangy man with an animated face and the most profusely bushy eyebrows that Noah had ever encountered. By comparison, her mum was a homely woman who seemed to be perpetually smiling. Noah suspected that if one had slapped Rose around the face with a wet haddock, she would have come up grinning.

Jim had shaken his hand. "You must bring Hazel back to Witney for a long weekend, Noah. I think you'll enjoy it."

The pair had enthusiastically waved goodbye as the Leggett's train had pulled out of the railway station, and an hour later Noah moved his stuff back into their bedroom. "Thank Christ they've gone home," said Hazel lustily. "I've missed having you keep me warm for the past two nights."

"I don't know about that," he goaded her. "It's been nice to have a break from your snoring." Luckily he saw her right hook coming and ducked in time.

It was a Saturday night and Sheppard and Leggett were on an overnight shift - working 10pm – 8am. It was the worst possible stint, because it was usually long and boring and cold. Noah hated it, because by the time they signed-off and got the bus home, they had to attempt sleep with the bright morning sunlight streaming through the curtains. Fortunately, they didn't work these tours of duty too often and this was their last rostered night shift. Tomorrow they could relax.

An hour before midnight they had timed their patrol so as to be outside Cundy's pub opposite Silvertown Railway Station, just in case there were any fights as the pub closed up for the night. But tonight was all quiet and the pub's patrons simply staggered out and went home. The doors were closed and the lights switched off. Silvertown was deathly silent.

"Shall we go over the line, my sweet?" asked Noah. It was their personal secret code which suggested they cross the railway line via the foot bridge where it was dark and isolated. There they could indulge themselves with long passionate kisses and cuddles without being discovered. She giggled. "I thought you'd never ask. Let's go."

Minutes later, in a dark spot in Factory Road, he had taken her into his arms and their lips had met in a passionate embrace. They had all the time in the world. They could patrol their beat as they saw fit, and needed only to occasionally call the station to advise the duty sergeant that all was well. They would ring the station again from the police call box located on the Silvertown by-pass once they returned back over the footbridge. But for now, their time was their own. He slid his hands under her tunic and gently squeezed her breasts and ran his hands over the warm soft curves of her body. She didn't resist.

Time slipped by as they indulged their passion. Even though they would be sleeping together when their shift had ended and they went home to their cosy house in Becton, he couldn't get enough of wrapping her in his arms and kissing those luscious lips again and again.

All of a sudden, they heard a dull detonation that seemed to originate from the far end of the factory complex site along the banks of the river in Thames Road.

"What the hell was that, Noah? It sounded like an explosion," she said, buttoning up her tunic.

"You're right," he agreed. "Come on. Let's go take a look." They set off at a brisk walk. Thames Road was beyond the railway sidings and would take them ten minutes at a fast pace.

They shone their flashlights through the metal gates of the Cooperative Wholesale flour mills and the Keiller marmalade factory at Tay Wharf, but found nothing untoward. The manufacturing plants were silent and closed for the night. The last company at the far end of Thames Road was the Thomas Ward ship-breaking yard. Noah tried the gate and found it open. They walked inside to look around. The acreage was littered with great piles of metal from ships that had been scrapped. Hazel swept her flashlight beam across the scrap-yard and saw several ships' funnels and a dozen or so old railway engines. Hazel discovered that the door leading into the office block was ajar and a scruffy van was parked outside. The building was silent. Noah shouted, "It's the police. Is anyone here?"

A minute went by. They went inside, sweeping their flashlights into dark corners. Noah repeated the call.

Then a man's voice called out from upstairs. "Hello. It's the night-watchman." A middle aged man appeared on the stairs from the upper floor. He lit the way with his torch and joined them on the ground floor. He was swarthy faced man dressed in a rain-coat and flat cap.

"Who are you?" asked Noah.

"I'm Vic Noone. I'm the watchman. I'm just doing my rounds."

"We heard what sounded like an explosion a while ago and wondered what it was," said Noah.

"Oh that. It was a bloody great steel boiler tube that fell over in the scrap yard," he explained. "It must have weighed at least ten tons. It made one helluva racket. It scared the life outta me."

"Is that your van outside?" asked Hazel.

"It certainly is," confirmed Noone.

"So, is everything under control?" asked Noah. "No problems?"

"Nah, it's all tickety-boo. I'll just finish my rounds and lock the gates behind me," said Noone.

"Alright then," said Noah. "We thought we'd just have a look around and make sure that everything was okay. Goodnight."

"Thanks very much. Cheerio mate," said Noone, and gave them a cheery wave.

The following Monday morning had started very pleasantly indeed. They were scheduled on the daytime shift. It was Noah's 25th birthday and he had awoken in their double bed to find Hazel grinning mischievously at him. A weak sunrise attempted to flood the room with light, but there remained another hour before they needed to get dressed. Through half-asleep eyes he had watched in fascinated amazement as she had slipped off her night-dress so that she was completely naked. Almost in silence she had climbed on top of him, straddling his body with her own. She had gripped his wrists and bent to kiss him tenderly. Several minutes elapsed before her hips began to grind into his groin and he quickly felt himself becoming erect. She was grinning impishly at him, confident in the knowledge that she could bring about the carnal desires to which he was helpless to refuse her.

Wisps of long blonde hair fluttered against his chest, and as she bent to kiss him, the hard nipples of her breasts rubbed against his chest hair. She reached behind her and guided him into the core of her body as she began to make long slow love to him. Throughout their lovemaking her eyes never left his face, but grinned at him wickedly. She bent lower and whispered into his ear, "Happy birthday, my darling."

She sensed his urgent needs and began to move her hips ever more rapidly, grinding them forcefully down onto his groin as she rocked back and forth faster and faster until their lovemaking reached its peak. They were carried along on a rising tide of emotion as a paroxysm of orgasm swept over him and Hazel felt his explosion within her. Sensing her own approaching consummation, she was spurred on to even greater effort, until at last she felt the intense climax explode deep within.

Afterwards, as the golden afterglow of their lovemaking dissipated, they lay entwined for several minutes, breathing heavily from their exertions. Both utterly fulfilled. At last she leaned over and whispered earthily into his ear. "That's your birthday treat finished, sunshine. Now get your arse out of bed. It's time to go to work."

That Monday morning also brought dreadful news. The duty constables were lined up for parade prior to going out onto their respective beats. Sergeant Ambrose made the announcement. "I know this will come as a shock, but I have to tell you that our colleague, Sergeant Charlie Ethridge died last night from a sudden heart attack." There was immediate chatter from amongst the ranks and Noah heard several fellow officers express disbelief that Charlie had gone. Ambrose held up his hands for quiet. "I'll let you know what the funeral arrangements are later this week. I'm sure that many of you will want to attend." Noah could detect a lump in Ambrose's voice and he looked visibly upset. He and Charlie had served together for many years as they had risen together through the ranks. On this occasion Ambrose didn't bother to inspect his police officers, but simply said, "Dismissed," and they went out on patrol.

The day brought even more unexpected news. DC Andy Summers found them as they worked their beat in North Woolwich. He was driving his unmarked car.
"All hell's broken out in Silvertown. Did you have any problems on your shift on Saturday night?"
"None whatsoever," said Noah, puzzled. "Why? What's happened?"
"The safe at Thomas Ward Ship-breakers got blown sometime during the weekend and thousands of pounds have been nicked."
Noah looked quizzically at Hazel. She looked equally amazed. He said to Summers, "Well, we did hear a loud noise around midnight, but we went to see the night-watchman at Thomas Ward's, and he told us that a heavy boiler tube had fallen over in the scrap yard," he explained. "But other than that, we didn't see anything."
Andy Summers looked from one to the other. He was clearly missing something. "You spoke to the watchman?"

"That's right. A bloke called Vic Noone. He was doing his rounds," Noah described his appearance. "Have you spoken to him yet? Andy?"
Summers face was set grimly. "It may interest you to know that Thomas Ward's doesn't employ any night-watchman."
"Then who the hell......?" stuttered Noah. He looked aghast at Hazel. It was beginning to dawn upon them that they'd been conned.
"I do believe that you were talking to the guy who blew the safe." Summers informed them. "You'd better come back to my office and make out a full report."
"Do you think that Vic Noone could be his real name?" asked Hazel, clutching at straws.
"I very much doubt it," said Summers. "In fact you could say his name another way. How about calling him No one?"

It was three days later and Summers had driven Noah and Hazel into London to scan through Scotland Yard's mug-shot gallery in the hope that the pair would be able to pick out a photo of the mysterious Vic Noone. "Of course we don't have any fingerprints," he said. "He was far too clever for that."

The mention of Vic Noone being clever brought back the embarrassment they had felt when word had flown around the station regarding them being conned by the safebreaker. Their fellow officers had enjoyed a good laugh at their expense.

"We might strike lucky because safecrackers, or petermen as they're sometimes called, are a rare breed amongst criminals," Summers explained. "The common or garden thief doesn't have the tradecraft or knowledge to deal with cracking safe codes or to use explosives. These things take years to master, so they're a small and exclusive branch of the criminal fraternity."

For over an hour they had sat looking through thick books of mug-shots. Each volume was cross-referenced for the type of crime and included photographs of common burglars in the hope that their man was amongst them. Each picture had only a reference number against it. No names were included in case it could be argued later in court that a witness had been influenced by choosing a name rather than an image.

Suddenly, Hazel said, "I think this is him." She slid the rogue's gallery album across to Noah and pointed at a darkly complexioned man in the middle row of photographs. Summers looked over his shoulder. Noah was nodding with certainty. "Yes, I agree. That's definitely him."
Summers took hold of the volume. "Hang on a minute. I'll just go check his name and last known address. Won't be long."

Summers was back in less than five minutes. He pointed at their chosen mugshot. "Are you certain that's the bloke who was the watchman at Thomas Ward's last Saturday night?"
"Yes," said Noah. "I'm absolutely positive." Hazel agreed with him.
"That's a shame," said Summers. "The chap you picked out has been dead for the past two years."

Charlie Ethridge was laid to rest with a heavy Metropolitan Police presence ten days later. Every officer who could be spared attended the funeral, as did dozens of police officers with whom Charlie had served over the years in various divisions. Noah was surprised to see Chief Superintendent Humber and a Commander from Scotland Yard in attendance, together with police motorcycle outriders providing an escort to the funeral cortege.
That same week, Percy Longstaff was promoted to station sergeant in place of Charlie.

14: The Orphan's Charity Fund

It was three weeks later when the duty watch assembled for parade prior to beginning their patrols. Sergeant Ambrose addressed the officers. "A very serious theft has occurred from the duty sergeant's office," he begun. "As you're aware, the police officers at this station have for many years, made donations towards the Orphan's Charity. The cash is usually kept in an old biscuit tin in the sergeant's desk, prior to sending it to the charity. That money, amounting to £31 10s, has gone missing." A number of outraged voices were heard. "Who the hell would stoop so low as that?" said Ronnie Baldwin. "Bastards like that ought to be hung," mumbled Les Jones. Ambrose called for silence. "We have no indication as to who took the money, but we can rule out any members of the public, because they don't have access to the sergeant's office." There were further outraged voices, because it seemed to point to a police officer being the culprit, or even Lily Branson. That was unthinkable. Ambrose held up his hand for quiet. "If anyone has any information, then inform myself or Sergeant Longstaff as soon as possible." He dismissed the parade and the coppers proceeded out on their patrols.

The next morning Noah was ordered to see Inspector Maitland immediately in his office. He knocked at the door and entered. Maitland was sat behind his desk and Ambrose stood to one side. Both looked in a serious mood. This didn't look good and Noah wondered if he had somehow blotted his copybook. Maitland indicated for him to sit.
"Constable Sheppard, there's been a very serious accusation made against you by a member of the force," said Maitland in a formal manner.
Noah was astounded. "But sir....what?" he began to protest, but Maitland held up his hand against interruption.
"This is a very grave matter, Constable Sheppard. An allegation of stealing from your fellow police officers has been made. It involves money that has gone missing from the station's charity collection for orphaned children."
Noah felt stunned that such an accusation could be made against him. "I've stolen nothing, sir."
"As you're well aware," continued Maitland, "the collection money is deposited in the desk in the sergeant's office before eventually being forwarded to the charity. Sergeant Ambrose and I have personally searched the office, and the cash has indeed gone missing. The amount of £31 10s has

been stolen. The complainant alleges that you have stolen this money and deposited it into your own personal bank account."

"Am I allowed to know who has made this allegation against me?" asked Noah. He immediately thought of McEachen.

"Erm, well we don't exactly know who it was. The complainant wanted to remain anonymous," said the inspector. He opened his desk drawer and removed a sheet of paper and laid it onto his blotter. "However, even though this person doesn't wish to be identified, the fact remains that the cash is without a doubt missing, and I am duty bound to investigate its disappearance."

Noah indicated the single sheet of paper. "May I have a look at that, please sir?"

Maitland slid it across the desk. There was a deathly silence in the office whilst Noah read it. The note was written in block capital letters and wasn't signed. It said,

AS REGARDS THE MISSING CASH FROM THE OPHANS FUND, YOU MITE WANNA CHECK SHEPPARDS BANK ACCOUNT. I SAW HIM SUSPISHUSLY HANGING AROUND THE SERGEANTS OFFICE, AND THEN LATER I SAW HIM WALK INTO TO THE BANK WIV A FISTFOOL OF CASH. I DONT WANNA BE IDENTYFED COS HE MIGHT BEAT ME UP FUR TELLIN.

"Of course, I wouldn't normally give any credence to an anonymous allegation of this kind," said Maitland, "but the fact remains that the cash is missing and the finger of suspicion has been pointed at you. I think we can safely say that the informant is a fellow police officer because he, or she, claims that he saw you hanging around the sergeant's office." He held out his hand for the return of the badly written and grammatically inaccurate sheet of paper.

"Sir, I know who sent you this and it's utterly untrue," said Noah, and for the next ten minutes he related the story of Patrick McEachen. He revealed the saga of the missing army stores in Bielefeld, and the Irishman's speedy discharge from the army, and the veiled threats recently made against him.

Ambrose had remained silent throughout these proceedings, but now he spoke up, "There's an easy way to prove or disprove this accusation. How about if I accompany Constable Sheppard across to the bank, and he asks for a recent bank statement? That would disprove this cock and bull story, wouldn't it, sir?" Noah was happy to hear that Ambrose was on his side.

Maitland lit up his pipe. "Is that okay with you, Sheppard?"

"Yes sir," said Noah. "It certainly is."

"Very well then. Off you go, and I'll expect to see you back here in about fifteen minutes with your bank statement."

Twenty minutes elapsed before Noah and Sergeant Ambrose returned to Maitland's office. He could tell by the gloomy looks upon their faces that it wasn't good news. Ambrose was holding a sheet of paper with the bank's logo upon it. He handed it to the inspector. "His statement shows that £31 10s in cash was deposited into his account yesterday, sir," said Ambrose.

Maitland examined the bank statement. There was the deposit in black and white. "Did you go to the bank yesterday?" he asked.

"Yes sir. I withdrew £3 to pay my utility bills." The inspector ran his finger down the debit column. Sure enough, on the line above the deposit was the withdrawal of £3. It didn't make financial sense. Why would Sheppard withdraw £3 if he already had over £31 in cash in his pocket?

He shuffled some papers on his desk. This, he thought, was turning into a very disagreeable matter. It wasn't good for his officers' morale to have these accusations made known around the station. But this sort of behaviour couldn't – and wouldn't - be tolerated within his command. He made an unpleasant decision. "Constable Sheppard, the allegation made against you has been shown to be substantially true. Therefore you are suspended from duty with immediate effect pending further enquiries. Do you have anything to say for yourself?"

Noah didn't know what to reply in his defence. Within the past few minutes his world had fallen apart, because someone - and he couldn't prove who - had deposited the cash into his account. He said, "This is a pack of lies that has been used against me by McEachen, sir, and I intend to prove my innocence."

Inspector Maitland wrote down Noah's reply and said, "Your statement is noted." He held out his hand. "You will now hand over your warrant card and leave this police station and not return until I send for you. Understood?"

After they had left his office, Charles Maitland sat for over an hour in contemplative thought. He was troubled. Something about this whole affair didn't sound right. He considered himself a good judge of character and he was rarely wrong in his estimation. He had always liked Sheppard, and considered him to be an honest and able police officer. He did a good job and carried out his duties to the highest standard. The successful outcome of the Mortinson affair and his interest in keeping kids out of trouble with sports activities sprang to mind. These matters showed that he was a dedicated police officer.

He wondered how much truth was in Sheppard's contention that McEachen was a crook. He went to the steel filing cabinet and removed McEachen's personnel file and laid it on his desk. He began to read it carefully, trying to read between the lines.

Patrick McEachen, stated the file, had been born the fifth of eight children in a slum tenement in the Coombe district of Dublin in 1926. Aged seven years old, he had been admitted to the School for Destitute Children located at Skinner's Alley. McEachen attended school until he was fourteen and Maitland could find no record of any school certificates or further education. After the war, aged twenty, he joined the British Army as a private in the Royal Army Service Corps. After three years service at RASC bases in Aldershot, Hong Kong, and Cyprus, he was promoted to Lance Corporal and transferred to the stores department. For the remainder of his army career he was posted to Bielefeld in Germany as a senior storeman where he appeared to have kept his nose clean – or not been caught. Then, aged 25, he resigned from the army whilst in Germany and joined the Metropolitan Police Force. He appeared to have received an honourable discharge, because there was no mention in the file of him having problems with large amounts of stores going astray. What the file didn't show was the wretched poverty within which the Irishman had been raised.

Hazel was almost tearing her hair out. She and Noah had just arrived for duty this morning, when Ambrose had called her into his office. He'd instructed her to proceed out on duty by herself. "But why, Sarge?" she had asked in surprise. "Is there a problem?" Ambrose was usually a genial character, but today he harshly said, "Just do as you're told." She had wondered if Noah would be joining up with her later in the day, but when he didn't, she worried herself sick

And now she had returned to the station after her duty shift, and there was no sign of Noah. She tapped on the sergeant's door and turned the handle. "Aah Hazel," he said, "I'm glad you dropped by. I need to speak to you." He told her matter-of-factly that Noah had been suspended from duty until further notice. When she had got over the shock and asked him why, Ambrose had said, "I'm afraid I can't tell you. It'll be up to him to put you in the picture."

When she arrived home, she found Noah sitting in the parlour staring into space. She rushed over and wrapped her arms around him. "Are you okay, love?"

He nodded morosely. "I suppose I'll survive, but this has come as a bit of a shock."

She kissed him on the cheek. "I'll go make us a nice cup of tea." She returned minutes later with two mugs and sat herself on the arm of his chair. "Tell me all about it," she said. He told her, in minute detail, everything that had occurred at the interview with Maitland and Ambrose, and which had culminated in his being suspended from duty.

"This has got to be McEachen's dirty work, hasn't it?" she asked.

"There's no doubt about that, but I can't prove it." He was deep in thought. "Even if I could prove that McEachen sent that note, the fact remains that the orphan's money was paid into my bank account. I'm sure that he stole it, and then paid it in. Anyone can pay cash into someone else's account."

She had a suggestion. "You could try asking the bank tellers if they remember who paid it in, couldn't you?" she suggested.

"That's a good point. I'll go to the bank tomorrow," he said glumly. "Other than that, I can't think what else I can do."

Back at North Woolwich police station, Inspector Maitland was thinking along the same lines. The story which Sheppard had told regarding McEachen selling off army stores at Bielefeld had a ring of truth to it. McEachen was a fairly recent arrival and had been on his force for less than three months. He remembered that he hadn't, as yet, called him in for a cosy chat. In fact, other than reading his personnel file, he knew almost nothing about the man. Maitland decided to interview him before too long.

Another thought occurred to him. The anonymous note had landed upon his desk via the station's internal mail; which meant that the informant was almost certainly a fellow police officer. The envelope had simply been addressed, *TO INSPECTOR MAITLAND*. He picked up the phone and spoke to DC Summers.

Minutes later, Summers was sat in Maitland's office. The detective, together with every officer in the station, was well aware of the missing cash. News had travelled fast. Maitland handed over the note and envelope. "I want you to test these for fingerprints. See what you can find." Summers handled the documents with a set of tweezers. "Who else has handled these, sir," he asked.

"Apart from the informant, Sergeant Ambrose touched them, then myself, and lastly, Constable Sheppard has seen them."

Summers nodded. He'd get straight onto it. He would take them to division HQ, where the boys in the fingerprint department could test for dabs within the hour. The prints of every officer on the force were kept on file just in case they manhandled any piece of evidence. He hadn't believed for one minute that Noah Sheppard would be mixed up in anything so blatantly underhand as to steal money that was meant to go to the orphans, so he was more than happy to help to clear his name.

"By the way," said Maitland, "would you kindly send a copy of the note and envelope to Constable Sheppard. Legally he's entitled to have copies of the accusation."

Bert Ambrose called Les Jones into his office. "You've been paired-up with McEachen for almost three months, haven't you, Les? What do you think of him? How do you get along together?"
Jones looked uncomfortable. "Just between ourselves, Bert, I can't wait for his training period to be over and done with. I can't stand the bloke. He's always spouting off about how clever he is. He seems to think that he's superior to everyone else." Jones was a 22-years service man. He was the next longest serving copper in the station after Ambrose and Longstaff and he was the only constable who could get away with calling Sergeant Ambrose by his Christian name.
Ambrose was pensive for a moment. "Do you think he's ready to be let loose on patrol by himself?"
"It can't come soon enough as far as I'm concerned, Bert."
"Very well," said the sergeant. "He can take over Sheppard's beat in Silvertown as from tomorrow. I'll shift WPC Leggett onto the Becton beat"
"Thank Christ for that," said Les Jones.

Noah reread the photographic copies of the allegation that had arrived in the post this morning. Attached to them was a personal note from Andy Summers in which he said that the scan for fingerprints had revealed only those of Ambrose, Maitland, and himself. The informant must have worn gloves so as not to leave any prints. He also said that if there was anything he could do to help, then just call.

Noah was despondent. Yesterday he had called into Lloyds Bank and asked the manager if anyone could recall who had deposited the sum of £31 10s into his account. It was a vast amount of money, almost five times as much as his weekly wage of £6 15s. Surely one of the bank tellers would remember? Enquiries had been made, but no one could recollect the transaction. It was a dead end.

He had now been on suspension for over a week and the mind-numbing boredom of being at home was grating on his nerves. He attempted to keep himself busy with keeping the house tidy or by taking long walks along the foreshore of the River Thames, but his every waking moment was overshadowed by the thought of McEachen privately laughing at his expense. He couldn't wait for the evenings, when Hazel would come home from work and they could talk about how her day had progressed or anything of interest. Even the most insignificant and mundane of crimes that she dealt with took on an exciting importance when compared to his daily dose of monotony.

He'd received a formal letter from Maitland that set out the terms of his suspension, but which stated that he would at least be on half-pay. He was aware that the inspector could have chosen to suspend him without pay, so he was grateful for the small kindness.

He and Hazel had been talking over a cup of cocoa. She snuggled up into his arms as they again discussed the main topic of conversation – his suspension. For the past week they had, without any success, tried to find a way out of the dilemma.

Amongst their fellow officers, it was an open secret that the pair were in a relationship, although, as far as they knew, no one was aware that they lived together. Noah was well liked by his fellow officers and several had said to Hazel that they didn't believe he could be guilty of such an accusation.

She was deep in thought. She sipped her cocoa and said, "It seems to me that this tale of woe appears to originate back in Germany. Something must have happened there that would cause McEachen to want to get his revenge on you." It was a new line of enquiry – something they hadn't yet explored. Noah's brow furrowed. He was in a contemplative mood and lost in his thoughts.

Suddenly he sat bolt upright. "Hazel, you're absolutely right. I'm going to travel over to Bielefeld and try to have a word with the quartermaster. It was him who discovered that McEachen was stealing truckloads of military stores. If he's still stationed there, he may be able to help me. I'll set off tomorrow morning."

"That's a wonderful idea," she said, kissing him on the cheek. "I'm coming with you."

"What? You can't just swan-off to Germany without so much as a by-your-leave," he argued.

"You've forgotten my darling Noah that I'm off duty for two days from tomorrow. If this trip takes any longer, then I'll tell Ambrose that I was seriously ill – or that I'm dead."

He knew better than to argue with her when her mind was made up. They discussed their travel plans; which would involve sailing via Holland on a ferry. He had a sudden brainwave. "Hey, how about I borrow my friend's car again? Then we could drive to Germany instead of travelling on trains." Buoyed up with a sense of purpose, he dashed off to ask his garage owner friend if he could again borrow the Morris Minor. The little car had been utterly dependable when they had holidayed in Devon last summer, and it would save them precious time, rather than having to wait around on cold railway platforms.

When he returned home with the car it was late evening. He found that she'd been busy. She'd packed two overnight bags, located their passports, and made up a picnic hamper.
"We'd better get an early night," he said. "It's going to be a long day's drive tomorrow."
"Bugger that," she replied with a saucy smile. "Let's go down the pub for a few drinks; and when we come home, you can drag me off to bed and take advantage of me."

It was still dark when they drove away from their house in East London to begin the long drive to Germany. Noah found it frustrating as they attempted to overtake the heavy trucks on the trunk roads, but at last, they arrived at the ferry port of Harwich.

The passage across the North Sea was interminably long and uncomfortable as the ship rolled around in a corkscrew motion, but fortunately they were allocated a small cabin with bunk beds and turned-in for the remainder of the voyage.

The sun had long ago dipped below the horizon when the ship docked at Hoek van Holland, but their car was quickly unloaded and they were on their way to Germany.

They found a decent hotel on the outskirts of Nijmegen and had a delicious meal of stamppot and spicy sausage with sauerkraut at a nearby restaurant. Tomorrow they had a three hour drive to Bielefeld ahead of them, so they turned-in early. The cotton sheets of the bed were cold and Hazel was shivering. "I'm freezing. Wrap your arms around me, Noah," she pleaded.
"I'll make you a deal," he whispered. "You give me a big kiss – one of your Leggett specials - and I'll give you a cuddle."
She laughed. "You drive such a hard bargain, Mister Sheppard."

They arrived at the gates of the British army base mid-morning and asked to see the quartermaster. Noah had been anxious in case he'd been transferred elsewhere during the past four years, in which case this would surely result in being a wasted trip. He remembered that his name was Major Bradfield and was delighted to discover that he still held the position. They were waved through the entrance and drove to the quartermaster's office.

Major Bradfield met them at the door. He was a short wiry man with wispy thin hair. They made introductions and were seated. Bradfield indicated their Morris parked outside his door, "Judging by your car, which has British registration plates, you've come a long way. How can I help you?"

"About four years ago, I was a national serviceman who was based here as a truck driver with RASC," explained Noah. "Since being demobbed, I've become a police officer with the Metropolitan Police." He indicated Hazel. "In fact, we're both police officers."

Bradfield rested his chin onto his intertwined fingers. "And what can I do for you?"

"I've come here to ask you for information regarding a former storeman called Patrick McEachen." Bradfield's eyebrows shot up in surprise and his face resembled a question mark. He was taken aback to hear McEachen's name after all these years.

Bradfield held out his hand. "I think I'd better see your police identification," he said coldly.

Out of habit, Noah's hand reached into his jacket pocket, but then he realised that his warrant card had been withdrawn by Maitland. He begun to mumble an explanation, but Hazel quickly produced her own ID and handed it to Bradfield. Bradfield derisively snorted when Noah informed him that McEachen had also become a police officer. He shook his head in amazement. "The Metropolitan Police must be hard-up for coppers if they took him on," he said in disgust.

Noah decided to hide nothing and tell the whole story of McEachen, including the fact that he was suspended and that he suspected the Irishman of planting the damning evidence. He showed him the copies of the accusing note and envelope.

"That wouldn't surprise me in the least," said Bradfield. His face became sombre. "How much do you know about McEachen's scams when he was based here?"

"Hardly anything at all, sir," said Noah. "Apart from him suggesting that I could earn some serious money."

Bradfield looked at his watch. "This may take a while to explain," he said, and for the next twenty minutes he described how McEachen would initially identify the valuable consignments of military stores that arrived at Bielefeld's huge distribution warehouse.

"His next step," said the major, "was to approach one of his extensive group of German business contacts and invite them to buy them from him. He basically conducted an auction. Whoever offered the highest price won the bid." Bradfield took a sip of tea from his mug. "Most of these people were ordinarily quite respectable citizens, but when it came to getting their hands on top class quality goods at a fraction of their retail price, they didn't ask too many questions about where they came from. It was just a few years after the end of the war, and Germany was struggling to get back on its feet, so they would buy their goods from wherever they could get them."

"This is fascinating," said Noah. "How did he get around accounting for the missing items? There must have been a mountain of paperwork that accompanied each consignment."

"Sometimes he simply burnt the papers, so that there was no record of the stuff even arriving in the warehouse. At other times he would doctor the documents and send only half the shipment to the correct consignee. The other half got sold to the highest bidder." Bradfield shook his head in frustration as he remembered the barefaced audacity of the Irishman. "On some occasions he would send a third of a load, and the storekeeper at the destination, in perhaps Hamburg or Munich, would miraculously misplace the paperwork, and they would both have a share of the profits. McEachen had dozens of people on his payroll, including the truck drivers, as you found out for yourself."

"So how was he caught?" asked Noah.

"It was simple really. I'd suspected for some time that consignments were going adrift, and one day I just walked into the warehouse and did a random stock check. The paperwork for a large consignment of bedding that had recently arrived from the UK was still on his desk, but the actual goods were long gone. He couldn't account for where they were and he was caught red-handed."

"But why wasn't he tried and convicted?" asked Noah.

"Aah, there's a question. I wish I had the answer," said Bradfield with dissatisfaction. "The army's own Special Investigation Branch – the SIB – began to investigate the case; but suddenly the whole thing was dropped. Mysteriously the case was closed, and McEachen was allowed to retire with an honourable discharge." He raised his finger and pointed upwards. "I suspect that the top brass would have been ignominiously embarrassed if McEachen's scams had become public knowledge, because questions would have been asked regarding how a half illiterate Irishman could rip off the mighty British Army. Mind you, after that debacle, the accounting procedures were tightened up considerably."

Noah was shocked. "It doesn't seem possible that he got away with it," he said.

Meanwhile Major Bradfield had made a pot of tea in the office kitchenette and came back holding three mugs.

"So, what happens next," said Major Bradfield. "The things that I've just told you may seem very interesting, but it doesn't help you an awful lot, does it?"

They had no answer to that and the three of them were scratching their heads for a solution. "Is there some way we could compare McEachen's handwriting with the note that he wrote to Inspector Maitland?" asked Hazel. "At least we could definitely identify him as the informant."

Bradfield nodded. "Certainly we can do that. We have a small SIB unit on the base and they just happen to have a detective who doubles up as a handwriting expert. But first we require something to compare your note with. Hang on a minute." He lifted the phone and dialled an internal number.

"Hello Tom," he said into the handset. "This is Jeff Bradfield. I'm after a favour. I've got some Met policemen in my office who've just arrived from the UK. They need a handwriting comparison done on our old friend, Patrick McEachen." There was a bellow from the other end and Bradfield laughed down the phone. "That's the one; the very same McEachen." The room was silent for a moment. "Thanks Tom, can you send him straight over. And could he bring the case notes relating to McEachen, please?"

Ten minutes later the SIB detective arrived carrying a bulky case file. He made himself comfortable and began to compare the abundance of McEachen's handwriting that was contained within the four year old file, and the note sent to Inspector Maitland. Minutes went by whilst they held their breaths. At last he said, "That's a positive comparison. Patrick McEachen wrote this."

"Are you quite certain," asked Major Bradfield.

"No doubt about it," said the detective. He pointed out several flourishes and distinct similarities in the handwriting with the aid of a magnifying glass.

"Well done. Would you kindly make out a report regarding your findings? I'll need it urgently," said Bradfield. The detective got ready to leave. He began to gather up the case notes, but the major stopped him. "Just leave those here, would you?"

When they were alone, Bradfield said, "There's a nice restaurant about a mile up the road. If you'd care to come back here after lunch, his report should be ready for you to collect. There will also be a note to your Inspector Maitland from myself. It's also possible that these large and bulky case notes relating to Patrick Seamus McEachen, may be left laying around where just anyone could find them and walk away with them. Okay?"

Meanwhile, back at North Woolwich police station, Patrick McEachen had been invited for a cosy chat with the inspector. The Irishman made himself comfortable whilst Maitland poured Earl Grey tea from a porcelain teapot. "Well now Constable, you've been stationed here with us at North Woolwich for the past three months. Have I got that right?"

"Oiy certainly have, sir. Oiy'd say ya hit the nail roight on da head, so I would." The thick Irish brogue was unmistakable.
"And how well do you get on with your fellow officers?" he asked. The loaded question had been deliberately designed so that he could complain about them if he so wished.
"Oh bejeezus, sir. They're a great bunch of fellas, so they are. Yae couldn't be askin' for better."

The inspector went on to asking McEachen some easy questions about his background and his upbringing in Ireland. They were simple enquiries - made in a friendly and genial manner. But more importantly, they were questions to which he already had the answers.
All of the Irishman's responses matched those stated on his personal file. All, that is, except one.
"What did you do after leaving school at the age of fourteen," asked Maitland.
"Well to be sure, sir, oiy discovered oiy 'ad a brain, so oiy took meself off to the university to study physics, so oiy did." Maitland suspected that this was a barefaced lie as there was no mention of him attending university, or any other place of learning for that matter, after finishing state school. He recalled a reference to a long-dead famous Irishman. "He's was so full of his own claptrap - he didn't just kiss the Blarney Stone - he swallowed the bugger."
Maitland smiled and decided to have some fun and to secretly test McEachen's new-found knowledge of physics. "What university did you attend?"
"It was Trinity College in Dublin. I was dare fur ages, so I was."
Maitland nodded knowingly. "And what do you think of Boyle's Law? Do you think there might be any truth in it?" McEachen was clearly stumped for an answer, but he recovered like an old pro and attempted to bullshit his way out. "Well sir, oiy look at it like diss," he said, waggling his outstretched hand from side to side. "It could go either way."

Patrick McEachen sat in the mess-room afterwards and scrutinized every detail of his discussion with his senior officer. He'd heard that the inspector was keen on having cosy fireside chats with his subordinate constables, so he hadn't felt as if he'd been especially selected for the interview and it was nothing to be suspicious of.

He did wonder if Maitland had an ulterior motive for asking about his relationship with his fellow officers. McEachen's lip curled in loathing when he thought about it. He would have preferred to have said to Maitland, "Oiy'd loik to shoot every last feckin one of you English bastards an' I'll make sure that you're gonna be the first." But that would have to wait for another time.

His thoughts flew back 25 years or so. He was yet to be born when the English army – The Black and Tans – had invaded his blessed Ireland during the Irish War of Independence in 1919, so he hadn't personally experienced the rough treatment of that violent period. But the tales of their brutality during those terrible times had been handed down from father to son and from mother to daughter. The English bastards had killed and wounded hundreds of unarmed civilian Irishmen before being disbanded in 1922 because they were hopelessly out of control. His Da would often recount the story of his poor mammy, who had been an innocent bystander in the street when she had been rifle-butted in the face by an English soldier. She lost two teeth and her jaw was dislocated. McEachen seethed with anger when he recalled that the recruitment of the Black and Tans had been the brainchild of Winston Churchill. He hoped that the fat bastard would rot in hell for his sins.

He remembered when he was a little older; when he could sit beside his Da and Mammy as they sang the Irish Republican folk songs down at the ale house. A vision of the filthy tenement building in which he'd been born ethereally swirled through the dark canyons of his thoughts. They rented a 2-bedroom Dublin apartment from some absent English landlord in which his Da and Mammy and many siblings had to somehow sleep in abject poverty.

When Maitland had asked him about his schooling, he didn't want to tell him that he left school with no examination certificate to his name. Why should he let the well-to-do fecker think that he was just another Irish simpleton? He'd decided on the spur-of-the-moment to embellish his academic achievements a little and award himself a university education. Now he wished he hadn't. But he wasn't gonna have that English gob-shite, sitting there in his shiny office, look down on him. An image of Maitland dressed in his crisp smart uniform and neat handlebar moustache sprang into his consciousness.

He'd get his own back on the English, just like he did in Germany. He remembered those far-off days after leaving school when he had been trying to scratch a living in Dublin, but failing miserably and almost to the point of starvation. He was a fully-fledged member of the secretive Irish Republican Army, but other than nervous respect from the general public, it brought very few financial benefits. Then he'd spotted a recruitment poster for the British Army and a plan began to form in his devious and scheming mind. He, Patrick McEachen, formulated a scheme to balance the books and strike a blow against the English. He remembered a quote by some long-dead philosopher, which stated, 'If you want to hide a tree – then plant it within a forest.' This is exactly what he would do. It was a long-term objective, but he had nothing but time on his idle hands. He would, he promised, enlist into the British Army and launch an attack from within. He discussed the plan with his senior officers in the IRA and received their blessing. The next day he marched down to the recruiting office.

He smiled with self-congratulation when he recalled how he'd ripped those bastards off for thousands of pounds. And when their military policemen had come calling, he'd simply reminded them that if they wanted to make a hoo-ha about it, then he, Patrick McEachen, would let the facts be known to the newspapers and politicians and the military top-brass; and embarrassing questions may be asked about how this thick Mick from Dublin could get one over on the invincible British Army. He grinned at his own analogy.

He'd put some of that army money to good use. Through Irish Republican contacts, he'd purchased a small amount of guns and explosives which he'd squirreled away in the garden shed of his rented house in the Docklands of London. When the time was right, some hard men would arrive from Ireland and cause death and mayhem for the British bastards. He couldn't wait for the day when he could strike a blow in revenge for his mother and the many dead Irishmen killed by the English. He would make those gob-shites pay dearly for their policy of interment without trial of his Irish countrymen. Meanwhile, his job in the police force was the perfect cover to act as the quartermaster for the IRA.

As for Noah Sheppard; he was certain it had been him who'd alerted Major Bradfield to the disappearing goods scam. And now, all due to his scheming and cleverness, Sheppard was up to his armpits in disciplinary problems. McEachen laughed to himself as he recalled how easy it had been. He'd watched Sheppard go over to the bank, presumably to pay a bill, or some such errand. He had then stolen the cash and paid it into Sheppard's account later that same day. He'd been amazed at how easy it was. He didn't know the account number, but the bank teller bent over backwards to be helpful. It had simply been a case of wearing many layers of clothing, a thick overcoat, some spectacles, and a woollen hat as a simple disguise. Then he sent the note telling the inspector where he'd find the money. It was as straightforward as that. He'd laughed his socks off when he'd heard that Sheppard had been suspended. Serves the bastard right!

Noah and Hazel had sped back from Germany as quickly as possible. He called Andy Summers just as soon as they arrived home. "Andy, could we meet up? I've got some important information." Summers was at their house within half an hour. All pretence at hiding their clandestine cohabitation was put aside for now, but he trusted that Summers knew how to keep a secret. Noah showed him the case files and letters from Bradfield and the SIB detective.

Summers whistled. "Blimey, you have been busy boys and girls, haven't you? These documents should help to blow McEachen's story out of the water."

Noah agreed. "Yes it should, Andy. But another aspect of the case is troubling me. If McEachen was stealing from the army on such a grand scale, then where's all the money gone? He must have salted it away somewhere. Is there any way of checking it out?"

Andy Summers deliberated for a moment. "Well, you can get to officially examine someone's bank account, but only if one obtains a court order from a judge."

"What about unofficially?" asked Noah.

Summers was cautious, "If I was found attempting to get confidential bank account information without a legal court order, then I could be in big trouble, Noah."

"I'm sorry, Andy. Forget I even asked."

Summers stood up and made ready to leave. He took McEachen's case notes with him. "I'll see what I can do," he said as he walked out the door.

Two days had elapsed when Summers returned to the house. Noah waved him inside. The detective had a grin as wide as the Mississippi River. Noah was intrigued. "What's happened? Come on Andy, spill the beans."

"For starters," said Summers, "I had our own people double check the army handwriting expert's findings, and they agree with them. McEachen definitely wrote that note."

"That's good news."

"Then I went to his bank and had an off-the-record chat with the manager. My God, Noah, you would never guess how much that man's got salted away in his account," he said, shaking his head in amazement. "It made me wonder why he chooses to be a beat copper, when he could be living a luxurious high life." He remembered an important point that had to be explained. "Of course, what I've just told you about his bank account is highly confidential and must never be divulged to anyone, otherwise my job's at risk. It's got to be investigated by CID first. Understood?" Noah and Hazel agreed.

"The next point is that Inspector Maitland thinks we've got sufficient grounds to apply for a court order so as to look into McEachen's account and financial affairs. It shouldn't take too long. You should be back on the beat in next to no time, mate." He was about to leave when he remembered an important point. He grinned. "By the way, Inspector Maitland sends you his best wishes and hopes to see you back at work soon."

Summers returned again the following afternoon. "Inspector Maitland wants to see you. He said you can bring Hazel, if you want." They squeezed into Summers' unmarked car and set off for North Woolwich nick.

The inspector was sat at his desk as they entered his office. Ambrose was with him. When they were seated Maitland said, "Well now, events have been moving rather rapidly since your return from Germany. DC Summers and other force experts have examined the documents and it has been proven that Police Constable McEachen had been the author of the offending accusation of theft." The remainder nodded knowingly, but aware that these facts were already known.

"After careful consideration," went on Maitland, "there were suspicions that McEachen's financial situation may be far more than he could rightfully account for." His eyes briefly looked at Summers. "Therefore I applied for a court order to officially examine his bank account and his home address."

He looked at them gravely. "When we searched his address, we found a considerable amount of arms and explosives in the garden shed." There were mutters of surprise from Noah and Hazel.

"This morning," continued Maitland, "Constable McEachen was questioned under caution regarding the origins of the weapons and of the huge amount of money that we found in his account. He couldn't provide an answer, and so he was arrested and charged with unlawful possession of firearms. However, he did at least own up to being the informant for the cash taken from the sergeant's desk – he could hardly deny it, could he? He's presently languishing in a cell in central London whilst further enquiries are carried out." They sat back, satisfied that the wheels of justice appeared to be turning in the right direction.

Maitland poured Darjeeling tea into porcelain cups and passed them around. He put some shag tobacco into the bowl of his pipe and lit it. He was smiling. "And now it's my pleasant duty to inform you that your suspension from duty is hereby rescinded and you are reinstated to your former duties at this police station with immediate effect. This matter will not appear on your personal record and you will suffer no loss of pay or pension rights. Is that understood?"

Noah was relieved beyond belief. The nightmare was over. He said, "Thank you, sir. I'm glad to be back." He glanced at Hazel who was sat next to him. She was deliriously happy and smiling. Noah had been anxious that this debacle may have caused changes to be made if their relationship were to be even suspected.

He said, "Can you confirm, sir that I'll still be on patrol with WPC Leggett?"

Maitland swivelled around in his chair and spoke to Bert Ambrose. "I can't see any problem with that – can you Sergeant? I think we can trust this pair of lovebirds to be discreet."
Hazel blushed. There it was – out in the open – kind of. Noah mumbled, "Thank you, sir."
Maitland stood up. The interview was concluded. He shook Noah and Hazel's hands in congratulations, as did Ambrose and Summers.

Bert Ambrose took them to one side. He said, "You've both been through a lot with your travels halfway around Europe, so take a couple of days off, okay? We'll put it down to passionate leave."

Minutes later they were waiting in the station's courtyard for Andy Summers to drive them back to Beckton. "Darling," she whispered, "did I hear Sergeant Ambrose correctly? I'm sure that he said we'll be on passionate leave. I think he must have meant compassionate, didn't he?"
He grinned. "Well if you're offering a passionate couple of days, then I'll take your offer."
"Oh you randy bugger," she laughed, "You're such a smooth talker."

15: Rose Blewitt

The Royal Arsenal Cooperative Society food hall in Kennard Street was busy during mid-morning as local shoppers purchased their food from the butchery or grocery department. Fresh food was mostly purchased on a daily basis, because very few housewives in the district possessed one of those new-fangled refrigerators. Instead they usually kept their perishable food in their kitchen larder. The daily cycle of food shopping entailed traipsing around the area's shops to buy fresh produce. However, the housewives didn't seem to mind, because it gave them the opportunity to chat with their friends and neighbours.

Accessible by a separate door was the Coop's drapery and hosiery department, whose range of clothing was often described as old-fashioned – or naff - as the locals would put it. They preferred to purchase any new clothes in the modern shops on the opposite side of the river, in South Woolwich, or in the market in Beresford Square.

To get there entailed taking either the Woolwich ferry or walking through the quarter mile long Woolwich foot tunnel; but the choice of shops was far superior. If money was really tight, then they would catch a bus to Rathbone Street Market and buy second-hand clothes from a stall.

Janis Beavis wheeled her pram into the Coop's grocery department and parked it just inside the door, first making sure that her five month old daughter Elizabeth was still asleep. She pulled the woollen blanket snugly around the baby's chin and walked the few yards across to the cooked meat counter. There she purchased a few ounces of luncheon meat for her husband's sandwiches and some tongue and corned beef. She glanced over at the pram and smiled. Elizabeth remained sleeping soundly. Janis needed some cheese, and so she crossed to the other side of the store and spent a few minutes looking at the dozens of different types of cheese on display. She chose some Cheddar and Red Leicester; and the white-coated shop assistant cut off a wedge with a wire cheese cutter. Janis bought a farmhouse loaf from the bread counter and headed for the entrance to collect her daughter.

She knew something was amiss as she approached the door. There were two other baby prams parked nearby, but neither was hers. She looked frantically around as panic set in. Where was her baby? She was positive that she'd parked her right here, just inside the entrance to the shop. Surely someone hadn't decided to take Elizabeth on a tour of the store, had they? She quickly searched the Coop's other departments. She asked the shop assistant at the cold meats counter, who had served her just minutes ago, if she had seen her daughter's blue and white pram. "No love, I ain't seen her. Are you sure you left her right there?" she asked, trying to be helpful.

Janis ran outside and looked up and down the street. She saw only a woman carrying her shopping bags towards Newland Street. There were no prams to be seen. Only the boisterous sound of children playing in St. Edward's Roman Catholic School on the opposite side of the street could be heard. She ran to the end of Kennard Street where it meets Albert Road and looked both ways. There was no sign of her baby. The few pedestrians that passed by were acting normally, whilst inside her head, her world was falling apart. Someone must have snatched her baby. She ran as fast as her legs would take her to the opposite end of the street and frantically searched up and down the length of Newland Street, but could see nothing out of the ordinary.

Janis Beavis returned to the Coop, hoping against hope that her baby had been found inside the store. The shop assistant from cold meats had meanwhile called the manager, Alfie Simmonds, down from his office. He listened whilst Mrs Beavis frantically told him what had happened, and as soon as it became clear that someone had taken her child, he called the police.

Rose Blewitt wheeled the pram into the hallway of her house in Winifred Street and carefully took the baby into her arms. She was still asleep. She took the little bundle into her front parlour and sat gazing into the distance and wondering what had possessed her to take the child. She knew that it was wrong and that she had broken the law; and she understood that she was causing heartache to the baby's parents, but some deep-seated maternal instinct had made her take the infant.

In her heart-of-hearts, Blewitt knew what had caused her to snatch the child. Three months ago her husband Danny had dropped a bombshell when he had announced that he was leaving her. They'd been married for a mere five years, and in those few short years she had tried to give him the child that he wanted, but she had sadly suffered two miscarriages. He said that he no longer found her attractive and refused to discuss patching up their marriage. He said that he was going and wouldn't be coming back. Within ten minutes he had packed a bag and he was gone. She suspected that he had another woman, but there was nothing she could do about it. Suddenly she was alone. Within days, as the desolation of being left high-and-dry became self-evident, the mind numbing loneliness set in. They had no children, and she had no close family to whom she could turn.

Just a half hour ago, it had all seemed so easy. She had completed her shopping and was about to leave the store when she saw the three prams parked inside the entrance. She happened to glance at the sleeping child in the blue and white Silver Cross pram and guessed that the baby was a girl because she was dressed in a pink woollen top with a pink bonnet. For just a few seconds she watched the child sleeping peacefully. Its puckered lips and cute upturned nose and soft unblemished skin simply added to the impression of innocence. Rose wished she could pick the baby up and smell it. She had smelt a baby once before; a newborn boy belonging to a friend, and she had instantly fallen in love with that unmistakable odour of a newly born infant. She didn't know what had triggered her need to hold the baby, but she knew that she couldn't simply take her out of its pram and cuddle it. The mother might return and cause a scene.

She quickly looked around the store. Everyone appeared to be busy shopping or serving behind the food counters. No one was looking at her. Without thinking she let off the pram's brake and pushed it through the door. Once outside she began to panic, but it was too late now and she walked quickly into Newland Street and began taking long strides until she came to Winifred Street, just 150 yards away. Within a matter of minutes she had arrived at the door of her house. No one had seen her.

Noah Sheppard and Hazel Leggett were on a rest day when they heard an urgent rap on the doorknocker. Noah opened the door to find Andy Summers. Parked outside was his unmarked police car. "Hello Noah," said a flustered Summers, "all hell's broken loose down in Silvertown. Someone's taken a woman's baby and we need some more boots on the ground. Inspector Maitland is asking if every officer can give up their rest day and come into work." Noah waved him inside.

Hazel came out from the kitchen where she was busy making a tray of bread pudding. "Hello Andy. What brings you to our humble abode?" she said grinning. Summers was the only police officer at the nick who was aware of their living arrangements, but they trusted him to keep this information to himself.

Summers went into more detail about the missing baby. "Sergeant Ambrose says that, seeing as Silvertown's your regular beat, then he needs you to come in."

Hazel said, "Give us a few minutes to get into our uniforms."

Minutes later, they climbed into Summers car and were whisked back to North Woolwich police station.

Ambrose met them at the station's reception desk. He explained that he'd called in officers from other patrol areas and was presently deploying them on door-to-door enquiries. Mrs Beavis' husband had been brought home from his stevedoring job in the Royal Albert Dock and was now comforting his wife at their home in Auberon Street.

He said to Hazel, "If you could be with Mrs Beavis, then that would be a great help. She probably needs another female with her right now."

He turned to Noah. "And if you could work with DC Summers. Try working backwards from the Coop where the baby was taken from." Summers and Noah signalled agreement.

They piled into Summers' car and headed for Auberon Street.

Rose Blewitt was panicking. The baby had awoken from her nap and was crying. She didn't know what to do. She examined her nappy and found it soiled. She'd never had to deal with an infant's soiled nappy before, and even if she had, she didn't have any available. She took the baby into the kitchen and cleaned her up as best she could with a tea-towel. However, the little girl was still crying and the strident noise reverberated around the house; so-much-so that she thought that her next door neighbours, who lived just the other side of the thin dividing walls, must surely hear the baby's screams.

To make matters worse she possessed no baby food whatsoever. She could hardly leave the child by itself whilst she went around to the Coop to buy baby powder and a feeding bottle and nappies. People would be out looking for the child. She couldn't risk it. She wasn't aware that the infant's parents lived just a short distance away, in the next street, at the far end of Auberon Street. What frightened her most was that there was no turning back. She could hardly trundle the pram back to the Coop and give it back.

She looked through the net curtains of the front parlour and panicked when she saw a policeman knocking on a neighbour's door on the opposite side of the street. They must be looking for the child. She was terrified that the police would knock on her own door. Should she answer it? What if the baby should begin crying again? It must be hungry. She opened a tin of vegetable soup and warmed it up on the gas ring, making sure that she mashed up any lumps.

Suddenly there was a rat-a-tat-tat on the doorknocker. She froze with fear. She decided not to answer it. She picked up the baby, holding it tightly as its own mother would do, and luckily the child just lay there gurgling happily. From behind the safety of the net curtains she saw a uniformed police constable give up and go next door and ring the doorbell. She listened to the conversation intently, almost holding her breath. The policeman was asking her neighbour, the elderly Mrs Cooper, if she's seen anyone wheeling a blue and white pram within the past few hours. He explained about the missing baby.

"Sorry dear, I ain't seen nuffink," Rose heard her say.

"Okay thanks," said the copper. "I tried your neighbour's house, but couldn't get any answer. Does she have any children?" he asked.

"Nah, she's by herself. Well, she is ever since her 'usband left her," she informed him.

"Does she go to work?" he asked.

"Yeah," said Mrs Cooper, "she works in Tate & Lyles."

The mention of her working at the sugar refinery brought about another dimension to Rose's already considerable worries. She was due to clock-on at work on the following Monday morning. She could hardly leave the baby alone, could she? Rose Blewitt heard the policeman thank Mrs Cooper and walk off to the next resident of Winifred Street. She had a sudden terrifying thought. That busybody Elsie Turpin lived just in the next street. The bloody woman made it her business to know everyone else's business. What if she came knocking? She wouldn't put it past the damn woman.

It was a moderately warm dry day and so she wheeled the pram outside the back door, where baby would be in the fresh air, but might not be heard by anyone calling at the front door. It was a bit risky but she would take the chance.

At the Cooperative in Kennard Street, Andy and Noah were in the manager's office taking statements from the shop staff. Alfie Simmonds had temporarily closed the store for business, because as Summers had succinctly put it – the store was now a crime scene. When the incident had occurred, Alfie had the good sense to check the time by his wristwatch. It had said 10:20. The shop staff had been questioned and they had tried their best to give descriptions of anyone they'd served between 9:30 and when the child was taken at 10:20.

Almost all of the shoppers were women, a majority of whom were regulars who shopped in the store several times per week and were well known to the staff. As most customers had a Cooperative Society dividend book, it was easy enough to look up their addresses so as to interview them. Without fail everyone had invited the police into their homes to clear their names as being likely suspects.

Noah suggested they check the till receipts so as to verify the number of customers served. "Good idea," said Andy. But it wasn't to be an easy task. All cash and till receipts were sent upstairs to the cash office by being loaded into a contraption called a "torpedo" and whisked up a series of pipes by a jet of compressed air. The torpedoes then dropped into a bin until someone got around to sorting through them. With all the drama going on, no one had found the time. Alfie Simmonds said he'd see to it. "Let's hope they've all got divvy books," he said.

The CID were using the Coop as their base, as it was from where the events had originated. Hazel stepped into the office. Summers looked up, surprised to see her. "I thought you were staying with Mr and Mrs Beavis?" said Noah.
"I'll be going back there in a moment, but there's something you might want to consider," said Hazel. "Mrs Beavis reckons that a maximum of three minutes elapsed before she noticed her daughter missing from the store. If you add another minute while she raced around the other departments searching for her, plus running to each end of Kennard Street, then our baby-snatcher cannot live more than seven minutes away at a brisk walk, can they?"
Summers was nodding agreement. "That's a good point, Hazel. How far do you think someone could have pushed the pram in that time?"
"I walked the same route just a few moments ago," she said. "Whoever snatched that baby couldn't have gone further than Auberon Street in one direction or to Muir Street going the other way. Therefore, I think we could focus our search area to just five streets."
"That's brilliant work," grinned Summers. "Have you ever thought about joining the CID?"
She laughed. "I did think about it, Andy. But then someone told me that I'd first be required to have my brain removed."

Hazel felt out of her depth. She sat in the Beavis' living room and had no idea what to do next. Mrs Beavis had already given Andy Summers a full explanation of what had occurred earlier at the Coop when their baby had gone missing, but Hazel asked her to go through the facts of the case once again. Andy seemed to have asked all the right questions, because there didn't appear to be any inconsistencies in her story.

But in the end it was the inquisitive nature of Elsie Turpin that solved the disappearance of Elizabeth Beavis. She had been hanging out washing on the clothes line when she heard a baby cry somewhere off to her left. She guessed that it emanated from a garden in Winifred Street that backed onto her own. She immediately became suspicious. She knew that the elderly spinster, Mrs Cooper lived at number 24 and Mrs Blewitt was at number 26, neither of whom had any children. She listened intently for several minutes. There it was again! It was that same unmistakeable baby's cry. Now there was no doubt in her mind.

Within minutes she was knocking on the Beavis' door, eager to be bringing the positive news of their baby's discovery. Hazel was in the sitting room with Mr and Mrs Beavis when the knock came. "I'll get it," said Hazel, getting out of her chair.

She was irritated to see Mrs Turpin standing in the porch, and naturally supposed that the insensitive Elsie had come to get up-to-the-minute information on the disappearance of baby Elizabeth. Her abduction was the hot topic of conversation on the streets of Silvertown, and Elsie Turpin, she guessed, would want to be *au fait* with the latest news.

But Elsie beckoned her outside - out of earshot of the Beavis'. "I might 'ave found their missin' baby," she whispered. "I heard a baby cryin' from a house over the back of me in Winifred Street just a few minutes ago."

"Are you quite sure?" asked Hazel.

Elsie grimaced with hurt pride. "I'm sure you've heard of my reputation. I know everythin' that goes on around 'ere, love."

"Fair enough. But let's go over to your house, so that I can hear it for myself." She called out to the Beavis' that she was going out for a moment, just in case it should be a false alarm.

Minutes later they were standing outside Elsie's back door listening intently. They could hear only the everyday industrial noises from Silvertown's factories. No sound of a baby crying.

"Maybe she's asleep in her pram, love. I'll go and put the kettle on," said Elsie.

Seconds later Hazel heard a baby's cry coming from a back garden house in Winifred Street. "Mrs Turpin," she whispered urgently to Elsie, who was making a pot of tea in the kitchen, "can you come out here, please. I've just heard a baby crying."

Elsie came out the back door holding two mugs of tea. "There's no need to be all formal, love. You can call me Elsie if ya like," but Hazel ignored her invitation to be her new-found friend.

"Can we have a look from your upstairs back bedroom? We may be able to spot the pram."

"Good idea, love," said Elsie. "Follow me."

Elsie slid the sash bedroom window up and they scanned the gardens of the terraced houses in Winifred Street that backed onto her own. Hazel made herself comfortable on the edge of the bed whilst Elsie's eagle eyes examined each of the neighbouring rear gardens from behind the safety of the net curtains. There was nothing out of the ordinary to be seen and it would simply be a matter of waiting for the baby to cry. They didn't have a completely clear view, because a pram could easily be hidden from sight by garden foliage, or be parked down the side alleyway of a house.

The room was silent as they waited. "How's your young man, dear?" asked Elsie, fishing for information. "Your Noah is such a nice fella, ain't he? Has he asked you to marry 'im yet?"

Hazel was shocked at the manner in which Elsie Turpin could blatantly ask the most personal information without batting an eyelid.

She gave her a sharp look. "He's not my young man, Mrs Turpin. Constable Sheppard is simply a colleague."
"Okay love. Please yerself," said Elsie, and continued watching intently.
Further minutes went by. "D'yew mean to say that he ain't even kissed you yet?" asked Elsie.
Hazel was becoming angry at the woman's interference. "No he hasn't," she hissed.
"Okay love," said Elsie. "Keep yer hair on."

A further ten minutes had elapsed when they heard the unmistakable baby's cry. Then moments later they heard a woman's voice as she came out to pacify the infant. "There there, my darling, sshhush. I'll get you some milk soon." Then they saw Rose Blewitt emerge into the open with the child cradled in her arms.
"That's Mrs Blewitt," whispered Elsie, pointing at the woman. "That ain't her kid, coz she ain't got any."
"Thank you very much, Mrs Turpin." She counted the houses from the end of the block. Mrs Blewitt's house was the tenth. "I think we'll leave things to the CID from now on."

Hazel walked around to the Coop and went upstairs to the office, eager to give news of the discovery. She knew that she would find Noah and Andy there, but was surprised to also find Inspector Maitland, who had dropped by to receive an update on the latest situation. As she reported the news, the room exploded with cheers and they were all grinning and shaking her hand.
Inspector Maitland said, "Well done, Constable Leggett. You've done a great job."
"Actually sir, its Mrs Turpin we have to thank for discovering the child in the first place."
"Very well," said Maitland, puffing on his pipe, "but all the same, you've done a good job."
"I hate to remind you gentlemen," she said, "but we still have to go and recover the baby."

The four police officers drove around to the house in Winifred Street and assembled outside the door to number 26. Seeing the coppers, the residents immediately piled out onto the street and gathered in large groups. Assumptions and supposition were running rampant as they waited for something to happen.
At the same instant, Elsie Turpin had got wind that events were about to unfold and so abandoned her surveillance from her bedroom window. She had marched around to Winifred Street to join the police

officers on the basis that she had every right to be in the forefront of the action because it was she who had discovered the whereabouts of baby Beavis.

Inside number 26, Rose Blewitt looked out from behind the net curtains of her front parlour and knew that her world was about to fall apart. Disjointed thoughts swirled around her mind. If only she had been able to have a child of their own, then perhaps her husband Danny wouldn't have left her and she wouldn't be in this predicament. She had taken the baby a mere five hours ago, and from the outset had understood that she would never be able to keep her. She held the baby tightly clutched in her arms as the police officers knocked on the door.

16: The Montana Brothers

It was late autumn when Noah knocked on the door of Elsie's new neighbour in Auberon Street. Hazel was stood behind him. She was nervous. Having had an innocent upbringing in the Oxfordshire countryside, she had no idea what they would find inside a brothel. Elsie Turpin had done an excellent job of keeping a log of the comings and goings of dozens of men who had visited the house. In her neat handwriting Elsie had comprehensively kept a record and description of each customer, including the five women who worked on the premises.
His knock was answered by a brassy looking blonde woman in her early thirties. Her face was as hard as nails, and one look told him she'd been around the track a few times. She didn't attempt to be civil.
"Oh God, it's the Old Bill. What do you want?"
He didn't beat around the bush. "I have reason to suspect that you're running a brothel at this address. May we come in?" He could faintly hear background music playing.
She sneered at him. "I dunno what you're talking about. You obviously haven't got a search warrant, otherwise you would have waved it under my nose, so the answer is – No you cannot come in."
Noah had been expecting this response. "I can go get a search warrant within an hour if you want to be difficult; or you can let us inside for a look around. We won't take long," he promised.

Before being detached to North Woolwich nick, Noah had helped raid several whorehouses around the Bethnal Green area. He was aware it would be extremely difficult to prove that this dwelling was being run as a brothel. In any case, he wasn't opposed to brothels *per se* – as long as they were run properly and didn't upset the local residents, then live and let live. He preferred that men use the services of a prostitute rather than perhaps commit rape or sexual assault upon an innocent young woman. After all, prostitution was the oldest profession in the world and brothels have been around since time immemorial, so had no wish to change the status quo. However, these decisions weren't his to make. Running a house of ill-repute was still a criminal offence and he would have to abide by the law.
The woman held the door open. "Please yerself. You can come in, but don't go upsetting my guests. And make sure you wipe your boots."
Noah kept things polite and did as he was told. "What's your name?" he asked.

"The name's Ingrid. What's yours?" They showed her their warrant cards.

They were shown into the small sitting room. Three women, all in their mid-twenties, lounged upon sofas reading magazines. They were in various states of undress. One of the girls wore a short sheer negligee whilst another was wrapped in a bathrobe and the third girl wore simple slacks and sweater.

"Afternoon ladies," said Noah, removing his helmet. "Sorry to disturb you. We're just having a look around." He glanced at Hazel and grinned. Her face was a picture. This was her first encounter with prostitutes, and to describe her expression as shocked would be an understatement. She was goggle-eyed.

"What you looking for then, handsome?" asked one of the women in a husky voice. "If you're looking for a bit of fun, then you've come to the right place." She pointed at Hazel. "You'd have to get rid of your girlfriend first though, I ain't into threesomes."

He disregarded her obvious attempt to embarrass them. "Thanks for the offer, but I simply want to know how many girls work here?"

"No one works here," interjected Ingrid from the doorway. "All these ladies are my friends and they come here to relax and sometimes invite their boyfriends over."

"Are there any boyfriends here at the moment?" he asked. He already knew the answer. Elsie Turpin had described a man who entered the premises 20 minutes ago.

"Cathy's upstairs with her boyfriend getting better acquainted," volunteered Ingrid.

Noah decided to be completely honest with her. "A record of the men and their descriptions has been logged over the past two weeks. Considering the short space of time they visited, points to the fact that you're running a knocking shop, so you may very well be charged with keeping a brothel."

She shrugged her shoulders. "You've got the wrong end of the stick, officer. I ain't running no brothel, and you wouldn't be able to prove that I am." Ingrid glared at him. "I've been quite civil wiv you and let you come into my house; but the next time you knock on my door, just make sure you're carrying a search warrant. Do I make myself clear?"

"Crystal clear," he said as they began to leave.

He was determined to have the last word. "You can pass on a message to the Montana brothers – Tell them we're going to shut them down. Understood?"

Most police officers were required to attend court on a regular basis to give evidence to an alleged crime in which they had been the arresting officer. Mainly, officers would attend the Magistrates Court to offer evidence for lesser crimes such as drunkenness or for minor theft. Magistrate's courts were usually presided over by a panel of three lay judges, or justices of the peace; and more serious cases would be sent up to the crown court to be heard by a judge and jury.

Noah and Hazel had given evidence at a score of appearances at Magistrates and Crown courts over the past year. Noah had appeared as a witness for the prosecution at the Old Bailey for the important Mortinson trial. He recalled how he'd felt alarmed at the prospect of standing in the witness box to give his account of events, especially since he had played such a major part in the discovery of the murder. The thought of being questioned mercilessly by the bewigged counsel for the defence, a corpulent man with a booming voice, had filled him with terror. But he need not have worried. Inspector Marston had coached him beforehand in the techniques of giving evidence, and had advised him to speak in a clear and concise voice. Don't mumble he had said, and stick to the facts. His enduring memory was of Raymond Mortinson staring hopelessly from the dock and seeming resigned to his fate as the irrefutable evidence unfolded and stacked up against him. After a whole day in the witness box, Noah had been thanked by the judge and dismissed.

Both he and Hazel had taken part in the Kensett trial for stolen export electrical appliances. They had also attended court for the appearances of the Peeping Tom and the abortionist, but both had pleaded guilty from the outset and they had been duly sentenced. Likewise it was looking like the Rose Blewitt case would be a simple guilty plea and she would perhaps receive a short sharp shock sentence together with some psychiatric help. The McEachen case was still being made ready for trial and wouldn't be tried for several months. Meanwhile, McEachen would remain on remand in Pentonville Prison.

Today the couple were attending the magistrate's court for the first appearance of an assault case. The court was located in South Woolwich on the opposite bank of the Thames and the pair had needed to walk through the foot tunnel which crossed under the river. Noah had spoken to the clerk of the court and ascertained that their alleged hard-man was well down the judges list of cases to be heard. This meant that they would be hanging around the court for hours on end. They had no other options, but to take a seat and await their turn.

Several simple cases came before the magistrates and were dealt with either with a guilty plea that resulted in a fine, or a not guilty plea with the outcome of either going back to jail on remand, or being released on bail.

The tenth case on the court list was for burglary. The accused came up from the cells below ground and stood in the dock. Meanwhile the alleged criminal's solicitor made himself known to the magistrates and pleaded not guilty on his client's behalf. Hazel and Noah were sitting at the back of the court gallery, neither of them paying attention to the case until Hazel happened to look up from her magazine.

Suddenly she dug Noah in the ribs. "Noah – look at the man in the dock," she whispered urgently. He looked up and studied the prisoner carefully. "Good God. It's Vic Noone."

"But according to Scotland Yard's records, he's supposed to have died two years ago," she said.

He was thinking furiously. "Hazel, you go call Andy Summers and ask him to come over here to the court. Meanwhile, I'll have a word with the court bailiff and see what this guy's name is. You can bet it won't be Vic Noone."

Summers arrived within the hour. Meanwhile, the prisoner, who appeared as Harry Ernest Roberts, was remanded in custody until his next court appearance. He would be going back to Brixton Prison in the paddy-wagon later this afternoon. Summers took formal statements from Hazel and Noah in which they stated that Roberts was the same man they knew as Vic Noone and that he had represented himself as the night-watchman at Thomas W Ward Ltd on the night that the safe had been broken into.

Andy Summers would make enquiries at Scotland Yard as to how this man could show up on their records as, not only dead, but be living under an alias. Summers wondered aloud if it were possible that Roberts'/Noone's fingerprints appeared on the Yard's files under two different names. He didn't hold out much hope of him being charged with the safe-blowing. Their evidence appeared to consist solely of identification by the two police officers. It could be argued by any half-clever legal counsel that his client was being identified after glimpsing the alleged safe-cracker for a matter of seconds in a pitch dark room with only the aid of a flashlight. He would also argue that the thief left no fingerprints and that the prosecution had no other evidence against his client, and so their case was flawed. "See what I mean?" said Andy. "We'd be ripped to shreds in court."

"Well, let's hope that he gets jailed for this burglary charge," said Hazel.

"I've just had a chat with the prosecution's counsel," said Andy, "and he's quietly confident that Roberts, or whatever his name is, will be doing a stretch of porridge for the burglary."

Noah was on foot patrol in North Woolwich for the first part of their shift whilst Hazel remained at the station typing up reports. He strolled aimlessly westwards along Woodman Street, the collar of his greatcoat pulled up to ward off the bitterly cold wind. He felt his ears and nose becoming numb. He looked forward to taking a refreshment break with a cup of sweet tea at George's Diner or perhaps a plate of pie and mash at Ryland's.

Suddenly a car pulled up beside him. It was big and black and looked powerful. With its flashy oversized tailfins, Noah identified it as an American model. The rear window slid down and a man leaned out – smiling a toothy grin. Noah didn't know him from Adam.

"Good morning, constable. What awful weather. You must be frozen." He was well dressed in a pin-striped suit and spoke with a foreign accent. His black hair was combed straight back and appeared to use a generous quantity of Brylcreem. He held a black Malacca walking cane with an intricately decorated silver head-piece.

The man handed a cardboard box out the window and Noah automatically, without thinking, took it from him.

"Enjoy your lunch," said the man.

Noah began to ask his name, but the man tapped the window with the cane and the driver took off. Within seconds the limousine had disappeared into an adjoining street. Mystified, Noah opened the box. Inside, wrapped in aluminium foil, was a seafood sandwich together with a selection of appetisers and a bottle of beer. Underneath the sandwich he found a business card. The name on the card said, Anthony Montana – General dealer.

Noah described the incident in a written report that landed on Inspector Maitland's desk. Maitland had read the account of Noah and Hazel's visit to the brothel, so he was already aware of the Montana brothers and their activities. This latest information instantly grabbed his interest. If the Montana's were attempting to set up shop here in North Woolwich, then they were in for a surprise. He made a phone call to a friend at Scotland Yard.

Noah got a call to go see Andy Summers in the CID office. He knocked and walked in. Summers was sat talking to a dark haired man in his early thirties. Andy made the introductions. "This is Detective Constable Dave Humphreys from the Flying Squad. He's been temporarily transferred here to North Woolwich to give assistance with the Montana problem." Humphreys leaned over and shook hands. He was dressed in a smart navy blue suit and tie with a button-down collar.

Noah pulled up a chair. "Have you had many dealings with the Montanas?"

Humphreys grinned. "We've been acquainted for a number of years. We do our best to make their lives a misery and in return they hate our guts." Noah noticed that Humphreys had a distinct East London accent.

"How do you manage to upset them?" he asked.

"We harass them any way we can. One time, we found one of the Montana gorillas walking across a busy road in Whitechapel, so we gave him a tug and arrested him for jay-walking. We threw him into a cell for the afternoon, until their lawyer came and bailed him out." He threw back his head and laughed. "Another time - just for the hell of it - we arrested one of the enforcers for wearing odd socks." Humphreys was laughing uncontrollably now, with tears of hilarity running down his cheeks. "We tossed him into the back of our car and took him for a leisurely drive out into the countryside. Then we made him walk home from Hertfordshire. That's the God's honest truth. That'll teach 'em not to upset The Sweeney." Noah noticed that instead of using the official name of the Flying Squad, Humphreys used the cockney version. Flying Squad rhymed with Sweeney Todd which was then shortened simply to The Sweeney.

"So why have they moved from Whitechapel to Silvertown?" asked Noah, bringing the conversation back to the matter in hand.

"We like to fink it's because we made life too difficult for them in Whitechapel. They're mixed-up in some very serious stuff; prostitution, illegal betting, loan-sharking, fencing stolen goods, protection rackets, drugs, armed robbery and even murder."

"Murder?" queried Noah.

"Yeah," explained Humphreys. "There was a fella down in Whitechapel called Seamus Flynn. He and his crew ran the local rackets. Anyway, Flynn got convicted of theft and went away for a five stretch. While Flynn was sewing mailbags in Parkhurst, the Montanas took over his business and expanded it to include armed robbery and drugs. When Flynn unexpectedly got early release for good behaviour, he naturally wanted back what he thought was rightfully his. The Montanas didn't wanna give anyfink back and suddenly Seamus Flynn disappeared off the face of the Earth."

"So how do you suggest we get rid of them?" asked Andy.

"Why don't you do what we did? How about you raid their brothel for starters?" Humphreys looked serious. "Sometimes you've got to fight them with unusual methods and be as underhand as they are. This is a war and it ain't no good pussy-footing around."

Just before the hour of midnight, the residents of North Woolwich came out of their houses to see in the New Year. Even the youngsters were allowed to stay up late. Over at the Henley Arms, on the corner of Albert Road and Fernhill Street, the pub was doing a roaring trade and everyone was getting sloshed. A dozen underage kids were sat on the steps outside, whilst their mums and dads were inside drinking themselves stupid. Every so often the parents would bring out a glass of lemonade or a packet of crisps or an arrowroot biscuit.

Noah and Hazel stood outside the pub watching the events. He had been present for the dawning of two New Years Eve's whilst stationed in London, but this was Hazel's first since joining the force. All her previous New Years had been celebrated in the quiet village of Witney in Oxfordshire.

But now, as midnight approached, the pub emptied out and everyone came outside to mill around on the pavement. Someone switched their wireless on and turned the volume up to maximum, and the whole street could hear the sound of Big Ben chiming her bells to welcome in the New Year. The street went wild. Everyone was shaking hands and hugging and kissing their neighbours and wives and husbands and sweethearts. Hazel slid her arms around his neck and her soft lips found his. She didn't care who saw them. "Happy New Year, darling," she whispered.

From up and down the street, and from every street in the east end of London, residents grabbed a pair of dustbin lids and slammed them together, making the most awful cacophony of noise. Others brought saucepans and lids from their kitchens and smashed them together to add to the noise. Then, from every ship that was berthed in the Royal Docks and up and down the River Thames, each brought in the New Year by sounding their steam horns and sirens for over ten minutes. Some horns were louder than others, but each ship seemed intent on outdoing their neighbouring vessel.

The couple found themselves linking hands to join a circle of revellers as they sang Auld Lang Syne. And as the songs final notes faded away, Noah found himself on the receiving end of numerous kisses from the ladies of Fernhill Street. One strapping blonde lady grasped his head between her hands and gave him a long and deep kiss. "Gaw'd bless ya, darlin," she giggled. In the raucous hullabaloo he found that he'd become separated from his police helmet and discovered it on the head of a woman dancing a rumba down the centre of the street.

Moments later someone slid their arm around Noah's waist, and he found himself in a conga line that snaked haphazardly along the street. In the general excitement, Noah had lost sight of Hazel. He swivelled his head around and spotted her twenty yards further back on the end of the conga line. She was laughing and having a great time.

On a cold afternoon in early January, Andy Summers and several beat coppers raided the house in Auberon Street. Dave Humphreys was on-hand to offer practical advice. Over the years he'd carried out dozens of house raids and his suggestions were invaluable.

Due to Elsie Turpin's eagle-eyed reconnaissance, they knew they would find four customers inside. This was good news. Not only would they arrest Ingrid for keeping a brothel, but they'd charge the young women with prostitution, and scoop-up the customers at the same time.

Andy rang the bell. The door was opened by Ingrid and her face dropped as soon as she saw the gaggle of coppers on her doorstep. Dave Humphreys was the first over the threshold. As he stepped past Ingrid he thrust a copy of the search warrant into her hand. "There you go, my love, here's summfink for you to read." Suddenly the house was filled with policemen who thoroughly searched each room. Frantic voices could be heard from the upstairs bedrooms as burly coppers interrupted the girl's afternoon assignations with their 'boyfriends.' One gentleman, who was found naked in bed with a female, was asked to state her name for the record. He hadn't the foggiest idea. "I've paid good money for a shag. I wanna refund," he complained bitterly. Each of the customers was asked the same question regarding their girl's names. They didn't have a clue and shook their heads. That put paid to Ingrid's boyfriend/girlfriend scenario.

Meanwhile, all across the parish and as far afield as Canning Town, the police were asking the area's shopkeepers and businesses if they had received visits from men demanding money for 'protection insurance.' Several had stated that they had recently been approached by menacing characters who had made it plain that if they failed to pay insurance, then they were certain to have problems. After suffering setbacks in Whitechapel, the Montana brothers were attempting to rebuild their empire. North Woolwich CID, with help from The Sweeny, intended to stop them in their tracks.

At one such establishment, a printing firm on the Victoria Dock Road, the owner had been left in no doubt that he must pay insurance, or else the outcome would be dire. They would be back to collect the first 'premium' on Thursday.

Just after midday Thursday, two heavily built men dressed in wide-awake suits entered the premises and made their way to the office. The firm's owner, on police advice, had made himself scarce in the storeroom.

At his desk sat Andy Summers.

The two men barged into the office. "Where's the guv'nor?" they demanded.

Summers looked up. "He's not at work today. I'm his son. What can I do for you?"

They exchanged uncertain glances, but nevertheless presented an intimidating presence. "We're here to collect the insurance money," said the tallest man. "We ain't here to bugger about. Where is it?"

Summers adopted a naive and innocent countenance. "You must be mistaken. We already have liability insurance. Why would we need extra cover? What's the name of your insurance company?"

The big enforcer's face and neck turned an ugly red. He swept a great pile of paperwork from the desk. "Don't get funny with us, sunshine, or I'll rearrange your face for you. Understood?"

"I understand perfectly," said Summers, holding up his warrant card. "And you two are under arrest for attempted extortion. Understood?"

He looked past them to the printing factory floor. Through the plate glass windows several officers were rushing to assist with the arrest.

That same afternoon Hazel was writing up crime reports in the reception area at North Woolwich nick. Noah hated paperwork with a vengeance, but she was intelligent enough to recognise that formalities were a necessary evil and that official procedures had to be complied with. Therefore she always volunteered to make out their reports. Anyway, whilst her handwriting was neat and precise, Noah's scrawl looked like a drunken baboon had attacked it with a meat-cleaver

A well dressed man entered the police station and presented himself at the reception desk. He was in his early forties with a suntanned face and an unruly mop of fair hair.

Hazel got up from her desk. "Good afternoon. Can I help you?"

He flashed a devastating smile. "Hello, my name's Eugene Chamberlain. I'm a solicitor and I'm here to represent my clients, Mister Foreman and Mister Hill. I understand they're being held in custody?"

The penny dropped and she realised he was referring to the two mobsters who were presently languishing in cells 2 and 7.

An hour later, after bail terms had been guaranteed, the enforcers walked free. Eugene Chamberlain was the same solicitor who'd represented Ingrid and her girls in the matter of keeping a brothel.

All across K division the police were harassing the Montana's business. As soon as the police discovered a brothel, they would raid it. If they detected illegal betting, it was shut down. The outfit's hard men were wary of collecting insurance premiums in case they were met by a bunch of coppers, and the incidence of robbery had dropped dramatically. The police were hitting them hard and their empire was in disarray.

The Montana's activities reduced to a trickle and they lay low to lick their wounds. Meanwhile, the policemen of North Woolwich were in seventh heaven. Their continued success had the effect of boosting the officers' morale and some had nicknamed themselves 'Maitland's Marauders.' Noah felt the lift in the spirits of every officer at the nick as they went about their duties with a smile and a spring in their step. Even Fag-Ash Lil had a permanent grin stitched upon her face. This felt like real crime-fighting.

Noah and Hazel were walking leisurely along Woodman Street, idly watching the rag n' bone man as he fed his horse a meal of oats from a nosebag. His cart was piled high with various metal goods which he would later sell to a scrap metal merchant. It was a hard existence and mostly one where he barely scraped a precarious living. An elderly resident came out from his house brandishing a bucket and shovel to collect the pile of dung which the horse had just deposited in a steaming mound. Horse dung was prized by gardeners for use as compost for their rose bushes.

A limousine glided to a stop beside them. Noah recognised it instantly. The rear window slid down and Tony Montana leaned out. This time he wasn't smiling.

"Constable Sheppard, the last time we met, I tried to be friendly towards you. I recall that I even gave you a small gift. And how do you repay my kindness? You and your colleagues have carried out many intrusions at the houses that my brother and I own and you have upset my tenants. Unless this interference into my business affairs ceases, then I shall look upon your activities as tantamount to hostile action and I shall hold you responsible. Understood?"

Noah was about to remind him that he was talking in a threatening manner to an officer of the law, when Montana smiled at Hazel and said, "What a pretty companion you have. Let us hope that no accident should befall her." He tapped the window with the tip of his cane and the car roared off with a screech from its tyres.

It was early afternoon when a car pulled up outside Barclay's Bank in East Ham High Street. Three men got out and walked briskly into the bank, pulling balaclavas down over their heads. The driver kept the motor running.

Across the street, above a shoe repair shop, six members of the Flying Squad kept watch. One of them, Detective Inspector David Hulson, looked at his watch. He spoke into a walkie-talkie handset. "Cars move in now. Box him in." He turned to his colleagues. "Okay, let's go. We'll get 'em as them come out the bank with the cash."

As they ran across the road, two unmarked cars, which had been parked out of sight, roared along the street and swung across the front and rear of the getaway car. In the same instant they heard the unmistakable sound of a single gunfire shot from within the bank. Seconds later the three villains ran out of the bank carrying bags stuffed with banknotes, and holding sawn-off shotguns. They got the surprise of their lives to find a squad of armed coppers waiting for them on the pavement. They'd been caught red-handed by The Sweeney.

Whilst the men were wrestled to the ground and cuffed, Hulson ran into the bank. It was pandemonium inside. Bank staff and customers were screaming and crying amid a strong acrid smell of cartridge propellant and wisps of white smoke hung in the air. Behind the counter, a man - presumably a bank cashier – lay racked with pain. He'd been shot in the upper leg and a pool of blood spread across the floor. Hulson grabbed a phone and called an ambulance.

Within the hour the wounded man had been taken to hospital for emergency treatment. He had lost a lot of blood and it was touch and go whether he would survive. Local police had been drafted in to tie up any loose ends and take statements from those involved.

The four bank robbers had been transported to North Woolwich police station for processing and questioning. The four men were all notorious villains and were well known to the police. Each of them had long criminal careers and had served time in a variety of prisons.

In an interview room, one of the men, Ronnie Stack, was nervous. His crew had been caught bang-to-rights with bags full of cash, so he was under no illusions that he would be sentenced to a lengthy stretch of porridge. On the opposite side of the desk, Big Dave Hulson, as he was known throughout the criminal fraternity, looked up and smiled. Hulson originated from Glasgow and his gruff manner of speaking was interspersed with a broad Scottish accent. "Well Ronnie, you've been a bit of a scallywag and landed yourself in a pickle, haven't you?" he said pleasantly. "Taking your previous record into account, I would guess that you'll be going down for a twenty to twenty five year stretch for armed robbery and attempted murder. If that bank cashier croaks it, then you might end up swinging from a rope."

"It wasn't me that shot him – honest!"

Hulson shook his head. "The law doesn't differentiate between who actually pulled the trigger. In English law there is a principle of common purpose in which you would be found guilty of a party to murder by joint enterprise. Cast your mind back to the Derek Bentley case."

Three years previously, in 1952, two young men, Christopher Craig and Derek Bentley, were carrying out a burglary in Croydon when the police turned up in force. Craig was armed with a revolver. He fired several shots, killing a police constable. They were promptly captured.

At their trial, Craig, aged 16, who had fired the shots, was deemed to be a minor and couldn't legally be sentenced to death. Bentley was 19 years old and consequently old enough to take responsibility for his actions. The case became a controversial issue when he was hanged at Wandsworth Prison six weeks later. Ronnie Stack's shoulders slumped in defeat as he realised that he could be facing execution.

Hulson changed the subject. "According to my information, you and your missus have recently been blessed with the arrival of a wee baby boy?"

Ronnie nodded, but remained silent, wondering where this line of questioning was leading.

Hulson rested his chin upon his intertwined fingers and smiled. "Even if they only convict you of armed robbery, I should imagine your kid will have left school by the time they let you out."

Stack knew that Hulson was trying to provoke him, but he recognised that the detective's statement was absolutely correct. He could imagine himself as an elderly man, with a face lined by years of regret and still banged up in Parkhurst Prison.

"However, not all is lost," continued Hulson confidently. "You'll be pleased to know that there's a way in which you can earn some brownie points with the judge and get yourself a much shorter sentence."

"How's that?" asked Ronnie eagerly. He was like a drowning man scrabbling for a lifebuoy."

"It's simple. You just tell me who provided the shotguns and who gave the go-ahead for the job." Hulson was aware that Ronnie's crew would have had to ask the Montana's permission to carry out the raid upon their turf and that the Montanas would have demanded a percentage of the proceeds. It was the way things were done within the criminal fraternity. You didn't carry out armed robberies within someone else's territory without asking beforehand. It was simply good manners.

What Hulson required was a signed statement from Ronnie Stack regarding the Montana's involvement. He lit a cigarette and relaxed as his prisoner sat weighing up his options – which were few in number.

Minutes later, as the inspector was emphasizing how Ronnie's family would suffer - whilst he would be sewing mailbags - a uniformed officer entered the room and whispered into his ear.

Hulson grinned. "Ronnie, I've just received good news. We've had a call from the forensics lab. They've dusted the shotguns for prints and come up with two perfect matches - yours and Tony Montana's."

Fifteen minutes later Ronnie Stack was signing a statement which firmly implicated both Tony and Joey Montana in multiple crimes.

The Montana brothers were sat in the back bar of the Connaught Tavern discussing the disastrous Barclays Bank raid. Their two minders stood guard nearby. So as to afford them some privacy, the bar had been cleared of other patrons. The minders had seen to that.

Joey Montana began the conversation. "We should begin making plans to scarper. If the bank teller should die, and we are implicated, we would be in deep trouble." Joey was usually the most level headed of the two and would deliberate any problem with a considered and logical approach.

"But what about our business?" said Tony. "It's taken us years to build it up. We cannot just walk away and let someone take it over."

Joey was surprised that his brother would even utter such an idiotic statement. "Perhaps you would rather be sewing mailbags, or even swinging from the end of a noose?"

"Okay," said Tony holding up his hands in surrender. "What do you suggest?"

"I recommend that we move overseas as quickly as possible. If Stack or his crew should talk, then The Sweeney will be searching for us. I think we ought to go abroad until the dust has settled, perhaps live in Spain for a while."

"How long do you think.......?"

Suddenly, one of the minders, who was keeping watch at the window, shouted out, "Boss, the Old Bill's turned up. They're getting outta their cars. You'd better make a run for it."

Without a second's thought, Joey was racing out the back door of the pub. He made for the courtyard at the rear where his car and driver were waiting. As he reached the wooden steps that led down to ground level, he swivelled his head around in search of his brother, who should have been right behind him. However, Tony was much too slow and Joey saw a copper's hand make a grab for his collar and Tony was jerked off his feet and unceremoniously dumped onto his arse. There was nothing Joey could do. He kept running. He wrenched open the car door. He screamed at his driver. "Quick, start the engine. Get outta here."

Later that day Josef Montana's limousine was parked beside a lonely track on Wanstead Flats. He sat in the back, brooding over what seemed to be an insoluble problem. His brother Anthony had been arrested by the police in connection with the bank raid in East Ham and they had him in custody at North Woolwich police station.

Joey lit a cigarette and attempted to solve their many problems. If Ronnie Stack – whose gang had hit Barclay's Bank in East Ham – should decide to grass them up to the cops, then their goose was cooked.

They had further problems to contend with. The Lloyds Bank robbery in Canning Town had unravelled when the revolver used in the raid was found at the home of George Fowler. Joey didn't know Fowler, but the man had promptly spilled the beans to the Sweeney and implicated Billy McKane and his crew who had actually carried out the job. McKane, of course, had sought the permission of Anthony and himself, because the robbery was to take place on their turf and the Montana organisation would be supplying the gun. The brothers would also be laundering the cash via their solicitor who would buy and sell stocks and shares on McKane's behalf. For this service the McKane crew would be charged 40% of the proceeds.

But now Joey was a very worried man. If Billy McKane or any of his crew should blab to the Sweeney in exchange for a softer sentence, then he and Anthony's days would be numbered. The atmosphere was getting too hot. It was time to leave London and find somewhere less precarious.

Their solicitor, Eugene Chamberlain, had been present when his brother had been interviewed by Inspector Hulson, and had reported that, to each question Anthony had answered, "No comment." That was good news.

However, things got worse, reported Chamberlain. Anthony had stupidly left a single fingerprint on the barrel of a gun which had been supplied to the Stacks outfit, and was facing charges of accessory to armed robbery. If the Barclays Bank cashier should die from his wounds, and it could be proven that he and Anthony had supplied the weapons, then they could potentially be facing charges of accessory to murder. It was a capital offence and carried the death penalty.

The lawyer had stated that, due to the severity of the charges, the chances of his brother being granted bail were slim. Joey had shouted and screamed at Chamberlain, "You're supposed to be our damn lawyer. We pay you handsomely to be our legal representative. So start earning your money and get my brother out on bail." But all efforts at securing Anthony's liberty had failed. Things weren't looking good. He would have to devise a plan to get him free. But what? To do nothing wasn't an option.

His mind drifted back to their boyhood days; being raised by their father in the backstreets of the Maltese capital of Valletta. Their father had brought them up to be tough strong-willed boys. He taught them to fight hard for whatever they wanted – because no one would simply hand it to them. He remembered his papa's advice. 'Always let your opponent think he's getting the better of you – then hit him with the unexpected.'

Even as young boys, he and Anthony had been staunch and devoted brothers; rarely out of each other's sight as they cruised the streets of Valletta looking for easy pickings. However, their father had insisted that they regularly attend school and gain an education. "It's no good making lots of money if you haven't got the brain to count it," he had wisely advised. Although there was just eighteen months separating them in age, he was aware that he and Anthony were as different in character and temperament as chalk and cheese. Whilst he judged himself to be intelligent and methodical in his approach, Anthony was more headstrong and didn't always think a problem though to its conclusion. He smiled fondly. His brother imagined himself as something of a fashionable dandy, with his smart suits, hand-made Italian shoes and that ridiculous Malacca cane. But even taking into account Anthony's shortcomings, he loved his sibling as if they were conjoined twins.

Anthony and he owned a sprawling ranch-style house on three acres of prime land on the edge of Epping Forest, yet he daren't set foot in the place because The Sweeney would surely be keeping a watch on the property.

He caught sight of himself in the car's rear-view mirror. The face that stared back looked tired and drawn, as if he were a survivor from some wartime transit camp. His straggly hair hung down in rat's tails and was becoming even greyer compared to the last time he looked. He badly needed a shave and a change of clothes.

He would use his father's wise words to get the better of the Metropolitan Police and secure his brother's freedom. But first he needed to acquire something with which to apply pressure; something to exchange perhaps. He thought hard. What single item, he asked himself, would force their hand and compel them to set his brother free?

Suddenly, Josef Montana had an inspiration and a plan began to formulate in his mind. However, his ordinarily sharp intellect was clouded by his raw need, whatever the consequences, to liberate his brother. On this rare occasion, Josef Montana wasn't thinking straight and his powers of reasoning had flown out the window. His usual logical thought processes had let him down and his reasoning couldn't progress further than his single notion that, whatever the cost, he must rescue Anthony.

The evening sky was as dark as a bailiff's heart as the big limousine cruised around Silvertown looking for a likely victim. In the front seats sat two of the Montana's powerfully built minders, Jake Moss and Jimmy the

Jock. In the back, separated by a glass partition was Josef Montana. The gangland boss had convinced himself that he could force the police to capitulate into setting free his brother in exchange for a hostage. All he needed now was a hostage to take prisoner. Almost anyone would be a suitable candidate, although he discounted elderly pensioners or disabled people, who would perhaps require special treatment and medications.

Up front in the passenger seat Jimmy whispered to his companion. "I dinnae think this is a good idea, Jake. I dinnae mind givin' some South London hard man a good pastin' if needs be, but the boss is askin' us to strong-arm civilians. It ain't right."

Jake stared straight ahead as he slowly drove eastwards along Newland Street. To their left was the tall creosoted dock fence and to their right was the stark outline of another wartime bombsite. "Yeah, I don't like it any more than you do, Jimmy, but at the end of the day, he's paying our wages." Suddenly the glass screen slid back. "Slow down," barked Montana. "Who are those people standing beneath the streetlight?" He pointed at two individuals in the adjoining street.

"It's just a couple of young lads," answered Jake.

Josef Montana's mind was whirring like a gyroscope – frantically tallying up the odds and probabilities of a child serving as a useful hostage. Obviously a child would need to be treated gently, and definitely not with any rough treatment. One couldn't simply lock the boy in a secure room. A kid would need to be fed and kept entertained. But on the plus side, his kidnap should create the maximum amount of sympathy for the boy's anxious parents and engender a willingness by the police to exchange Anthony as a means to securing the boy's liberty. Josef Montana made a quick decision. "That's our target. Go snatch one of them."

They started to quibble. "But boss, we can't just...."

"Do as you're told," screamed Montana. "Go snatch one of those kids."

Out of sight, in Tate Road, Noah and Hazel were keeping an eye out for the two lads they'd spotted playing at 'Knock Down Ginger.' The boys had scarpered around the corner as soon as they'd spotted the officers and had made off towards Newland Street. Noah wasn't about to make a strenuous effort to apprehend them; after all, small boys have been knocking on doors and running away since time immemorial. Noah could even remember playing the game himself.

The police officers turned the corner by the Royal Albert pub and spotted the boys up ahead beneath a streetlight. They appeared to be about nine or ten years old. Noah glanced at his wristwatch. It said just after 7pm. It was about time for the boys to be home indoors.

Suddenly a car screeched to a stop beside them and two men got out.

Hazel heard them shout something unintelligible and the smallest of the boys was literally scooped off his feet and dumped unceremoniously into the rear of the car. The vehicle was clearly an American automobile with white-wall tyres and tailfins. Within seconds the car had made off at high speed.

Noah and Hazel ran towards the streetlight. The second boy stood almost trance-like as tears ran down his cheeks. He was traumatised by what had occurred and his chest heaved with sobbing.
Hazel put a comforting arm around him. "Are you alright?" she asked. He nodded.
"What's your name, son?" asked Noah.
"Kenny Walker," the boy whispered. He was clearly frightened.
"Did you know the men who just took your friend away, Kenny?" he asked. The boy shook his head.
"What's the name of your friend?" asked Hazel.
"It's Billy Baldwin. He lives in Muir Street."
Hazel whispered, "Jeezus Noah, that's Ronnie Baldwin's boy who nicked the Mars Bars last year." They were aware that Ronnie was presently on-duty patrolling his beat in the Custom House district.
"Where do you live, Kenny?" asked Noah. The boy also lived in Muir Street, a few houses away from the Baldwin's. Noah suggested that Hazel take him home whilst he finds a phone and calls the station. The abduction of the boy would be categorised as a major incident and he was keen to get the ball rolling.

The limousine drove just a few hundred yards and pulled up outside a house in Winifred Street. The houses were quiet and no one was outside in the street. Perfect. The boy's arms and legs had been bound with rope and he'd been rolled up inside a piece of carpet. A length of sticky tape had been sealed around his mouth. Whilst Montana opened the front door, Jimmy the Jock quickly carried the bundle inside and laid the boy onto the bed in an upstairs room.

Meanwhile, Jake Moss drove away from the scene. Any luxurious car parked in a residential street in North Woolwich would be sure to attract unwelcome attention. Joey Montana had given him orders to dump the car. He drove via the quiet back streets towards the bascule bridge that spanned the locks entrance to the King George V Docks. Going across the bridge, he motored just a mile along Manor Way until he found the track that led between the Tate & Lyle sports ground and the ancient Gallions Hotel. The path was deserted as he drove steadily over the rough terrain. Minutes later the track met the swirling waters of the river. He got out and checked that no one was around. Satisfied, he leaned through the window and put the car into gear. Slowly the car crept forward and he watched as the limo went over

the edge of the dock and splashed satisfyingly into the muddy waters of the River Thames.
Jake watched until the car had completely disappeared beneath the water, then trudged off towards the bus-stop to catch a ride back to Winifred Street.

Back in Tate Road police colleagues had turned up in force. Sergeant Ambrose arrived with Les Jones, Dave Roberts and George Cheeseman. Before leaving the station Ambrose had arranged for Inspector Maitland and Andy Summers, to be called in to assist. He'd already called the police station at Canning Town so they could set up a road block on the Silvertown Way. Likewise K division would do the same on Manor Way, the road leading off the peninsula that, in effect, formed an island. It was a long-shot, but Ambrose argued that any large American automobile would be easily spotted at this time of the night on the otherwise deserted roads.

The sergeant, accompanied by Hazel, went around to Kenny Walker's home in Muir Street to try to extract a decent description of the two men and the car. Young Kenny was clearly nervous of being questioned by police officers and was only able to tell them that the men, and likewise the car, had been big. Meanwhile Noah and the other officers had been knocking on doors of houses in Tate Road in the forlorn hope that someone may have seen the incident as they perhaps glanced from behind their net curtains; but of course, no one had seen anything.

Ambrose sent word for Ronnie Baldwin to be brought back from his beat in Custom House. The abduction of his son was obviously going to have an emotional impact and upset Ronnie badly. He had lost his wife to cancer last year, and now his boy's life was being threatened. Ambrose decided that he would grant Ronnie indefinite compassionate leave.

At the house in Winifred Street, Joey Montana was beginning to understand how difficult the task of keeping the boy contained would become. For starters the lad was constantly crying for his father as big fat tears ran down his cheeks and a rivulet of snot ran from his nose. Ordinarily he would have given a grown-up a slap around the chops and told him to be quiet, but of course, he couldn't treat a young boy in that fashion. He handed the kid a handkerchief.
"Are you hungry, boy?" The kid silently nodded. He was starving and hadn't had his tea. Montana stuffed some coins into Jimmy the Jock's hand and told him to go get portions of fish n' chips.
"What's your name, son?"
The boy looked up with innocent eyes. "My name's Billy Baldwin and I'm almost ten years old."
Montana was completely bewildered. Apart from when he was a youngster,

he had never had occasion to have a conversation with a young kid before. In his everyday life he usually gave out orders, and his employees or minions did whatever they were told. He couldn't quite get to grips with having to treat this innocent child with kid-gloves.

"Where do you live, Billy?"

"I live in Muir Street. I want my dad," the boy said plaintively.

"You'll have to wait a while, but we'll let him know that you're okay."

"When can I go home? I don't wanna stay here," the boy said.

He tried explaining the situation in the simplest of terms, so that the boy would understand. "I know you don't," he said, "but my brother, whose name is Anthony, is being held against his will. As soon as he's set free, then you'll be able to go home as well. Understand?"

"Who are the people who won't let your brother come home?" asked the lad.

Montana was beginning to wish he'd not taken the boy, but had instead targeted a grown up. An adult would at least understand that they were a hostage and he wouldn't need to constantly explain the situation.

Montana thought it best to stick to the truth, rather than get tied up in a bunch of lies with this kid. "They're policemen," he said.

"My dad's a policeman," announced Billy with a hint of pride in his voice.

Josef Montana was dumbstruck. The boy's pronouncement came as a bolt from the blue, and he wasn't sure whether the lad's father being a copper was helpful or detrimental to his plan. He'd give it some thought.

One thing was for sure. He was going to need some help with keeping the kid entertained. The last thing he wanted was the boy to get stroppy and throw a temper tantrum. He didn't think he could handle an outburst from some bolshie kid. He could imagine him screaming the house down and alerting neighbours that someone was in residence.

He had purchased this property several months ago after the last tenant, a woman, had committed an offence and had been sent to prison. He bought it for a bargain cash price and decided to leave it empty for the time being.

A few days ago, when he was planning this course of action, he had thought it was a stroke of genius on his part to use this empty residence, located just a stone's throw from where the abduction was to take place. The police would be expecting him to have fled to some far-flung bolthole and not remain right here within their midst. Now, with the boy presenting potential problems, he wasn't so sure it had been a good idea.

What he needed, he decided, was a woman to look after the boy. Women were far better at handling children than men. It came naturally to them. He smiled to himself as an idea surfaced in his mind. He knew exactly where he would find just the person he required.

Eugene Chamberlain leased an office in Aldgate. He had gained his law degree from Oxford University in the late 1940s, and apart from a short stint at a central London law firm, his sole clients thereafter were the Montana brothers. His work with the Montanas mostly comprised the purchase and conveyance of properties, buying stocks and bonds on their behalf, income tax matters – which primarily included income tax evasion - and representing them and their associates in courts of law. The Montana's employees – who were mostly local hard men - were mainly accused of small-time offences whereby an arm or some fingers may be broken, but he could usually make the matter disappear after a chat with the complainant and some money changing hands.

Chamberlain's phone rang. He picked up the handset and a familiar voice said, "Listen very carefully to what I have to say. My brother Anthony is being held by the police for no good reason. I wish you to inform the police that, if they do not set him free immediately, then the missing boy, Billy Baldwin, will disappear off the face of the Earth. Have you got that?"

The news of the missing boy had swept across the Docklands as the police operation had swung into action. The lawyer had even heard it broadcast on the radio. Chamberlain answered, "I'll pass on your message, but as your legal representative I have to advise you that you're in serious trouble. By abducting that little boy, you have not only perpetrated kidnap – which carries a potential life sentence, but you have lost any credibility that you otherwise may have had. I also have to advise you that if you persist in carrying out this kidnap, then I can no longer act as your solicitor."

Josef Montana was half expecting Chamberlain's gutless reaction, so he wasn't worried one way or the other. The lawyer could go to hell as far as he was concerned. However, he decided not to respond unpleasantly. He may require his services in the short term.

"Are you going to tell me where you are?" asked Chamberlain.

"It's better that you don't know," answered Montana.

"As your solicitor, whatever you divulge to me is treated in the strictest confidence."

"I understand, Eugene, but when the police ask you if you know my location, I don't want to put you into a position of having to lie to them. Therefore, it's better that you don't know."

They exchanged a few further pleasantries and Montana rang off.

Eugene Chamberlain sat for a few minutes giving some thought to his future. The Montana brothers were on their way out – and will probably spend a lengthy period behind bars. He would need to find new clients. It was such a pity, because the Montana business paid handsomely. His mouth turned down in disappointment. This lucrative period of charging them exorbitant fees may be over.

In a back room of the telephone exchange near Aldgate East tube station, two men sat at the switchboard, listening intently. The older man was an employee of the General Post Office and worked for their telecommunications division. He adjusted his earphones as he traced the incoming telephone call to the solicitor's office just three streets away.
The other man was a member of The Sweeney. He wrote down a summary of the dialogue, even though a tape deck was recording every word of the telephone conversation. Beside him was a copy of the Telephone Intercept Order signed by a Home Office minister.
As the call ended, the GPO man gave the thumbs up. He wrote down a phone number and looked up its location. "The call was made from a public telephone. The call box is located at the junction of Albert Road and Fernhill Street in North Woolwich." He extracted the tape reel from the recorder and handed it over to the police detective.
Minutes later, the man from The Sweeney leapt into a car and was driven at high speed to North Woolwich police station. His boss, Big Dave Hulson, would be eager to listen to the tape.

It was dark when Jake Moss knocked on the door of the house in Auberon Street. Ingrid answered the door. She was well acquainted with Jake and invited him inside.
"The police have been here," she told him. "They're looking for a missing kid. They had a look around then buggered off. What's going on?"
He decided it wasn't his job to enlighten her. "Boss man wants to see you. He says to bring a fresh change of clothes. Enough for a few days."
"What does he want? Where have I gotta go? What's it all about?" she asked.
Jake was non-committal. "You'll find out when you get there."
"What about this place?" she said, indicating the brothel. "Who's gonna run it?"
"Let one of the girls run it. C'mon, let's go."
She packed a bag, and minutes later, was accompanying him to the house in Winifred Street.

Inspector Hulson lit a cigarette as Maitland explained the measures he'd taken in relation to the abduction of Billy Baldwin and the manhunt for Joey Montana. Maitland poured tea into delicate porcelain cups and used silver sugar tongs to drop in a sugar cube. The two policemen were well acquainted from back in the day when they were lowly beat coppers in the Poplar and Whitechapel districts.

They finished listening to the tape. Hulson said, "Well Charles, it's all becoming clear. Joey Montana hasnae left North Woolwich. He must be holed-up somewhere nearby with the wee boy. My guess is that he's in a private residence."

Maitland nodded. "He must be somewhere near the telephone box. With everyone searching for him, he wouldn't want to be out walking the streets too much, would he?"

Hulson agreed. "He obviously doesn't have a telephone in the house. That's why he's had to resort to using a public call box. In any case, most houses which do have a telephone, have to share a party line. I cannot imagine Montana wanting his neighbours listening-in to his phone conversations."

Maitland said, "Montana must be crazy if he thinks we would let his brother walk free. Obviously our main objective must be to find young Billy Baldwin and rescue him, but we cannot even think of exchanging him for an offender." Hulson nodded. He said, "Charles, I suggest that your men make the local door-to-door enquiries. We need maximum publicity in the newspapers and on the radio."

"I agree," said Maitland. "I'll make the arrangements."

"Meanwhile," continued Hulson, "I'll get my fellas talking to the local villains. Usually they won't talk to the police, but none of them wants to be involved with anyone abducting bairns. We may get lucky."

"Good idea," agreed Maitland. "We'll bring in some extra coppers from other divisions to help out. I shall also put the word around in the local factories for them to keep their eyes and ears open for anything suspicious. We'll swamp the district with policemen."

Ingrid accompanied Jake into the back parlour of the house in Winifred Street. Her boss, Joey Montana, wearing his customary fancy brocade waistcoat, was sat beside the coal fire sharpening the blade of a knife with a small file. A skinny brown haired boy sat at the table leafing through an old magazine. When the police had searched the brothel, they'd made it plain exactly who they were looking for. This had to be him.

She pointed at Billy Baldwin. Her eyes hardened. She was livid. "Is that who I think it is?" she spat out.

Montana seemed unconcerned. "He will remain here until Anthony is released," he said calmly.

"Are you outta your mind?" she said. "Every copper in London is out looking for him."

Jimmy the Jock wasn't comfortable with kidnapping the kid. He waded-in with his thoughts. "She's right boss. Ah'm no tryin' to poot a dampener on things, but I dinnae think the police are ganna exchange Tony for the wee laddie."

Joey pointed the blade in the Scotsman's direction. "When I want your opinion, Jimmy, I'll ask for it. In the meantime, just do as you're told."

He turned back to Ingrid. "When my brother is freed, then I shall let him go home," said the crime-boss. "In the meantime I require you to look after the boy. Women are naturally better at caring for children."

She knew better than to go against Montana. He ruled his empire with a strict regime of fear, and the women working in his cat-houses were kept in line by the threat of being slashed with a blade. She backed down and wisely decided to comply with his orders.

"Has the boy been fed?" she asked.

"He had some fish n' chips last night."

She went across to the boy and pulled out a chair. "My name's Ingrid," she said. "What's yours?"

His innocent blue eyes looked up at her. "My name's Billy. Can I have something to eat?"

She squeezed his hand and smiled. "Let's see what we can find, shall we?" She rummaged through the pantry and found a fresh loaf and a jar of strawberry jam. She cut off three thick door-stoppers and put them on a plate. The boy ate them ravenously.

Ingrid wrinkled her nose. The boy smelt awful and needed a change of clothes. She suspected he'd had an accident in his underwear. "When was the last time you had a bath," she asked

"My dad usually gives me a bath every Friday night," said Billy. It wasn't unusual for Eastenders to bathe on just one night of the week.

"I think it's about time for you to have another bath night," she told him. She went outside and retrieved the tin bath from where it hung from a nail on the back wall.

Whilst the boy bathed before a roaring coal-fire, Ingrid took his underwear and washed it in the kitchen sink. The poor boy had clearly had an accident in his pants and the smell pervaded the room. Ingrid didn't have children of her own, but in a maternal way she felt sorry for the lad. It wasn't his fault. Joey had probably frightened him so much; he had shit himself in fear. She didn't have any clean underpants which he could wear, so she hung them above the mantelpiece where they would dry quickly.

Elsie Turpin's eagle eyes didn't miss much. She was in her upstairs back bedroom when she happened to gaze through the net curtains and spot something strange in the garden of a house directly opposite in Winifred

Street. The reason that Elsie found it odd was because smoke was wafting from the chimney and the tin bath that normally hung on the neighbouring back wall was missing. The house had previously been rented by Rose Blewitt; but since she had been convicted of abducting the Beavis baby some months ago, the house had lain vacant whilst Rose had served a short prison sentence, and the bath had consequently not been used. Elsie wondered if the landlord had rented out the house to new tenants. She resolved to find out.

Noah and Hazel ambled into Auberon Street. They knocked at the first house and spoke to the householder, a middle aged woman who wore a wrap-around pinafore and a head full of curlers. She was asked if she'd seen any sign of little Billy, but the woman shook her head.

On the opposite side of the street, Les Jones and another copper from East Ham were knocking at doors as they made enquiries. Across the length and breadth of the parish, policemen were searching for young Billy Baldwin. Beat bobbies from outlying districts had been drafted in to help with the search. Householders were being asked to search their garden sheds in case the lad had somehow escaped from his kidnappers and taken refuge in an outhouse. Yesterday Noah and Hazel had accompanied Inspector Maitland into the Tate & Lyle sugar refinery, where he had addressed hundreds of employees in the canteen and asked them to keep an eye out for the lad. Likewise at factories up and down the area, they had talked to employees in works canteens and on the factory floor – but all to no avail. No one had seen anything.

Noah knocked at Elsie Turpin's door. Elsie answered with a grin. "Hello you pair of lovebirds, how ya doing?"
Hazel looked at her sharply. "Mrs Turpin, how many times do I have to remind you? Constable Sheppard and I are simply work colleagues."
Elsie took a drag on her Woodbine. "Please yerself, luv. D'yew wanna cuppa tea?" They followed her inside and she made them comfortable in the parlour.
"Any news regardin' the boy?" she asked as she poured a brew. Virtually everyone in the neighbourhood had heard about Billy and the circumstances of his abduction by Joey Montana. They shook their heads.
Elsie indicated the brothel on the opposite side of the street. "At least they've had the decency to close for business, seeing as that Maltese crook's kidnapped Ronnie Baldwin's little boy."
Ronnie was well known in the area and Elsie had personally known him for years. "How's Ronnie doing? He must be worried sick about his boy."
They nodded. Baldwin had been granted indefinite compassionate leave and advised to stay at home on the off-chance that his son should unexpectedly

return home. Ronnie hadn't been idle. His every waking moment was taken up walking the streets and shouting out his son's name in the forlorn hope that Billy would answer.
Changing the subject, Elsie said, "Has Rose Blewitt been released from jail yet after snatching the Beavis' baby?" Rose Blewitt had been sentenced to a nine month prison sentence with a stipulation that she undergoes psychiatric treatment. Taking into account time off for good behaviour, she should soon be eligible for release on parole.
Noah wondered what had triggered the question. He frowned. "Why do you ask, Elsie?"
"I wondered if she's moved back into her old house in Winifred Street," she said, jerking her thumb in the direction of the neighbouring terrace of houses. "I noticed that it's been rented out, coz someone's definitely living there."
Hazel was equally mystified because, only yesterday, she had knocked at the door of No. 26 Winifred Street as part of a door-to-door sweep of the area. There had been no answer and the curtains were closed. "What makes you believe the house is occupied, Mrs Turpin?"
Elsie grinned. She was proud of her investigative skills. "Coz the tin bath, which usually hangs on the back wall, was missing yesterday, and now it's back in place. Also there's smoke from a coal fire coming outta the chimney pot."
Hazel rose from her chair and went to check it out from the rear kitchen window. She returned and nodded to Noah. "She's right. It's smoking like a kipper factory," she confirmed.

Noah and Hazel discussed this possible new lead in the search for Billy. It was a small coincidence that the house in Winifred Street, where Hazel had attempted to make enquiries, was in fact occupied by new tenants. There could be several reasons why no one had answered her knock yesterday. Perhaps the residents were at work or had gone shopping. Who knows?
They held a whispered discussion. Noah idly wondered if Inspector Maitland could obtain a search warrant for the property; but other than a roaming tin bath and a puff of chimney smoke, they had scant evidence to justify a warrant being issued.
Meanwhile, Elsie had been gazing through the net curtains. "That old tart from the brothel's just left the house," she announced. "She's with some bloke." The pair joined her at the window. Sure enough, Ingrid was leaving the premises accompanied by a well-built man. She was carrying a heavy shopping bag and walked quickly in the direction of the dock fence. "I wonder where she's going," Hazel idly speculated
"I'll soon find out. You stay here," said Elsie. She grabbed her coat and was

out the front door in pursuit. Hazel was dumbfounded at her nosiness. Elsie had elected herself as the areas self-imposed Nosy Parker and nothing was going to stop her quest for titbits of information.

Elsie returned within minutes. She had a triumphant grin on her face. "Just as we thought," she said. "She went into Rose Blewitt's old house – the one with the missing tin bath."

Billy Baldwin sat at the table, playing cards with Ingrid. He liked Ingrid. She was a nice lady. The three men who had snatched him sat around the blazing fire. The man who was their leader wasn't English. Billy didn't like him. He had a gaunt cruel face and constantly fiddled with a sharp knife. He was scary. His skin was the colour of tough leather and he spoke with a strange accent. He sounded foreign.

The other two men were big and ugly. One of them had a scar down one side of his cheek. He spoke with a Scottish accent. The leader called him Jimmy. Jimmy was okay. Last night he went out and bought portions of fish n' chips. They were delicious; but now he was hungry again. He didn't know the third man, but Jimmy had referred to him as Jake.

Billy wanted to go home, but the gang leader told him he couldn't go – not until the policemen let his brother Anthony go free. Billy desperately wanted to go home. He missed his dad. He wished his mum was still alive. If she was here, she would give him a big cuddle and tickle his ribs until tears of laughter ran down his cheeks. He wished she could come back.

"I wanna go to the toilet," he said to the man who was called Boss.

The man looked down his nose at him. "Can't you hold it until later?"

"I wanna go for a poo," explained Billy. "If I don't go soon, I'll shit myself."

The boss relented. "Okay son, but don't be all day." He gave Jimmy his instructions, "Take him to the toilet, but don't let him outta your sight."

Like all the houses in Woolwich, the toilet was located in the alleyway outside the kitchen door. Jimmy escorted him outside and held the toilet door open. The toilet was clean and consisted of a typical cast iron cistern with a pull-chain flush system. Billy went inside and sat on the seat. Jimmy closed the door. "Don't yae be takin' all day, wee man."

He could hear Jimmy the Jock loitering outside as he lit a cigarette. He gave it a few more minutes, and then called out. "Can you get some toilet paper please? There's no paper in here." He heard Jimmy grumble and go look for a fresh toilet roll from the kitchen cupboard. Quietly, Billy opened the door, and once outside, made a dash for the back wall like his life depended upon it. He shimmied over into the neighbouring garden of a house in Auberon Street, although he had no idea where he was. He heard Jimmy shout, "Hey you wee bastard, come back here. Git yer arse back here wee man, or I'll crush yer skull fer yer."

The boss-man came out into the garden. "Where's the boy?" Billy heard him say.

"He was in the lavvy an awent intae the hoose tae get the laddie some bog roll, an' he done a runner."

"Come back inside the house, Jimmy. No use in letting the whole world know about it."

After climbing into a neighbouring garden, Billy opened the back door and went inside. He heard voices coming from the front parlour. He walked into the room and was amazed to find two police officers chatting with the house-owner. They looked surprised to see him. He recognised them instantly. They were the same pair who had caught him nicking Mars Bars last year from the Co-op. He remembered that the kindly woman police officer was called Hazel.

He ran into her arms and she held him tightly. The terrifying ordeal he'd endured was over and now he felt safe. It was like being back in his mum's arms. Tears ran down Billy's cheeks and he began to cry.

"Shuush," she said soothingly. "It's all over now, Billy."

Meanwhile, Noah focused on the serious business of apprehending Josef Montana. "I'll go call Inspector Maitland. We need to get that house surrounded," he said, indicating Rose Blewitt's former home. He went out the door.

At the house in Winifred Street there was panic. With the boy having escaped, Montana no longer had any leverage to get his brother freed. In any event, in his heart of hearts he'd already recognised that the police would never allow Anthony to walk free, even if it was in exchange for a policeman's young son. He knew that he must give up any notion of helping his brother. Now it was time to scarper before a whole bunch of coppers come through the door. Having ordered Jake to dump the Chevrolet in the river, Josef Montana was without any means of transport and already he was regretting his decision.

Jake, Jimmy and Ingrid were gathered in the living room. "The police will arrive soon," he told them. "Let's get out of here. They'll be looking for four people, so I suggest we split up."

Once outside, they went different ways. The two henchmen - Jimmy the Jock and Jake Moss - walked together along Newland Street, somehow feeling safer together. They were arrested an hour later as they strolled along

Victoria Dock Road. Ingrid scarcely bothered to escape. She sauntered back to Auberon Street, where she would be among her friends and fellow residents of the brothel. As she arrived at the door, she was observed by Elsie Turpin and was picked up later that day.

Josef Montana had just one means of escape. He caught a bus which was bound for Canning Town. It proved to be a good decision, because even though the trolley-bus trundled over the cobble-stones at an excruciatingly slow speed, it arrived in Canning Town safely and without incident. He went into a telephone box near the railway station and put through a call to Eugene Chamberlain's number in Aldgate.

He didn't beat around the bush. "Eugene, I need you to gather together as much money as possible. The police will be looking for me and I'll need to leave the country. Therefore I'll require some funds. Go to the bank and get it. I will be at your office in one hour.
Chamberlain began to argue. "I can't lay my hands on much money straight away without giving 24 hours notice. The banks set strict limits on how much can be withdrawn from an account. I'll try my best, but it won't be much. I'll need some time to sell your stocks and bonds, Mister Montana. You could send me your address when you're settled in another country, and I'll get it to you."

Eugene Chamberlain smiled to himself. As the Montana brother's lawyer and treasurer, he was tasked with investing the proceeds of their crimes into untraceable accounts, the identity of which only he was privy. With the two Maltese brothers about to either go into prison or go on the run, he would have access to the lion's share of their money – which was considerable. He would, he decided, fob-off Joey Montana with a pittance and become a very rich man.

In the back room of the Post Office telephone exchange, the tape recorder listened in to the conversation whilst the caller's location was traced.

Meanwhile, back in Woolwich, Billy Baldwin was the hero of the hour for using his initiative and escaping from Montana's gang over the garden wall. He was currently sat in Elsie's front parlour eating thick slices of bread n' dripping. A car pulled up outside and Elsie looked through the net curtains to check. "Looks like your boss just turned up," she announced. She answered the rap on the door-knocker. Andy Summers was accompanied by Inspector Maitland. She peered out into the street and was pleased to note that a crowd of neighbours had begun to gather. She was delighted, because a visit from a senior police officer was bound to enhance her reputation and standing in the community.
She led them into the parlour. The inspector saw young Billy and had a

satisfied grin on his face. He shook hands all round. "Well done," he said. "You've done an excellent job."

Noah introduced Charles Maitland to Elsie and explained that, if it hadn't been for her eagle-eyed observations regarding the chimney smoke and tin bath, then this case may have turned out very differently. "That's wonderful," said Maitland, shaking her hand again. "I wish that every resident was as observant as you are Mrs Turpin. You're a credit to the community"

Elsie was grinning like a Cheshire cat at such rapturous praise. She gave him the benefit of an exaggerated wink and laughed out loud. "You're welcome, Charlie. Anytime you need to know what's going on, then just pop around," she said.

Maitland took her exaggerated friendliness in his stride. "Well now, perhaps we'd better get young Billy home to his father. As far as I'm aware, he doesn't yet know he's safe." Maitland suggested that they take him home in the car. He wanted Noah and Hazel to accompany them.

Outside in the street the crowd had swollen with inquisitive neighbours. They were about to drive off. Billy was sat in the back of the car between Hazel and Noah, whilst Maitland was up front with Summers. Suddenly the rear door was yanked open and Elsie somehow squeezed in beside them. "Ya didn't fink you were gonna go without me, did ya?"

Inspector Hulson, still at North Woolwich with his crew, received the call over his car radio regarding Joey Montana's phone call and gathered his crew together to brief them. "We'll keep Chamberlain's office under surveillance and arrest Joey as he comes out. Hopefully he'll have a sizeable amount of cash about his person. Then I'll also be able to arrest Chamberlain for laundering the proceeds of crime. All understood?" His men nodded and made ready to go apprehend Josef Montana.

Outside Ronnie Baldwin's house in Muir Street, a sizeable crowd had gathered. The boy had been safely returned to his dad and the atmosphere inside was ecstatic as Ronnie protectively held his son tightly in his arms. Maitland, together with Noah and Hazel were gathered in the small front parlour, whilst Elsie stayed outside amongst the crowd as she basked in the knowledge that she had played no small part in Billy Baldwin's freedom.

Hulson's car swung into the street and screeched to a halt outside Ronnie's house. Hulson ran inside and quickly brought Maitland up to date on Montana's intercepted phone call. "I'd like to take some uniformed officers with me. Can I borrow Sheppard and Leggett?" Several years ago, at the trial of a particularly violent hard-man on charges of assaulting one of his men, the defence lawyer had argued that his client had been unaware that

the person dressed in a grey suit was a police officer and that his client was simply defending himself from a random attack. After that debacle, Hulson always liked to have a uniformed officer present at the arrest. In any event they'd had the most recent contact with the Montanas.
"No problem old boy," said Maitland. He turned to Noah. "You two go help out Inspector Hulson. You'll be under his orders for the time being."
Events moved rapidly. Within minutes Noah and Hazel were riding with Hulson in his Wolseley unmarked car into central London. The inspector drove fast and furious as he led a convoy of his crew towards Aldgate.

In London, in a side street near Aldgate tube station, Eugene Chamberlain sat at his office desk. He heard the stairs creak as someone came up to his office. He knew it would be Joey Montana. The Maltese crime boss could be an explosive and violent individual whose volatile mood swings were legendary. The lawyer was scared stiff. The door opened and Montana came into the room.
"I hope you have a substantial amount of money to give me," he said coldly, "Otherwise you'll have a problem."
Within the past hour, Chamberlain had indeed been to the bank and had withdrawn a substantial amount of money. He had intended to fob-off Joey with mere peanuts and keep the rest. But now, with Montana standing there looking intimidating, he didn't feel so brave. "Erm, I wasn't able to withdraw as much cash as I would have liked, Joey. The bank has limits I'm afraid. I could only manage £70." He began to count out the money onto his desk.
"Do you take me for a fool?" said Montana in a cold menacing voice. "My brother and I have trusted you with our financial affairs for many years, and now you attempt to cheat me." He whipped out a knife and held it against the lawyer's neck. The pearl handled knife, with a six-inch serrated blade, had been a 15th birthday present from his father. With his free hand he delved into Chamberlain's pockets and quickly discovered the missing sum of money. Eugene broke out in a sweat. He could feel the blade of the knife against his carotid artery.
"Where's the rest of my money?" screamed Joey.
Eugene could feel the blade pressing into his skin. He began to stutter. "There's no more money here, Joey. Everything's in the bank or in stocks and shares. I'll need more time to sell them through a stockbroker."
Joey Montana whispered into his ear. "You're a lying cheating sonofabitch. You just ran outta time." He drew the blade in a slashing motion across the lawyer's neck and a great gout of dark red blood gushed onto the desk. The

lawyer collapsed to the floor as copious pools of blood soaked into the carpet. Eugene Chamberlain's eyes closed as he took his last breath and lay still.

Inspector Hulson, together with Noah and Hazel and his Sweeney crew were parked outside in three unmarked cars when Josef Montana burst out of the building. Judging by his wild-eyed appearance and a sizeable bloodstain on his jacket, Hulson immediately knew that something serious had occurred. He began to get out the car, but the Maltese gangster spotted the welcoming committee and made a run for it. Hulson was surprised at the speed with which he could move, because within seconds the gang boss had put a respectable distance between himself and The Sweeney. Without warning, Noah and Hazel leapt out and began to give chase.

Hulson made a quick decision. He turned to his deputy, Detective Sergeant Eric Oliver. "Eric, go check out Chamberlain. Judging by the amount of blood on Montana's clothes, he might be in a bad way. Let me know the outcome when you can."

By now, Montana was 200 yards away and disappearing amongst the crowds of office workers thronging the pavements. Hulson could see the two uniformed constables chasing after him and closing the distance. Hulson and the remaining two detective constables climbed back into the car. "He's heading towards Leadenhall Street. Get after him. Put your foot down."

They sighted Montana as he attempted to merge into the crowd near Holy Trinity Church, but he spotted them and disappeared into the nearby maze of narrow streets and ancient alleyways. Hulson and his crew frantically searched, but Montana had vanished into thin air. "I think he's heading towards the river," observed Hulson as they hunted through the narrow cobble-stoned side-streets.

Meanwhile, A half mile away, Josef Montana had made good progress. He had no idea where he was headed, but simply needed to put some distance between himself and The Sweeney. He seemed to have shaken off the two uniformed coppers, but he was tired and gasping for breath. He walked under the raised viaduct of Fenchurch Street Station and found a small park located between The Tower of London and the Royal Mint. He was exhausted. He sat upon a wooden bench in this quiet oasis, whilst all around him the roads were clogged with heavy traffic whizzing to and fro.

Any thoughts of liberating his brother from police custody were now forgotten as he focused on escape. He was well-acquainted with Inspector Dave Hulson. The Scottish policeman had tried to shut down his illegal operations many times in the past; all without success. The Sweeney had been only partially successful in closing down his criminal empire in Whitechapel, but he and Anthony had simply moved their business into the docklands of Silvertown.

He took the sharp bladed knife from his pocket and slid it into his sock, then stuffed his bloodstained jacket into a nearby litter bin. He dragged himself off the park bench and began making towards the river, subconsciously wondering if he could escape aboard a boat or hide onboard a ship. He was walking along the approach road to Tower Bridge. He was so tired that he could barely drag one foot in front of the other. To his left was Saint Catherine's Dock; which as usual was busy with the loading and discharge of ocean-going ships and coasters. Across the road sat the commanding citadel of the Tower of London, scene of many beheadings and executions of traitors.

Two hundred yards away, Noah and Hazel had lost their quarry and were frantically searching down the maze of side streets. Hazel stopped several office workers to ask if they'd spotted anyone with Montana's description; especially anyone wearing bloodstained clothing, but each of them shook their heads and went on their way.
"Noah, we'll be able to cover more ground if we split up. I'll dive down this street and head towards the river. What do you think?"
"Okay my love. That makes sense, but don't take any risks."

Hazel searched the narrow cobbled side streets and crossed under the railway tracks on the approach to Fenchurch Street station, but always heading towards the distant River Thames. It was just a hunch, but Hazel guessed that Montana would try to put as much distance between them as possible by crossing one of the bridges into South London. She knew that Noah would be searching the parallel streets, and Hulson and his team would likewise be searching frantically. She could hear police sirens in the distance.

Adjacent to the Tower of London, Hazel came upon an open space with a wooden bench surrounded by several tired looking bushes and foliage. Her legs were weary, so she rested on the bench for a moment. Nearby she spotted a jacket which had been stuffed into a waste bin. She pulled it out and discovered it was soaked with blood. Joey Montana, she guessed, must be nearby.

Hazel again set off in search of the gangster. She headed for Tower Bridge and saw Montana in the far distance walking along Tower Bridge Road. There was no mistake. He was wearing his fancy brocade waistcoat. He was attempting to blend in with the multitude of pedestrians making their way towards the bridge. She jogged off in pursuit and was soon closing the gap.

Hazel caught up with Joey Montana. She placed her hand on his shoulder. "You're under arrest, Joey. You'd best come quietly. We don't want any trouble, do we?"

Montana had no intention of coming quietly. His eyes scanned the immediate area for other cops. She appeared to be alone. She was reaching behind her to take her handcuffs from their pouch. Reaching down, he found his flick-knife and pressed the release button. The blade flashed open. Without a second's thought he lunged for the copper.

Hazel saw Montana leap towards her, then felt a sharp pain in her left arm as the blade sliced through her uniform tunic. Bright red blood began to spurt out of the wound and she automatically clamped her hand over it.

"That'll teach you to come after me you stupid bitch," sneered Montana.

Hazel could hardly believe she'd been stabbed. She was livid. Without a second's thought she sprung forward and kicked Montana hard in the groin. His eyes bulged as he doubled over in excruciating pain and his legs buckled from under him.

Hazel suddenly recalled Noah's advice all those months ago on her very first day on patrol, "Just remember that the only weapons you have to defend yourself, are a truncheon and a police whistle." She tugged on the lanyard and put the whistle to her lips and blew hard.

Two hundred yards away Noah heard the whistle and guessed that it might be Hazel calling for help. He raced down the centre of Tower Bridge Road, his long legs pounding along the tarmac. Cars and trucks swerved out of his way. He came upon Hazel. She was sitting on the pavement as passers-by stopped to help her. He saw the blood running down her arm and bent to cradle her in his arms.

"Don't worry about me. This is only a flesh wound. Montana's run off towards the bridge," she said. "Go get the bastard."

Montana was aware that his appearance was unkempt and dishevelled and that he stood out in the crowd. He began running towards the bridge; wanting to disappear within the morass of pedestrians heading for the south side of London. The police were closing in. Behind him an authoritative voice called out, "Stop right there, Montana." He glanced backwards and saw Constable Sheppard in the distance running after him. Other policemen were getting out of a police car. He attempted to run towards the bridge, but he was still in severe pain where the girl had kicked him in the testicles.

But he was too late. Up ahead, the traffic had come to a halt as the bridge gatekeeper had closed the barriers in readiness for a ship to come through the bridge. Montana was on the bridge approach road now and there was no way back. He was trapped. He glanced to his left and saw a cargo ship with its attendant tugs making towards the bridge. The two roadways were silently lifted vertically so as to be fully open and allow the vessel entry into the Pool of London. He reached the barrier, where a crowd of waiting pedestrians and cyclists had gathered. He pushed them aside and climbed over the barrier. Behind him he heard Sheppard shout, "Stop him. Grab hold of him."

He could run only a few yards before he came to the water's edge. He frantically looked around. Sheppard was climbing over the barrier. Behind him, Hulson and members of The Sweeney were closing in. He looked down into the swirling waters of the River Thames. The tide was ebbing at a fast rate and deadly whirlpools formed around the bridge's granite base where it met the dirty contaminated water. The ship was coming through the bridge. It was stridently sounding its horn. Montana looked around. The mass of commuters were staring aghast. Noah Sheppard was just yards away and would grab him any second. "Give it up, Montana. You cannot get away," shouted the policeman.

Josef Montana made a decision. If the police caught him, then he was under no illusions that he would either spend a considerable time in prison or swing from a noose. He took a deep breath and jumped. The water was bitterly cold as he hit the river and went under. He felt the strong tide buffet him violently against the underwater foundations, forcing the air from his lungs. Seconds later he was sucked further beneath the swirling vortex and felt his mouth and lungs fill with the polluted water. He struggled frantically to fight his way to the surface, but the strong current held him down. The river was so polluted that no sunlight permeated beneath its surface. His lungs were bursting from lack of oxygen. He couldn't hold his breath any longer. Everything went black. The ancient River Thames had claimed another life.

17: Follow the Money

It didn't seem possible to Noah. One minute they were up to their armpits with an organised crime gang in their midst, and suddenly they was back to dealing with boisterous schoolboys playing pranks. But they weren't complaining. Almost overnight the crime rate had sunk to the insignificant levels they'd typically experienced in Silvertown before the Montana gang arrived on the scene.

The River Thames gave up Montana's body two weeks later when it washed ashore at Greenwich. The money which he had taken from Eugene Chamberlain was found in his trouser pocket, and his pearl handled knife was tucked inside his sock.

A hearing at the coroner's court was convened in relation to the death of Montana and the murder of Eugene Chamberlain. Noah, Hazel and Detective Inspector David Hulson of the Flying Squad were the principal witnesses and gave their version of events leading to the gangster's drowning.

When asked by the coroner how he and his team came to be keeping watch outside Chamberlain's office, Hulson stated that he followed the basic instinct of the criminal mind.

"And what may that be?" asked the coroner irritably.

"Always follow the money," said the detective. "Wherever the money is – there you will find someone who wants possession of it."

Over the following months Noah and Hazel and other police officers appeared in court as witnesses for the prosecution. Tony Montana was the primary defendant and unsurprisingly, he was sentenced to life imprisonment. Ronnie Stack and his gang received stiff sentences for the East Ham armed robbery and malicious wounding charges. They had been lucky that the bank cashier had made a complete recovery; otherwise they would have been facing capital murder charges. Astonishingly, Jake Moss and Jimmy the Jock – whose correct name was revealed as Campbell – got light sentences after young Billy Baldwin testified that the pair had appeared reticent to be party to the kidnap, but been browbeaten into it by Josef Montana. Lastly, Ingrid Blackwood, who ran the Auberon Street brothel on behalf of the Montanas, was released without charge after she cooperated with the police and closed down the cat-house. Her girls dispersed to pastures new. Hazel had heard on the grapevine that Ingrid was now living a respectable married life in Essex.

Closing down the Montana crime gang had been a major feather in the cap for the Metropolitan Police and especially for The Sweeney; but the role played by Noah and Hazel had also been recognised as above and beyond the call of duty.

And so it was that on a cold winter's afternoon, the officers of North Woolwich nick were on parade as the Chief Constable awarded commendation medals to Hazel and to Noah in recognition for the part they'd played.

In the evening, after the top brass had departed back to Scotland Yard, the coppers of North Woolwich again mustered at The Royal Pavilion pub for a right royal booze-up.

Hazel was at the bar, surrounded by Noah and many of their colleagues who were eagerly admiring her medal and parchment commendation.

"Well done, Hazel," said Ronnie Baldwin. "You've had an amazing year since you arrived. "What's been the best part?"

Hazel gave it some thought. She laughed. "The bit I enjoyed the most was when I kicked Joey Montana in the nuts!"

They had slipped back into the easy going routine of pounding their Silvertown beat, almost as if nothing had happened to disturb the largely crime-free atmosphere which had prevailed before the Montanas showed up.

Hazel commented about how much had changed since her arrival over a year ago. "Back then," she said, "most of our colleagues would rather have had their teeth pulled out, than work with a WPC; but now I think, they've accepted me as someone who can do the job just as well as they can."

Noah nodded. "Yes, I think you're right. Nowadays they look upon you as one of the boys." He decided to tease her a little. "I hereby promote you to an honorary bloke"

She elbowed him in the ribs. "You're talking gibberish. Shut up Sheppard."

The pair were strolling along Woodman Street. Hazel had things on her mind. Something she needed to get off her chest. She would have liked to have been holding his hand, but they'd long ago agreed they daren't risk it.

"Noah my love, can I ask you something?"

His mind was elsewhere and was unaware of the thunderbolt that was about to land. He grunted, "Of course you can."

She stopped and turned to face him. "Do you love me?" she asked seriously. He awoke from his dream-like reverie. "But of course I do. What on earth made you ask?"

"I'm fed up with all this ducking and diving and keeping our relationship a secret," she said. "I want us to get married."

He grinned. "My goodness, Miss Leggett, you sure know how to surprise a fella, don't you?"

She laughed. "I try my best. So partner, what do you say?"

He would like to have crushed her into his arms and given her a passionate kiss, but that was impossible in public – and certainly not outside Lizzo School. He smiled. "As always, your timing's perfect. I was going to ask you this week, but you've beaten me to it. I guess I'd better go see your father and ask for your hand in marriage."

She agreed. "Let's go next weekend."

A serious thought came to her. "There have been rumours that the top brass won't stand for a married couple on patrol together. They may split us up and we'd be on separate beats."

"Don't worry. I had a word with Ambrose and asked what police regulations say regarding married officers working together."

"What did he say?"

"He said there are absolutely no rules regarding married officers, because the problem had never arisen before. He couldn't see any problem with us being on the same beat; just so long as we didn't hold hands and canoodle in public, he couldn't see any difficulty."

She let out a dirty laugh. "In that case, you may have to take me for a smooching session underneath the arches."

Printed in Great Britain
by Amazon